HER MIDNIGHT SIN

SOFIE DARLING

🌸 Created with Vellum

1

———

LONDON, 14 SEPTEMBER 1825

If you're goin' to have a wife, you might as well tup her right.
That bit of wisdom came courtesy of a father long lost to John Nylander, but the essence of the sentiment had somehow stuck after all these years.

A man didn't need to love his work to do it well.

This belief had taken Nylander far, from cabin boy to captain of the *Fortuyn*, the East Indiaman currently being defreighted beneath his watchful eye on the banks of the muddy Thames. If he no longer derived pleasure from the work, he did, at least, experience the cold satisfaction of a job done with skill and precision. It didn't need to thrill him.

A breeze swirled off the river and cooled the beads of perspiration coating his neck. Pleasing, that north wind on the exposed patch of skin, even if it did little to lower the heat of exertion that didn't want to abate. It was as if he contained a furnace inside his chest. Of a sudden, his head went light, and he reached for the rail at his side. The feeling passed as quick as it had come on.

"Captain?"

The First Mate stood at his side, a sheaf of papers extended and an expectant look in his eye. How long had the man been standing there? And how was it Nylander hadn't noticed?

"Yes, Mr. Smythe?"

"The final accounting, sir."

Nylander accepted the papers with a curt nod. He shuffled through the stack, a cursory glance confirming the numbers all lined up, and handed them back to the mate. "It's ready for the hands of Danner."

"I'll rush it to the warehouse now, sir." Mr. Smythe pivoted on his heel, his efficient step already on the move.

From his vantage point at the base of the main mast, Nylander watched a group of sailors set about rolling fifty barrels of spices and dyes—payment for delivering a pair of high-spirited Thoroughbreds to an Ottoman sultan—down the gangway to the warehouse to be readied for distribution through England. Escaped from the poop deck, a flock of chickens clucked past, brushing Nylander's trousers with their affrighted wings. A swift apology on his lips, the mess boy raced behind them and attempted to contain the fractious birds.

Nylander shifted his gaze toward the waist of the ship, where the cooper set about repairing gunpowder barrels damaged by a rough night of roiling seas off Cape Vares. Beyond the cooper, a group of men inspected the rigging and sailcloth for rips and signs of wear beneath the watchful eye of the boatswain.

Temptation, sly and magnetic, tugged at Nylander. In a matter of an hour, they could weigh anchor and be gone from London, a town he'd never had much use for. They'd already waded through the necessary bureaucracy of the Pool, and the last of their small cargo was now rolling off the ship. Their work here was nearly done.

But it wasn't anything related to his trade that stayed the command to weigh anchor in his mouth, rather it was a personal tie. He'd promised his oldest friend in the world that he would attend a dinner tonight, and he wouldn't beg off. Even if it was a meal that would consist of, at minimum, seven full courses soaked in butter, cream, and salt. What did a man need with such rich fare that was like as not to give him gout?

He breathed out a snort. What sort of man was Jake now that he'd become the noble Viscount St. Alban? The two of them had been inseparable in their youth and early manhood spent aboard small sloops, trading up and down the coasts of the Orient, before they'd graduated to the larger merchantman vessels that could handle the open sea. A few years younger, Nylander had observed Jake with the keen eye of a worshipful little brother, and Jake had treated him as such, though no blood connected them. The Van Rijns, Jake's Dutch mother's family, were a tight-knit bunch, but not so insular that they hadn't been able to admit an orphan of eight years into their midst and raise him as their own.

Now Jake existed in a rarefied world that Nylander hadn't the faintest notion of.

He shook his head free of the thought. He may not know Jake's new world, but he knew the man. Jake hadn't asked for this life, hadn't wanted it. For his own part though, Nylander couldn't understand why. If he had the opportunity to own land, *English* land, he'd seize it with both hands and never look back. A man put roots down in land. The sea was a shiftless, impermanent mistress. He would take land over water any day.

Of course, water was all he'd ever known, all he would ever know. He'd accepted that fact years ago. How many orphaned boys were offered the opportunity to rise as high and amass the amount of wealth as he had?

"You might have a problem," sounded a voice behind him.

Nylander jerked around. Tall and lean to the bone, the man before him personified the word *trouble*, wolfish light glimmering in his dark eyes and silvery scar racing along the sharp ridge of his right cheekbone. He'd picked up the man in Gibraltar, accepted his coin for safe passage, and spoke not another word to him for the duration. He'd expected the passenger had made his way off the *Fortuyn* with the other cargo.

He squared up to the man and crossed his arms over his chest. "What problem?"

"The *Free Reaver*."

Nylander didn't need to ask the man to explain himself.

"It followed us all the way from the Bay of Biscay until we came within sight of Cornwall." The man's gaze glittered. "Never knew a pirate barque to allow an East Indiaman with cargo to pass without incident. Curious, wouldn't you say?"

Nylander unclenched his jaw. "Might you be making an implication?" he asked on a low rumble of menace.

A sardonic twist to his mouth, the man shook his head. "More of an observation. You know who captains the *Free Reaver*, I expect."

"Aye," Nylander grunted. "There's not a sailor in the Atlantic who doesn't."

The man nodded and shifted his carryall bag to his back. "Then I'll be taking my leave." The man's hand shot out for Nylander to shake. "My most sincere thanks for the ride, and Godspeed, Captain."

Nylander's brow creased as he watched the man stride down the gangway. To his ear, a note had ribboned through the man's final words that ran counter to his initial assessment. Just now, the man had sounded aristocratic.

Nylander gave his head a shake. It mattered not. What mattered was that he was gone. A history lay within that man, one he didn't want to get tangled up in.

You might have a problem.

There was no *might* about it. He had a most definite problem with the *Free Reaver* and the pirate who commanded her.

And no solution.

Around Nylander, the pace of the crew began to slow, the day's end drawing near, as was tonight's dinner. Beads of sweat had coalesced into a narrow rivulet that now trickled down his spine. The north wind grew stronger, threatening to pick up into the sort of gale that could give a ship trouble on the open sea. His eyes cast upward to the blue sky darkening into steel gray. A chill stood the hairs of his arms on end, yet the furnace raged on inside him.

Directly above his head, a loud *pop* and *snap* of hemp ripped through the air, followed by the swift *zhush* of rope rushing through rigging at a too-rapid velocity. Just as his brain registered that an object was falling, *fast*, he heard a shout. "Captain!"

Nylander's gaze shot up in time to see an object... a *man*... closing in on him as quick as gravity allowed. He ducked backward before the man crashed down on his head, but at the last moment, reactively, he reached his arms out and stabilized his feet for the coming blow. The man slammed into him with the force of a thirty-six pound cannonball at short range, but his arms held, even if his legs didn't. In an instant, he was flat on his arse, the inert weight of the man sprawled across his legs, and struggling to catch the breath that had been knocked out of his lungs.

Through a haze black at the edges, Nylander watched the crew roll the man off him and onto his back. As if from a great distance, he saw it was the cabin boy. Well, *boy* might be a stretch, the man was two and thirty years, but he was small as a lad of twelve. Nylander had a strict policy of refusing any crew member under the age of seventeen.

A sailor bent low over the cabin boy's supine body, his ear pressed against the man's mouth. The ship went so still, one could hear a pin drop. The sailor's head popped up. "'E's alive!"

The men erupted into a raucous, relieved cheer. "Ye saved 'im, cap'n!" one of the crew called out. Another crewmate held up a ragged end of rope. "Snapped clean through. Rot, I expect."

Several slaps of good cheer landed on Nylander's back as he came to his feet by slow increments, his body angered at what his mind had commanded without a second thought. What the blazes had he been thinking? He hadn't. It was ever his difficulty in a situation that called for quick, decisive action. He saw a problem and became the solution before he thought.

He paid the price later, without fail. Like now.

He ran his hands through loose hair that brushed his shoulders and reknotted the leather tie that held it in place

at the nape of his neck, tucking a few errant strands behind his ear.

"Sure as I stand 'ere, 'e'da bin done for if ye'd not been
steppin' in," Nylander heard behind him and tried not to
flinch at another jovial slap to his back. He needed a long
soak in a steaming tub. His back, his arse, his entire body
barked its displeasure from head to toe, unwilling to understand that he hadn't a choice. The man would have
died.

Not on his watch.

Watch. He fumbled his timepiece out of his pocket.
Bloody hell.

The long soak would have to wait. He had just enough
time to sponge off the grime of the day's work and don his
one set of fancy clothes. He swallowed back a surge of
nausea, ignored the heat pulsing through him in waves and
the nascent ache in his head, and willed his body to
straighten to its full height before pointing his feet in the
direction of his cabin.

He had an aristocratic dinner to attend in his too near
future when all he really wanted was to lie down for the
next, oh, three or four years.

HER BOOTS a swift *click-clack* against cobblestones that
matched the gray sky above, Callie kept her chin high and
her mien calm. The outside world needn't see the storm
that swirled inside her.

Her raging case of nerves came down to two factors.
One, she was in London. Two, she hadn't the faintest idea
why she'd been summoned five days ago.

It couldn't be good. *That* she knew with certainty.

She loathed London. Its haste, hustle, and bustle. Its
grime. Its stench. Its buildings, narrow and long, crammed
shoulder to shoulder, and possessed of the vaguely mili-
tary look of tall, skinny soldiers holding their collective
breath. She'd only been here once before, and that was
enough. Already, she was champing at the bit to leave.

Her grip tightened around the worn leather handle of her travel bag to still her tremble. Again, the question pressed in: Why on earth had the Viscount St. Alban beckoned her?

The man hadn't invited her all the way from the north coast of Devon to meet face-to-face and discuss agriculture. She'd been running Wyldcombe Grange since her late husband Georgie's death and before this new Viscount St. Alban had taken up the reins of the viscountcy. The man had never once expressed a desire to know her better, or at all, as the case was. Which further begged the question: What did the man want?

She rounded the corner onto Cleveland Row, scanning the houses to her left and right. Number 3 lay ahead. A most disagreeable possibility for the viscount's summons poked at her. Namely, he was a man, and she a woman. Like a majority of men, he might be uncomfortable with a woman in charge. She'd met plenty of that sort of man these last few years.

Caution in her tread, no small amount of anxiety, too, she ascended the four wide steps of Number 3. She'd only stayed here the once, and that was years ago, in the first year of her marriage. Her preference for the country had suited Georgie's preference for Town perfectly.

Her head tipped back until her neck ached as she took in the measure of the mansion. In the dusky light of impending night, the manse gleamed and shone, announcing to the world that though it might be part of it, it was also above it. Even the fetid London air smelled better here.

Shoulders squared, she tapped the door knocker once, twice, thrice for good measure, and waited. If St. Alban had called her here because she was a woman, well, she wouldn't surrender with a whimper. Male or female, she was the first person to run the Grange in the black in twenty years.

Like a nagging muscle ache, a familiar thought wiggled into her mind. Another option did lay open to her. *You can walk away.*

She was still somewhat young, having been widowed

two years ago at age three and twenty. It wasn't outside the realm of possibility that her father could arrange another marriage for her. She wasn't naive enough to hope for a love match, Georgie's reaction to her physical person was a testament to that impossibility. But a woman didn't need the conditional love of a man, not when she had the unconditional love of her child.

She could quit the Grange and pursue that life. Wife, mother, the roles she'd been promised, that had been denied her. But...

She loved the Grange. And, in some ways, wasn't it like her child?

But does it love you back?

Of course not. But the work was satisfying, and she had a knack for it. She wasn't about to give it up, not without a fight.

On silent hinges the Viscount St. Alban's front door swung inward, and an elegant, liveried servant stared out at her, a question in his eyes for three heartbeats too long. Awareness of the country bumpkin she must appear crept through her. Her woolen travel pelisse and gown, unadorned brown and a good five years out of fashion. Her boots, black and practical, possibly still coated with Devonshire mud. And, of course, her duck-cloth travel bag, drab gray and frayed at the edges.

She'd never managed to be *in* fashion, or to care that she wasn't. It was simply out of the realm of possibility for her. She was too unfashionably tall; her body too unfashionably skinny; her eyes too unfashionably brown; and her hair too unfashionably red and frizzy for her to have ever been a fashionable Miss, even in the very first blush of her youth. So, she'd shrugged her too bony shoulders and stopped trying.

Now, standing on the stylish doorstop at this most fashionable address, she considered that she could've given it more of an effort.

At last, the servant took pity on her and spoke. "May I be of assistance?"

Callie resquared her shoulders and drew herself up to

her fullest height, which was half an inch shy of six feet. "Inform the Viscount St. Alban that the Viscountess St. Alban has arrived." A hesitation. "Please."

The servant's eyebrows shot skyward. Aristocrats didn't say please. Ever. "The Viscountess St. Alban? I believe his lordship is fully aware of the Viscountess St. Alban's whereabouts as she and he are in the drawing room with their guests." A heavy beat loped past. "*Together.*"

The hot splotch of a blush spread across Callie's chest and up her neck, and she silently thanked her lucky stars for her unfashionably high collar. Her preference for blouses that buttoned all the way up to her chin made it impossible for anyone to know that she blushed three times a day, at a minimum. She cleared her throat and attempted to right the conversation that had gone horribly sideways. "The *Dowager* Viscountess St. Alban."

On a deferential bow, the servant retreated three steps and swung the door wide. "Of course, my lady. If you will follow me."

Callie stepped inside the bright and spacious foyer. As a child, she'd imagined the homes of the aristocracy stuffed to the brim with every expensive thing in the world, like her parents had done with their nouveau riches. But when she'd actually entered one of those homes upon her engagement to Georgie, she'd found the opposite to be true. Those with power and privilege allowed a few priceless pieces—a Ming vase, a Roman Venus—to speak their wealth for them. Understatement shouted infinite privilege like no amount of gilded finery ever could.

And she had no use for any of it, never had.

Footsteps echoed as she followed the servant into the study, pleasantly dark with rich woods and floor-to-ceiling shelves surely packed with every book known to mankind. She'd only ever been in this room once, but she was certain not one book had populated it when Georgie had been its master.

"If you will please wait here, I shall see if his lordship is in."

"You said he's in the drawing room with his wife and

guests. Of course, he's *in*." Callie never had an ounce of patience for London manners.

A smile teetering on the edge of distress creased the servant's face. He bowed in polite goodbye before shuffling through the doorway and out of sight.

"For pity's sake," Callie exclaimed to the empty room. Getting to a viscount in London was like peeling away the layers of an onion to reach its stinking center.

In Devonshire, it wasn't possible for a lord to remain so insulated from the world outside the manor. That wasn't to say a country lord couldn't try. Georgie had, an effort that had run the Grange into the ground.

Movement caught at the corner of her eye. A man radiating confidence with every step strode into the room. He could be none other than the Right Honorable Jakob Radclyffe, Fifth Viscount St. Alban, the personification of the ideal aristocratic lord. And the exact opposite of the Viscount St. Alban who had preceded him in both appearance and bearing.

Georgie hadn't been so very tall. Or so very imposing. Or so very unabashedly handsome. Except this man's handsomeness wasn't at all pleasing to Callie's eye. His were the sort of looks that could be used as a weapon. With the man's arrival in the room, the tremble had returned to her hands.

"If it isn't the Dowager Viscountess St. Alban," he said, the words spoken on a friendly enough note, even if a slender thread of irony might have woven through them. "Nice to put a face to the name." He gestured toward a plush leather chair opposite the room's grand oak desk. "Would you care to have a seat?"

On a silent nod, Callie lowered herself to a perch on its firm edge and settled her travel bag at her feet, keeping it close at hand. She wouldn't be making herself comfortable. Her fists clenched tight at her sides, and her nails dug deep crescents into her palms, the pain enough to stay the tremor. Across shiny oak, eyes the disconcerting blue of a pale-eyed sheepdog observed her. They were the sort of blue that bore into skin and bone, straight to the essence. Her heart banged out a hard, unsteady thud.

St. Alban slouched deep into his chair, at absolute ease. "I take it the roads were clear. We weren't expecting you until the morrow."

Callie willed a steady voice. It wasn't that she lacked the courage to deal with this man, but it so happened that her future lay in his hands. "Yes, your lordship." The words emerged soft and skittish, unlike the confident and commanding voice her workers at the Grange knew. How she hated London, this room, and this blasted cocksure man, what they reduced her to. "There wasn't a drop of rain the entire journey."

"Remarkable. And you came here straightaway?"

"From the Gloucester Coffee House."

"In Piccadilly?"

"That was the final stop. I walked from there."

"Most ladies don't walk in London, particularly those unfamiliar with its environs."

Callie shrugged. "It's not a far distance by Devon standards."

St. Alban drummed contemplative fingertips on solid oak a few rounds. He gave one final tap, shot to his feet, and strode to the brass whiskey cart situated near the bay window overlooking a garden. Callie intuited he wasn't the sort of man who sat still for long.

"Would you like tea to be brought in? You must be exhausted after all your breakneck journeying and walking." He held up a crystal decanter possessed of the amber glow that characterized a fine whiskey. "Or perhaps you'd prefer a drop more bracing?"

"Neither, my lord," she spoke around the lump in her throat. If she could hear it, surely he could, too.

He poured a few fingers into an etched crystal tumbler before returning to his seat. Again opposite each other, they resumed staring across the desk. It was possible she would crawl out of her skin if the man didn't state his business soon.

"You're wondering why I summoned you to London."

She nodded. Her voice had proven unreliable.

"How long have you resided at Wyldcombe Grange?"

"These last five years." She swallowed. "Upon my marriage to the late Fourth Viscount St. Alban."

"And do you enjoy the Grange?"

"*Enjoy?*" she asked, nonplussed despite her nerves. "Enjoyment has naught to do with it. The Grange is my life."

St. Alban's head cocked, assessing. He was trying to decide what kind of woman she was. "I appreciate your forthrightness, so I'll return you the favor. Simply put, I'm selling the Grange."

2

---

allie's stomach performed a nifty trick and flipped before dropping straight down to her toes. Her heart raced to catch it, and perspiration sheened every square inch of her skin as her body went hot, clammy, then hot again. She opened her mouth to speak, but words refused to budge.

She tried again. "You're *selling* the Grange?" The question nothing more than a whisper uttered on the hope that she'd misheard him through the wool plugging her ears.

Cool, contained, St. Alban continued. "The fact of the matter is the estate is unentailed." He lifted empty, indifferent hands. "And I haven't the faintest interest in it."

"No interest? But it runs at a profit." Her voice clawed its way to the surface and grew stronger with each word she spoke. "In the last year, the sheep flock has doubled in number. The dairy is producing enough milk and cheese to sell in the Barnstaple Saturday market. And, since we learned how to properly prune the apple trees, the orchard is exceeding all expectations. Our cider has gained a bit of renown throughout Devonshire and our first batch of brandy will be ready for market in the spring. We even have our own—"

She stopped wasting her breath. This man didn't care that the Grange had its very own rare Charentais alembic still that would produce fifty barrels of apple brandy this

13

season alone. Or that she had an appointment with a London distributor tomorrow morning to discuss a potential arrangement for its distribution. If he cared about those details, he wouldn't be selling.

Further, he likely viewed her intense unladylike display with distaste. In a matter of seconds, she'd gone from being utterly unlike herself to too like her unvarnished self. Mayhap there was a middle ground. She sought it by asking the most obvious and pressing question. "Who is buying the Grange?"

"I'm offering it to a friend."

"A friend?" The question emerged an eek, a croak, incredulous. She wasn't sure whether to laugh in hysterics or explode in outrage.

"A friend, yes, he's—"

"From Devon?" Even as her heart sank into the floor, a dark and primal anger surged up.

St. Alban shook his head. "But he has experience running things."

"*Experience running things?*" Disbelief swelled with each word. "How do you know he will want the Grange?"

"He will." The reply came succinct, certain.

Cold steel wrapped around Callie's heart. "And what is this *friend's* occupation?"

"He captains an East Indiaman."

"A ship captain?" she scoffed. "What does a man like that know about running the Grange?"

"*A man like that?*" St. Alban's eyes narrowed, guarded and wary. "I take it you don't have a high opinion of sea traders."

Callie almost snorted. *Almost.* That was the important part. "We see our share on the north coast of Devon. They're a cagey lot."

"I captained a ship before I came into the viscountcy."

She'd put her foot in it. "Undoubtedly, there are exceptions."

The words rang hollow, and she knew that he knew she didn't mean them. Beneath his implacable visage, she might have detected a glint of humor, but she couldn't be sure.

Subtly, through the riot of emotion assailing her, slinked the sly, familiar nag. *This is your chance.* The opportunity to walk away from Wyldcombe Grange and claim the life her heart had wanted since the moment she'd agreed to marry Georgie.

But how could she give up on the Grange and everyone it supported? This had been their most successful year yet. And if the quantity of apples populating the orchard was any indicator, this would be their best cider and brandy season yet, too.

She couldn't... she *wouldn't* leave the Grange in the hands of an outsider who didn't know the first thing about it. Someone who would run it into the ground. Someone who didn't love it.

But does it love you back? came the unwanted refrain.

It wouldn't sway her. She had a duty, and she wouldn't shirk it.

She stiffened her spine and sat forward. Her voice found itself. "I'll rephrase my question. What does your friend the ship captain know about running a six-thousand-acre agricultural estate?"

The viscount shifted the slimmest fraction in his seat. But she caught it. That shift spoke of unease. "He's a quick learner."

A nervy feeling swelled inside Callie. She had nothing to lose. "So you haven't offered the Grange to this *friend* of yours yet?" The word *friend* refused to sound like anything other than a curse from her mouth.

The viscount steepled his fingers before him and narrowed his glacial gaze. She knew this look. It was the look that formed when a man began to understand her true nature, that beneath her skin and bones ran an iron will. "I'll put the question to him tonight. It was to have been arranged before you arrived tomorrow."

Silently, Callie blessed the dry heavens above that had allowed her to arrive a day early. She gathered herself, willing her voice not to shake when she spoke her next words. They needed to be absolute steel. This was a man she was dealing with, and a man's world she was navigating. A woman's voice, quaking with emotion, wasn't respected here. "Give me a chance."

"My lady," began the viscount, "I have considered that. Perhaps you would like the position of estate manager. We might be able to arrange—"

"To buy it," she bit out, only stopping herself from adding *you nodcock*. No good could come from calling a viscount a nodcock. Even if he was one.

St. Alban set his hands to rest on the desk before him. "When I arrived in England nigh on a year ago, it was my lot to sort through your late husband's papers."

He hesitated, the tips of his forefingers *tap-tap-tapping* each other meditatively. Callie braced herself for what he would say. If someone pulled the chair out from under her, her body would remain locked in its seated position, she was sure of it.

"And debts. A mountain of them, in fact." His countenance softened, grew conciliatory. He was attempting to let her down gently. "You've done an excellent job of managing the Grange and rehabilitating it back into the black, but I don't see how you have the necessary funds to purchase it at its current value."

His words gave the ember of anger that had been glowing inside her the oxygen it needed to flare into a full bonfire. "I've earned the right to buy the Grange." She all but banged her fist on the desk for emphasis.

The viscount let her words blow past him. A full minute dragged out beneath the silence, and Callie's mind raced, even as she acknowledged he only spoke the truth. She had no ready cash. Every year, she reinvested every last farthing of the Grange's profits back into the estate, which left her, technically, penniless. Still, what could she say to convince him not to do this awful thing?

Her attention shifted beyond his shoulder and fixed on the garden outside. In a symphony of color bloomed blue plumbago, purple aster, and white bugbane. Fall flowers had always been her mama's favorite. *Nature's last little gift before winter.*

Mama… An idea struck.

Words began falling out of Callie's mouth before the import of them fully formed in her mind. "My mother left me monies enough to buy the Grange."

Disbelief communicated itself in the skeptical lift of the viscount's brow. "It seems I should have known about these monies sooner."

Callie unstuck her tongue from the roof of a mouth gone dry. "Well, they aren't exactly in my possession, but I can access them through my father. A little time is all I need."

"How much time?" St. Alban asked. "This matter was to be resolved by tomorrow."

"Until—" Her mind raced. *Think.* "Until… after the Baptism of the Duke of Muck."

St. Alban's brow knitted in perplexity. "*The Baptism of the Duke of Muck?*"

"It's our harvest festival." Her mind performed a quick calculation. "About four weeks from now."

St. Alban held her gaze, searching. "You'll have one hundred thousand pounds at your disposal?"

The number nearly knocked Callie to the floor. *One hundred thousand pounds?* She struggled to hold steady. She'd gone too far, and this man surely knew it. "Mayhap we can work out a plan for payment if I give you"—again, her mind calculated—"twenty percent up front. That's twenty thousand pounds."

An unconvinced, "Mayhap," was all he gave her by response.

She must say something, *anything* to plead her case. No, not *anything.* Only the truth would do. "I've earned the right," she repeated, this time softly, the words a quiet force, the legitimacy of them plain and irrefutable.

St. Alban sat forward, clearly arrived at his decision. Callie's breath froze in her chest, and her head grew light, as if it had floated clear of her body and was watching these events unfold from above.

He extended his hand. "You have a deal."

Before he could change his mind, her hand shot out to seal his words. If he felt its cold clamminess against the dry warmth of his own, he betrayed not a hint. The man was a gentleman. Grudging thought.

Callie reclaimed her hand, and relief surged forward on a wave of misgiving. What she'd done was less than honorable. Those monies of her mama's, well, they weren't quite the truth of the matter. In fact, they were an outright lie. But those phantom monies had done their job: they'd bought her time. Four weeks' worth.

There was her appointment with the spirits distributor tomorrow. It would have to be canceled. No honest deal would yield her the funds she needed as fast as she needed them.

Honest. Her mind snagged on the word and twirled it around, testing its weight. Another solution presented itself, one that had been proposed to her only this past spring, one that had naught to do with honesty. It was an offer practically in hand. All she had to do was reach out and take it.

In truth, this particular solution was underhanded and dirty, but... *possible.* That was the important part. Unlike those phantom monies from her mother, this possibility existed.

No, no, no. How could she even consider it? The mistress of Wyldcombe Grange didn't enter into business deals with notorious pirates.

Urgency swelled inside her to bursting, and she shot to her feet. She hadn't a moment to lose. Unlike her apples, solutions weren't exactly growing on trees. "My lord, if you will pardon me, I must return to the Grange posthaste." *And see to the securing of monies that don't officially exist,* she didn't add. "As you may or may not know, the apple harvest is under way."

St. Alban had the sense to appear somewhat abashed by the unspoken fact that he'd pulled her away from the Grange at its busiest time of year. "Night is falling, my lady, surely you'll wait until the morrow."

"I shall take the mail coach. It travels by night, and I'm most keen to be on my way." Vast understatement.

"The *mail coach*?" St. Alban's brow creased in disbelief. "You didn't arrive by—"

"Mail coach? Of course not. I traveled the stage by day."

"*Stage*? Not by hired post-chaise?"

Callie only just didn't roll her eyes at this privileged aristocrat. "To travel in such luxury would be an egregious waste of the Grange's resources."

Did the man think she was made of money? Well, he did think she had thousands of pounds at her disposal, so maybe he did.

He released a long-suffering sigh. "Lady St. Alban and I are having a few guests to sup tonight, please stay and join us. I'm certain we can arrange a more suitable travel conveyance for your return journey."

Callie opened her mouth to refuse the viscount's generous offer—why did the man have to be so blasted honorable?—when a long shadow stole into the room. She glanced right and found a massive figure filling the height and breadth of the doorframe.

"I haven't arrived at a bad time, have I?"

St. Alban's head whipped around, and a smile spread across his face, instantly transforming his visage into someone Callie might be able to like under different circumstances. He shot to his feet and crossed the room in a handful of exuberant strides. "Why if it isn't Captain Nylander, as I live and breathe."

Captain Nylander.

Dread filled Callie's gut as she watched the two men shake hands and manfully clap each other on the back. These men were most definitely *friends*.

"St. Alban," the captain replied, the words succinct, but their tone warm.

His voice was deep enough to shake the foundations of this mansion loose. Certainly deep enough to rattle Callie, her breath shallow and her mouth dry. She rose to a stand by slow increments and stood so silent and so still that she imagined she might be forgotten. Then the captain's gaze met hers over St. Alban's shoulder, and all hope was lost. His eyes narrowed in question, and she lifted a single, imperious eyebrow in response. The Grange knew that eyebrow well, and she sensed it was her best defense against this man in this moment.

Before her stood the man who would never be her friend. He was her rival... her *enemy*. Soft gaslight caught the golden strands of his unfashionably long, slightly unkempt hair and the glint of clear blue sky in his eye. For all his modern English attire, the man could have been a Viking, a Norse god even, from the tales of yore come to life. All he lacked was a shield in one hand and a hammer in the other.

Callie's breath had no choice but to catch in her chest. Her enemy was imposing, yes, but did he also have to be so blasted, devastatingly... *god-like?*

GREETINGS and back claps out of the way, Jake stepped back. "You're looking well, my friend. How long has it been? Six months?"

"Thereabouts," Nylander said, distracted, his eye steady on the curious woman beyond Jake's shoulder. She stood quietly, a straight vertical line of a woman, tall and not a curve on her. Her hair shone the fiery red of an East Indian sunset.

Jake cleared his throat. "Shall we toast to your safe arrival?"

Nylander jutted his chin toward the woman. "If you've still some business to conduct, I can wait."

Jake's brow darkened, as if unhappy to be reminded of her. "Just finishing up some business with the Dowager Viscountess St. Alban."

A Dowager Viscountess. *Right.*

She stepped into the light of a gas wall sconce. She was all long limbs, gangly like a colt who had yet to grow into her legs. High cheekbones. Strong nose. Eyes, not conventionally blue and round, rather dark and almond shaped. A mouth too wide and full to be called pretty, but appealing. Her individual features were none of them fashionable, but they synthesized to form a face attractive and compelling. She was a difficult woman to look away from. He couldn't if he wanted, so strong was the magnetic pull of her.

Yet she stood glaring at him with the hostility of a woman who had a serious bone to pick. He'd never encountered her in his life; he would've remembered. So why was she looking at him like she would strap lead weights to his ankles and toss him into the sea rather than lay eyes on him ever again?

Jake glanced back and forth between them, a deep furrow in his brow. "Shall I introduce you?"

"There shan't be any need for that," she said tightly.

Shame, bitter, hot, and familiar, sliced through Nylander, a shame he'd never been able to shed. Its stigma wrapped tentacles around him and squeezed. Though he was dressed in the finery of a nob, this woman wasn't fooled. People of quality always saw straight through to who he was, who he *really* was. Jake didn't see it, because he loved him like a brother, but this woman did with those coal dark eyes of hers that pierced and burned. She knew him for what he was: an orphan, a cast-off, a man to be used and discarded when the whim suited her.

Perhaps not that last part for her. Unlike many a lady before her, she clearly wanted nothing to do with him, not even the pleasure his body could offer hers.

A throat cleared behind them. "My lord, another guest has arrived."

A flash of annoyance crossed Jake's features. "Show the guest into the drawing room. Lady St. Alban will know what to do with him. Aren't we to go into supper any moment?"

"To be sure, my lord. But this guest—"

The remainder of the servant's words were cut off by a series of shocked gasps and a few startled eeks in the foyer. Jake's eyebrows drew together, and he brushed Nylander's shoulder as he raced from the room.

That left only him and the woman. Their eyes collided, and an odd tension charged the air. He'd met any number of people who'd looked down their noses upon him, but never one who so nakedly hated him at first sight. Not like this woman clearly did.

He swept his arm toward the empty doorway, gesturing for her to precede him out of the room. It was the gentlemanly thing to do, even if he wasn't one. Her mouth set in a resolute line, she swept past him with nary another glance. He reckoned she didn't have much of a care for the dirt beneath her shoes.

He tugged at the cravat that was attempting to strangle the life out of him. How did these London dandies do it? One hour in this garb and he was ready to set sail for the South Seas where three articles of clothing were two too many. He swiped at a bead of sweat trickling down his temple. The furnace that had begun in his chest had spread through his body and hadn't cooled by a single degree.

At the woman's heels, Nylander found a foyer much altered from the empty one he'd passed through not five minutes ago. Presently, it was crowded with a dozen wide-eyed lords and ladies dressed in the first stare of fashion.

This altered foyer did share one similarity with the earlier one: its dead silence. But this silence wasn't peaceful or static. It pulsed with a latent energy that begged to be allowed its head as everyone focused on a single point near the front door. He followed the collective gaze toward the object of their rapt attention and found a lone man standing at the foot of the grand staircase.

Recognition hit him. The man was none other than the mysterious passenger he'd picked up in Gibraltar. Except now, he was clean, shaven, and buffed to a noble shine in his evening blacks. The man was still too thin and called to mind a lone, rangy wolf, but it was clear as day that he was one of *them*, a lord.

Jake stepped forward, a bewildered smile on his lips. "My good sir, I'm afraid you have the wrong address for your evening out."

A petite blond woman gasped as one hand flew to her

mouth and the other to her belly large with child. Jake glanced at her, concern radiating from every cell of his being. Two facts were immediately clear. She was Jake's wife, and she knew that man.

A regal silver-haired gentleman stepped forward. "Percy?" he asked, the name carried across the room on incredulous wings.

Jake's brow furrowed, and his hands clenched into fists at his sides. That dark look didn't bode well for this Percy. Lady St. Alban's hand wrapped around her husband's upper arm. She knew it, too.

Beside him, Nylander felt the flame-haired woman's presence. She was following the action like him: as an outsider, as clueless about the shadowy undercurrents eddying through this room as he. She observed, curious, speculative, as if she was accustomed to taking in gatherings as an outsider. It connected them in a strangely tangible way.

Across the room, Percy said, "Papa, the servants told me I would find you here." His gaze shifted. "And, Lady St. Alban, may I congratulate you on your nuptials and—" He gestured in the direction of her ripe belly.

Like a coil breaking free of its tension, Jake sprang across the foyer on a low, guttural growl, and the room burst into utter chaos. Without pause, Jake's right arm reared back and shot forward in a quick, well-aimed jab to Percy's nose, surely breaking it for all the blood that spewed forth and sprayed across black-and-white marble and wrought iron balustrade.

"Oh, well landed," a lady's voice rang out. It was Lady Nicholas, a pleased smile on her lips. Nylander hardly knew her, having transported her to Paris last year, but it wouldn't be a stretch to imagine her reaction entirely in character. She was just that sort of woman. Her husband was a lucky man.

Ahead, a large quantity of blood dripped down Percy's chin, a scarlet stain spreading across his formerly white shirtfront. Nylander had seen his share of bloodied broken noses in his day, but had there been quite this much of it? Was it possible that one nose had so much blood to spare?

Heat blazed through him. He blinked and swiped the back of his hand across his damp forehead. The room was going gray at the edges, and with each thud of his heavy heartbeat, it went ever blacker. He shook his head. Rising voices and shouted obscenities shrilled through the air, but they were muffled as if he was hearing them through a tunnel at a very great distance.

Pinpricks of sweat surfaced from every pore on his body, and his stomach lurched. He reached out to steady himself and found himself grasping the arm of the woman beside him. She tried to wrench her arm away, but his grip only tightened. Somehow, she was the only barrier between him and the floor.

Then that wasn't true anymore as the floor rose to meet him, and his head clattered against cold marble. The last thing he saw before the room went completely black was the woman's dark eyes staring down at him.

The last thing he heard from the far reaches of the dark tunnel was, "Who would've thought the sight of a little blood could fell a man like you?"

And the last thing he wondered was what he'd done for her to treat him like she loathed him with every last fiber of her being?

3

TWO DAYS LATER, SOMEWHERE IN SOMERSET

Blasted *malaria.*

The diagnosis—well, not the *blasted* part—that had placed Callie inside this carriage, careening down a soggy country road with a noisome, querulous nurse squeezed in at her side and a feverish, possibly concussed, intermittently raving ship captain splayed out across from her, both lost to the world in slumber.

Disgusted, Callie stared out the fogged-up window and took in the uneventful countryside racing alongside her. How had it come to this?

One moment, she'd been watching a scene straight out of a French farce in St. Alban's foyer, and the next, she'd been cradling the captain's head, dripping with perspiration and hot to the touch, lest he hit it again on the checkered marble floor and this time crack it clean open. She still couldn't recall the thud of his skull against unforgiving marble without her stomach giving a lurch.

Next thing she knew, St. Alban was barking orders that a carriage be brought round to transport the Viking to the nearest inn and that a doctor from the Westminster infirmary be instructed to meet them there. The concern was that the captain had a fever and that it was contagious. A few hours later, St. Alban returned as supper was concluding to assure his family and guests that the doctor had diagnosed the captain with a malarial flare up—*They're not uncommon in the Far East*—and a possible concussion—*You saw the way his head bounced when it struck the floor?*

Then he'd pulled Callie aside and asked the fateful question. "Will you take Nylander back to Devon with you?"

"I... I should think not," she'd all but exclaimed.

The viscount's head cocked to the side, and his eyes went ice cold. A shard of foreboding stabbed through her. "He shouldn't stay in London."

"And why is that?" Callie had never been more taken aback in her life.

"London is a cesspool, and the close quarters on his ship would be a misery. Clean country air is what he needs to recover. Then once he's well enough, you could show him the workings of—" The man had enough sense to stop.

Callie silently finished the sentence for him. *The Grange.* But it wasn't this argument that would sway her.

It was that St. Alban's petite, blonde viscountess was a good six months gone with child. She was glowing and gorgeous and perfect in the specific way only a very pregnant woman could be. Callie had had to swallow a surge of envy. What if the physician was wrong and the captain was contagious with smallpox or scarlet fever? Callie couldn't bear the idea of causing the loss of a child due to her selfishness.

And that had settled it.

Callie was offered a night's accommodation in the Cleveland Row house, which she grudgingly accepted, her departure effectively delayed a day. In the deep of the night, however, she did have a curious incident.

Restless, she'd wandered out into the back garden to collect a few sane thoughts from this mad whirlwind of a day when she encountered a girl of middle-teen years— Miss Radclyffe was her name—lying flat on her back on a patch of springy turf, gazing up at the twinkling sky through a small telescope.

Due to all the confusion, Callie's introduction to the girl had been overlooked, but she had noticed Miss Radclyffe's quiet presence at the opposite end of the supper table. She was of a height with Callie, unusual in itself, and quite possibly the most strikingly beautiful girl Callie had ever beheld. It was clear that Lady St. Alban wasn't Miss Radclyffe's mother by blood, but rather a woman from the Orient. From St. Alban's life before he'd become a viscount.

Callie apologized for intruding on Miss Radclyffe's stargazing.

"No need. The stars are entirely indifferent," she'd replied. "I was hoping to catch a few last remnants of the Epsilon Perseids."

"The Epsilon Per—?" Callie trailed.

"It's a meteor shower. But, alas, it seems to be done for the year."

"For the year?" Somehow, Callie found herself being drawn in and charmed against her will. As much as she wanted to loathe St. Alban and everyone connected to him, she couldn't. His family were, quite annoyingly, treating her with respect, kindness, and generosity.

"Oh, yes, meteor showers return every year. They're quite predictable, unlike us humans."

"Quite," had been Callie's dry reply. The last day had certainly reinforced the truth of human unpredictability.

For the hundredth time inside this cramped carriage, her gaze fell on the most unpredictable Captain Nylander, drawn in as if by a lodestone. He was hard to ignore, sprawled out as he was, taking up three quarters of the carriage interior, if an inch. A harness had been devised to hold him in place and prevent him from sliding to the floor. The leather held fast and true, even as it was tested to its limit by the combination of jostling carriage and massive man.

She rested her forehead against the window. The translucent gray cloak of encroaching night was beginning its descent, chasing away vibrant daylight and dimming the green of rolling hills into slate gray. They would have to stop at a coaching inn for yet another night on the road. Only fools traversed the Exmoor after dark.

Annoyance seethed inside her. Over the last few years of widowhood, she'd become accustomed to bending circumstances to her will, not the other way around. And this was one set of circumstances that refused to bend. At least St. Alban's carriage took the road more smoothly than the average stagecoach, and its plush leather seat was, if she was being honest, quite the most comfortable she'd ever set bum upon. Still, she'd have rather returned home by post coach than be saddled with her present predicament.

Through some strange trick of fate, she'd become obliged to care for the man who would buy her home out from under her, if given half a chance. It defied all belief. Well, that wasn't precisely correct. Mrs. Bickle, softly snoring at her side, was the woman sent by the Westminster infirmary to nurse the captain. Callie shifted away from the woman's bony elbow cutting into her rib cage. In truth, the woman wasn't much of a nurse.

The following day, when Callie and St. Alban had arrived at the inn to begin the journey west, Mrs. Bickle had jutted her sharp chin at Callie and spoken her words to St. Alban. "Yer sayin' this woman is to be the boss o' me?" The question ballooned with incredulity with each word she spoke. "Why, she ain't dressed no better than Margie down the street."

Callie hadn't the faintest idea who Margie-Down-the-Street was, but it wasn't a compliment.

"It's an odd state of affairs, I kin tell ye," the woman continued, "when the 'elp is dressed better than the missus."

It was true that Callie didn't believe in finery, abjuring silk in favor of the more practical Devonshire wool. But she kept her appearance neat and her person clean, which was more than Mrs. Bickle could say for herself.

Chin lifted, Callie stepped forward. "If you plan on being in my employ, that will be enough." Her words emerged in the haughty voice provided her by the best finishing school in Exeter. "You will be reporting to *me*, not the viscount." She glanced at St. Alban and detected an appreciative glimmer in the man's eye. "If you take issue with this state of affairs, I suggest you see yourself back to whence you came."

She half hoped the woman would. Instead, Mrs. Bickle had mumbled the approximation of an apology and followed the lads lugging the captain to the carriage.

Before he'd left, St. Alban had a few final words for Callie. "I've sent word to Nylander's ship and had his personal effects retrieved."

Callie had nodded when she'd really wanted to shrug. These details made no difference to her.

"And," St. Alban continued, and Callie's ears perked up at a particular note in the syllable. "Have you any experience with malaria?"

"Not in the least."

"It's a fickle affliction. You'll need to keep your eye on him."

Callie scoffed. "Isn't that Mrs. Bickle's job?"

The viscount raised his eyebrows. "You need to know that it can be tricky. Best to be aware."

On those strange parting words, the man had left her responsible for an unpredictable man and his churlish nurse. Now, here they were, a cozy little trio rattling through the wilds of Somerset.

Again, her eyes landed on Captain Nylander. Somehow, in the dusky interior of this enclosed carriage, the light sought out his features and illuminated them to their best advantage. The twin crescent-moons of golden eyelashes resting against his cheeks. The bold ridge of a cheekbone. The firmness of lips parted in abandoned sleep. Even the three days' growth of his beard didn't obscure the deep cleft of his chin or the strong line of his jaw. His beard was red. *Like Thor's*, came her next thought.

Mama had loved the Norse tales and told them to Callie a hundred times over. Gorgeous and bold and possessed of a glorious red beard, Thor had been her favorite. It could've been no accident that Father's beard was red, although now streaked with gray.

And the man slumped in restive oblivion across from her? He would've made Mama's knees buckle. Even with his resemblance to Thor, *ungodly* handsome was what he was.

He was impossible to behold.

He was impossible *not* to behold.

Callie nestled her shoulder deeper into the little corner and closed her eyes. She'd been staring at that man too long. They must be nearing the coaching inn by now.

Tomorrow, they would complete the final leg of their three-day journey and, at last, reach the Grange. The thought should've comforted her. Instead, it sent a clamor of anxiety straight to her gut. She had just about four weeks to secure the Grange from her god-like rival. The fictitious money from Mama that had saved her in the moment wouldn't save her in the end.

There would be no money from her father, either. He'd visited the Grange on the first anniversary of Georgie's death, looked her up and down, commented that she'd *gone to seed*, and hadn't returned since. If she lost the Grange, the last vestige of her marriage into the aristocracy, there would be little, other than her title of Dowager Viscountess, left to show for her father's strides into the upper tier of Exeter Society or for her entire adult life, for that matter.

Her hands coiled into tight fists. No one was going to take it from her. Not the Viscount St. Alban. Not the Viking sprawled out across from her. Even if she had to make a deal with the devil.

"You could make a pretty penny, and the tax man would be none the wiser."

Those had been the notorious pirate Jack Le Grand's exact words during their first and last meeting at Hawkset Cove a few months ago. They taunted her now, their illicit wisdom hard to deny in the face of her desperation. She would never see as much quick profit from her brandy using a law-abiding London distributor.

Could she go through with it? Could she humble herself to the outlaw whose offer she'd so haughtily rejected in the name of all that was right and honest? The humiliation she could bear, but the loss of principle and the high ground, to be on the same level as such a man…

That would be an outcome difficult to tolerate.

If she went through with this idea and *if* St. Alban ever learned of it, he wouldn't sell her the Grange. It was that simple. He might even have her arrested.

Well, he wouldn't find out.

Voices from outside the carriage began shouting back and forth, and the vehicle slowed. Callie poked her head forward, nose pressed into the window, steaming the glass, and made out the open gate and circular courtyard of a coaching inn.

As the viscount's team of four clattered to a stop across rough cobblestone, Mrs. Bickle startled awake. Eyes wide with terror, she grabbed Callie's arm. "What in the feckin' 'ell is this?"

"Mayhap you were still too deep in your cups this morning to have taken notice of our departure from the Red Lion in Salisbury?" Callie asked, unable to restrain her distaste. The woman's drinking habits really were a source of concern. "We've arrived at our inn for the night."

Mrs. Bickle released Callie's arm with a nettled smack of papery lips, drew her shoulders back, and exhaled a piqued huff. If the woman had been a cat, the hairs along the ridge of her spine would've been standing on end. Callie buttoned her pelisse and clutched her reticule in general readiness to vacate the carriage. She wouldn't bother soothing the woman's wounded pride. She hadn't spoken a word that wasn't true.

A gruff cough sounded from the opposite bench. In unison, she and Mrs. Bickle turned to find the captain twisting his body from side to side in a stretch that seemed testing and intentional, the leather strap surely strained to its limit. Long, golden lashes fluttered off high cheekbones, and a blue gaze, clouded and disconcerting, stared out. Callie froze, her breath caught in her throat, and waited. He did this periodically, tried to push through his fever to wakefulness. Then his eyes slid shut, and he slumped back into his seat. The breath Callie had been holding, released.

"Well, wadn't that a close one?" Mrs. Bickle exclaimed on a relieved, short laugh.

Callie couldn't help but share the sentiment. What would she do with this hulking Viking if he awakened inside the carriage with little to no idea how he got here? It was the stuff of night terrors.

Well, he wasn't *hers* to do anything with. He was Mrs. Bickle's problem. This time tomorrow eve, they would arrive at the Grange, and she would thoroughly wash her hands of him. At a house and estate as sprawling as Wyldcombe Grange, she would be able to avoid the man entirely, even after his recovery. Of their own accord, St. Alban's words returned to her:

Then once he's well enough, you could show him the workings of—

Good thing he'd stopped, for she would've had to tell yet another lie by assuring the viscount that, of course, she would show Captain Nylander the workings of the Grange. Which she hadn't the slightest intention of doing. Did the man take her for a fool?

Callie reached around Mrs. Bickle, still bristling with offense, and twisted the brass handle. She cut across the short distance and pushed the door open before hopping down from the carriage. The flummoxed coachman, Thomas, stared out at her, his empty hand extended to assist her descent. She exhaled a short, unladylike snort. City servants were a different breed from Devonshire ones. Still, she should let the man perform his duty and assist her once in a while, like a good lady.

Again, she snorted. She wasn't any good at being a lady, not since Georgie died.

She pointed her face to the sky and inhaled a deep sip of fresh country air. Around her, the courtyard teemed with hustle and bustle: the cacophonous clanging of the arrival bell, the sharp clatter of horse hooves against well-worn cobblestone, the harried shout of the hostler to a stable lad. "Kip, make play!"

The boy, who couldn't have more than a dozen years on him, directed a crude gesture at the hostler's back, and his step, if anything, grew slower. While Callie had no doubt the impertinent Kip had a firm handle on how to make his way in the world, she couldn't like the fact that he was doing so at such a young age. It was the same in every stable throughout the country.

"And you must be the most esteemed Dowager Viscountess St. Alban?" Callie heard at her back. She pivoted, just as Mrs. Bickle brushed past her and made tracks to the tap room. The man before Callie was lowered into a bow fit for the Queen of England. She cleared her throat, and the man rose, not to his full height but to one deferential to his betters, who happened to be her at present.

"Am I to take it you're proprietor of this establishment?"

"I am, my lady."

Again, he bowed. *For pity's sake.* She had little use for the idea that she was better than anyone else for no reason other than she had a title. On the Grange, when she was picking apples or milking a cow, none of that mattered.

"Have you enough rooms to accommodate our party for the night?" she asked, straight to the business at hand.

"The best the Dog and Duck has to offer, my lady."

"My coachman will require the assistance of two, likely three, strapping lads to assist one of our party to his room. Thomas?" she called out.

At the sound of his name, the driver broke off his conversation with a local serving woman, her eye possessed of the specific saucy twinkle that had Callie averting her gaze. Thomas ushered the obsequious innkeeper to the carriage as to acquaint him with the same problem their party had encountered at the coaching inn from last night: the transport of a feverish, possibly concussed, man from carriage to room, which likely involved stairs, judging by second-floor windows buffed to a mirror shine.

The place did appear clean, at least. Like as not, comfort would be an altogether separate issue. It didn't matter. All she needed was a hot bath, supper in her room, and a place to lie horizontally, preferably in a bed with fewer than ten lumps and more than fifty feathers. Based on recent experience, it was the most she could hope for.

While the men began extricating the captain from the carriage, Callie stood silent sentinel beside the front door and observed the now-familiar process. The leather strap holding him in place was released. With the assistance of gravity, he slid to the carriage floor while his body was pushed out by one man behind and tugged forward by another in front, his massive form emerging feet first. On a series of moans, groans, and guttural grunts from both patient and helpers, the Viking was hoisted by the arms onto the shoulders of a strapping lad to either side of him.

At the bottom edge of her vision, she caught movement in the general area of the captain's boots. Yesterday and this morning, he'd mostly been dragged across the courtyard of the Red Lion. But just now—

There!

There was the movement again. His feet were attempting to keep in step with the men assisting him, which could only mean…

Her eyes flew up to meet the narrowed blue slits of his already trained upon her. She went still as a woodland creature caught in the crosshairs of a hunter's bow, and her heart banged out a series of hard, rabbity thumps. His gaze wasn't clouded, not in the least. Instead, he stared straight at her—straight *into* her. Piercing, lucid were those eyes the blue of a Devon sky on a clear wintry day. An electric instant passed before his lashes dipped once, twice, and fell to a close onto high cheekbones.

Her parted lips uttered a soft, unconscious "Oh," and she startled into self-awareness. The captain drew level with her at the doorway, and she glanced at his feet. His eyes might be closed, but his boots continued moving in step with the stable lads. One foot in front of the other, the trio shuffled across the threshold and past her, but his gaze didn't meet hers again. Was it possible he was recovering?

Once inside the main tap room, she trailed behind her party and inhaled the scents of roast joint, tobacco, beer, and unwashed body blended into the particular humid fug that she recognized as the unmistakable scent of the English coaching inn. Locals and travelers alike had gathered for an evening of food, drink, and song, judging by the fiddler tuning his instrument in the corner nearest the fireplace, which glowed orange with recently stoked embers. Up the stairs, she followed the huffing and puffing lads as they negotiated the Viking up, one heavy step at a time, stopping for rest on the landing midway before reaching the top.

"My lady," the innkeeper began, gracelessly squeezing past her in the narrow, second-floor corridor. "You are in Number One. Our very finest room." He turned the key in the lock to their left and flung the door open with a flourish.

Callie paused and allowed the innkeeper to precede her into the room. She chanced a final glance in the direction of the Viking, half expecting to meet his lucid blue eye again, every muscle tense with the possibility. But a silhouette of his profile was all she was presented as the lads fumbled with the door one down from hers.

A frisson of heat lit inside her, strange and discomfiting. Goose bumps raised along her arms, down her spine.

Then he was ushered into the room next to hers, leaving her in the corridor, alone. She stood rooted in place, kept company by the muted opening strains of fiddle song seeping up through thin floorboards. Not once in her life had she reacted to another living being the way she had to that man just now. Shaken, she stepped inside her room.

She cursorily glanced at the wall to her right, papered in a garish green that had been fashionable at no point in history. She and that man would share *that* wall. She could only hope he kept his feverish ravings to himself tonight. But... was he still fevered?

It wasn't any of her business. Now that they were free of the carriage and inside their separate rooms, he was Mrs. Bickle's concern.

"Have water for a bath sent up along with a light supper," she said to the innkeeper. "I'll be keeping to my room for the duration of my stay."

The man inclined his head, and light glinted off a centrally located patch of bald scalp. "Your wish is my command, my lady."

He scurried off to perform his duties, and Callie kicked the door shut. She paced to the room's lone window and stared unseeing at the courtyard, a hive of buzzing activity below.

What if... *what if* the Viking was emerging from his sickness? Further, had there been something in his piercing blue eyes? Beyond lucid, she'd have sworn they were *knowing*. What could they possibly *know*?

A knock sounded on the door, and Callie nearly jumped out of her skin. "Yes?"

"Your dinner, milady," came a muffled female voice through hollow oak.

"I'll be right there."

Callie tamped down the uncharacteristic flight of fancy and crossed the room. The contact between his eyes and hers had lasted the flicker of an instant, no more. There was nothing in it. *Nothing*.

Tonight, she would lay her head on her rather feeble pillow.

Tomorrow, she would arrive home.

And such matters would be relegated to the travel weariness they surely were.

4

C allie's eyes flew open.

A moment later, she gathered her bearings and remembered where she was. The Dog and Duck coaching inn, in her room, her ears attuned to whatever odd sound that had cut through the inn's general cacophony to jar her from an already fretful slumber. For there was such a riot of noise: mail coaches clattering in and out of the courtyard below; the arrival bell announcing said mail coaches and late-comers; the ongoing drone of the ground floor tap room, periodically punctuated by raucous proclamations and spikes of laughter.

But, no, none of those sounds had startled her awake. A different sound, one clear and intentional, had done it. Still as stone, she lay, eyes wide, ears waiting for it. Scratchy eyelids grew heavy and her blinks ever longer as exhaustion pulled her into seductive slumber. Perhaps it had been a dream.

A sudden *thump-thump-thump* drummed at her headboard, and through the wall came a muffled shout. She shot upright. *There!*

What in heaven's name was happening? Was there a lunatic or an injured person on the other side of that wall? The next instant, her brain caught up with the question. This was the wall she shared with the Viking. According to Mrs. Bickle, his fevered ramblings were worse at night.

Callie reached for a pillow and dragged it across her face. That should do the trick. For a moment, it seemed to. Then, through sparsely populated goose down, another shout sounded. How long could this go on? Where was Mrs. Bickle?

One minute passed, then another and another, as she reached for sleep. But she couldn't find it, not with the random bang of a fist against the wall at her head, accompanied by the odd exclamation. At last, she gave up.

She swept blankets off her body and jerked on her nightrail. Cautiously, she poked her head through the crack in her door. When she saw that no one occupied the corridor, she traversed the short distance to her neighbor's door, her feet a quiet tiptoe against floorboards. Not that she needed to bother. A solitary woman's footsteps couldn't compete with the bedlam below.

Electing not to knock, she twisted the handle and tentatively pushed, expecting to find it locked. Instead, it opened on surprisingly silent hinges. A scold ready on her lips, she strode inside, scanning the room for Mrs. Bickle, who was most assuredly passed out from too much drink. The nurse's cot, however, was empty, and the privy corner, too.

Of a sudden, she felt *it*... a presence. Her body and her breath stilled; her mind and her heart raced. To her left lay the bed...

And the Viking.

Inch by slow inch, her gaze traveled up the foot of the large central bed, over feet and legs covered by blankets, her body heating up by a degree with each inch spanned. The blanket ended at his hips, and she braced herself. She released a sigh of relief when she saw that the upper half of him was clothed in a white linen shirt, his trim waist widened all the way up to broad shoulders that took up nearly half the bed. He was such a very large man, not an inch of excess on him, just massively built.

She inhaled a deep breath and, at last, reached his head, hair strewn about in golden streaks. The word for his hair, the one that had been on the tip of her tongue for days, came to her: lustrous. The man had *lustrous* hair.

At last, she made herself meet his eye, which was surprisingly lucid and decidedly unimpressed. "All done?" his voice rumbled deep and grumpy down the length of bed.

Callie opened her mouth to reply, but words refused to form. She snapped it shut, her throat gone dry as the desert, and clutched her nightrail tight to her throat. It wouldn't do for him to see her blush.

"Is it possible I've been kidnapped?"

"Hardly," came her retort before she could control it. The very idea! So, he didn't remember her from St. Alban's manse? Well, she would be a forgettable sort of woman to a man who looked like a Viking god. "You are here at the behest of Lord St. Alban."

"And *here* is?"

"The middle of Somerset."

His eyebrows drew together and released in an instant. "This conversation promises to be a long one. Before we continue, can you bring me another pillow? This one is flat as a flounder. I'd get it myself but"—he shifted, and for a breathless second Callie thought he might rise, but as quickly he fell back—"I can't seem to find the strength. And a cup of water," he added. "My throat feels as though I drank a pint of sand."

Callie glanced about the room, its furnishings consisting entirely of a bed, side table, wardrobe, privy screen, and cot, and located the washstand near the open window. Since the room was no longer or wider than three strides in any direction, she had a water pitcher in hand in a matter of seconds. Hand shaky, she poured a tin cup halfway full, the Viking's slitted eye upon her the entire time. Her heart raced as fast as a hummingbird's in spring. The way he was ordering her about, he must think her a servant, possibly a nurse.

If he'd been a sheep with, say, foot scald, she'd move him to another pasture and have him well on his way to recovery in a matter of minutes. But this man wasn't a sheep, and he certainly didn't have foot scald. And she certainly was no nurse. Still, she could give him a pillow and a cup of water without inflicting too much harm.

Cup in one hand, she reached for the pillow on Mrs. Bickle's cot. Where was the blasted woman? Hesitant, wary, Callie crept closer, stopping two feet away from him. His form covered by a pile of blankets, he didn't look so much like her enemy as a man in need.

"Which do you prefer first?" she asked, her tone at once brisk and wobbly. She alternately held up the cup and the pillow.

He rolled onto his side, facing her. "The pillow."

She stood, pillow extended, her feet rooted to the floorboards, perplexity increasing with each second that ticked by.

He cast an impatient glare over his shoulder. "Well?"

Oh. He meant for her to tuck the pillow behind him.

She took a few steps forward and set the cup on the bedside table. The distance separating them—less than a foot now—was about the closest she'd ever come to a man who wasn't her husband, and, even then, she hadn't come much closer to him.

Eyes clenched shut, she bent over, careful not to touch any part of him, and wedged the pillow between his back and the bed, giving it a few pushes for good measure. In all, the task took no longer than three seconds, but in that time her brain was able to sift out one prevailing sensation: the heat of him. Not the expected clammy heat of fever, but the heat of a large body pulsing with banked energy. He might be weak as a kitten now, but soon, too soon, he would be a jungle cat, up and moving, vibrant and curious, and entirely too much for her to handle.

Even as a frisson of warning crawled through her, she experienced another sensation, one more tangible and immediate in that three second span. Humid and searing, his breath filtered through her nightrail and shift, reaching the bare skin of her thighs in short, shallow bursts. Warm, liquid heat snaked through her, pooling in the pit of her stomach, and even lower to her—

She shot upright, every muscle in her body aligned in

the ramrod straight line of utter, complete, soul-deep shock. "That should do it."

He rolled onto the flat of his back with an accepting grunt and thunked his head solidly on the oak headboard. "Water," he growled, eyes closed on a wince.

She almost felt sympathetic, but she had a more pressing concern. How was she going to get the water into this man? Without… without coming close to him?

She cleared her throat and reached for the cup. Angling her body so only the parts that absolutely had to come close, came close, she pressed the cup against his firm lips. When they parted to admit the drink, she tipped the cup, and he swallowed. Her eye followed the undulation of his throat, the muscles connecting to collarbone and shoulders below his shirt, the beat of his pulse visible on his neck. So strong, so vulnerable. He was all heat and vitality and man.

His eyes flew wide, and alarm shot through her. At once, he began coughing and wheezing, the strangely intimate moment instantly transformed into sputtering chaos.

"What can I do?" She'd never felt so inept.

He shifted to his side until his coughing fit resolved. "Water," he croaked again.

"Are you sure? It didn't go so well the last time. Perhaps all you need is a little—"

"*Water*," he repeated.

Blindly, he reached out to grab the cup from her hand, just as she reached forward to place it there. Time stretched and slowed as water sloshed into the air on a high arc before landing with a splash on the Viking, soaking his hair and shirt to the skin, turning white linen disconcertingly translucent. What a lot of mess a little water could make.

"Will I never quench this thirst?" he growled, his eye catching hers and holding. "Nursing might not be your calling."

"I'm most definitely *not* your nurse," she shot back.

It was almost laughable the way his eyebrows met in confusion, but he wasn't wrong. She was a terrible nurse, and she hated being terrible at anything. Work and diligence always made her the best at any endeavor she set her mind to, except this one. She might have to concede the possibility that even the slovenly, drunken Mrs. Bickle was a better nurse than she.

Mrs. Bickle… Of course.

What Callie was good at, however, was knowing exactly what action to take when the moment required it. She held up a staying forefinger when the captain opened his mouth to ask the inevitable bevy of questions. "If you'll excuse me."

She caught another bewildered knit of his brow before she fled the room and flew down the staircase toward the main tap room as fast as her feet would carry her. She would wager every last acre of the Grange that Mrs. Bickle was there.

It was only when she reached the bottom step that it hit her: she was clad in a nightrail, a shift, and not a stitch more. Mumbles and whispers crackled in the air, and eyes darted left and right to gape at her. She raised her chin a notch and cinched the sash tighter at her waist. Her bare feet squirmed on the sticky floor. There was no turning back from here.

A room much altered from its earlier incarnation greeted her. Then, it had been warm, cozy, its pace slow and inviting. Now, it was hot, smoky, cacophonous with strident fiddle and shouted conversations from a dozen tables.

A loud, brassy laugh rose above the din. Instinctively, Callie pointed her feet in the direction of the sound, weaving through the densely packed room in a series of starts and stops as she attempted not to brush against anyone else's person and failing miserably.

Again, the laugh sounded, closer now. She rounded another two tables, and there her quarry appeared before her, sitting on one man's lap while flirting with another. What sort of nurse was Mrs. Bickle anyway?

Callie stopped directly in front of the cozy trio. At times, she could use her height to great effect to gain attention and a grudging respect when she needed it. This was one such occasion. "Mrs. Bickle."

The woman tipped her head all the way back on her neck and met Callie's eye. She expected to find distress there, or at least a bit of sheepishness at having been caught out in the dereliction of her duty, but she encountered no trace of guilt in the woman's bold gaze.

"My, oh, my," Mrs. Bickle began, clearly having knocked back more than a few pints of the inn's house brew. "If it ain't the lady of the manor." Mrs. Bickle made a big show of eyeing Callie up and down, inviting a few snickers. "Yer a long 'un, that's sure."

Callie ignored the woman's rude appraisal. She'd been called worse. Still, she clutched the closure of her nightrail tighter at her neck. "Your patient needs you."

Another brassy laugh erupted from the nurse, and she snuggled deeper into the man's lap, who gave a lecherous waggle of bushy eyebrows. "There's no 'elp fer that man. Just let the fever run its course and see whut's on the other side. Never know, the bloke might still be alive." She let out a boisterous guffaw before draining the last dregs of her pint, belching the loudest burp ever to cross a pair of female lips, and calling out for another.

Callie knew when she'd been dismissed, soundly. Without another word, she swung around and retraced her steps toward the staircase, catcalls, whistles, and hoots trailing in her wake. The absolute nerve of that woman.

She could take Mrs. Bickle's advice and leave the Viking to sweat it out. Perhaps the innkeeper could find her another room, one that didn't share a common wall. But it wouldn't do. She had a responsibility to the blasted man.

Dread carving grooves into her gut, she stomped her way up the stairs. She arrived at his door and slowly twisted the handle, unable to fully commit to the decision she'd made only seconds ago. Perhaps providence had taken mercy on her and delivered a miracle to this room by plunging him back into fever and unconsciousness.

She poked her head inside and found no such mercy

had occurred. The Viking now sat completely upright in his bed, his lucid stare trained entirely on her.

"And she's returned," he said, his tone dry, his voice rumbly. "For a woman who *most definitely* isn't my nurse, you're remarkably concerned about the state of my health."

"It's not *concern*," Callie retorted. "I'm responsible for you, you nodcock."

The insult had been lying dormant in her belly for days, and its release felt good. Then his eyes narrowed, and his head canted to the side, speculative. Perspiration pin-pricked her skin, and her sense of bold triumph tucked its tail between its legs and scuttled away.

She might regret her acid tongue yet.

MEMORY TEASED at the edge of Nylander's consciousness. He should recognize this woman, he was certain of it, but memory refused to make itself known.

"We've met," he said, slowly, a statement of the obvious that would earn him another *nodcock* if he wasn't careful.

She breathed out a long-suffering sigh. "In London. At St. Alban's manse."

That was it. How could he forget the way those eyes of hers had seared into him? Though they'd lost a measure of their former intensity, they were no less hostile. "My memory of that day is a bit foggy."

"No surprise there, considering how hard you cracked your skull on St. Alban's marble floor."

That would explain his wallop of a headache. A memory of the world going black at the edges pushed for-ward. His collapse must've quickly followed, its cause becoming increasingly clear, given his current state of fogginess and bone-deep exhaustion. He pointed toward the table beside her. "Bring that here."

She glanced down and appeared surprised to find the discarded cup of water near at hand. She gazed at it as if it filled her with dread.

"You left it there when you hied off like the three Furies were at your back."

On an irritated roll of her eyes, the woman grabbed the cup in an unceremonious slosh and walked it carefully over. Then she shuffled backward until her back hit unyielding wall. He suspected she would disappear through stone and plaster if she could. What a confounding, difficult woman.

Cup drained, his eyes couldn't help closing in satisfied bliss. They opened to find her gaze steadily fixed upon him, her eyes those familiar onyx orbs of hostility. "So, Somerset," he said by way of a conversational bridge.

She nodded once, tightly, as if the affirmation cost her. "On our way to Devon. St. Alban thought it would be best if you recovered in the country from your—"

"Malaria," Nylander rumbled, low, more for himself than for her. "And he sent *you* with me."

She shifted on her feet. "Something like that."

Interesting. "So, if you aren't my nurse, then who in the blazes are you?"

"Just the country bumpkin relation of a grand London aristocrat," she replied with the shrug of an indifferent shoulder. The movement, its intent, struck a wrong chord. Though he hardly knew this woman, he understood at a fundamental level that she was indifferent to nothing.

Another memory skirted the edge of recognition. They'd been introduced at St. Alban's manse, but he couldn't grasp the details, except that her adamantine eyes had been the last thing he'd seen before his complete descent into darkness. This, he also knew: she was telling him something important. But he had neither the strength nor the patience tonight to pull the truth from her. An altogether more immediate issue was foregrounding itself. Namely, the noxious fumes emanating from his person.

He eyed the woman up and down, and, again, she shifted beneath his scrutiny. She didn't care for his appraisal. "I find myself weak as a cub and in need of your assistance, but you might not be strong enough."

"I'm plenty strong," she retorted.

He couldn't help himself, he smiled. This particular grown woman's petulance was surprisingly winsome. "In that case, I require your help to remove my shirt."

Her face soured as if she'd swallowed a lemon, whole. "Why?" she squeaked around it. "We've established I'm no nurse."

"Well, you're *here* and better than nothing—"

"I wouldn't be so sure of that."

"—And in case you haven't noticed," he persisted, "I smell as if I've been keelhauled through London's sewers and hung out to dry on the beak head of an East Indiaman that hasn't been to shore in six months." Her eyebrows met in confusion, and her face took on an ashen hue. "To be clear, I need a bath, and the only way to do so effectively is to remove my clothing."

"You don't need—" The sentence died in her mouth. "You do stink to high heaven."

"Then if you'll assist—"

"But," she cut in, "you must be too weak for a bath."

"A sponge bath will do."

She dipped her pinky into the washbasin, and relief stole across her features. "This water is cold. We can't have you catching pneumonia on top of malaria."

It was almost comical how little she desired to do with him. *Almost.* His desire to wash the sweat and stink off his body was the greater of their two desires. "I'm a sailor, I can handle a little cold water. Now"—he bent at the waist, shifting his upper body forward—"let's get this shirt over my head."

He stilled and waited. She might bolt. It was entirely possible. Except she didn't seem the type. A stubbornness hung about her, one that insisted she see a matter through to its end. Why else had she returned to his room? It certainly wasn't out of a liking for him. Still, he couldn't help adding, "I don't bite, unless—"

Her eyes widened, and he stopped. Her ears went red to their very tips. She knew how that sentence ended.

Bloody hell. Now he'd given her every reason to bolt. "It was a sailor's poor attempt at a joke, forgive me." An uncertain moment passed, then her body relaxed by a fraction so small he sensed rather than saw it. "I've worked the hem up to my hips. All you need do is hoist it over my head and off." He made it sound so simple, matter-of-fact, like it would be no strange thing to help a man she hardly knew undress. "Got it?"

She nodded.

"Ready?" he prompted, unsure of her.

She squared her shoulders. "Of course."

That a girl. He inched his shirt to mid-torso. "That's about as far as I can get it."

Her eyes darted lower, beyond the edge of his shirt, toward his exposed stomach. She went stone still. "You've never seen a man's bare midsection?" he asked.

"I'm from the country and have four brothers, of course I have." She hesitated. "Loads of times." Another hesitation. "Just maybe not like yours."

He snorted. And he thought he'd heard it all. On another woman's lips those words might've been flattery, an invitation, but not on this woman's. "Can we get on with it?"

She inhaled a deep breath, coughed a little—he really did reek—and stepped forward like a martyr braced for the flames. Through the dregs of his odor came other scents: fresh citrus, flowery apple. For such a sour woman, she sure did smell like a sweet confection, the sort a man could gobble up in three bites and be left wanting more.

His cock jumped, and he gave himself a mental shake. Where had that come from? If he wasn't careful he would give her considerably more to view than his bare chest.

For her part, she couldn't have noticed the state of his partial arousal for she'd clenched her eyes shut to grab the hem of his shirt. The back of her hand brushed against his skin, cool and fluttery, as she lifted in one great heave, up, up, up, over chest, shoulders, head, his hair the last of him to slip free. Her eyes opened, and a startled "Yip!" escaped her in the instant before they squeezed shut again.

"I thought you'd seen a shirtless man before." He was unable to resist adding, "*Loads.*"

One at a time, she blinked her eyes open. "You have, um," she stammered, clearly searching for the correct word.

Ah. It wasn't his body that shocked her speechless. It was his skin. Or rather the designs inked into his skin. A few tense seconds passed before he took pity on her and provided, "Tattoos."

"*Tattoos,*" she breathed out.

"Have you never heard tell of them?"

"No, I mean, yes, I have. But I've never seen one." She rolled her bottom lip between her teeth. "Or four."

"Mmm," he grunted, a heavy sense of exhaustion replacing his interest in this conversational thread. He allowed his eyes to drift shut and propped his head against the headboard, gently. "About the sponge bath?"

"Yes?"

"If you could gather the requisite materials?"

"Oh, of course."

Eyes closed, he listened to her spring into action, at once sliding the washstand next to the bed before opening and closing and opening the drawers of the wardrobe, the muted sounds of her rifling through fabric, presumably to find a suitably clean cloth for washing. "Ah-ha," she crowed. His eyes slid open to find her holding up two cloths in triumph. In a thrice of seconds, she'd set them on the washstand next to a rather dingy bar of soap.

She backed away one step, then another, until she reached the door, hand on handle, her entire being poised on the edge of flight. "If that will be all..." she trailed.

"You're not going to finish the job?"

"I, um," she stammered.

A guffaw escaped him, and her eyes went flinty. Really, she made ruffling her feathers too easy. "Another poor excuse of a joke, forgive me," he apologized. Even he could hear that he only half-meant it. "I have all I need."

Her baleful eye lingered on him a beat longer than was strictly necessary before she pivoted on her heel and fled the room.

The woman didn't need to be told twice.

5

S ilence.
Dark, persistent, absolute silence that might last until the end of eternity roared in Callie's ears. How long was this blasted night doomed to drag on?

She flipped onto her other side, annoyed she only had two, and doubled the pillow beneath her head. All had gone quiet within and without the inn, providing the perfect combination for a restful night's sleep, yet the swarm of activity buzzing about her brain kept chasing it away. *That* moment kept returning to her.

"You've never seen a man's bare chest before?"

She'd screwed up her every last bit of courage to peek her eyes open. She'd most definitely not seen one like his. Broad shoulders, muscled chest, segmented stomach exposed all the way down to the level points of hip bones, which his blanket had blessedly cut across the lower half of him.

If a body could be a sin, his was.

But it wasn't his body that had shocked her speechless. It was his skin. Or rather the drawings stained into his skin. One covered his entire right pectoral, another smaller one lay to the left above his heart, yet another wrapped around his left shoulder, and one more inked into his right forearm.

What sort of man had ink needled into his skin? What sort of man was the Viking... her *enemy*?

In her fluster over naked torsos and sponge baths, she'd forgotten that not insignificant detail. The man was her enemy. He would take the Grange from her, if given the chance.

Did he have more of those tattoos on other parts of his body?

Likely.

Had they been painful?

Doubtless.

Were they still painful?

Why wouldn't her mind settle and sleep? The man was more interesting than he had a right to be.

Had Mrs. Bickle returned to mind her charge? *Mrs. Bickle*. The woman was a trial at every turn.

Callie tossed onto the side she'd abandoned not a minute ago. But, really, had Mrs. Bickle returned? She hadn't heard another peep through the wall, which was in all likelihood a very good thing.

It could also be a very bad thing.

She snorted in frustration, swept the covers off her body, and retraced her steps to his room. This time she really did have to be careful not to make a sound, quiet permeating the air at a level that begged to be disturbed by the errant creak of a floorboard.

The door closed behind her on a muted click, and she went still, her eyes adjusting to the darkness whose only source of light was the pale moon streaming through the open window. On quick cat feet, she made her way to the bedside, noting on her way that Mrs. Bickle's cot lay empty, and found the Viking lost to slumber, blankets pulled beneath his armpits.

He was in no mortal danger. She could leave now. But her feet refused to obey her good sense. The position of the moon had its rays washing over the still figure, as if displaying him. Glorious and golden, he lay. His red beard remained. He hadn't shaved it off, and, strangely, she was glad.

Her timidity slid away, and her curiosity drew her in. She'd seen plenty of men stripped to the waist during harvest season, yet none of them were like him. They lacked his presence and his beauty, and none of them had *tattoos*.

Each appeared to have been done by a different hand. The one on his right pectoral was simple in concept, swirling lines thick, bold, and a soft black that faded into his skin as if it had been there a very long time. The same was true of the smaller one on his right forearm, a simple black anchor. The one at his shoulder, however, possessed a different character. Its lines twisted about in intricate, braided patterns that were familiar. It might've had origins in the ancient tribes of Ireland or Scotland.

But the small one left of the center of his chest intrigued her most. Delicate and perfectly symmetrical, it consisted of three vertical columns of what appeared to be lettering from an Eastern language of the sort she'd seen at the British Museum upon her one and only visit.

What did it say? And why had he placed it directly above his heart?

Nothing about the tattoos would have been remotely civilized in the eyes of English society. What did they feel like? Not the experience of having them on one's body, but to touch beneath one's fingertips. As if a person outside of herself guided her actions, she leaned in, and her breath hitched, catching in her lungs his newly clean scent. Trembling fingers reached out to hover a hairsbreadth above his shoulder for a collection of one, two, three seconds before touching tips to flesh.

The tattoo felt like... *skin*, warm to the touch, as if the sun had just kissed it. A quick glance confirmed the rest of his arm was tan. This man spent his days beneath an open sky. They were similar in that regard.

She shook her head. It wouldn't do to think of any similarities between them.

Of a sudden, his hand shot across his body and strong fingers closed around her wrist. A shocked yelp escaped her, and she startled backward, but she didn't get far as his grip only tightened. Her eyes met his blue gaze steady upon her, not an ounce of surprise in their depths.

Her stomach dropped to her toes, and mortification swept through her. He'd been watching her watching him and... *touching* him. Again, she tried to draw back, but he held fast onto her wrist and her gaze. How long had he been observing her?

Her heart threatened to thunder out of her chest. She didn't know this man. They'd been in close proximity for days, but she knew him not at all. She knew not what sort of life he led, what those tattoos said about him. The man was a *sailor*, which wasn't a solid marker of good character.

Most importantly, he was her rival for the Grange. How could she have lost sight of that? Well, the sight before her was how.

As suddenly as he'd grabbed her, he released her. Reflexively, she reached up to clutch her nightrail to her throat and found nothing there, only bits of flimsy linen. Alarm streaked through her. She was clad simply in her sleeveless shift.

He rolled fully onto his side, eyes assessing, propped on an elbow, his unclothed torso stretched before her. She rolled her bottom lip between her teeth and went very, very still.

Again, he reached out and caught her wrist, this time gently. His thumb began stroking its inner pulse point, and his blue gaze burned into her. "Is that a blush pinking your pale cheek?"

Oh, the tumult his words, the gravel of them against the back of his throat, unleashed in her. That numb feeling of acting outside herself returned. It was just him and her and the moon.

She swayed forward, and he released her wrist, his fingers catching at the indent of her waist, his eyes never leaving hers for an instant. "What a lovely curve."

His gaze, his touch, his *words* stole into her. No man had ever spoken of her thus.

Straight. Flat. Tall. Mannish. Unnatural. Those were the words Georgie used.

Yet in this deep hour of an endless night that existed in a limbo between reality and fantasy, a different narrative called out to her, one that whispered of her *lovely* curves.

His hand trailed higher, and the breath froze in her chest. A fingertip circled the tiny pink birthmark near the top of her arm, once, twice, before moving an inch over and brushing the outer curve of her breast. A smile, shadowed and knowing, curled about his mouth. "So sweet."

She should be outraged, livid. She should storm out of this room. Yet it didn't feel right in this oh-so-wrong moment. A reality unlike any she'd ever experienced held her in its grip. His words, his touch, his smile struck fierce, hidden longing into sudden flame.

His hand curled around her ribs and pulled, the sinewy muscles running the length of his forearm flexing, tugging her closer to the bed, to *him*. Sudden doubt spiked through her, and she went rigid, her body transforming into an unyielding plank. His eyebrows creased together, and his smile fell. Alarm pulsing off him in waves, he shot upright and swung his legs off the bed, a strip of blanket now only covering... Quite a bit of him. Her blush doubled in ferocity.

"Have I," he began, discomfiture in his words, writ across his face, "misinterpreted the situation?"

"What situa—" She stopped.

Oh. *The situation.*

Yes, she should say *yes*, that he'd misinterpreted everything. But it was a lie. Her body, warm and liquid and vibrating with novel sensation, had known all along what her mind hadn't: she wanted him, and every cell in her body combined into collective desire for this *situation*.

He'd misinterpreted nothing.

"Stay."

Further melting occurred inside her. A man had never touched her, looked at her, not like this, not like his world would collapse if she didn't *stay*. Something shifted into place. *Desire.* She'd never been desired, a fact well-established by three years of marriage to Georgie, and she'd never experienced desire for herself.

To have the object of her desire begging her to *stay?* She was powerless to resist it.

With a confidence she'd never dreamt of possessing, she stepped into the parted V of his legs. The darkness lent a strange anonymity to the moment, even granting her permission to proceed in a way she never would in the light. She wasn't sure how much more out of character she could act tonight, but she was about to find out.

She took his upturned face between her hands and lowered her lips to his, unprepared for the heat of his skin upon hers. Large, strong hands wrapped around her waist, and she never felt so feminine as when he pulled her into him on a low, gravelly groan. His tongue touched hers, and she startled back on a shocked, "Oh!"

"What did I do?"

"I don't know." She bent forward, her mouth a hairsbreadth from his. "Do it again."

Who was she right now? It mattered not. It felt right, being this woman.

Well, it didn't feel *right*, but it did feel *good*, oh so good, when his mouth strained up to close the distance between their lips and touch his tongue to hers again. Warm, slippery skin on hers. Soft. Firm. Inviting. Exacting. Lava pooled in her belly, seeped into her veins, pulsed through her body, lit her skin alive.

Oh, this felt *good*. It had to be right.

His hands shifted to her bottom and pulled her into him. He broke from her mouth, and she cried a protest at the loss. His lips found the crook of her neck, his tongue tickling, teasing, tempting her to venture down this path of sin with him. She'd never felt so physical, so carnal, her body understanding what her mind hadn't until now: she was made for this. She'd never felt more like a woman.

With a knowledge of their own, her legs slid up his muscled thighs until she straddled either side of him. Here, she hesitated, her quim hovering above his manhood. She could turn back, forget this reckless, wanton night ever happened.

His tongue slid across her collarbone, and she knew:

she would never forget this night. Why not make it worth remembering?

She took her shift in hand, inching it up fold by fold, breathless to feel *him* against her naked flesh.

"Wait," he spoke into her neck, his breath deliciously warm and humid against her, his beard one part scratchy, one part soft. Oh, how she liked his beard. "Are you ready?"

"Ready? I've never felt more ready for anything in my life."

His hot laugh skated across her skin, and a different sort of heat ribboned alongside her desire. She'd amused him, and it felt good. His fingers slid along her legs, and the thought fell away. One hand clasped her thigh, steadying her in place, while the other feathered across the sensitive inner flesh. Her breath caught in her throat, and her quim throbbed, ached. She waited and craved.

Then he touched *her*, his finger a wet slide along the slit of her sex. A shudder ripped through her, and a deep animal moan sounded from a part of her she hadn't known existed. Ephemeral tingles of desire, pleasure, and need glittered through her, transforming her into a heavenly being, no longer bound to this earth.

His finger slipped inside her crease and touched, *oh!*, a part of her too sensitive to be touched, yet it begged, pleaded, for more of that sweet pressure.

"Your cunny is so wet for me."

What absolutely filthy words. She wanted more of them. "How wet?" she heard herself ask.

"Mmm, let's see."

Again, his long finger feathered along her slit, before pressing into her center. She inhaled a sigh. What novel sensation, to have him *inside* her.

"Oh," she breathed out when he began moving, his finger a slick, slow slide. Pleasure cascaded through her in tiny ripples. Her lips found his neck, salty, sweetish, and she licked up to the lobe of his ear, taking it between her teeth and giving it a testing nibble. He groaned and increased his rhythm. With a will of their own, her hips began to move in unison, and a sudden craving to touch him, all of him, intensified.

She reached between their bodies, her fingertips brushing the hardened muscle of chest and stomach until the solid velvet of his manhood throbbed against her fingers. Reflexively, her fingers wrapped around him. How very large this part of him was.

"Firmer," he groaned.

She squeezed her fingers. His eyes drifted shut, lost to the pleasure she gave. Then they slid open, and a smile curved about his lips, a smile so sure, so confident, it would have sent her running in the other direction on a different night. But not tonight. Tonight, his cocksure smile emboldened her, spiked her craving higher.

"I think you're ready."

He took his cock in hand, and, instinctively, she placed both hands on his shoulders and lowered to touch her sex to the tip of his manhood. With his other hand, he cupped the back of her head and drew her face toward his, her hair falling to form a curtain around them. It was only him and her at the center of this night where time had left them to their own devices.

"You're trembling." His words formed an intimate whisper, a caress.

"Am I?"

His lips touched hers, and the pure carnality of the moment slid into something softer, something more intimate. His hands clasped her waist, and he began to enter her with a slow sureness, her quim stretching to accommodate him.

Oh. He was large, so very large. The sensation wasn't exactly pleasurable, but it wasn't unpleasurable either. She shouldn't enjoy it, this pleasure mixed with pain, but her body wanted *more.* On mindless impulse, she lowered as he continued to penetrate. How much of him was there, anyway? Could there possibly be *more?*

He tensed beneath her, and his eyes flew up to meet hers, a question forming about his mouth.

She pressed a shushing finger to his lips.

She understood.

He'd reached her maidenhead.

He removed her finger from his mouth. "I don't deflower—"

"I want this."

A hesitation. A clench of his jaw, until finally, "You're certain?"

On wicked impulse, she twisted her hand and grabbed his, bringing it to her lips, her tongue tracing along his forefinger and slipping it inside her mouth. She sucked, and he moaned. Her hips bucked as he thrust upward, fully impaling her, and her maidenhead was no more.

Breaths heaving, mingling, he and she went still as her body adjusted around him. It burned. She'd known that would happen. It ached, too. But, oh, how sweet the ache. And, oh, how she wanted more of this ache, an ache borne of pain, pleasure, and desire.

She moved up, then down, slowly, developing a rhythm on him, his hands at her waist, steadying her, even as he took the tie of her shift between his teeth and tugged. The garment fell open, revealing her breasts. Self-consciousness flared through her. "I'm sorry. They're so—"

"Lovely and"—he kissed one nipple—"pink and"—he kissed the other—"perfect." He took the hard bud into his mouth and sucked.

The pain, the self-consciousness, all the world fell away, and she was no longer herself. Her hips bucked, and she rode him.

"Do you feel it building?" he groaned against her breast, his fingers digging into her hips.

She clutched his hair at the scalp and held on for dear life as sensation swept through her. "What is *it*?"

He slowed his rhythm and met her eye. "*Bloody hell.*"

Panic streaked through her. "Don't stop," she pleaded. He couldn't, not now. "What did I say?"

"You'll have your pleasure, too."

Without another word, he slipped his hand between them and touched a fingertip to—oh—what must—*oh*—be the most sensitive spot in her body, rubbing, sliding along it as his hips began to move in smooth strokes.

"Do you feel it now?"

"Yes," she exhaled, caught up in sensation she couldn't name.

She ground down on his fingertip, even as he continued to penetrate her. Her eyes closed, she reached, she strove for a place just out of grasp. He took a nipple between his teeth and bit down, his tongue flicking across the hard bud. Of a sudden, the elusive place opened to her, and she hung suspended on the edge of a precipice.

Driven by wild animal instinct, he thrust into her, and his fingertip worked her, and she fell headlong into an oblivion of bliss, her quim clenching, then pulsing its pleasure around his hard cock. He drove harder, stroke by delicious stroke, and shouted his release into her clavicle, his rhythm slowing to an eventual stop, the ragged in and out of their combined breaths, the only sound in the room, his forehead heavy on her shoulder.

A strand of dismay twined through her. What was she to do next?

His hand began feathering up and down her spine, and she longed to sway into the light pressure. It very closely resembled... affection?

She needed to leave... *now*. She pressed one foot, then the other, to the floor and slid off him. Even in the moonlight, she could see the satisfied smile curling about his mouth. "Must you?"

Yes. She absolutely must.

She cleared her throat. "Why don't you lie down while I"—she glanced down at her thighs, smears of blood dark against her pale skin—"wash up?" He needed a little washing up, too.

She snatched the unused cloth off the washstand and made quick work of cleaning herself. She turned to hand him the cloth and saw that he'd drifted off to sleep. She made to wake him and stopped. Why on earth would she do that? Tomorrow, the humiliation of this night would be difficult enough to bear. Why start tonight?

She placed the cloth on his manhood, which even in its sated state was no small thing, and cleaned him. After all they'd done, this act felt as intimate. She tossed the thought into the rubbage bin along with the stained cloth. If Mrs. Bickle noticed it, well, she was just the sort of person who could intuit what had happened tonight with a single glance, for that was where the woman's thoughts resided.

Callie's rational mind was beginning to reassert itself, and it didn't like at all what it would need to contend with in the hours and days to come. Drat it all, what had she done?

Shame warred for primacy over another feeling: a bright gloriousness, full to bursting. Did all coupling feel like this?

Something else tugged at her: the possibility of a babe. After all, new life was the natural consequence of what they'd just done. It was possible she could have the estate and a babe, all she ever wanted...

Ridiculous thought. After one coupling? She'd observed enough animals in the farmyard to know it usually took more than once. Still, a thread of hope that wouldn't be snapped by mere reason shimmered through her.

She gave herself a mental shake. It was high time she remembered who she was and her place. She wasn't a farmyard animal. She was Lady Calpurnia Radclyffe, Dowager Viscountess St. Alban, skilled at all she put her hand to and as frigid, Georgie had assured her, as the North Sea wind in January. *That* was who she was, and she mustn't forget again.

She rushed to the door, sparing one final glance for the man laid out flat on his back and fully asleep. Oh, how was she to face him in the clear light of day?

His handsomeness wasn't merely superficial. Somehow it radiated from the core of him, so bright it burned. It really was near impossible to look at him directly, which suited her perfectly. She would never be able to look at this man directly again.

Not with the knowledge of this night in his eyes.

NEXT MORNING

A proper, indifferent dowager viscountess for all the world to see, Callie drew her shoulders back and lifted her chin. She was the only still point in the courtyard that had transformed into a hub of hustle and bustle with the dawn. Not a whiff of the lusty hussy she'd been in the dark of the night hung about her.

Oh, what had she done? And she would have to sit inside an enclosed carriage across from the man she'd done *it* with? A wave of nausea threatened to topple her.

"Kip!" came a shout from the inn's main doorway.

The boy sauntered around the corner and shouted back, "Whut?"

The innkeeper burst forth and snarled. "You'll show a little more respect and snap in your step if you expect to earn your keep!"

"Beg pardon," Callie cut in without thought.

The innkeeper stopped dead in his tracks and pasted a smile, false and obsequious, onto his face. "Why, Lady St. Alban, I didn't see you standing there. I trust you had a restful night?"

Callie cleared her throat. She wouldn't be discussing last night with this man, or anyone else for that matter. She nodded toward Kip. "What's your business with this boy?"

"He's in my employ, your ladyship."

"He isn't a relation of yours?"

The innkeeper shook his head, scorn in his scoff. "The boy has no relations to speak of."

Her mind made up in a snap, Callie addressed the boy directly. "How would you like to come to Wyldcombe Grange with me? You can enroll in the local school and train to be a groom, if you like."

Kip's mouth screwed up to one side as his eyes narrowed on her. He was testing her words for the truth. "I ain't settin' foot in no school, milady," he stated. "A groom is foin wi' me."

"Now see here," the innkeeper began, his obsequiousness losing to his true nature. "You can't sweep in here and steal my labor without consequence. Or recompense," he added on a sly note.

It wasn't difficult to see what the man was about. "This boy isn't chattel. He can't be bought and sold. He comes with me of his own free will. If you wish to keep your labor, my advice is to treat them like human beings." She turned to the boy. "Now, would you like to sit inside with us?" She wasn't sure how to fit him, but she'd find a way.

"Out on the boot is foin wi' me. Better 'n' foin." With that, he trotted past her and hopped onto the back of St. Alban's carriage.

"Don't you need to gather your belongings?" she asked, slightly nonplussed.

"I ain't got nuthin' worth takin'." He pulled up his feet and wriggled his bony bum into place. Clearly, he wasn't new to this.

Like that, Callie had picked up another stray. Between the boy, the Viking, and Mrs. Bickle, she'd accumulated quite a few on this journey. Speaking of her strays...

Movement beyond the innkeeper's shoulder pulled her attention from his livid scowl and toward a matter more pressing: Captain Nylander's blond head making its way through the main tap room. Panic spiked through her in time to her racing heart. Her moment of reckoning was on its way.

When he appeared at the doorway, confusion replaced panic. The Viking was, once again, being helped along by two strapping lads. His feet were moving, but his gaze stared out, clouded and unfocused on a distant point that wasn't—oh, could it be?—*her*.

"What is this?" she called out. "Isn't Captain Nylander recovered?"

The lads grunted in dissent. "Found 'im like this," said the one. "'Is nurse told us to bring 'im down," said the other. The trio shuffled past. The lads struggled to settle the Viking into the carriage, even rousting up a dubious Kip from his perch to help.

All the while, Callie stood back, careful to tamp down the pure, unfettered joy that threatened to spring to life. She should be ashamed of wishing ill health on a person, but she wasn't. She'd never been so happy to see someone so helpless.

Maybe... Perhaps... Could it be all wasn't lost? Was it possible that he wouldn't remember last night? Had the heavens offered her a reprieve from her midnight sin?

At last, the lads emerged from the carriage, beads of sweat trickling down their faces. Thomas the coachman slipped them a bit of coin, and Kip bounced back up onto the boot.

"Your ladyship," Thomas said, "we're ready to depart."

Callie allowed the man to do his job and hand her up into the carriage. Once inside, she gave the captain a quick once-over to ensure he was strapped in properly before settling her gaze on the view outside her window. She was just about to give the ceiling a quick double-tap to let Thomas know she was ready to depart, when a voice cried out, "Oi!"

In the next instant, Mrs. Bickle was rapping on the carriage door. With everything else going on, Callie had clean forgotten the woman. She twisted the handle and pushed the door open. Mrs. Bickle shouldered her way inside the carriage, along with her particular fug of stale beer and unwashed body... Or was that *bodies*? Distaste shuddered through Callie.

"Thought ye could git rid o' me that easy?" Mrs. Bickle asked, her usual fractious self.

"I would never in a million years dream that getting rid of you would be so simple a feat."

The woman harrumphed and jutted her chin toward the Viking. "This 'un made it through the night. Whut did I tell ye?"

"No thanks to you."

The woman shrugged an indifferent shoulder.

"You know, Mrs. Bickle, I'm beginning to have a few doubts about you."

"Oh, yeah?"

"Did you ever receive instruction on how to be a nurse?"

"Depends on 'ow ye define *instruction*."

"And given the company with whom I've seen you cavorting these last few nights, I doubt the existence of a Mr. Bickle altogether."

"Worked that one out, eh?" Mrs. Bickle barked a short laugh and immediately groaned, rubbing her fingers against her temples. The woman was clearly experiencing the aftereffects of a night of carousing, and who knew what else. Actually...

Callie did. Heat flared. Oh, how she knew. *Intimately.*

She didn't dare look at the man opposite her for fear of what her gaze might reveal. But she didn't need to look. She needed only count her lucky stars. It was possible the gods had granted her a reprieve this once.

She might not be so lucky a second time.

6

THREE DAYS LATER

Nylander inhaled. *Fresh, feminine.* He tasted. *Salty, sweet.* He touched. *Silky cream, burning velvet.* He beheld. *Shadowed cherry, temptation.* He licked…

His eyes flew open. A grand twenty-foot ceiling towered above his head. This wasn't the low beadboard ceiling of the captain's quarters on the *Fortuyn*.

He shut his eyes and ignored whatever strange reality awaited him beyond his eyelids. He struggled to reclaim the dream that flirted, teased, taunted, enticed at the edge of consciousness, but never committed. If he could just make out her face…

The door to the room opened and clicked shut, and the dream was gone. Reality must be contended with. His eyes slitted open. A chambermaid crossed dense, quiet carpets, set down a water pitcher, and threw open the curtains, a burst of brilliant light catching dust motes midair, transforming the room from dark to light in an instant. A soft hum on her lips, she finished her duties, blissfully unaware of her silent observer, and vacated the room, her lilting song fading in her wake.

No longer could Nylander avoid reality. His body stiff and achy, he pushed himself up and slumped back against the headboard. Lush goose down below him, the slide of fine linen across his skin, it was possible this was the most comfortable bed he'd ever lay arse upon.

65

The room was spacious, both in breadth and depth. So, too, was it spotless, elegant, upper-class, and without doubt English. Alongside that certainty came another: he'd never set eyes on these four walls in his life. Walls golden with warm afternoon light, if he was reading the day correctly.

A flash of lucidity came to him. *London. Jake's foyer. Blood everywhere. Unrelenting heat. A pair of coal-black eyes, hostile, watching him sink into black-edged oblivion...*

Malaria. He hadn't experienced a flare-up in years, but when it circled back around, it was always quick to remind him of its power and its potential for devastation.

Was he still in London? *No.* The afternoon sunlight was too bright, the air too fresh.

He wasn't clear about the precise *where*, but a memory of the *how* pushed forward. *Interminable jostling, jolting, rattling. Claustrophobic, confined space.* He'd journeyed here by carriage over days, the nights spent in coaching inns.

He swept blankets aside and touched toes to lush Persian wool, intent on making his way to the window. He stood and experienced a wobble. Some amount of time had passed since he'd stood under his own steam. He shifted his weight from foot to foot and, at last, gained his balance.

He shambled over to the floor-to-ceiling bow window. Beyond, a great swath of countryside spread out, verdant stretches of land segmented into animal and crop enclosures by low stone walls. To his left, defined rows of an orchard ate up an entire hillside, and to his right, a blue sky dotted with puffs of white clouds met the horizon on a distant green hill.

Devon. He was in Devon to recover. Who had given him that information?

The country bumpkin relation of a grand London aristocrat.

Another certainty came to him: it wasn't a dream.

Dark shadows. Citrus, apple, salt, heat. White linen. Creamy flesh.

His lover hadn't been a strumpet like he'd begun to dread. He didn't use strumpets. Disease was the reason he gave his men, but it wasn't the truest one, and he wouldn't be the sort of man who contributed to that particular misery.

No, a distant familiarity hung about his memories of his lover. He'd known her in some way. Impressions of her remained: the feel of her, the scent of her, the curtain of her hair, a birthmark, cherry red and heart shaped on the inner flesh of her upper arm. So perfect was it, he could've believed it a tattoo.

What had gotten into him? Where the bloody hell was she? And, more importantly, precisely *who* the bloody hell was she?

He shuffled toward the armoire, each step a careful negotiation. There wasn't a bit of him that didn't ache from head to toe. Inside lay his personal effects—shirts, trousers, boots, toiletries—laid out like he was a respected guest.

Once he'd convinced his body to wash, shave, and dress, he ventured into his strange, new reality and stepped out into a dim corridor. Alone, he gathered his bearings in its eerie silence, carpets stretching dozens of feet to either side of him. This place set his teeth on edge.

A skivvy maid with no more than sixteen years on her rounded a corner, a bucket in one hand and cleaning rags in the other. Her eyes widened on him, and she bobbed a neat curtsy. "My lord," she said and slipped past.

Nylander's brow furrowed. In what world was he a *my lord*?

His ears picked up the drone of voices, muffled, distant, and he followed the sound, through the corridor, down the carpeted, walnut staircase, across a great, empty foyer, down another, less grand flight of stairs, until he stood just on the outside of a lively, bustling kitchen in the full swing of dinner preparations. Servants rushed about, attentive to their duties. Polishing silver, kneading dough, washing dishes, barking orders, taking orders, each aware of their individual role that contributed to the collective operation. One could happen upon a country bumpkin relation here.

"Where is that Kip with me eggs?" shouted a rotund, red-cheeked woman wearing an apron and an air of authority. It was clear who was in charge.

The intoxicating scent of hot currant buns fresh from the oven woke Nylander's stomach on a roar, and he stepped forward. The kitchen ground to a dead stop, ten sets of wide eyes upon him, curious and unblinking. The cook's hand stole up to her mouth, unable to contain the, "Oh, my word," that escaped her lips.

Nylander never felt so large and obvious in his life. "May I trouble you for a pot of coffee? And one of those buns?"

The cook nodded toward a scullery maid, who scurried into action. "How many spoons of sugar and dollops of cream do you take?"

"I take it black."

A few seconds passed before she nodded her acceptance of this preference. She clapped her hands together in two short bursts. "All right, you lot, dinner won't see to itself. Now you've seen *him*"—her chin jutted toward Nylander—"time to get on wi' it."

Her words set the room into motion, and Nylander was able to relax a measure. The cook gestured toward a stool, and he perched against it, taking in the workings of the lively kitchen. At last, he was presented a pot of coffee.

"Black, as you like it. I'm Mrs. Bailey."

"My thanks."

The brew's sharp, pungent scent hit his nostrils before it met his taste buds, and he couldn't contain a small groan of appreciation. That was the stuff. He could face this day and the strange world he'd landed in. Time to get some answers. "I'm Nylander. Perhaps you would be so kind as to tell me where precisely I am?"

A passing footman shot him a skeptical glance as if he'd grown another head and tossed out, "You're in the kitchens."

Nylander took another sip of his coffee and swallowed a rough answer to the man's smart-arse remark. *Patience.* "And where are these kitchens located?"

"Wyldcombe Grange," offered another passing footman.

At last, he was getting somewhere. "Devon?"

Mrs. Bailey huffed, exasperated. "North coast."

It was clear she wanted to finish with a *you dolt*. But she didn't, and for that he was grateful. However strange this situation was to him, it appeared equally strange to the staff.

"And where can I find the master of the house?"

"*Master?*" The servants looked at each other as if he'd asked them the way to Siam.

Nylander inhaled a snort of frustration. This was growing tedious. "Am I correct to assume this house has a master?"

Another moment's hesitation. Then Mrs. Bailey called out, "Kip!" No such boy presented himself. "Someone fetch him. On my word, that lad has no more substance than an apparition. One moment, he's there, and the next—*poof!*—he's gone."

A flurry of activity followed Mrs. Bailey's words. Clearly, the woman ruled this roost with the power and certainty of a monarch. Within the minute, a footman produced a young lad, fist clutching the boy's shirt as if he might, indeed, vanish into thin air.

"Now, Kip," Mrs. Bailey said, "take this man to the *master*." A few muffled snickers floated about the kitchen. "You'll be knowing where to go?"

"Aye." The footman had released Kip, and the lad was already half out the door. Nylander took this as his cue to follow.

"And don'tcha come back without a few eggs!" Mrs. Bailey called at their backs.

But Nylander paid no mind to it. A breeze of earth, dung, salt, and sun scented the air. Aye, they were near the coast. A measure of his misgiving slipped away. Nothing was too wrong in a world that had him near the sea.

"Been here your whole life?" He called out to Kip's back as they trod down a row of the kitchen garden's brushy root vegetables. A few hens clucked about, the poultry yard to the right. Winded from trying to keep up, he hoped the question would slow the boy's quick feet.

"Nah," the boy tossed over his shoulder. "Been 'ere as long as you."

"And how long is that?"

"Goin' on three days now." The boy seemed entirely indifferent to the matter.

Kip led them through the narrow gap between two outbuildings, a barn and dairy judging by their sounds and smells. They emerged from the narrow, dark space into an open field. Kip stopped and pointed toward a group of riders on a distant hillside. "There."

Nylander squinted into the distance and made out three men, two facing the one. The master and his right-hand men, presumably. "Your master is there?"

The boy flicked him an impudent smile. "Aye, there she be. Me *master*."

She? Strange slip of the tongue.

On the move again, they strode across tall grasses, navigated around grazing sheep, one pasture, then another, and another. Distant, fuzzy details began to sharpen into focus. The set-apart rider, while of a height with the others, possessed subtle differences. He was whippet-thin and bore himself stiffly. He guided his horse around, pointing somewhere even farther distant, his back now to Nylander. Beneath a black wide-brimmed hat trailed a thick braid the red of a banked ember down to the small of his back.

Nylander blinked. *Could it be?* He blinked again. It could.

The master of Wyldcombe Grange was, in fact, its *mistress*.

"Is she wearing—"

"Aye," Kip answered before Nylander could finish his sentence.

"Odd," came out of Nylander's mouth without thinking.

The woman wore *trousers*, like a man. Of course, how else could she sit a horse astride?

The boy sucked his teeth. "Ye git used to it."

Half a pasture away, snippets of conversation and individual words spoken between the riders carried on an easterly wind. *London distributor. Deal. Cliff barn.* At that last bit, the two men gave each other a look. Nylander knew that look. They didn't agree with their mistress.

Nearer, he and Kip came, and an entire sentence floated past. *I'll have my wishes heeded.* This from the mistress. It was clear that her wishes were commands, and they were to be obeyed.

More words. *Kegs. Mine.* The men exchanged another round of doubtful looks.

Nylander and Kip were now close enough that the conversation was clear. So intent were its participants on each other, they hadn't yet noticed them.

"That field borders the Exmoor," one of them said, "and Tom hasn't maintained the wall like he should've these last few years."

The other man spoke up, "Sheep ain't got no business in that pasture."

"They're doin' well enough where they are, if you don' mind me sayin', milady."

The woman's back drew up into a long, rigid line, making her sit taller in her seat, confirming his initial impression of her. She didn't like being nay-sayed. "Will you speak with Tom about it? Or shall I?"

"If 'e ain't on a bender," one of the men grumbled.

"Get him dried out and back to work, if you please. I expect the sheep to be moved to the easterly pasture within the week."

Nylander only noticed the dog at her horse's feet when it barked once and advanced a few steps in warning.

The two workers' gazes shifted and sized him up in silent scrutiny, their eyes saying what their mouths didn't. He wasn't one of them, so he should state his business. Kip scurried away in a flash, even as Nylander planted his feet. With two clicks of her tongue, the woman tugged on her horse's reins to face him.

Untraceable emotion flickered across her face, and Nylander's breath left his body in one great *whoosh* as if he'd been gut-punched. He'd found *her*: the mistress of Wyldcombe Grange, the country bumpkin relation, and his lover from the inn combined into the form of one slight woman.

Her gaze narrowed upon him and grew harder, if such a thing was possible. From her elevated position, her head canted to one side, as if she was evaluating an insect she would very much like to squash.

So, it was like that. She wouldn't acknowledge their... *relations?* She was no different from every other lady of her class who gazed upon him as a lower being. Except, of course, when they wanted something from him, they sang a different tune, more like a *coo*. But that was over quick enough, and the world went right-side up again.

Fine. He'd play the game her way. It was all the same to him.

The dog barked once again. "That'll do, Chance," she said. The black and white sheep dog circled back to his mistress, his mismatched blue and brown eyes never once wavering from Nylander.

"Lazarus wakes." Her voice had gone hard as the onyx of her eye. "You shaved your beard."

Nylander's brow furrowed at the observation. Unexpected. "Aye."

"And nicked yourself."

He ran a hand across his smooth jaw. "More than once."

She shifted in the saddle. "Do you know where you are?"

"Word has it Wyldcombe Grange."

A blast of wind gusted up, and she just caught her hat before it sailed away. She resettled it before addressing her men. "Will, Cam, I believe our business for the day is concluded. Are your instructions clear?"

"Aye, milady," one worker said. The other nodded. They clicked commands to their horses and galloped away. Latent resentment hung about the men, but Nylander dismissed the observation. This woman's strained relations with her men was no concern of his. *Cold. Haughty. Diffi-*

cult. She was the sort of woman who didn't care if she was liked.

"Now, Captain Nylander, as for the *why* of your whereabouts—"

"It's Nylander."

"I believe that's what I called you."

"Captain isn't necessary. Just Nylander."

Copper eyebrows came together in bemusement, and she shifted on her horse. "That's bold."

A beat passed, and the certainty grew that he didn't like this woman.

"Like a woman wearing men's trousers?" he asked. *Or like a woman stealing into a man's room for a midnight tryst?* he left unasked.

This woman had plenty to teach him about boldness. Yet, even with the proof before his eyes, it didn't seem possible *this* woman was *her*.

THE BEGINNINGS OF A BLUSH, splotchy and hot, began a slow creep up Callie's body. Silently, she blessed the high neck of her blouse.

She wouldn't give oxygen to his opinion on her choice to wear men's trousers. It was a decision that had rubbed more than one man the wrong way. And she cared not a whit. Trousers were a practical and functional garment for the work she did.

"There are different levels of boldness, I suppose," she replied. "Mayhap you're wondering how you came to be here." A pause, a breath. "Mayhap you don't remember due to your fever. You were quite delirious. Who knows what sort of wild imaginings entered your mind."

Breath held, she waited for the leering lift of an eyebrow, a smirk, something, anything that betrayed *knowledge*. But there was not the faintest sign, not a flicker of recognition. Was it possible he didn't remember? She wasn't sure whether to feel relieved or insulted.

"Why don't you refresh my memory?" he asked in his low, velvety baritone.

She cleared her throat. "At Lord St. Alban's request, I brought you to the Grange to recuperate from your malaria and for you to get a lay of the land in case you want to—"

She stopped before she could finish the sentence. *Buy it out from under me.*

He didn't know about that. How could he? St. Alban hadn't the opportunity to tell him before he'd passed out and cracked his skull on the floor. This man had no idea that this land would be his in a few short weeks if she couldn't gather the necessary funds. She had a choice: to tell or not to tell.

She made a decision on the spot. The Viking was Lord St. Alban's friend, after all, not hers. He was her rival, her *enemy*. What sort of fool helped her enemy?

He glanced about. "How far are we from the sea?"

"Not a mile."

"I knew I smelled salt on the breeze."

"You're the captain of a ship, correct?"

"The *Fortuyn*. My crew will be wondering where I'm off to."

"I believe Lord St. Alban handled that bit of business."

"The man always was efficient."

"He is certainly that." An edge so sharp ran the length of her words they practically glinted in the sun.

Nylander cocked his head, his eyes narrowed on her. He was wondering about that sharpness, its origin. The man hadn't the faintest clue, and she planned on keeping it that way.

He jutted his chin. "What sort of estate is this?"

"A typical one for Devon. Sheep for their wool. Cows for their milk and cheese. Root garden for the winter. Apple orchard. We're in the middle of picking season."

"I heard you discussing kegs with your men."

"For cider."

"Must be a profitable venture if you need more storage space."

Her heart kicked up a notch. "Last season was profitable," she bit out. She wouldn't be discussing the Grange's profitability with this man.

"You need a barn repaired? I have some experience—"

"That won't be necessary," she cut in. "We are quite capable of managing our own affairs."

He snorted and shifted his gaze. "Quite a few moving parts on a place like this. And you run it?"

He was impressed. Gratification stole through her. She couldn't help it. She wasn't sure a man had ever been impressed by her.

"And, if I may inquire further, what might your name be? I can't quite call it to mind."

Callie blinked, nonplussed. For all their conversation, and, ahem, *history*, it hadn't occurred to her that he might not remember her name. "I'm the Dowager Viscountess St. Alban."

His eyebrows knitted together. "I'm not versed in the intricacies of the English peerage. That would make you...?"

"The widow of the Fourth Viscount St. Alban, the current Lord St. Alban's predecessor. You may call me Lady St. Alban."

He nodded slowly and kept his thoughts to himself. He did that a good bit.

Her grip tightened around Arrow's reins. The gelding felt the movement and tensed beneath her, ready to ride at her command. "I wish you a speedy recovery from your fever, but I don't anticipate any reason for our paths to cross again. Wyldcombe Grange is a big house and an even bigger estate, and you have the freedom of both at Lord St. Alban's request. Do you ride?"

He shook his head.

"Pity." She didn't mean it, and, judging by the skeptical glint in his eyes, he knew. "Without the ability to ride, you won't be able to take in the Grange's many workings."

A cynical smile pulled at the corner of his mouth, but he remained silent. Those blue eyes of his pierced straight through her. How terribly, terribly attractive this Viking was. His hair shining golden in the sun. The anchor tattoo peeking out from the bottom of a rolled-up shirt sleeve.

"A good day to you, sir." Her thighs gave a light squeeze, and Arrow responded with a gentle trot forward. "Chance," she called. The dog sprang into motion and raced ahead.

As she galloped away, she felt his eyes on her back. Her heart had no choice but to race. Oh, traitorous body. It was good news that he didn't remember her or *that* night. Then why didn't it feel good?

She wouldn't press her palm to her stomach. Or think about what could be growing there. Or hope for it. Her mind knew it would be a disaster, even if the deepest part of her soul didn't.

Better to hope he never did remember. What would a tup with her mean to a man like him, anyway? It was absolutely for the best that she had no ties with that man, who too closely resembled a Viking from the days of yore, washed up on these shores to strip her of her land.

Guilt twisted inside her. She should have told him about the sale of the Grange. That he was St. Alban's first choice if she couldn't get the monies together.

But why? The man was a ship captain, who couldn't even ride. What business did a man who couldn't ride a horse have running Wyldcombe Grange? The master of the Grange—or *mistress* as the case was—must have that skill. It was a minimum requirement of the job.

Her resolve strengthened. Her plan to save the Grange had already been set into motion, the meeting with Jack Le Grand set for two nights hence. If all went well, she would have her money and all her doubts would be for naught. She wouldn't feel an ounce of guilt regarding the problematic man she'd just left in her dust.

Did it matter that her gains would be ill-gotten? They would be for the greater good. She wouldn't see the Grange run into the ground by a man who knew nothing about the land.

The man couldn't even ride.

7

TWO DAYS LATER

Inside the ill-lit warren of the Devil's Books' tap room, Nylander sat under the low ceiling and anchored his elbows on smooth oak. He took a long, deep draw from his first pint of the night. He knew in his bones there would be a second, and, possibly, a third. The ale, red and strong, worked its way through him, flowing from the base of his skull and spreading by warm increments.

Mostly recovered from his fever, he'd awoken this morning restless and jittery, needing to occupy himself with something, anything, that had purpose. But he'd found nothing. The servants mostly avoided eye contact, uncertain about his status in the household. He felt like a ghost that everyone would rather be rid of, beginning with the house's mistress.

True to her word, the *Dowager* hadn't crossed his path since he'd watched her gallop into the hills two days ago. No surprise there. She was a stuck-up lady who didn't feel the need to show the likes of him anything more than the thinnest facade of courtesy. Her kind wasn't obliged to his kind. She'd gotten what she'd needed from him.

He took another sip of his bitter.

Tomorrow morning, he'd leave a note, informing her of his departure and thanking her for her hospitality. He'd be halfway to London by the time she opened it.

Even with this plan in place, he'd been unable to suffer

through another solitary night beneath Wyldcombe Grange's silent, sprawling roof. So he'd prowled the house until he happened upon a passing footman and asked for directions to the nearest town.

"That'll be Upper Wyldcombe Lacey. 'Tisn't more than half an hour by foot." The man cocked his head. "You'll be wanting a public house, I reckon?"

"Aye."

"The Devil's Books on High Street is the one you want. Tell Jeb that Ollie sent you, and he'll treat you right."

The man hadn't been wrong. The Devil's Books combined the necessary elements of the perfect English tavern: ale, warmth, company in the tap room, if one was inclined, and solitude, if that better suited the mood. Nylander took another draw of his ale and caught Jeb's eye.

"Curious name, the Devil's Books." He found himself more inclined toward conversation than he'd been in a good number of days.

Jeb poured an ale halfway and spoke as he let the head settle. "Well, a curious sort of bloke built it more than a hundred years ago. We got four floors representing the four suits of a deck of cards. You're on the diamond floor. Each floor has thirteen doors and fireplaces for the number cards in each suit. And to top it off, we have a total of fifty-two stairs in the place." Jeb finished the pour. "Ale up!" He started another pint. "Rumor has it the man made his fortune off cards, but no one knows. He died a childless bachelor, and the place was bought and converted into this public house. Who knows why the original owner chose such a *quixotic*"—the man pronounced the word as if he'd just learned it—"name for his tavern."

Nylander gave an agreeable nod and tapped his drained glass for another. Jeb had hardly set a full pint before Nylander when a loud, brassy voice rang out, "Why if it ain't *the* Captain Nylander, or me name ain't Liza Bickle!"

Every last hair on Nylander's neck prickled to a stand. He knew that voice, and clearly it knew him. He swiveled on his stool and faced the woman, whose words had drawn every eye upon him. She was short, buxom, and possessed of a specific promiscuous charm welcome in every tap room around the world.

"Aye," the woman called over her shoulder as she stacked half a dozen empty pint glasses and carried them to the bar. "'Tis ye aw'right."

"Have we met?" he asked, cautious.

"'*Ave we met?*" A rough laugh scraped across her throat. "Guess I can't expect ye to remember, seein' as 'ow ye were out of yer bloomin' mind the 'ole time."

Dread crept in at the edges of his confusion. There was a question he must ask, an answer he feared. "Were you my nurse on the journey from London?" He seemed to recall some rough treatment. That it would've come from her hands wasn't too far a stretch.

"Aye." She sucked her teeth. "But *'Er 'Ighness* put an end to that the minute we rolled up to her big, fancy 'ouse. Slicked me palm wi' a few quid, then sent me down the road without a reference." The woman's voice quaked with umbrage. "I coulda made the finest nurse the world ever seen!"

"Liza, I got summat you can nurse!" one of the patrons called out, followed by a lively round of catcalls and whistles.

The woman gave a dismissive toss of her head, even as she adjusted her low-slung bosom to its best advantage. Her tale of woe continued. "Good thing Jeb needed a serving lass or Liza Bickle woulda been out on 'er arse. But me ma always said *Liza lands on 'er feet.* So 'ere I be."

Jeb rolled his eyes and busied himself with another pour.

The woman's eyes glinted. "'Er 'Ighness tell ye to turn out, too?"

"Not in so many words," Nylander replied, gruff, dismissive. He had no inclination to continue conversing with the fractious Liza Bickle. She was the sort to expect their conversation to lead to a place he had no intention of going with her.

His brow furrowed as a question occurred to him. Where had Liza Bickle been that night? It was Liza Bickle the Dowager Viscountess had sought when she'd left his room the first time.

Like a strike of lightning, a very specific memory sparked. The creases on his forehead deepened into tense grooves. The woman he'd had in the inn had been a *virgin*, which meant...

The Dowager was a widow *and* a virgin. How in the blazes was that possible? She'd been a man's wife. And she was a virgin?

Or, more accurately, *had been* a virgin.

He inhaled the groan that wanted release.

I don't deflower—

She hadn't let him finish the sentence.

"Oi," a man called from across the room. "Didn't I see you out in the fields a few days back?"

Nylander recognized him as one of the men who had been arguing with *'Er 'Ighness*, to borrow the phrase from Liza Bickle. Her Highness suited the woman better than the Dowager.

"Aye."

Another man piped up. "Will, 'ow do you know 'e's not 'er spy?"

"That'll be enough, Walt," Will cut in. "Anyone with eyes can see this man works with his hands. Besides, her ladyship ain't got no spies. She may be a lot of things, but she ain't no sneak. Does everything on the up and up, her ladyship does."

A few men grunted in grudging affirmation, and that settled the matter. About Her Highness, that was. Nylander could see they still had their doubts about him. He was a stranger in their village haunt. It was up to him to make them comfortable with his presence. A sailor most of his born days, this was nothing new.

"I sailed with the current Viscount St. Alban for over twenty years," he said by way of provenance.

"Was that before 'e was a nob?" The question garnered a smattering of amused snorts.

"Aye," Nylander assented easily, no offense taken. "I got laid low in London and came here to recover. Seems the

Devon air agrees with me." A bit of regional flattery never hurt in these situations.

"Aye, aye," the men chorused, and the mood settled. He may be a stranger to these parts, but, at heart, he was one of them.

However, Will wasn't finished with the churlish Walt. "What do you mean speaking all disrespectful about her ladyship like that? The last few years of her running the Grange been the most prosperous the place ever seen."

Nylander settled his elbows back onto the bar and let the men talk. Silence usually yielded more answers than questions.

"*Modernized* it, you mean?"

"Nah, she ain't modernizing, not the way you're saying. She ain't replacing no man with no machine. A *diversity of interests* is what she calls it. There's enough for every man to put in an honest day's work on the Grange. That's the long and short of it."

A man, wizened, decrepit, and clearly the elder of the group, spoke up. "Those other viscounts"—he pronounced it *vis*-count, derision in the word—"ne'er cared a whit for the runnin' of the Grange or what it meant to the village. They just wanted their dues without payin' in." The man spat on the floor. "Not 'er ladyship. Within a fortnight of that last viscount dyin', she got the roofs on the estate and in the village fixed. Those roofs 'ad been leaking fer years. I canna tell ye 'ow many buckets I 'ave in my collection."

"And then it was the school," Jeb chimed in. "And the schoolmarm she brought in. The proper sort with London credentials, teaches the tots a different word every day. Sally comes 'ome and teaches 'em to me. Quixotic was the word today. *Quixotic.*" He spoke as if each syllable was newly invented. "Can you imagine such a word?"

"Then she started in on the animals and land. Got that apple orchard all pruned and the wheel mill brought in."

"Aye, 'tis the cider that'll make the biggest difference. Mark me words."

"She's worked a wonder, truth be told."

Walt gave a grudging nod. "But that ain't to say she ain't a right 'oity-toity one."

No one would hear Nylander arguing with that assessment.

Will nodded. "She's got her airs, but she mostly just keeps to herself."

"Neither is she one to be naysayed. Ain't shy 'bout bullockin' right o'er a man, if she don't agree with 'im."

Again, the estate worker nodded. "Took a bit of gettin' used to, truth be told."

"'Oo's gittin' used to it? Upsets the nat'rul order fer a woman to be commandin' a man."

Some men grunted their agreement, others waved a dismissive hand and pshawed.

The elder man of the room spoke again. "The woman gets results better than any man in my lifetime."

This silenced everyone for a minute. Nylander signaled Jeb for another red bitter.

Another man, who had been quiet, shifted forward, a conspiratorial edge about him. "If she'd just listen to reason, we could be a sight *more* prosperous."

"No more of that talk," Will said, stern.

"Why not?" the man defended. "Ain't no 'arm in a little apple business on the side. Everyone knows the Grange 'as that brandy still, and Old Pete 'as been usin' it. I 'eard there's a stockpile of a 'undred kegs of the stuff."

Kegs. Nylander could only reckon they related to the conversation he'd heard two days ago. He gave a mental shrug. It didn't involve him.

"Freebooters would be in on the action faster than you can say Jack Robinson. Free money is whut, I say."

"Until the excise man catches wind and confiscates it all," Will spoke up. The man might not agree with everything about Her Highness, but he was loyal to her. "The Wild Hair is too smart for that."

"*The Wild Hair?*" Nylander found himself asking, unable to help himself

A flurry of sheepish glances passed among the men. A devilish glint in her eye, it was Liza Bickle who spoke up as she settled her ample rump onto the lap of a man who looked like he'd won a lottery. "Just a little nickname the village 'as for 'Er 'Ighness. If ye stay around long enough, ye'll see why." She gave him a saucy wink.

Her Highness did have quite a mane of wild red hair.

Moonlit room, the silky slide of hair across his skin, shorts bursts of humid breath hot on his neck...

"Anyone else hear about a freebootin' ship spotted near the cliffs at Hawkset Cove?"

Nylander froze. Ears attentive, he listened.

"Ye hear which one?"

"I 'eard it whispered 'twas the *Free Reaver*."

One of the men gave a low, long whistle.

"If that ain't *quixotic*, I don't know what is."

"That ain't no mere freebootin' vessel. Those men are right out 'n' out pirates."

Nylander considered the possibility of coincidence. Mayhap the ship that had followed him from the Bay of Biscay to Cornwall happened to arrive on the north coast of Devon around the same time as he. Could it be?

Not bloody likely.

He drained the last dregs from his pint, thanked the men for their hospitality, and placed a few shillings on the bar. He caught the barkeep's eye.

"Which way to Hawkset Cove?"

SOMEHOW, Nylander was lost.

For the last hour, it had been his lot to stomp through a never-ending stretch of knee-high scrub, bracken, and moor grass. He was bound to run out of land eventually and find himself on the edge of a cliff, wasn't he?

While his seafaring directional skills were quite refined on the water, they were sorely lacking on dry land. At sea, all one needed for navigation was a clear night sky and a compass. He glanced up at stars twinkling at him in mockery, their constellations no useful guide for him here.

He stopped and assessed his surroundings. A sound

caught his ear. An animal racing across the coastal heath, underbrush crackling beneath swift, sure feet. Instinctively, he crouched, hoping to blend into the landscape and not startle the creature.

The waxing moon crept out from behind a cloud, its mellow light gently illuminating the surrounding landscape. It wasn't an animal, but a man...

Running.

Hackles raised, Nylander poked his head up and scanned the heath for the man's pursuer, but he saw no one else. His gaze narrowed on the runner. Familiarity lay in his tall, whippet-thin form...

Recognition streaked through him. It was no man. Across the heath ran *Her Highness*, the Dowager Viscountess St. Alban.

He glanced around for her dog, but saw no sign of the animal. Once she'd passed, he scrambled to his feet, hoping to keep her in his sights, but the woman was fast. Under normal circumstances, when he wasn't recovering from a ten-round bout with malaria, he might be able to keep up with her, but, in all honesty, he wasn't sure.

Where was she going? What was her purpose? And, most importantly, why was she *running*?

Not a walk. Not a dash. But a measured run, each footstep in time with the last, her arms pumping in perfect rhythm with her feet. Her body moved fluidly, without hurry, assured, as if she'd been born to this sort of activity. She'd done this before. She was running for, what... *pleasure?*

A note of the familiar threaded into the extraordinary, at the very notion of pleasure in relation to this woman, in the way she moved. He knew the movement of her, intimately. A quick burst of lust shot through him, straight to his cock.

He followed at a distance, her sure step indicating she knew this land as well as any wild animal. He stumbled on a clump of moor grass. He could've slapped his forehead with sudden understanding.

She wasn't the *Wild Hair*. She was the *Wyld Hare*.

*Wyld*combe Grange. Ran like a *hare*.

Ahead, she slowed to a walk before stopping and bracing her palms on her knees, presumably to catch her breath. Beyond her lay the cliff's edge, the Bristol Channel glittering in the distance, a barque sitting atop its placid surface. In his bones, Nylander knew the name of that boat.

The confounding woman straightened and set her gaze across the cove. She couldn't miss the pirate's barque.

The blood froze in Nylander's veins. The rumors were true. 'Twas the *Free Reaver* in Hawkset Cove.

And the mistress of Wyldcombe Grange didn't seem the least bit alarmed at its presence.

8

Callie's feet cut around a jagged rock that would've been invisible beneath the cross-leaved heath even in the daylight. She could run this path blindfolded. Her shoulders relaxed and, at last, she experienced the release in her body that only a run beneath a late-night sky could grant her.

A thought, like a hungry barn cat, came round: she wasn't with child. She picked up her pace, but she couldn't outrun it. Her menses had arrived this morning, informing her that there would be no trace of her encounter with the Viking.

It was good news. Of course. The best news. Really.

The pang of loss spiked through her. But she took another step forward, then another, and another, and another. Her stride confident and swift, she left the feeling behind. Fourteen years ago, she'd become an expert at it, this leaving feelings behind in the dust of a run. And when the feeling came back, as feelings inevitably did, well, there was always another, even longer, run just on the other side of her doorstep.

Another barn cat thought slinked into view.

The Viking.

He would soon mend and be gone, no ties between them. It was only a matter of days before he found his way back to London and his ship. Of course, when he reached

London, Lord St. Alban would inform him of his intent to sell him the estate. He would know that she'd withheld the information. She cast aside the pesky needle of guilt that tried to push its way in. It wouldn't matter a jot if all went to plan with tonight's meeting.

She rounded a large boulder and veered onto the sheep path, her step more delicate along the cliff's crumbling edge. At last, her feet slowed from run to jog to walk to stop, and, panting, she stared down at Hawkset Cove below.

Beyond the place where moonlight rippled across the shallows, she saw the ship, its three masts swaying almost imperceptibly on the gentle roll of dozy waves below. Closer to the water's edge, she caught another movement. A small dinghy, three men inside, rowing to shore. Who knew smugglers were punctual?

Twin slivers of anxiety and dread snaked through her. She couldn't help feeling wrong to have invited those men to shore. She might've bitten off a bigger bite than she could chew. Meeting with them tonight was such a big risk.

But what choice did she have? Was there a risk too big if it meant protecting the Grange from ruin? To protect the only work that had ever given her life meaning? And what was the alternative? To do nothing and lose the Grange to a man who knew nothing about it? A man who would, in all likelihood, grind her efforts of the last two years into dust?

That wasn't an option. Not for her. Not for the tenants and the village. They wouldn't have their livelihoods and domiciles run into the ground by yet another ignorant master.

Not while she had breath in her lungs.

She stepped onto an inches-wide path, dug into the cliffside by years of erosion and feet, both human and animal, and wended her way down to the rendezvous point on the beach below. She reached the bottom and located the highest ground. There, she waited, the dinghy and its occupants drawing ever closer, their oars a light slap and sloosh in the otherwise still night.

At last, they beached their small vessel and splashed onto dry land. Callie steeled her resolve and notched her chin higher. She took these last few moments to take the men's measure before they stood face to face with her. Two were short, slight, and had the bearing of men accustomed to serving the third man, the infamous Captain Jack Le Grand.

He stood half a head higher than her. Except he wasn't only tall, but broad, too. His was the body of one much younger, but his face instantly dispelled the notion. Weather-beaten and rough, a long scar cut down the left side of his face from hairline to jaw. It was easy to see how this man had come by his fearsome reputation.

His eye caught hers and rendered the other features of his face insignificant. Twinkling, bright, and alert were those eyes. Paradoxically, they made Callie feel the seriousness of this situation more keenly.

She was alone and outnumbered on a secluded beach with a band of pirates. Right. Mayhap she should have informed a servant of tonight's run. And its route.

The pirate stopped and gave her a frank up and down, arms akimbo, feet spread wide. "Thought ye were a man." He loosed a broad chuckle, his cohorts echoing a beat behind him.

Callie had grown so accustomed to wearing trousers, sometimes she forgot that not everyone considered the practice normal. Still, a measure of tension released from her body. The man had broached familiar conversational territory. "You wouldn't be the first man to speak those words to me."

The pirate flicked a dismissive wrist. On any other man, it would be effeminate. "Lah, I was havin' a bit o' fun. Truth is, ye should be associatin' with a better quality o' man, if that's what ye be hearin'."

Her mouth snapped shut, struck dumb by the pirate's words. The fact was it had been her late husband who had spoken those words to her. What better quality of man than an exalted peer of the realm?

The pirate cleared his throat, the rough sound echoing off the cliffs that surrounded them on three sides. "Well, luv, ye got me here, which tells me yer reconsiderin' me offer. Now, what kind o' deal ye be willin' to make?"

Callie swallowed and took a deep breath, her heart pumping blood through her veins so fast she could hear its slushy *whoosh-whoosh* in her ears. This was the moment. She dug a silver flask from a pocket, twisted off the cap, and extended it.

Jack Le Grand's head cocked to the side. "What's this?"

Callie held her tongue as he accepted the flask and drew a measured sip of apple brandy. His eyes screwed up to the heavens and his lips pursed, he swirled the liquid around his mouth, entirely concentrated on the task of taste, like a connoisseur.

His eye met hers. "This here is the *eau de vie* the Second Viscount St. Alban was producin' before ye were a speck in yer father's eye. Still got Pete producin'? The man must be ninety if a day."

She must open her mouth and speak the words she'd come here to say. Or not speak them. That option was still available to her, for once she spoke them, there would be no returning to the time *before*. Jack Le Grand wouldn't take kindly to a deal broken.

"I..." she trailed. She began again. "This is from the first batch we casked two years ago."

The pirate tilted the flask philosophically. "It's right interestin' that yer here at the stroke o' midnight offerin' me up a taste. 'Specially considerin' ye told me where I could stick my mizzen mast only a few months back. Makes a man wonder."

He was going to make her say it. "I shall allow you to sell my brandy in Portugal, Spain, and the Colonies."

She'd spoken the words, and the world hadn't fallen about her ears... *yet*.

His eyebrows lifted, and he glanced around at his crew, a quick smile flashing across his face. "You'll *allow* me?" He set his shrewd blue gaze back on her, and his head cocked. "Now that's a bright gel."

An ominous note of portent shivered up her spine. She must speak up before she lost her nerve. "On two conditions."

A low chortle escaped the pirate, and his cohorts shared in it. "The gel has conditions, ye hear? Can't say I'm mightily surprised. What'll they be, luv?"

Callie wasn't amused at all. Quite the opposite, in fact. "First," she began with a bit too much force, "you must clear your ship out of these waters until the cider pressing and casking is completed. Your ship has been spotted, and people are talking."

A serious glint entered the pirate's eye. "Now, don't ye be tryin' to control the *Free Reaver*, luv, ye'll get nowhere with that. We know our game. Besides"—he jutted his chin toward the cliffs behind her—"there be caves in there that have ample storage."

Her heart slammed against her rib cage. "Storage?"

She had no interest in expanding the terms of their bargain. What had she been thinking by coming here and striking a deal with a pirate like he was an honorable business partner?

Wasn't that rather the point, though? That he wasn't honorable, and her profits would remain untouched by the excise man's hand?

"Aye, they're high up, like. But the less ye know 'bout it, the better."

Righteous umbrage fired through Callie. She must stand this bit of ground. "Now, wait a minute, these cliffs belong to the Viscount St. Alban, you can't just do what you please—"

"Oh, that's exactly what we do, luv, make no mistake." His eyes glinted in the moonlight, hard as diamonds. "Now that we've reached an understandin' about yer first condition, what be yer second one?"

Callie drew on every ounce of courage left inside her and cloaked herself in it. "I'll expect twenty thousand pounds up front."

Incredulity spread across the pirate's face, as if she'd grown horns before his very eyes. "Ye'll have to explain that one. I don't know much about complex economics, like."

"I can't allow you to abscond with my brandy without surety."

"Lots of fancy words there, luv. *Abscond. Surety.* One more time fer the uneducated, if ye please."

Was he having a bit of fun with her? For her ear had caught a singular note in his voice. As if a natural refinement lay within it that he was trying to cover up. He knew the meanings of those words, she'd lay odds on it.

"You can't take my brandy without paying me first."

Theatrical understanding blossomed across his face. The man certainly had a knack for drama. He tapped a finger to his temple. "Yer a smart one, that's sure. But me? I can be slow on the uptake. Here's an example. I'm wonderin' what payment would that be?"

"Half of what you expect to receive in Portugal, Spain, and the Colonies for—"

She hesitated, her heart in her throat. This was it. This was the only way to save the Grange.

"—For the next five years."

He whistled through his teeth. "Five years? Yer wantin' to be partnerin' with the likes o' me fer the next *five years?*" His gaze needled into her. "What ye be needin' all that coin fer?"

"That'll be my business," she stated, curt, final. "It'll be well worth your while."

"Oh, I ain't got no doubt 'bout that. Business dealin's always be worth my while, yer ladyship, have no doubt." He sucked his teeth. "Ten."

"*Ten...* what?"

"If you'll partner with me for five years, who's to say ye won't for ten? Twenty thousand pounds is more than a dozen men see in a lifetime."

Callie swallowed a roil of bile. She wouldn't be sick in front of this man. But...

Ten years? She could barely see her way to the end of

October, much less five or ten years. Time had become an abstract concept.

"Ten years," she heard herself speak. She'd become mired in the quicksand of this deal, no way out. Struggle would only make it worse. "It's a bargain."

Unlike time, money wasn't an abstract concept in the least.

"Yer a bold one. Anyone ever told ye that?"

Just two days ago, she didn't say. It wouldn't do to think about the Viking just now. This had nothing to do with him. Well, it did, but not directly.

"Ye expectin' this'll be worth me while?"

"Our harvests are bigger every year."

"Nah, I ain't talkin' 'bout this year. We got that all sewn up. How about the next five, ten years? Ye think I'm an upright businessman or sumpin'?"

"I wouldn't go so far as to say *upright*."

He barked a jolly laugh.

"But you are a businessman."

He nodded, contemplative. "I have a question fer ye now. Ye think ye can keep word o' what we be discussin' quiet?"

"I won't be advertising it in the papers."

"I ken ye won't, but here's the thing: ye ain't been sellin' it."

She swallowed. "The estate runs in the black with the cider and our other interests. No one pays attention to the brandy."

"The excise men haven't caught wind of yer little venture?"

"Again, it's not publicly known."

"And yer men won't notice a little freebootin' on the side?"

"I'll handle my men."

He glanced at his crew. "Lah, I like her spirit, that I do. All right, luv"—he spit on his hand and held it out—"ye got yerself a bargain."

"In gold," she inserted. "I'll accept your payment in gold."

"Is there any other form of payment?"

"All will be ready after the Baptism of the Duke of Muck."

"Eh?"

"Our harvest festival in a few weeks. You can't take it before then. There are too many workers on the estate right now. After the festival, the seasonal workers will be gone, and the Grange will be quiet. You can take it then."

She glanced down at Jack Le Grand's extended hand. He expected her to respond in kind. There was no help for it. She inhaled a deep, salty breath and spit in her hand. All three men chuckled when she and the pirate sealed their deal. After it was over, it was all she could do not to wipe her hand clean on the wool of her trousers.

The men began wading to their boat, and Callie called out, "How will I contact you when it's ready?"

The pirate met her eye over his shoulder. "Ye needn't worry yerself about that. We'll know when the time is right."

Without another word, the men sloshed into the dinghy and began rowing. Except for the soft splash of the oars, the night was quiet. Callie remained rooted to the ground as she watched them grow smaller with each stroke.

She'd just made the biggest mistake of her life, the knowledge sunk deep into her gut.

And it was too late to take any of it back.

Sudden sweat slicked her skin. She clawed at the buttons at her throat. Once open, she closed her eyes and let crisp night air caress and cool her.

Her heart settled, and she saw her reaction for what it was: fear. That was all. The pirates wouldn't receive the brandy if they didn't pay. And neither of them would win in that case.

She'd made a good deal. The best deal possible for her tenants and the village. It would come out all right.

It had to.

There was no other option, really.

Then why didn't it feel that way?

HER HIGHNESS the Dowager Viscountess of St. Alban, the Wyld Hare, started up the cliff's path, and Nylander slid back from the edge, his stomach scraping against underbrush even as he was careful to avoid its telling crackle.

His mind raced to fit pieces together that had no business being joined. What, precisely, had he just witnessed?

A bargain struck, that was what.

He hadn't been able to make out a single word spoken, but words weren't necessary. That handshake spoke all the volumes he needed to hear. A deal had been sealed between Her Highness and Jack Le Grand, the most notorious pirate this side of the equator, the one who had outlasted all the others, the heyday of pirating having passed years ago.

He tucked his face into the earth, moor grass tickling his nose, and decided against confronting her. The pungent scent of heath and soil hit his nose, the churr of a nightjar sounded in the distance, and the crunch of her ascending footsteps grew closer. He needed to puzzle this out before he relayed the information to Jake.

No good could come of Her Highness striking a deal with Le Grand, of that he was dead certain. Did she know nothing of the man's reputation?

If not yet, she would soon. No one came out of a deal with the pirate unscathed. She was an intelligent woman, but an inexperienced one.

Her head poked up above the low hedge of heath lining the cliff's edge, and her body followed a few beats behind as she struck out east along the coastal path. It was a stroke of good luck that a dense mist was rolling in from the Bristol Channel, blanketing the cove in a wet cloak of gray night.

He kept his head down and counted out ten slow beats. He glanced up just as her feet kicked into a trot. She was on the run again. He waited a good thirty seconds before pushing to a stand, dusting dried flecks of shrubbery off his clothes, and trailing in her wake at a generous distance.

In the space of ten minutes, his plans had changed, and it seemed he would need more time to recover from his fever. While here, why not learn every minute detail about Wyldcombe Grange? Who better to teach him than its mistress?

And if he served as an embarrassing reminder of one night's shame, well, he wouldn't lose any sleep over it.

9

NEXT DAY

Callie placed one foot in the stirrup and swung the other over the saddle in a swift, practised motion. Arrow stood steady as a post. "Kip!" she called out. "Will you fetch a flask of water from the kitchen? I'll be out all morning."

She settled in and waited, even as Arrow grew restless beneath her. He was itching for his ride, as was she. A productive morning spent seeing to the apple orchards was just what she needed.

Beyond the roofline, the sky began its fade from black to blue, the night's transformation into day. What was keeping the boy? She liked to get out and moving before dawn, so as not to get in the way of the apple pickers. She tended to make them nervous. They liked her ideas and results, but they didn't necessarily like *her*.

No matter. She didn't need to be liked. She only needed to be useful.

In the brightening light of dawn, she saw her bargain with Jack Le Grand was nothing to feel guilty about. She'd done right by the Grange.

If a flock of nerves fluttered about her stomach every time she remembered the pirate's shrewd gaze... well, she could ignore them.

They weren't useful at all.

"Your ladyship," came Mrs. Bailey's voice, her breath huffing and puffing, her feet a brisk click-clack. Kip followed close at the woman's heels. "You'll be needing more than a flask of water this morning."

She handed up a knapsack stuffed with provisions likely including, but not limited to, a buttered crumpet and a buttermilk scone, a wedge of hard cheese and a freshly baked Cornish revel bun. Oh, and a large chunk of shortbread.

"Thank you, Mrs. Bailey," Callie called down, tucking the food into the saddlebag at her back. Never in her life had she met anyone so determined to plump her up a bit. "What would I do without you?"

"Likely wither and blow away in the breeze."

Callie let the observation pass, finding any discussion of her physical person repellant. She'd never heard a good word about it. Not that she held Mrs. Bailey's words against her. They came from a place of affection.

At last fitted out for the day, Callie guided Arrow around and was about to set out when a short, sharp whistle pierced the air and brought her up short. She caught sight of a figure just beyond the edge of light. He stepped into the flickering glow of the stable yard's lanterns, and she went dumb.

The Viking.

The light had no choice but to play in the sun-kissed streaks of platinum that ran through his hair, pulled back into a low queue. His neck was a column of muscle that conveyed strength and *man*, below which a fine dusting of hair trailed into the loose, open V of his shirt.

Her eyebrows crinkled together. He was dressed as a laborer, or a ship captain, as the case might be. What he wasn't dressed like was a gentleman. But, then, he wasn't one, she supposed.

"May I help you, Captain Nylander?" She insisted on calling him *captain*. The formality of the word placed needed distance between herself and the man, whose mere presence made her squirm with discomfort.

Mere presence? The man's presence was quite a bit more than *mere. Massive. Ungodly handsome. Implacable.* Those were the truths of his presence.

"I awakened this morning with the urge to see the workings of the Grange."

Nerves and suspicion hitched her breath in her chest. Had he learned that St. Alban wished to sell him the Grange? Or, perhaps, he remembered their night of—

She searched his eyes for that particular knowledge and discerned no sign of it. "And why is that?"

He shrugged a shoulder. "Curiosity?"

She jutted her chin toward Kip. "I'm sure the lad would be amenable to assuaging your curiosity with a tour." Kip's capacity for exploration knew no bounds. She expected he'd trod every inch of the Grange by now. "If you'll pardon me." She tugged Arrow's reins, letting action speak for itself.

"I should like to accompany *you*," the blasted man called out, bringing her up short. "I'd wager coin that no one understands the workings of the Grange better than you."

"That is surely the case," Mrs. Bailey chimed in, beaming with pride. Callie had forgotten her presence. The Viking had a way of obliterating her awareness of every other living being.

"There is but one problem." A smile, no doubt mean and petty, curled about her mouth. "I have a busy morning ahead of me and a good deal of land to cover. And you, Captain Nylander, don't ride." She settled into her saddle with smug satisfaction. She had him there.

Again, he shrugged a shoulder. "I can't imagine there's anything to it."

She startled upright, muscles locked in tension. "Pardon?" She couldn't have heard him correctly.

"I've always wanted to try it."

"Horse riding is a skill that takes some time to learn," she said, measured, controlled, and the very opposite of the panic that wanted to rise.

"Mayhap."

His piercing gaze held hers, and she knew she'd lost. This man wanted to ride a horse, and he would. "Kip," she called. "Saddle Buttercup for Captain Nylander."

Kip's eyes went wide. "*Buttercup?*"

Callie nodded. Buttercup had only escaped being named Satan's Curse thanks to the head groom's sardonic sense of irony. When Kip opened his mouth again, to lodge a stronger protest, she cut in. "Buttercup is the only horse in our stable sizeable enough to support Captain Nylander's person."

Her body wanted to blush at that last bit. She knew exactly how sizeable Captain Nylander's *person* was. Best to stop right there.

Refusing to meet his eye, she alighted from her mount and began fiddling with various bits of tack—saddle, blanket, stirrups, straps—until Kip returned with Buttercup.

The moment she saw the horse, restive and annoyed at having been roused at dawn, she smiled. The Viking would be returning to the house within five minutes of their ride. She'd be shocked if he made it far enough to view a single apple tree.

Kip led Buttercup in a wide circle before proceeding to instruct Captain Nylander on the correct way to handle the beast. The captain ran his hand over the horse's velvety snout and along its mane. Buttercup snorted, but remained passive. Then Kip began a tutorial on how to mount. The Viking placed his foot in the stirrup and attempted to mimic the boy's smooth, lithe motion. But the stirrup wobbled out from beneath him, and he fell back onto his bottom, a billowy puff of dust clouding the air around him.

A chirrup of laughter escaped Callie, but the Viking paid her no attention. Instead, he pushed to his feet and dusted himself off. Again, Kip demonstrated the sequence of motions, this time slowly. Again, the captain tried his luck. This time, the stirrup wobbled a bit, but he didn't fall.

There the blasted man sat, mounted on Buttercup, a smile of accomplishment on his face.

She'd never seen the man smile. Not once. His wasn't a

symmetrical smile. In fact, it was lopsided. But, oh, what it did to his face. Somehow, it made him more handsome, and something else, too. It made him charming.

A strange note of the familiar hung about that lopsided smile, like she'd seen it on someone. Before she could lay a finger on the who, when, or where, it was gone, and he was a hair less devastatingly handsome. A hair less godlike. A hair more human.

"We have a morning of riding ahead of us. Do try to keep up," she said, all brisk business. "But feel at liberty to turn back if the need arises."

"Not a chance, my lady."

She let out a short whistle, and Chance bounded out of the shadows, ready for a day's work. She gave her mount a light squeeze of her knees, and she was on her way, Arrow's hooves a hollow *clip-clop* that echoed between manor house and stables. The Viking at her back, they reached the end of the paved drive and rounded a long barn onto packed gravel.

"I was surprised to see that Wyldcombe Grange has no formal gardens," his masculine baritone rumbled behind her. "They seem to go on for miles behind other great houses."

"The Grange did have formal gardens." She pointed toward the simple square structure to their right. "Last year, I had this barn and a new cow house built to replace them. Formal gardens are of no use to anyone."

Behind her, silence. Mayhap he was shocked. Or not. He didn't seem like the sort of man who would be taken aback by such an action. Georgie, ever aware of his viscountly place in the world, had surely rolled over in his grave.

In the quiet of a clear, breaking dawn, they rode eastward, leaving behind manor house, barns, dairy, cart shed, and ash house, an open sky and gently rolling hills before them as they passed segmented pastures to either side.

"May I inquire where we're going?"

His solicitousness brought a smile to her lips. It was at

complete odds with the way she viewed him. He was the Viking, after all.

"The orchard," she called over her shoulder.

"Do you mind if we ride side by side?"

Her smile fell. She minded very much. "Not at all."

She slowed her mount and allowed the Viking to draw abreast with her. For his first time on a horse, he was doing remarkably well. It seemed Buttercup had taken to him.

"So what's the purpose of the orchard?"

"We produce cider from the apples." She wouldn't mention the brandy. The less he knew, the better.

"Are cider apples different from the apples you buy from a fruit seller?"

She threw him an exasperated look. "They are." How had he known to ask that question? "Whoever planted them decades ago knew what they were doing. The Grange's orchard has thirteen varieties ranging from bitter to sweet. My guess is that a former Viscount St. Alban visited Normandy and was converted into a cider connoisseur."

"Is it necessary to have so many different apple varieties to make cider?"

"It's about the taste. Depending on the mixture of bitter to sweet, it does affect the complexity and flavor." She found herself warming to his line of questioning.

"You've really made a business of it."

She couldn't miss the appreciation in his voice, and a wave of gratification swept over her, despite herself. How satisfying to have an outsider admire the Grange.

"Our cider's renown is growing." She couldn't seem to stop gushing. "Only last month, an innkeeper from Exeter requested ten kegs of this year's brew for his tap room. We've even had requests ranging farther afield than England. In fact—"

She stopped herself right there. What was she going to reveal next? Her intention to sell her apple brandy illegally through pirates, instead of using perfectly legal distribution that would be subject to taxation and therefore cut into her need for immediate cash?

She was in danger of becoming entirely too comfortable with the Viking. Which wouldn't do, not at all.

She cleared her throat. "It's certainly a brisk morning. Winter will be upon us before we know it."

loody hell, Nylander cursed to himself.

Just when he'd gotten the woman talking, she'd shut herself up like a clam. All right, then, he'd find another way. "What's your name?"

A laugh startled out of her and earned him a confounded side glance. "You know my name. I'm the Dowager Viscountess St. Alban. Lady St. Alban to you."

He could hardly contain a sarcastic snort. She'd been something other than a lady to him less than a fortnight ago. But they weren't acknowledging that. *Right.* "You can't have more than twenty-five years on you. Such an aged name for a young lady."

The long length of her spine went ramrod straight above the trot of her horse. That couldn't be comfortable. "I fail to see how my age has anything to do with my name."

"What's your *given* name?" he asked, trying the question a different way.

What had started as a ploy to keep her talking had turned into genuine curiosity. What was the woman's name, anyway?

Her head canted to the side, and he couldn't help noticing that, above her high collar, her neck was as graceful as a swan's.

"Why do you want to know my given name?"

"I'm wondering if it matches the one I have in my head."

She stabbed him with a glare that would've been described as murderous in a dark alley. "And what name would that be?" The question came low and wary.

He gave her a slow appraisal from head to boot. "Gertrude."

"*Gertrude?*" she all but shouted.

"Not Gertrude?" he asked, all wide-eyed innocence.

"Most certainly not," she huffed.

Another name occurred to him. "Obedience?"

She stared at him as if he'd sprouted two heads. "Do I look like an *Obedience* to you?"

"Perhaps not." This was fun. "I can't imagine any Obediences riding about in men's trousers."

"I'll have you know that these trousers are specially fitted to me, which makes them, in fact, *ladies'* trousers."

"No doubt about that, milady," he said, his voice gone to gravel in his throat.

His gaze raked up said trousers from shiny boot up the length of long, slender thigh. The woman was correct. Her trousers were, in fact, well-fitted.

He cleared his throat, hoping to clear his mind. He wasn't here to think about her particularly well-fitted trousers and what they were doing to the crotch area of his. He shifted on his saddle, hoping to adjust himself. Buttercup snorted in warning.

A splotch of red had crept above her high collar. Her Highness blushed in the specific way of redheads, like a subterranean wildfire sprung to the surface, sudden and full-blaze. It made her less elevated. Less lady, more *woman.*

"One more guess?" he asked.

Her lips pinched together and her gaze trained straight ahead, she nodded.

"Mildred."

"*Mildred?*" Incredulous eyes swung around to meet his. "You truly think my name Mildred? I'm beginning to wonder if I should feel insulted."

"I'll have you know that I've met many a lovely Mildred in my time."

"I don't care about being—" She hesitated. "Lovely." Her eyebrows drew together. "Since you likely won't stop with these ridiculous names, I shall tell you. My given name is Calpurnia."

"*Calpurnia?*"

"Does that come as a great surprise to you?"

"In truth, I thought you might be a Rosalind."

"A Rosalind? After the Shakespeare character?"

"Aye."

"Because I wear men's trousers?"

He nodded.

"You read Shakespeare?" The question sounded like an accusation.

"Not regularly."

Calpurnia was a strong name, a graceful name. An unexpected name. In all honesty, he'd half-expected one of those others to be correct. But he could see now that Calpurnia was the name that fit this woman.

"*Callie*," he murmured, half under his breath. He liked the sound of it.

Her head snapped around. "Why would you call me that?"

"Seems more natural than Calpurnia. That name carries considerable heft." The honesty fell from his lips of its own accord.

"That was the intention of it." She trained her gaze straight ahead. "My father didn't allow anyone to call me Callie, not even my brothers on a tease. Only my mama was afforded the liberty. Callie is the name of the girl who serves pints at your local public house or shovels coal into your fireplace. A Callie doesn't ascend higher than the lower-to-middling classes. Calpurnia, on the other hand, well, with the right connections and a large fortune, a Calpurnia can rise all the way to the upper tier of Society and elevate her entire family with her." An acid note sounded in her voice. "Through a strategic marriage, of course."

"This happened when you became the Viscountess St. Alban?" Nylander wanted this to be clear as glacial water. It was another layer peeled away from this woman.

Her mouth pulled wide into the semblance of a smile. "Social status achieved."

The mood took a strange turn from playful exchange to dead serious admission. It wasn't difficult to intuit the marriage hadn't been a happy one. Truth be told, he wanted to know more.

To what end? He was here to find out why this woman had made a deal with Jack Le Grand last night. He wasn't here to sort out capital "L" *Lady* problems.

Every *Lady* he'd ever met had a variation of this problem: all the money in the world, but a toad for a husband. And they wanted nothing more than to use Captain Nylander to soothe the problem into submission for the amount of time it took to reach climax.

Just like this one had done. *Right.*

"How about you?" she asked.

"How about *me*?"

"What's your given name?"

"John," he stated flatly.

Her brow lifted. "John? That's all?"

"What did you expect?"

A smile that contained no small amount of wickedness pulled at her mouth. That smile nearly knocked him from his horse. "Honestly?"

He nodded. Honesty was all he wanted from her.

"Ragnar."

His brow furrowed. "*Ragnar?*"

"Or some such Viking name from the tales one hears as a child." Her gaze went soft, and she pulled her reins, drawing her mount to a stop. "Oh, look at that. It's glorious every single time."

He tore his eyes from her and wrestled Buttercup to a fitful stop. Not a hundred yards in the distance stood row upon row of apple trees, heavy with ripe fruit, the rising sun peeking through lush green boughs in a warm golden glow. It inspired awe, stillness, and reflection. It was magic. This view wouldn't get old in an eternity of years.

A short series of three sharp barks broke the spell, and Her Highness's dog, Chance, shot down a narrow bridle path and disappeared into the orchard.

A gasp and a short cry emerged from her. "Look," she cried out, pointing. "Cows!" Then she, too, was off like a shot, spurring her horse faster with each stride.

Nylander squinted into the distance and, at last, saw what she and the dog were on about: in the aisles between the rows of trees lay several cows on their sides, their chests rising and falling in quick, shallow pants. He squeezed his knees to spur Buttercup on, just as Kip had instructed, but the infernal animal simply craned his neck and pinned him with a stubborn glare. The only thing preventing Nylander from jumping to the ground and coaxing the animal forward was the doubt that he'd be able to remount the beast.

"Oh, come on, Buttercup," he bellowed. To his amazement, the surly brute jolted into motion. He only just tightened his grip on the reins before he was left in the beast's dust.

By the time he caught up to Her Highness, she'd already dismounted and was kneeling beside a groaning cow, her hand rubbing along the animal's great, round stomach. "They've gotten into the apples. See how her belly is distended with gas?"

As if to illustrate her point, the cow farted the greatest gust of wind Nylander ever had the dubious pleasure of observing. He'd been raised on ships surrounded by men well-versed in every crudity known around the world. It was saying a great deal.

Her Highness didn't bat an eye. "There must be a dozen of them." Her eyebrows drew together. "How did they get here?"

"Strong breezes unlock gates all the time round these parts, I'd wager." It was as good a guess as any.

"That may be true, but it's more than a simple gate between these cows and this orchard. You saw the lay of the land. The way the pastures are configured..." she trailed, lost in her thoughts. "And the location of the barn where these girls would've been... It doesn't make sense. They couldn't have just wandered over."

"Are you saying that someone deliberately led them here?"

Her eyes flew up to meet his, and he saw the truth there: it was precisely what she wasn't saying. Her gaze shifted. "No, of course not."

She was lying. He had no doubt of it.

She gave another cry of distress and raced toward another afflicted cow. Every hair on his body stood on end, root to tip. Such a cry could easily be mistaken for a different sort of cry... a cry of exquisite distress the moment before a woman broke in release.

Her cry of exquisite distress before *she* broke in release.

He gave his head a good shake and tamped down his body's response before dismounting from Buttercup and following her on foot.

"She's choking." Her Highness dropped to her knees beside the afflicted beast, whose eyes were rolling back in her head, frantically swallowing and getting nowhere.

Her hand wrapped around the cow's chin and tipped the animal's head back, her eyes closed as she felt along its throat. "*There*." She frowned and seemed to arrive at a decision. "I don't think there's any other way."

"Any other way?" Slow dread crept along the question.

"She has an apple lodged in her throat."

"Should I fetch the animal surgeon?"

She shook her head. "There's no time for that. Besides, I've heard it's been done successfully."

The creeping dread solidified in his gut. "What is *it*?"

Her dark eyes locked onto his. He saw decision there. Determination, too. "We must pull it out."

Exactly what he thought she'd say.

She shrugged off her coat and unbuttoned her right sleeve before rolling it up in a series of jerky motions. "You will hold her head while I—" She hesitated. "While I reach my hand down her throat and pull the apple out."

"Won't she bite you?"

Her eyes narrowed on the animal. "I don't think so. Cows are docile creatures. But, um"—her certainty faltered—" perhaps you wouldn't mind holding her lower jaw in place?"

Nylander gave a curt nod by way of answer and began rolling up his sleeves. Just as she turned to her task, her eye snagged on his forearm and she stilled for a silent heartbeat, long enough for him to catch the look. His anchor tattoo. Which was the worst offender to her ladylike sensibilities? The tattoo? Or his bare skin?

She bent over the cow's head and, in a slow, soothing stroke, brushed her fingertips between the animal's eyes to the side of its mouth, where she began feeling around. "I think it would be best if you straddled her head. Use your knees to keep her immobile and her jaw open."

Nylander nodded. It was a good plan.

He maneuvered around the distressed cow, careful and slow, but it wasn't only for the animal that he exercised caution. It was for Her Highness, too, who had positioned herself directly across from him. His body's awareness of hers on high alert, he placed his feet to either side of the beast's head and met Callie's gaze, no more than a foot from his. "Ready?"

Her eyes wide and tense, she nodded, her tongue nervously skating along her bottom lip, leaving behind a thin sheen of moisture that had him transfixed for a long beat of time. He blinked to speed it away and wedged his fingers inside the cow's mouth, one hand taking hold of its upper jaw, the other the lower, readying himself to pull them apart. "The next time she belches, I'll secure her mouth open. Got it?"

Callie nodded.

He steadied himself and waited for the inevitable. At last, the cow discharged yet another belch. He averted his face from its noxious stench, even as he pulled her mouth all the way open and held. "Now," he barked, the syllable a rough command, every muscle from fingers to forearms to biceps to back straining to hold the cow's mouth wide.

Callie started to insert her hand and hesitated. He knew what that hesitation meant. She would have to trust him. Her eyes met his.

"I'll not let go, not until you're safe."

She gave a barely perceptible nod, sucked in a shaky breath, and plunged her hand into the cow's mouth.

He'd expected her face to screw up in disgust, for her to have a woman's reaction to it, but she didn't. Instead, she committed fully to the task. She sidled her body around, toward his, so her arm could slide deeper inside the cow. He caught her faint scent of citrus and apple blossom over the cow's stench.

"It's so strange," she began, as if she was talking to herself. "I can't feel... *There*... There it is," she said, her face awash in relief. Amazed eyes cut toward his. "I've found it."

"Can you get it out?"

Her face scrunched in concentration. "I just need to..." She shifted further around so that the entire left side of her body was pressed against his right, her shoulders and her hips digging into him for leverage as her arm dove deeper.

His body sprang to awareness, even as he attended to his one task, which was to ensure this cow didn't remove her ladyship's arm at the shoulder, for that was how far she'd sunk inside the great beast. It was entirely possible this woman would climb all the way inside the animal, if that was what it took to save it.

By now, she was panting hard, her breath puffing in and out, and he realized his was, too, in rhythm with hers as they strained toward their mutual goal: the removal of the stubborn apple.

"If I can get my fingers around..." Her movements became more subtle as she turned, the front of her squeezed hard against him. "There it is... I have it."

So close was she now, that when she'd spoken that last bit, her lips brushed against his throat. Her hot, humid words sent a shiver racing down his spine. A raw intimacy lay within this moment, unlike any he'd experienced with any other living being.

"I'm removing my arm now," she said. She hadn't noticed his reaction.

Her arm began emerging from the distressed, farting beast, slowly, by increments, so as not to harm the animal. Her body shifted away from his, too, and the ache of loss shot through him.

How long had it been since he'd had her? Since the night at the coaching inn, which was what? A fortnight past? Even though he regularly abstained longer than that when he was at sea, that night had left his body primed for more, reducing him to a man who lusted after a woman, who baffled and bedeviled him, through a putrid fog of cow farts.

Her hand appeared, clutching a mangled, slobbery apple, glistening in the newly risen sun. She tossed a triumphant smile his way. Muscles strained to their limit, he held the cow's jaws until he'd stepped over and behind the wild-eyed beast. Then he let go and jumped back.

The cow vented all her frustration and annoyance in a long, "*Moo!*" She kicked her legs a few times to gain momentum before rolling to her feet. Immediately, her confusion seemed to fall away, as if not much of any importance had just occurred, and she ambled off, presumably to swallow another apple whole.

In tacit agreement, Nylander and Callie collapsed to the ground, both panting, enervated heaps. An exhausted smile played about her lips. "I imagine your arms feel like jelly."

He made a show of trying to lift them before letting them flop to the ground. She exhaled a gusty laugh and slumped against the tree at her back. He'd never seen her so relaxed, so un-self-aware. He rather liked this Dowager Viscountess St. Alban.

His eyes drifted shut, the symphony of dawn surrounding them. The musical trill of birds risen with the new day. The sough of a gentle, easterly breeze rustling the leaves of the trees. The short in and out of her breath, soft and subtle and, oh, so familiar. Again, an ache, sexual and distinct, pulsed through him, and he instantly tamped it down.

His eyes blinked open and slid over to meet hers, already upon him. Something he couldn't identify resonated in their depths. Time slowed.

Of a sudden, as if the ground had turned to molten lava, she broke the contact and shot to her feet, busily dusting off her trousers. Time picked up its pace.

She spared him an impatient glance. "I must retrieve some men to get the cattle back to the cow house. Will you be able to ride?"

Nylander's arse protested beneath him that it wasn't getting back onto a horse today, perhaps ever. Besides, it seemed Buttercup had found other matters to attend elsewhere. "I prefer to walk."

This pulled a commiserating smile from her. "Best walk now while you can. Tomorrow, it won't be so easy."

From his low vantage point, he watched her grab her horse's reins in one hand and place a sure foot in the stirrup. On a quick hop, she swung her other leg across the animal's back and mounted in a swift, sure motion.

His prick jumped. Her *ladies'* trousers did quite a fine job of outlining the contours of her arse. He ran a frustrated hand through his hair. Thoughts like that would get him nowhere. Not with this woman.

Just before she spurred her horse into a gallop, she called over her shoulder, "And you can find your way back on your own?"

"I'll manage."

Without another word, she sped away, leaving him alone with nothing but his thoughts and an orchard full of groaning, belching, farting cows who had their own worries. He rose, one slow increment at a time, his muscles already growing stiff. She receded into the distance, and he shook his head.

He couldn't help it, he half-admired the woman. She was capable. She was brave. The woman had *heart.* She didn't shy away from doing what was right when the moment required it.

And that was what had him stumped. Why had she done such a wrong thing by making a deal with a man like Jack Le Grand?

The circle of the Dowager Viscountess St. Alban, *Callie*, didn't square.

11

TWO DAYS LATER

"Should feel like you're running on a cloud."
Callie took the boot in hand and turned it over, testing its weight. She peered inside, then touched fingertips to soft, springy wool. "This is marvelous, Jane. How did you manage it?"

Callie bent to untie the laces of her boots and kicked them off her feet. Her stockings quickly followed. She wanted to feel the cloud against her skin. She slipped one foot, then the other, inside, and her eyes involuntarily drifted shut in bliss.

"Well, pet, it wasn't too tricky once I had the idea." Jane loved to explain her creative process in detail. "I separated the upper part of the boot from the sole and cut the wool to the exact shape. Then I sewed it all together. You'll see a bit of wool peeking out along the edge, but it shouldn't make any difference in the wet. Wool is impervious to the elements. Do you like them?" she asked, uncertainty in the question.

"Like them?" Callie's toes wiggled around in luxury. "Jane, you're a genius."

A shy smile lit across Jane's round face, a light blush pinking her cheeks. "Shall I fetch us a spot of tea?"

"I would enjoy that," Callie replied while the other woman retreated to the kitchen. Jane wouldn't want her to follow, so she remained in the cozy drawing room, her feet luxuriating in her friend's glorious invention.

Her friendship with the efficient, trustworthy Mrs. Jane Smith still took her by surprise. Callie had never been one for the deep attachments so many other girls and women cultivated with one another. But when she'd arrived at the Grange upon her marriage to Georgie and found herself in need of a necessary, and private, item, a servant had directed her to Smith's Emporium in the village. The store was rather less grand than its name suggested, but one could find a surprising number of goods within its narrow walls. It was there Callie first met Jane.

From the outside, Jane fit perfectly into the conventional world she inhabited. A petite, smiling woman, the sort who drew one in, not with her physical beauty, but with the beauty that shone from her warm eyes and smile. She took a diminutive role in the family business, was the mother of two boys and two girls, and employed a house maid like the prosperous business owner she was. Yet Jane wasn't entirely conventional, which was where her friendship with Callie had begun.

That first day, Callie had walked into the shop, not at all comfortable with asking for her necessary, and private, item. After circling the emporium's wares for a period of time that was beginning to foreground itself, Jane had sidled up to her and asked sotto voce, "Is there something special you'll be needing?"

"Well, I," Callie began and paused. "I need a pair of trousers." She paused again. "With the thinnest fabric possible."

Jane's head canted to the side. "For the viscount?"

How Callie wanted to say *yes*, but it wouldn't do. Georgie was three inches shorter than she and three stone heavier. "No."

"Is it true then?" Jane asked, a twinkle in her eye, her tone conspiratorial.

"Is what true?" Callie asked, fearing the answer.

Jane glanced around to make sure they were alone before leaning closer. "That you hie across the heath like a rabbit fleeing a wolf beneath the full moon?"

Callie opened and closed her mouth, mortified heat suffusing her body. "I think I'll go—"

Jane wrapped a staying hand around Callie's forearm. "No, pet, stay. Pardon my bluntness. It's one of my principal faults." She released Callie. "Now tell me about these trousers you're needing."

Callie explained that the pair she'd been using for years, cast-offs from an older brother, had become so threadbare that they'd begun to fall apart.

Jane's eyebrows drew together in concentration as she paced around Callie in slow circles, appraising her for a full minute. At last, she stopped. "Come back for a fitting at three o'clock sharp tomorrow."

"Oh, I don't need them fitted to me," Callie said in a rush. "A general size will do."

"Oh, no, it won't," Jane protested. "You're dealing with the best seamstress between here and London. I'll not be selling you a pair of ill-fitting trousers. Besides, I'm curious."

"Curious?"

"Since you run in them, mayhap we can make a modification or two that will render them more comfortable. Do you ever get abrasions when you run around?"

"Oh, um," Callie stammered, this turn of conversation taking her quite by surprise. "As a matter of fact, I do."

Jane nodded her head and uttered an affirming, "Mm-hmm."

Mr. Smith strode into the store, and Jane's face returned to the distant affability of a friendly proprietor. "Remember, your ladyship, three o'clock sharp tomorrow for your fitting."

And, like that, their friendship was struck.

Every time Callie came to Jane with a problem with her trousers for chafing or her boots for blisters, a twinkly light entered the woman's eyes and a secret smile curled about her mouth. Jane enjoyed helping Callie defy convention. Further, she delighted in being a co-conspirator in the defiance.

It was the one act of rebellion in Jane's otherwise perfectly conventional life, and Callie was immensely grateful that it was she who inspired it. The woman was lightning with a needle, possessed of a rare combination of imagination and skill. Callie had yet to present her with a problem she couldn't solve. She liked being Jane Smith's little rebellion.

Jane bustled into the room, bringing with her tea, her specific aura of good-natured energy, and baby Pris, bright blue eyes trained on Callie, contented thumb stuck in her mouth, and affixed to Jane's chest with a series of crisscrossing straps. "Little pet woke from her nap," Jane said in a sing-songy voice meant for the babe.

"You're sure it isn't painful for Pris to be stuck onto you like that?" Callie asked. She still hadn't grown accustomed to this strange device that Jane had constructed.

"Not in the least," Jane breezed, setting the tea service onto a shiny, walnut sideboard with a light clink. As if to illustrate her mother's point, Pris's thumb popped out of her mouth and she started blowing bubbles of delight while her chubby legs kicked out. "Since she started crawling, it's the only way I can get any work done."

"Oh, that reminds me," Callie said, reaching into her reticule. She pulled out a small jar. "Mrs. Bailey made a fresh batch of apple sauce this morning."

"Pris, you see that? Your auntie Calpurnia has brought your favorite."

Pris expressed her delight with another round of slobbery bubbles, and Callie's insides went light with warring feelings of joy and longing.

Jane set the jar aside. "Now, Calpurnia, word has it that you have a visitor at the Grange."

Callie indulged an inward groan. The brightness of the room dimmed a few shades. "'Tis true," she had no choice but to admit.

A muted hum on her lips, Jane prepared the tea before settling across from Callie with Pris still strapped to her chest, twin sets of saucer-like eyes staring out at her with curiosity. "He's the talk of the village, you know," Jane stated.

"I can only imagine."

Jane brought her teacup to her lips and blew, cooling breath rippling the surface of the tea. "I've yet to see the man, mind you, but I've heard him described as a Viking by Mrs. Mayhew and as an angel warrior by Miss Patchett." Conspiratorially, she sat forward. "Mrs. Finch said he was too handsome to look at directly."

Callie swallowed a great, scalding gulp of tea, avoiding a coughing fit by sheer strength of will. "I'd say all those descriptors hit the mark."

Jane slumped back in her chair and exhaled a breathy, "Oh, my."

An intolerable, dreamy silence followed. Callie decided to insert some reality into this conversation. "The man is utterly insufferable."

"How so?" Jane wasn't immune to the lure of a good gossipy chat. Callie liked that about her friend more than she cared to admit.

Callie held Jane in her thrall as she gave an abbreviated account of how Captain Nylander had ended up her "guest" at the Grange. "Or *Nylander* as he insists on being called," she said finishing up.

"Simply *Nylander*?" Jane asked.

Callie nodded. A secret smile formed on Jane's lips. A shiver had possibly run up her friend's spine. *For pity's sake.*

That she'd omitted the part about Lord St. Alban wanting to sell the Grange to Captain Nylander, or even that St. Alban wanted to sell the estate at all, was of no consequence. No need to worry Jane about an event that wasn't going to happen.

"But what is it that makes him insufferable? Isn't he a useful sort, being a ship captain and all?"

Callie swallowed another gulp of tea. "I suppose he has his uses."

An image popped into her mind: his forearm muscles, hardened steel rippling beneath his skin, struggling, straining, to hold the cow's jaw open. He'd been quite useful at keeping her arm intact.

"It's just now that he's recovered, he turns up everywhere." The complaint emerged sour and pettish. "You don't have him hidden in your pantry, do you?"

Jane giggled like a girl in the schoolyard sharing a naughty joke. "Tell me more."

Callie proceeded to tell Jane about the way he'd made himself indispensable to Mrs. Bailey in the kitchens. Apparently, the man had amazing abilities with egg gathering, chicken coop repair, and root garden upkeep. She'd even heard the word *magical* applied to his butter churning abilities. "I can't seem to escape him, except when I run, of course."

Jane clasped her hands before her, the picture of rapt delight. "I did wonder at you arriving two hours before your usual time today. And at my back door. You gave Dorrie quite a fright, I can tell you."

Callie grimaced. "Please offer her my apologies. I didn't know how else to slip the man. Somehow, he turns up everywhere I am."

"Are you sure," Jane began and stopped. Was that a blush pinking her cheeks? "Are you sure he's not interested in you?"

"*Interested*? How—" Callie stopped. Her eyebrows drew together. Jane meant... *Oh*. "Interested in *me?*" Incredulity swelled up, and she barked out a hearty laugh. The idea was so ludicrous, it defied belief. "It's clear you haven't laid eyes on the man."

"Why is that?"

"Men like *Nylander* don't notice women like *me*," she stated with a lifetime of accumulated certainty.

Jane's head canted to the side. "You're a compelling beauty, pet," she said in that straightforward way she had.

Distress furrowed Callie's brow. "*Me? A beauty?*"

"Have you never taken a look at yourself in the mirror?"

"Oh, Jane, please let's not speak of this." Callie's discomfort grew roots.

"I'm sure Shakespeare could say it better, but your hair is the deep red the sun gets just before it sets in the western sky."

"Oh, I don't know, Jane, you might give Shakespeare a run for his money. My hair is orange."

"Oh, pish," Jane dismissed. "And I've always envied your height with those long legs of yours."

"Two spindly sticks. That's what my legs are."

"And the bones of your face are fine. Even your freckles are dainty and charming."

Callie harrumphed in dismissal. But her heart raced, and heat flushed up.

"If none of that is true," Jane continued, "then you must ask yourself a question."

"What is that?"

"Why is the man following you about?"

Callie went still. She'd been so annoyed with the blasted man that the question never occurred to her.

"Well, pet, it's clear as day to me that the man is besotted with you." Jane sat back in certain satisfaction. Somehow, Pris managed to mirror her mother's expression.

Callie set her teacup down in a too-loud clatter. "Jane, I just remembered a pressing engagement back at the Grange."

She shot to her feet and bolted toward the front door and the blessed freedom of the outdoors. Anything to escape Jane's absurd, erroneous, impossible conclusion. It was too much. The man didn't even remember their night together.

She was halfway through the entrance when she stopped dead in her tracks, instantly realizing her mistake. She should have left by the back. Not twenty feet away, *he* stood across the bustling High Street. Their eyes collided and held. Surely, the pummel of her heart against her rib cage would leave bruises.

"Calpurnia," she heard behind her, "you forgot your boots."

Callie swiveled and snatched the boots out of Jane's

hands, hoping to make it fast so Jane wouldn't notice the blasted man, who was now ambling toward them.

"Why if it isn't Lady St. Alban," she heard at her back.

Her stomach curled. He'd already reduced the distance between them in half if the proximity of his voice was any indicator.

Lady St. Alban. Two days ago, he'd called her *Callie.* His voice had been a low, attractive rumble in his chest as if her name had brushed across crushed velvet to reach her. That rumble had made her knees go weak. It felt as if he'd claimed her name, and a deep, intractable part of her responded to the claiming.

Jane lifted onto her tiptoes and peered over Callie's shoulder. Her eyes went round as saucers, and Callie suppressed a groan. "Oh, my."

It was too late.

Unable to avoid the situation any longer, Callie sucked in a bracing breath and swiveled to face reality in the form of the approaching Viking. He stopped before them and offered a short bow, like a gentleman at ease with anything life threw at him. She couldn't quite summon the same quietude, not with Jane at her side, ogling the man like she'd never seen one.

In all honesty, it was likely she'd never seen a man like this one.

Callie cleared her throat. "Mrs. Smith, may I introduce Captain Nylander to you?"

"'Tis my pleasure, good sir." Her words were as bouncy as her curtsy. Pris clapped. Traitorous baby.

He nodded, his massive form diminishing Jane's front door stoop. "The pleasure is mine."

Jane looked as if her knickers had melted off her body. Just as Callie thought to slip past and leave the two to their graceless salutations, Mr. Smith stepped up to join their awkward, little party, a questioning light in his eyes. Breathless and flustered, Jane introduced her husband to Captain Nylander.

"My dear," Mr. Smith began, "might you be in need of a lie-down? You appear flushed."

"Right you are, Mr. Smith," Callie inserted. "I think we might all be in need of one. Now, if you will excuse me..." she trailed. She slipped past the trio and down the front steps, her heels a swift click-clack across the worn cobblestones of High Street.

Not a dozen footsteps later, she heard them, *his* footsteps quick at her heels. She wasn't getting away so easily, it appeared. Really, it was strange the way the man kept appearing at her side. Was there something to Jane's words?

No. That wasn't it.

Then why was the blasted man following her about?

He drew abreast of her and slowed his pace. Apparently, they were to walk together. She may as well ask him the question that had her curious. "Does that happen to you often?"

"What is *that?*"

She almost snorted. "Truly, you jest."

"I fear not."

"I'll have you know that Jane Smith is one of the most logical, curious, and plain-spoken women I've ever known. Yet upon meeting you, she was reduced to a tongue-tied puddle of jelly."

"You heard her husband. The woman was feverish." The Viking's tone had gone hard and oddly flat.

"*Feverish?*" Callie couldn't contain an unladylike snort. "That's certainly one way of explaining your effect on the woman."

Although she was neither touching nor looking at the man beside her, she sensed a gathering tension in him, as if all the muscles in his body had clenched into a tight fist. She couldn't help feeling she'd been unkind in some way. *Strange.* Most men would rise to her observation like a rooster in the hen yard. Yet for this man, the subject seemed like a raw spot that she'd scraped with a fingernail.

Tense silence filled in the space between them, and Callie was at a loss for how to bridge the distance. Fortunately, the Viking had better manners than she. "This is my first time seeing Upper Wyldcombe Lacey in the daylight. Is it always this busy?"

"Everyone is preparing for the Duke of Muck."

"There's a Duke of Muck?"

"The Baptism of the Duke of Muck," Callie clarified. "It's our town's harvest festival."

"Interesting name for it."

"It's mixed up with a bit of town history. But I can't imagine you'll be here to see it as your recovery seems well on its way."

She wasn't being subtle about her desire to see him gone. But the time for subtlety was past. High time the man cleared out.

He pointed toward a cartload of apples trundling up the street from the opposite direction. "Are those apples from the Grange?"

She shook her head. "They're from neighboring land-holders. In fact, I believe those apples are headed for the Grange. We're buying apples from everyone who will sell to us."

"For your cider?"

She nodded.

Every ten steps or so, a villager acknowledged, "Your ladyship," with the tip of a passing hat or a sheepish smile. Callie responded with a gracious nod, which was all that was expected of her. The Viking at her side elicited more than a few lifted eyebrows accompanying the morning's greetings.

Once they'd maneuvered past a makeshift grouping of fruit and vegetable sellers, shouting their wares, he cleared his throat. "I believe this is the first time I've seen you dress like a—"

"Woman?" Sudden humiliation, hot and bright as an August sun, streaked through her. *Straight. Flat. Tall. Mannish. Unnatural.* The words flung themselves at her in familiar refrain.

Clearly, the man didn't remember that there had been one occasion when he'd seen her not only as a woman, but as a desirable one, too.

12

W oman.

She'd spoken the word as if ice ran through her veins, yet Nylander sensed a brittle crack running the word's length. The slightest touch would surely break it open to reveal a raw, throbbing center.

"It isn't the first time, though," she continued, determined, recovered.

This woman—yes, *woman*—was tough. He would do well to remember it.

"I was wearing a dress at Lord St. Alban's manse in London."

He kept forgetting their brief encounter preceding the foyer's burst into pandemonium and his descent into fever. He reached back into his memory and located his first sight of her... And her welcoming scowl. Indeed, she'd been wearing a dress. In fact...

He gave her a quick up-and-down. She'd been wearing *this* dress, plain, brown, modest wool. Was it her *only* dress? What sort of woman was this Callie?

"I only wear trousers for estate work and—" She hesitated. "Other purposes."

Like her moonlit scarpers across the heath. But he wouldn't reveal that particular knowledge, nor that he wished she'd put them back on. They snugged to her in all the right places.

He couldn't help noticing more than a few askance looks from passersby. "Are we doing something wrong?"

"Such as?"

"The townsfolk. They keep casting confounded glances our way."

A laugh broke loose from her. "*I* am the town oddity, and *you* are a stranger. *Together?* We may be too much."

Nylander held out his arm at a ninety degree angle. "Perhaps we would excite less village gossip if you placed your hand on my arm while we stroll together." It seemed the most conventional course.

Her brow furrowed. She was weighing the wisdom of his words against her desire to be free of him. Eyes fixed firmly ahead, she lifted her hand and lowered it onto his arm, her palm lighter than the perch of a sparrow.

A few degrees of her heat penetrated the wool of his overcoat, the linen of his shirt, and found its way to his skin. As much as she would like to convince him and the world that she was an ice queen, this gave her away.

Familiarity stirred. He remembered her heat, the vitality of it, pulsing with life and passion, so opposite the woman she'd chosen to present him ever since. Which was the real Callie? He had a feeling he knew, and she didn't want him to.

"I'm surprised you can walk." She was referring to his dawn ride on Buttercup.

"I might've had a bit of trouble making it to the chamber pot the last couple of mornings."

He expected her lips to purse in the firm line of a silent scold. Instead, a reluctant smile played about her mouth. Emboldened, he said, "Most ladies would chastise me for the indelicacy of my speech."

She shrugged. "I don't mind plain words. I have four brothers, all of whom are older. There was no room in that house for missishness."

"Same on a ship." Interesting point of connection. "Did you enjoy growing up with brothers?"

"Very much."

He smelled an opportunity to peer into her past. "Yet you didn't return there after your husband's death."

"Wouldn't dream of it." She shot him an inscrutable glance. "It sounds harsher than it is. I could have returned to Kingsbridge, to my father's house, and perhaps I intended to, but it didn't work out that way. After Georgie's death—"

"Your late husband?"

She nodded.

A thought occurred to Nylander. Was it possible her husband died between "I do" and the wedding night? Before they could consummate their marriage? Her virginity had begun to nag at him, and this would explain it. "How long was your marriage?"

"Three years."

"*Three years?*"

Her brow lifted in silent query at his outburst.

Three years of marriage explained nothing at all. It only unearthed more questions. The woman carried more secrets than a priest.

"After Georgie's passing," she continued, "I decided to stay on at the Grange. I'd grown too independent to return to anyone else's household." Her words came slower now, as confessions were want to do. "I quite like abiding by my own rules."

"Wouldn't your mother have welcomed her only daughter home?"

"My mother perished before I reached my thirteenth year." Hard and impenetrable was the statement, as if she'd built a fortress around it. "Besides, my father had no further use for me. I'd done my duty."

The same thick strand of bitterness wove through her words as from two days ago when this subject had first been broached.

"At the Grange," she continued, "I'm able to take charge and set ideas into motion and see them bear fruit, literally." She gestured toward an apple cart clamoring past. "I could never go back or take it for granted, not like you men."

"I take no part of my life for granted," Nylander all but

growled, surprising himself with a sudden ferocity of emotion.

Wide eyes, less certain than they'd been seconds ago, rounded on him. "No?"

"I've striven tooth and nail for every opportunity, every bit of coin, every single possession I own."

Silent, she nodded. He detected empathy in her eyes. The moment elongated, and a specific intimacy permeated the air. It was the intimacy of understanding. He relaxed beneath it.

She averted her gaze and fixed her attention straight ahead, their forward-moving feet leaving the moment behind. Which he was only too happy to do. He'd revealed more of himself than he liked. Time to right this ship. "What do you consider your greatest achievement at the Grange?"

"Reclaiming the apple orchard from the wild when I arrived five years ago."

"Before your husband passed?"

"Aye. He cared not what I did to pass the time while he was in London."

A clearing appeared to their right, its only building a simple, clapboard structure. Fresh whitewash gleamed bright in the midday sun.

"This has the look of another improvement," Nylander observed.

"I don't consider upkeep of the village school an improvement. Rather, it was a basic necessity that wasn't being tended properly."

Their footsteps slowed to a stop when a group of a dozen or so children burst through the building's side door. Amidst the cacophony of wild shouts and laughter, the children played as if their very lives depended on them having as grand a time as possible in the limited time allotted. Nylander was certain he'd never felt that free in his life, especially not as a child.

The woman beside him went still and silent, her dark eyes luminous and watchful. What he saw in there was impossible to miss. Longing so naked and raw, he knew he should respect her privacy and look away. But he couldn't.

Instinct drove him to ask, "Why did you agree to your marriage?" The question, and his desire to know its answer, had nothing to do with the Grange or bargains with pirates. But for some unholy reason he needed to know if what he saw in her eyes was true. "You don't seem concerned with social standing."

"I don't give a fig what the world thinks." She shrugged one shoulder, her gaze inward. "Why not marry? Don't most women marry once in their lives?" Something sounded in her tone. *Distaste.*

"So you would never marry again?"

"I never said that."

A little pulse of confirmation shot through him, and he remained silent.

"Marriage has its pitfalls, but it has its benefits," she continued.

"Yet you don't seem to be interested in any of them."

"I wouldn't go that far."

"Name one."

"Children come of marriage."

There. What he'd seen in her eyes was true. She wanted children. He couldn't help the tug of sympathy with this difficult woman who looked at him like he was the spit beneath her shoe. And yet...

She'd been a virgin. The woman who'd married for children had been a *virgin* for the three years of her marriage. Her circle became more impossible to square at every turn.

"You'll have noticed there is no child," she stated on a humorless laugh. "The marriage didn't quite go to plan."

"Many plans find a way of slipping out of our control."

Her head snapped around, and she cut him a sharp glare. The silence that followed combined to speak volumes. He'd rattled the woman. Was she wondering if there was an undercurrent running below the surface of his words? If he could possibly know of a plan that might slip away from her?

Perhaps it would be kinder to put an end to this charade, to tell her that he knew she'd made a bargain with a pirate and that, although he didn't know the details of it, he knew with certainty it wouldn't go to plan.

But he wouldn't.

This woman hadn't made a deal with just any pirate, but with Jack Le Grand. Nylander needed more information before he confronted her with that particular truth.

She pulled her hand off his forearm. He'd hardly registered its loss before she was striding away, her feet beating a determined tattoo against stone. He jogged a few steps to catch her. She would have to do better than that if she wanted to shake him off.

"This is a damned long main street," he observed.

Her nostrils flared in annoyance. "It's just over one mile in length. The longest in England according to the locals."

Ahead, its end came into view, dozy waves of the bay lapping at the dark, sandy shore not a hundred yards distant. "It runs into the sea."

The observation was met with silence. He looked around and saw she no longer walked beside him. She'd stopped where the road met sand.

"I believe this concludes our tour for the day." She was finished with him.

Which left one problem. He wasn't finished with her.

"The tide is low."

Her brow lifted as if to say, *You call yourself a master of the sea? Anyone can see that.*

Implicit insults aside, he didn't want her to leave. "Those caves"—he pointed toward the limestone cliffs in the not-so-distant east—"are they only visible at low tide?"

"They become completely submerged with the tide. Every spring, youths must be cautioned about them. Before I arrived, there was a tragedy involving a pair of young—" She bit off the final word of the sentence.

"*Lovers?*"

She nodded. "Which means the rumor about the caves must not be true. Otherwise, they could've made it to higher ground."

Nylander cocked his head. "Rumor?" Experience had taught him there was always a nugget of truth located in local rumors.

"That they connect to the silver mine."

"*Silver mine?*" A tingle of foreboding crawled up his spine. "Those cliffs have a silver mine?" This conversation became more interesting by the word.

Callie shrugged. "Not in that cliff precisely. A little farther east. But they haven't been operational in over a decade. No one ever figured out how to run them at a profit."

Nylander needed to slow this conversation. Information was coming at him too fast. "You're saying the mine didn't stop operating because the silver vein ran out?"

"Not at all. It's not the sort of enterprise that I want to become involved with."

"What does it have to do with—" It hit him. "Where is the main vein located?"

"Beneath the Grange's lands, of course."

One thought tumbled over another: What game was she playing? Did Jack Le Grand know about this silver mine? Ridiculous question. Of course he did. Would her ladyship here know that Jack knew? Was that at the heart of their bargain?

"Who knows about these mines?"

Her eyebrows drew together in befuddlement, and a short, confounded laugh escaped her. "Everyone in Upper Wyldcombe Lacey, to be sure. Everyone in England, possibly. Silver from the mine was used in the crown jewels. Queen Charlotte wore a piece worked in Devon silver—a brooch, I believe—for an official portrait. It's rather a large source of pride for the area."

Nylander cared not one whit for any of that. "Why did operations cease?"

"The tunnels became unstable, and there were some deaths." Her head canted to the side, assessing, suspicious. "You're quite interested in this subject."

"As a man of the sea," he said, thinking fast. *Think.* "I'm fascinated by how goods are acquired on land."

With a single lift of an imperious eyebrow, she reminded him that she was Her Highness and that she didn't believe a word he'd just spoken. She cleared her throat. "I have work to get on with. Good day, Captain."

With that, she pivoted on her heel and stalked away, boots dangling by their laces at her side. Was that wool he'd glimpsed inside them?

Her back receding into the distance, Nylander found himself wishing she was wearing her *ladies'* trousers. She filled them out rather nicely.

Tearing his gaze away, he returned his attention to the caves. They were the key to Callie's bargain with Jack Le Grand. Nylander's gut churned with the certainty. But...

Did she know? Had the silver mine been an explicit part of the deal? Somehow, Nylander didn't think so. Callie's love for the Grange ran deep and wide. She wouldn't invite a renowned pirate to destroy it.

But that didn't mean the silver mine hadn't been part of the pirate's deal with her. It was all a matter of perspective. Every transaction with Jack Le Grand contained multiple subterranean levels. Nylander couldn't rid himself of the feeling that Callie didn't know about those levels.

Aye, she'd made a bargain with the man, but what bargain, he hadn't a clue. He needed to uncover the truth before it was too late and blew up in all their faces.

If Callie thought he'd become closer than her shadow of late, she hadn't seen anything yet.

13

NEXT DAY

"**I**sn't it rare that calves are born in autumn?"

Callie gazed down at mother and calf in their stall. She'd had a hunch about the choking cow, and it had been correct. She'd been pregnant.

"It's uncommon, but not unheard of. Nature does as it wills, not as we humans will it." Mr. Hawkins stuffed the implements of his trade into a weathered green duffel bag. He was the only veterinary surgeon for miles around. "Now, if you'll pardon me, I must see to Farmer Kenning's sheep. They're in need of a good drenching."

With that, Mr. Hawkins left the cow house and Callie alone in the stall, unable to take her eyes off the calf suckling his mother's teat. In moments such as these, a profound sense of accomplishment and hope for the future of the Grange overwhelmed her.

Today, however, the thought didn't feel as wondrous as it had in the past. Nothing did anymore. Not since she'd made the bargain with the pirate, which now hung above her like the executioner's ax, poised to fall and separate her head from her body at any moment.

Many plans find a way of slipping out of our control. Oh, how the Viking's words haunted her. How had he known to speak them?

Her eye on the labor-exhausted cow and calf, her gut

told her those cows hadn't wandered into the apple orchard by accident. But...

What reason could the pirates have for releasing the animals into the apple orchard? Their profits depended on the apples being converted into brandy, as much as hers did.

She exhaled her paranoia on a huff. If life on an agricultural estate had taught her nothing else, it was that coincidences and accidents happened. It was possible that a series of miscommunications, forgotten tasks, drunkenness, and plain laziness had led to the dairy cows finding their way to the apple orchard. Honestly, it was the only explanation.

Time to carry on.

She rolled up her sleeves, grabbed her bucket, and vacated the stall. Certainty in her step, she strode down the long, central aisle of the cow house to the other side that housed the dairy cows. It was time for their morning milking.

She enjoyed the everyday details of running the Grange. They gave a life purpose. She'd never understood why so many of her sex and class were content to lead such idle and boring lives. Not even their children occupied the women of her class, as they left much of the child-drearing to nannies and governesses.

That wasn't the life for her. Maybe Georgie had been correct, and she was *mannish* and *unnatural*. But those descriptors, beyond their unnecessary cruelty, had never sat right with her. She didn't feel like a man. She just felt like a very different sort of woman.

Jane Smith came to mind. She, too, was a different sort of woman. She was a dutiful wife and mother, an exceptional seamstress and shopkeeper, and co-conspirator in keeping Callie outfitted for her midnight dashes across the moor. Her life had purpose and industry beyond her femininity. Yet Jane was the least mannish woman Callie had ever known.

But here was Jane's particular talent: she looked like every other conventional woman. It was a talent Callie didn't possess. She'd never learned the trick of appearing one way and being a different one.

As she drew near the milking stalls, the giggly murmurings of milkmaids busy at their morning's work increased in volume. Fortunately, the first stall she reached was empty, save a cow placidly chewing her cud. Callie pulled up a short, three-legged stool and felt along the cow's engorged udder until she reached a teat.

Oblivious to their mistress's presence, the girls chattered on, which suited Callie perfectly. Her presence made the girls nervous.

But here was the thing: that gaggle of giggly milkmaids made her nervous, too. They were so fresh and vibrant. Though they weren't much younger than she, they were so entirely her opposite.

But, oh, how she loved it when, like today, she was able to slip inside a stall unnoticed and be surrounded by their giggles and their gossip, which simultaneously informed Callie of the latest Grange tattle and provided entertainment. It wasn't that she was sneaking about, but she knew it would ruin their good time if they knew she was amongst them.

Today, they were bandying about a frequent subject of theirs: a young man.

"I'd say 'e knows 'is way around a hoe."

"Aye, 'e'd make my soil right loose and smooth after a day's plowin'."

Laughter echoed all the way up to the rafters. As these young lasses' employer and guardian of their good virtue, she should be shocked. But Callie couldn't quite muster the outrage today. Instead, she found herself stifling a laugh.

"I 'appened to see 'im loading cider barrels onto a wagon yesterday," one of the girls said.

"And?" asked a second girl.

"Don't keep us in suspense, Becky," spoke a third.

"Well, the work must've got 'im all het up, because 'is shirt was open down the front—"

"Oh," sighed one maid.

"Was 'e all muscular?" whispered another.

"Aye, that 'e was, but that weren't all."

"What else could there be?" asked the sighing milkmaid.

"Becky, you know what else there be, no *could* about it!"

"You saw 'is—?"

"Course not," said the maid who held all the information, "but listen to this. 'E rolled up 'is sleeves, and you know what I saw?"

Callie's breath suspended in her chest, and her pulse quickened.

"'E 'ad those markin's sailors get on their skin."

"*Tattoos?*"

"Mm-hmm, that 'e did."

Callie went still as stone. Today, the milkmaids weren't gossiping about just any young man. Today, they were gossiping about the Viking.

"Wouldn't mind seeing where 'e might be 'idin' any others."

Callie could tell the girl. Not that she would, but she could. In detail.

Her body heated up by a degree. These girls' wonderings and speculations, Callie *knew*. Biblically.

"You know what 'e looks like?"

A few whispery giggles floated on the air.

"A Viking."

That did seem to be the general consensus.

"And you know what Vikings do, don't'cha?"

"What?"

"*Plunder.*"

Here was the thing about all this talk of Vikings and plunder. There was an ugly past when Vikings literally laid waste to entire English villages and took what they wanted with brute force. But when words like *Viking* and *plunder* were applied to Captain Nylander, well, they took on a different meaning. Any plunder that would occur between that man and the woman lucky enough to wander into his path would be entirely consensual.

The riot of raucous laughter the word elicited exhibited no signs of stopping until, suddenly, definitely, it did. Curious, Callie poked her head above the stall and immediately ducked down on an inhaled gasp, her heart a hammer in her chest. It was *him*, looking every inch these girls' fantasy.

Eyes fixed firmly on the cow's pink udder, she resumed milking, a steady *squirt-squirt* of milk resonating against the solid wood pail. Perhaps he would state his business and leave without noticing her.

It was possible.

Then the possible became the impossible when he appeared at the hind end of her cow. She kept her attention firmly fixed on her task. Perhaps he would receive her message and skulk away. Over her stall drifted the shuffle of fleeing feet as the milkmaids cleared out.

She was alone with the Viking. *Again.*

Sudden pique flared up as, at last, she faced him. There, he stood, watching her, an inquiring glint in his eye.

"It's you," she exclaimed, her frustration with this situation, with this man, at last, finding its vent. "Of course, it's you. It's *always* you."

Instead of hanging his head in apology, the blasted man did the opposite. He smiled.

And to add the insufferable to insult, her body warmed to his smile as if the full heat of the summer sun shone upon it. It was a smile a woman could bask in.

"Did you miss me?"

The cheek!

Still, a tidy question reared its annoying, little head: Had she?

***

QUICK ON THE heels of Mrs. Bailey's command to fetch a bucket of milk from the diary, Nylander's feet hit packed earth, purpose in his step, a crisp, sea-salted breeze against his skin.

"You're a man used to work, so I may as well put you to

it," she'd said. "There's no butter where there's no cream, so off wi' ya. Tell Becky it's for me."

He tilted his face toward the wide blue sky and let the English sun pour what little warmth it had into him. He missed the sun of a hot climate. A sun that gave one no quarter as it saturated every pore with its fire and turned a man's skin brown and vibrant.

The sun of the north Devon coast was a stingy sort, as if it had a scant allotment of light and heat that it must portion out like a miser. In the few weeks he'd been here, the days had grown shorter and the air had turned sharper. The sun was beginning to settle in for the winter.

But the oranges and yellows of autumn had something to say before winter reached out and encased this half of the world within its icy claws. Autumn energy possessed a specific crackle that set people into motion. The warm equatorial sun lacked its northern counterpart's ability to inspire such industry. He found himself warming to this crisp Devon sun, its particular energy soaking into him.

On the other side of the poultry yard, he caught sight of a youth loping toward him. This lad wasn't from the Grange. It wasn't only his cautious way of taking in his surroundings that marked him as different. His brown curly hair, golden-tipped and near the same color of his skin, did, too. He was of mixed African descent, and no one at the Grange, Upper Wyldcombe Lacey, perhaps all of Devon, resembled him.

Jack Le Grand had sent this lad his way. Nylander hadn't any doubt of it. Jack would send three invitations, three days in a row. It was ever the same when they shared the same stretch of air.

Wordlessly, the lad stopped before him, blocking his path, and extended a slip of paper. Nylander accepted the note and gave its contents a quick scan. He closed his fist, crushing it in his palm. "That's all the reply he'll get." His words, their tone, brooked no rebuttal. It was the same reply Jack always got.

"'E don't like that answer, not one bit." A cocky smile tipped at the side of the lad's mouth. He was possessed of the gangly arms and legs of a boy about to become a very tall man. Nylander had been the same at that age. Complete with cockiness, too.

"Off with you, now," Nylander said.

He watched the lad disappear down a hill and uttered a muted litany of curses. Jack Le Grand knew he was here. *Bloody hell.*

He should've seen this coming. Jack made it a point to have land connections in every port. It was the only way a pirate of his advanced years—all sixty-five of them, if memory served—kept his neck out of the hangman's noose. The man was likely better apprised of land matters than those who lived on it.

And then there was the not insignificant matter of the way he'd shadowed Nylander from Gibraltar. Jack had something he wanted to say to him. Too bad. He wasn't interested. That ship sailed five and twenty years ago.

He snorted a humorless laugh when, in reality, it wasn't funny at all. It hadn't been then, and it wasn't now.

He reached the cow house and stepped inside its wide open double doors. Its cavernous expanse smelled of dung and animal and rich, dense earth. The scent wasn't unpleasant. It was the essence of life, of beginnings.

He picked up a low drone of voices and followed the sound, which was punctuated by a giddy laugh every few seconds. He began to be able to pick out distinct, fully formed words. Words like plunder and Viking.

Viking?

He rounded a corner and found a neat row of four indifferent cows crunching idly on hay, each being milked by a different milkmaid.

"Would one of you be Becky?" he asked, setting off another round of giggles, but no direct answer to his question.

The gaggle of girls stood in unison, sidled around him as a group, one indistinguishable from the other, and fled the barn. For a moment, he thought he was alone. Then he heard it: the squirt of milk hitting the side of a bucket in the next stall. He peeked around the hindquarter of an unbothered cow, expecting to find Becky. Instead, he found Her Highness, actively, persistently avoiding his gaze.

He waited. She would have to acknowledge his presence, sooner or later. It did give him time to observe her profile. How pretty it was.

That night flashed before him. *Her silhouette limned by the soft glow of distant moonlight... Mouth open, short bursts of breath specific to the rhythm of coupling... A bead of perspiration catching a moon ray...*

Her unsurprised gaze shifted to meet his, and a blush peeked above the high collar of her blouse. Redheads couldn't pretend indifferent when they weren't. It was their particular curse, but he felt glad for it. He liked the look of her. She was the very image of a dairymaid, wholesome and fresh, the energy of satisfying work filling in the space around her.

And, just now, when she spat annoyed words at him, he couldn't hold back a smile. He liked that she reacted to him, that he could burrow beneath her skin. It was childish, perhaps, this need of a boy to tweak the girl who thought herself too good for him. She broke their eye contact and squeezed the cow's teat, another hard stream of milk hitting the side of the bucket.

"I've been wondering why I couldn't find you in the early mornings."

"Well, you've found me." Her grip on the teat slackened. "Am I to assume you'll state your purpose sooner or later?"

He held up his bucket. "Mrs. Bailey won't allow me back in the house until this is full."

"You can take mine in a few minutes." She returned to her task.

Nylander watched the rhythm of her hands squeeze and release, the sound of the milk hitting the side of her bucket filling the space between them. Though she was hard and uppity, she was intriguing. "Do you milk the cows daily?"

She heaved an exasperated sigh. "You think I'm too good for this sort of work?"

"Not I, but—"

"*I* would think so?"

"Most lords and ladies do."

"After Georgie died, that's what everyone around here thought, too. That I considered myself above it." She swiveled on her stool and faced him square. "Well, I'm not. No one is too good for this sort of work. I lo—" She stopped.

"You love it."

Her serious, coal-black eyes upon him, she nodded. No one could doubt her love for this place. A question occurred to him, the obvious one, one that should have been obvious to her, too. If this place was her life, her true love, then why was she gambling it with a man like Jack Le Grand?

She pivoted and gave him the hard angle of her shoulder. "A few more squirts and the bucket will be full."

"I don't have much experience with livestock."

She shrugged, her hands intent on their work, the cow utterly indifferent.

"I've always wondered what it would be like to milk a cow," he said, surprising himself.

She didn't miss a beat. "Can't imagine it would be congruous with life aboard a ship."

"Would you mind showing me?"

"Mind showing you what?"

"How to milk a cow."

Her hands stopped mid-squeeze, and the stall went silent, save the persistent sound of the cow chewing her cud. Wide eyes rounded on him. He'd made her go speechless.

He rather liked that.

14

"**B**ut I... *you*," Callie stammered.

"Would you humor a guest of the estate?" Nylander asked, knowing full well he had her there. Good manners dictated that a considerate host indulge the request of a guest, no matter how odd or inconveniencing.

On a huff that might have been petulant, she stood and gestured toward her vacated stool. "Of course."

He stepped forward and stopped. Knowledge lit within her eyes. The stall wasn't wide enough for them to switch positions without close proximity. It was possible their bodies would brush against one another, probable, even. Tension, deep and sinuous, coiled inside Nylander, anticipatory, ready.

He inched forward. She inched forward.

He stepped to his left. She stepped to her right.

She emitted a nervous laugh and darted in the other direction at the same moment he did.

Another nervous laugh sounded, this one less amused by their unexpected pas de deux. Her skittish gaze held his for a heartbeat, and he went still. She pressed her back flat against the wooden slats of the stall, her message clear. Only a narrow gap existed between cow and wall, and he was to step through it without touching her.

Into the opening, he moved, and she shuffled sideways,

the front of his body and the front of hers now separated by inches. Her face averted, her chest heaving, she looked as if she would fuse with the boards at her back, if it meant not having to touch him.

In this strange way, they maneuvered around each other, he stepping forward, she sidling over, her movements stuttered against uneven boards. He wouldn't be surprised if a splinter wedged its fine tip into her back.

He caught her scent—*citrus, apple, fresh, clean*—and time slowed. Into the slim inches that separated them pushed *that* night. Her breath released on a trembly exhale, and chills raced along his skin, raising fine hairs as it went. That exhalation, its particular tenor, its particular tremor, pushed him to push her. Her continued denial of that night, of *this* now, poked something ugly into life inside him.

He would be known. He would be acknowledged.

"There was a woman," he rasped.

Wide eyes met his. She had the look of a trapped animal. "We do abound."

"In my room." His voice was no louder than a muted rumble. But it didn't need volume, so close were they. A musky scent mixed into the air. It was coming from her. It was the musk of fear.

"Your former nurse, Liza Bickle, is a woman."

"Not her," he said, pushing toward the edge. He wanted her to jump off and speak the truth aloud. "A different woman."

"I—" She hesitated, the heavy throb of her pulse visible above her high collar. "I went into your room." She swallowed. "We spoke. I helped you. Then I went back to my room."

'Twas true these were all facts, but there was one more fact she was excluding: her return later.

"Aye," he replied. Reason stepped in and bade him say no more. What did he hope to accomplish by bringing her shame into the light? Further, what did he hope to gain? "I reckon 'twas naught more than a dream," he finished. The charge in the air fizzled and went flat. He felt oddly deflated.

Her eyebrows drew together, and she blinked. Then she slipped past, breaking free of their dance, of him. "You'll want to roll up your sleeves." Control replaced the wobble in her voice with each word she spoke. "Otherwise, you'll soak them with milk spray."

He nodded and unbuttoned his cuffs, releasing the reckless moment to the past. As he rolled his sleeves to his elbows, he caught Callie's eye snagged on his anchor tattoo. "I believe you're familiar with my tattoos?" Did the woman really have such delicate sensibilities? "Not many gentlemen possess tattoos, I suppose." He didn't like the way the word *gentlemen* sounded like a sneer from his mouth.

She gave a small shrug. "I wouldn't really know, but—" She hesitated. "Can I ask you a question?"

He nodded.

"Where did you get your tattoos?"

He ran his fingers across the faded black anchor. "This was my first. Got it when I was sixteen in Le Havre. It was infected for six weeks."

"Did you get your others in Le Havre?"

He shook his head. "They're from places I've visited. Siam, New Zealand, and a few others."

Her head canted to the side, genuine curiosity writ across her features. "Why would you do such a thing over and over again?"

He couldn't help laughing. She seemed so perplexed. "It isn't as serious as all that. I think of them as the transportable souvenirs from places I've traveled. Evidence of my time at sea."

"But," she began, hesitant, "they must've been painful."

"Like bloody hell," he said. "Some more than others. It depends on the method for delivering the ink into the skin."

"Do they still hurt?"

He shook his head. "They just feel like skin. Would you like to see the others?"

Her mouth gaped open and instantly snapped shut. He'd gone too far. She gestured toward the stool. "You'll want to grab a teat between thumb and forefinger at the base of her udder."

He did as instructed.

"Not that one."

He dropped his hand and darted an inquiring glance over his shoulder.

"It's already been milked. Each teat needs to be milked to prevent mastitis."

He pointed to another. "This one?"

She nodded. "Now squeeze."

No milk flowed. Not even a drop as it remained stubbornly dry. Unaffected, the cow continued chewing her cud.

Callie stepped closer until he felt her hovering over his back. He might've felt her breath whisper across the nape of his neck, and a shiver might've purled up his spine.

"Release the teat and repeat the steps, slowly."

Again, he followed her instructions, and, again, no milk.

"Ah," she breathed into his ear. His loins tightened. "I see what you're doing wrong. Here"—she reached around and covered his hand with hers—"like this." Her thumb and forefinger wrapped around his thumb and forefinger, and she squeezed. "Not all of your fingers at once, but in a wave motion." Middle, ring, and pinky fingers squeezed, one after another in sequence. *Middle, ring, pinky... middle, ring, pinky.* "See?"

His mouth gone dry, he nodded.

"Mind to keep squeezing and releasing thumb and forefinger to allow more milk in." Her hand dropped from his, and a pang for its loss stole through him. "Try it."

He was tempted to fail again, just to have her touch him again. Instead, he followed her instructions and succeeded in coaxing a thin stream of milk. A little chirrup of triumph sounded in his ear, and, before he could register the action, his hand shot up and caught her wrist.

The instructive moment transformed into one he understood well, propelled by an elemental urge. She went still and watchful, and what he saw in her eyes took him by surprise.

If he was reading her correctly, she wasn't opposed to the possibility of where this moment could lead them. In fact, she might be more than *not opposed*.

He tugged, and she swayed forward. His thumb rubbed light circles on her wrist, and she exhaled. "Captain Ny—"

"*Nylander*," he growled.

"I believe," she whispered, "you've gotten the knack of it."

Still, he held her in his grasp.

Still, she didn't pull away.

"I have the knack of a great many things."

EVEN AS THE breath froze in Callie's lungs, her heart beat a rapid tattoo, sending blood zinging through her veins. All the better to deliver the feeling to every cell in her body.

Desire. Her knees weak with it. Her skin *alive* with it. She was helpless against it.

A not-too-distant shout spiked through the air. Then another, and another, until it became a riot of shouting. She shot upright and broke from his grasp. Later, she wouldn't countenance the pang that had streaked through her from the loss of his touch.

"Do you hear that?" she asked, her feet already on the move.

"I believe the dead can hear it," she heard close at her heels.

"It's coming from the cider house."

Only a truly terrible occurrence would warrant the level of shouting that could be heard through stone walls from hard men who never spoke a word more than the moment required.

Driven by panic, Callie cut across the stable yard, between the dairy and cart shed, the straightest line to the cider house. She crashed through the closest door, which opened onto the first floor fruit loft. The crisp, floral scent of crushed apple met her nose.

Her feet took the short flight of steps to the ground floor two at a time. No one stood at the cider press. She kept running. She reached the end of the loft, and the barn opened above and around her. Ahead, the horse who pulled the millstone was being led away, allowing her a view of the accident.

The stone wheel had tipped off its circular track, and a worker was trapped beneath, with Will and Cam attempting to prevent the great stone from slipping farther and crushing the man. Jess was his name, and he had a young family at home depending on him.

Callie's stomach dropped to her feet, her voice caught in her throat. If those men didn't get that stone off Jess in the next minute or so, he would be crushed. Will and Cam's strength couldn't hold forever. Just as she hurried forward to lend whatever paltry help she could, the Viking rushed around her. She'd forgotten about him.

"Not like that," he shouted as he moved forward. "You'll throw out your backs trying to lift the stone that way." He wedged his massive body between the two men. "Like this."

He crunched into a tight ball and wedged his shoulder beneath the stone.

"You," he called out to Will, "grab him." Jess had gone eerily silent. "And when I count down and say *now*, you pull him out. And you," he said to Cam, "position yourself on the other side, like me. And use your legs to lift. Everyone understand?"

The men nodded and scurried into place, each understanding they had one shot at this. That if they lifted the stone and allowed it to come back down on Jess, it would mean his life.

Nylander was good at directing people. Beyond good. He was a natural-born commander. Unlike her, who hadn't been able to utter a word of command since she'd entered this room.

She'd never been comfortable with that side of her role. She enjoyed the work of planning and implementation, but she didn't enjoy the leading. An undercurrent always ran below the men's acceptance of her orders, as if it were unnatural to take direction from a woman. They'd never once looked at her the way they were looking at Nylander, with appreciation and not a little bit of awe as he inched his shoulder farther beneath the stone. A small note of envy tinged through her, accompanied by a begrudging gratefulness. Her feelings were all set to odds when it came to this man.

"*Three*," he barked, his left palm flat on the ground, his right gripping the stone at his shoulder. "*Two*"—his back muscles bunched into hard readiness beneath his shirt— "*One*"—the breath caught in Callie's chest. She wanted to look away, but she couldn't, not if she expected to meet the eye of any man who worked her land ever again—"*Now!*"

On a loud roar, the muscles of Nylander's back, his great thighs and arms, tensed, his entire body strained in the concentrated task of relieving enough of the stone's weight off Jess so he could slip out. The stone shifted an inch, maybe two, but it was enough for Will to give a tremendous heave and pull Jess free.

"'E's out!"

Mirror images of each other, the Viking and Cam scuttled out from beneath the unwieldy stone and allowed it to drop to the ground with a sickening thud. Callie's breath released. Body flat on the ground, Jess groaned in pain and clutched at his right shoulder with his left hand.

"I'd say it's yer collarbone that's broken," Will said. Cam nodded in agreement.

Jess closed his eyes and groaned again.

"You know what that means," Will continued.

"Aye," Jess grunted.

"Let's get some whiskey in you before it begins."

Before it begins. The words, ominous and grave, sent a shudder through Callie.

Jess rolled onto his uninjured side and, with the assistance of Will and Cam, made it to his feet by slow, arduous increments. Callie started to follow when she noticed Nylander hanging back, an assessing eye on the wheel mill. His eyebrows were drawn together in concentration, one might even say concern.

"What is it?" she couldn't stop herself from asking.

"It's just that—" He hesitated.

"*It's just that* what?"

He shook his head. "Nothing, likely."

An alarm bell clanged through Callie. What wasn't this capable, natural-born leader of men not telling her?

"How old is this wheel mill?" he asked.

"It was brought in before last year's harvest. This is its second season in use."

He squatted beside the broken plank and ran his fingers down its smooth length to the break. "This wood has been compromised. Mayhap it was rot or a boring insect." He sounded unconvinced by his own words.

"Rot isn't possible. It's practically new. I inspected every board and joint. They were solid as the stone they held."

He nodded, distracted, deep in his thoughts. "Unless—"

"Unless?"

Dread filled her belly. What he wasn't saying was exactly what she didn't want to admit to herself, much less hear voiced aloud.

"Unless"—he shook his head—"it was the sea air."

Callie's fists clenched at her sides. While she didn't want to hear her worst fear confirmed aloud, she certainly didn't wish it withheld from her.

"The men will need all the help they can get setting that collarbone." Nylander had unfurled the long length of his body and was already on the move.

"You know how to manage a broken collarbone?" What didn't the man know?

"I've set a few in my day," he said over his shoulder, and was gone.

She stood, flummoxed, astonished, and, oh, *impressed*. Of course he'd set a few collarbones in his day. The man wasn't only a natural-born leader of men, he was a natural at everything he set his hand to. He'd ridden Buttercup on his first try. He'd milked a cow on his first try.

Well, setting a broken collarbone was where she drew the line, content to leave it to him and the other men. It was a grisly business that she had no stomach for. Her eye returned to the broken beam, and acid curdled in her belly. First the cows in the orchard, now this. A man had very nearly been killed. Something wasn't right. Perhaps...

She couldn't finish the thought. It couldn't be the pirates. Why would they sabotage their own interests?

Mayhap it was a disgruntled tenant who wanted her gone. She'd thought she'd reached an accord with the locals these last few years, but there might be a hold-out now making his voice heard. But would someone on the estate risk one of his fellow workers' life? Releasing cows into the orchard to eat apples could be a harmless prank. Not this, though.

Or was it the most recent addition to the Grange... Captain John Nylander? Had he discovered that Lord St. Alban would sell him the Grange if she failed? Wouldn't he benefit the most from sabotaging her primary source of income? Even scare her away in the process?

Except, he didn't seem the type to use underhanded tactics to reach his objective. But she didn't know him, not really. And he'd been following her so closely...

What if the Viking was sabotaging her efforts, her *livelihood*?

Sudden doubt sprouted and grew quick roots inside her: she wasn't certain she could best him.

But she must try. She must fight. She must draw out what the man knew. Tonight. Not sometime in the indistinct future, but tonight. She must hit this head-on and hard.

She would ignore the quake of anxiety rattling through her.

And she would forget what had passed between them in that stall. That, perhaps, she'd felt neither *mannish* nor *unnatural*. That, perhaps, she'd been wanted. Figments of her overwrought imagination, surely.

She would tend to matters grounded in reality.

Tonight.

15

NIGHT

Nylander leaned over green baize and gazed down the length of the billiard stick. His arm reared back in short practised strokes, once, twice before striking the cue ball with too much force and sending another ball flying, red-stained ivory ricocheting off a wood-paneled wall before sinking to a stop in dense Persian wool.

Third time tonight.

Disgusted by his lack of concentration, he let the stick clatter to the billiard table and ambled toward the dart board. He took a dart in hand, aimed, and threw. He repeated the sequence three times, all the darts flying wide of the bull's eye.

He'd never developed the knack for landlubber games. He spent, at minimum, three hundred days a year on water. What use was a billiards table on the rocking horse roll of the open sea?

He prowled the length of this room, the house's gentleman's retreat, back and forth, bored, hoping to find something of interest that he'd missed these last several nights. He'd even tried to convince the footman, Ollie, to join him for a round of billiards. The man had refused, citing work obligations, but Nylander understood the truth of it. The man was afraid Her Highness would sack him.

All her servants gave her a wide berth. When they looked at her, they saw a strange woman, a Wyld Hare,

155

someone they could neither understand nor predict. After all, she wore men's trousers. They couldn't see through that exterior to the woman below. But he'd glimpsed *her*.

And those *men's* trousers… Well, she was correct. They were ladies' trousers, on her. Devoid of vanity, she saw them as nothing more than a functional item of clothing, necessary to the demands of her work. She hadn't the faintest notion of how those trousers presented her body, specifically the womanly curves of her arse, in full, loving glory.

He'd give himself a cockstand if he wasn't careful. A cockstand and nowhere to go with it.

The back of his hand still tingled with awareness from her touch earlier. The pulsing heat of her skin, the humidity of it. The entire essence of his being concentrated into the place where her skin touched his. He'd never felt so animal, so *male*, and so outside of himself, as if he'd both transcended his physicality and sunk deeper into it at once. It was as if he'd had a spell cast on him. By her.

Except he knew the spell she wove wasn't intentional, rather the opposite. He'd never encountered a woman so unwilling to own her desire, so at odds with it, the struggle evident in her sway forward, her pull back, the repetition of the cycle.

It intrigued him. *She* intrigued him, this woman who saw him as nothing more than the dirt beneath her boot. Remnants of the anger that had surged in the cow stall prickled back to life. How he'd wanted to strip a confession from her. He still wanted it, if he was being dead honest.

But it was a reckless desire, this need to be a sin acknowledged, and one that would get him nowhere with that confounding woman. And she really was confounding. She was capable and brave. She cared deeply about the land and everyone who lived off it. Considerations which had him swinging full circle to the question that had been bedeviling him for days: Why had she struck a deal with Jack Le Grand?

While these days spent tracking her movements hadn't

turned up any substantive answers, they had yielded some curious scraps. The cows in the orchard, who had certainly been intentionally let loose there. The silver mine, whose deposit wasn't fully exhausted. No doubt, Jack would be interested in that morsel of information. And the wheel mill accident today...

It hadn't been an accident. A dense concentration of small holes had been painstakingly bored into the wooden plank connecting the stone wheel to the central pivot, compromising its integrity so that the combination of the stone's weight and the pull of the horse would snap it clean through when put to work. Those holes were too perfect and symmetrical to have been caused by insect or rot. They were man-made.

Her Highness had a problem. While the specific nature of her problem hadn't made itself clear, he understood it in a general sense.

Jack Le Grand.

Nylander would wager the entirety of his hard-won fortune on it.

He found himself at the far end of the room, a pair of buff leather chairs and two cases of bookshelves flanking either side of the fireplace. He scanned a row of books at random and stopped dead on one title. *The Complete Works of William Shakespeare.* He pulled the book and thumbed through its thousands of pages, scanning plays and character lists until he found the one he sought.

As You Like It. The one with the heroine who wore trousers. Mayhap Shakespeare could provide instruction on how to deal with one such woman.

He sank into cushioned leather and dove into the play. The Dowager Viscountess St. Alban was similar to her Shakespearean counterpart in more ways than one. Aside from their penchant for trousers, they were both noble, headstrong, and intelligent.

A throat cleared behind him. The smile that had found its way to his lips, dropped. He glanced over his shoulder to find Ollie returned. "Change your mind?" he asked, annoyed at being pulled from the play. He snapped the book shut.

"Her ladyship requests your presence in her study."

Nylander's brow lifted in surprise. "She does, does she?"

"If you will follow me."

Within minutes, they'd reached the study door, a golden stream of light running up its cracked-open length. Nylander stayed Ollie just as the footman's hand reached for the handle.

"No need for announcements." Nylander fancied observing Her Highness inside her inner sanctum, unobserved.

"But, her ladyship—"

A hard glower silenced the younger man and sent him hurrying off. At times, Nylander's massive size had its benefits. He pushed the door open on silent hinges and stepped inside the room.

Stretched before him lay a long, cavernous room lit at the far end. Scents of leather and wood, even the hint of cigar, lingered in the air from the men who'd once populated it. But no more. Now, this room had a mistress. One who hadn't bothered to make a single feminine change to it.

There *she* was, flame strands wisping about her face, nightrail shut tight at her throat, brilliantly lit as if she were a stage performer, bent over a large oak desk with, at least, six books open, fingers moving from one to the other, her gaze darting in a measured rhythm as if she was reading all six at once. She really wasn't an ordinary lady.

Quite the opposite, in fact.

The sort who made deals with pirates, in fact.

He cleared his throat. Her head startled up, and she gasped. Recognition, deep and elemental, spiked through him, and his lust from earlier sparked to life.

"Who's there?" she called out, squinting into the shadows, nervous fingers tucking those loose tendrils behind her ears. He wished she wouldn't.

He stepped into the light and left the thought behind. This was Her Highness he was dealing with, a woman determined to keep the shame of him her dirty secret. The ugly strand of annoyance that skated the edge of anger earlier pulled taut, reminding him of its presence. He could ignore it. He had years of experience. "'Tis the man you summoned."

Her body visibly released in relief. "You certainly have a way of entering a room. You must do the world a favor and consider tying bells around your ankles."

He approached the desk and perched a hip on its edge. She drew back, startled at his audacity. Good. She needed someone to set her back on her heels every once in a while.

"How is Jess's shoulder?" she asked.

"Set." He'd spare her the sickening details. He flipped idly through the pages of the nearest book at hand. "I see you're settled in for the night with a bit of light reading."

She reached out and snatched the book away. "I'll thank you not to disturb my place, sir."

He pointed toward a drawing in the center of the desk. He pointed toward the blueprint. "What is this?"

"It's a survey of the estate. I commissioned it last spring."

He leaned over, settling his weight more fully onto the desk, and took a closer look at the books surrounding the survey. Each was an illustration of various types of linking geometrical patterns. "What are these?"

"Pasture designs." She spoke haltingly, as if the words were being pulled from her. "Some are English, some American. I was hoping to find differences that would be of use, but mostly they're the same."

"Allow me?"

She gave him a long look before relenting and sliding two texts toward him. "Rectangles, gates, and such. Some useful-looking new types of gates that I'd like to implement, but not much by way of new designs. I need more control over my sheep and cattle."

She was referencing the cows in the orchard. Silent, he

studied the texts, while her gaze rested hot upon him. He pointed toward the blueprint. "May I?"

She slid the large, flimsy paper across polished oak. "Of course."

"And those if you please?" He indicated the pencil and paper at her elbow.

Her brow gathered in question, parallel crease lines between her eyebrows. Still, she acquiesced.

Half an eye on the survey, his pencil began scratching across blank paper, an idea fleshing out as quick as it formed in his mind. She followed every movement and mark. Minutes passed, and the idea took solid shape. At last, he drew back and laid pencil to rest. "How about this?"

She sidled around the desk to get a better look. Her scent of citrus and fresh air met his nose, and he inhaled. He couldn't help himself.

"What precisely am I looking at? Is it a flower?"

He shook his head. "What if you get rid of all the rectangles and, instead, arrange all the pastures like petals, if you will, around this." He pressed his forefinger dead center. "A central holding yard. All the individual pastures would lead here. Of course, the animals will need to go to the barn periodically or move to other areas, which would necessitate an aisle that runs from the holding yard to the exterior. For example, if the milk cows got through their individual pasture gate and managed to squeeze through the holding yard gate, too, the worst thing that could happen is they would make their way down the aisle and into a barn. You could implement versions of this throughout the estate. In fact"—he traced a fingertip across the land survey—"this land with the large barn would be a perfect area to try it first as it has the cliffs providing one boundary and the barn another."

"No."

His brow furrowed. "*No?*"

"That won't work."

"If you look here"—perhaps she wasn't viewing it properly—"you'll see that it's quite perfect."

"It isn't. There are issues with that barn which cannot be resolved."

Head canted to the side in complete absorption, she scanned his work. His heart beat a hard hammer in his chest, fueled by no small amount of annoyance. Something else, too. Was he crestfallen? Did her good opinion mean so much to him?

"But that isn't to say this"—her forefinger dug into his drawing—"isn't *brilliant*."

Her praise spread through him with the rapidity of a Mozart arpeggio. The sunken low he'd experienced seconds ago was instantly replaced by an effervescent high.

He might like it too much. Or not at all. He couldn't be sure. Of one thing he was absolutely sure, however: he couldn't trust a feeling that blew cold one second and hot the next. Better to squash it now than allow it to grow roots.

Lest he forget, this woman neither liked nor respected him as an equal.

He cleared his throat. "There are, of course, potential problems with my drawing."

"Such as?"

"It might be time-consuming, not to mention costly, to implement."

Her eyes fast on his drawing, she shrugged.

"Also"—why was he seeding doubt into the plan he'd just proposed?—"there might be a problem with water."

"Not so. See here?" Her finger trailed across the survey. "Several small streams cut through the estate. Water isn't an issue." A frown formed about her mouth. "You're not accustomed to praise, are you?"

Her words caught him off guard. He pushed off the desk and planted his feet, ready to dig into the meat of their conversation. "You didn't call me into your inner sanctum to discuss pasture configurations."

Her head whipped around, and her gaze found his. A beat later, she'd moved on. Her long body ramrod straight, she set about closing and stacking her agricultural books into a neat pile, the openness of moments ago fading fast.

When finished with her tidying, she took a seat in her too-large leather chair and regarded him with the hauteur of an aristocrat staring down her ignoble subject.

"I have a matter of some delicacy to ask. But before I begin, I request that anything we discuss not leave these four walls, as it won't become common knowledge for some weeks yet."

"And what matters of delicacy could you and I possibly have to discuss with one another?"

WAS the man toying with her?

There were so many *matters of delicacy* that had accumulated between them, and his tone was so suggestive, it was impossible to tell. Hallelujah that she and he were separated by an oak desk no smaller and no less dense than the tree itself must have been in life.

"You mistake my meaning. The matter of delicacy refers not to you and I, rather to the sale of the Grange."

His brow furrowed. "You're selling Wyldcombe Grange?"

Surprise, coupled with no small amount of relief, spiked through her.

He hadn't known about St. Alban's intention to sell the Grange for he hadn't even known St. Alban owned it.

Nylander hadn't been sabotaging her efforts.

"You have the wrong end of the stick, I'm afraid," she said. "Wyldcombe Grange isn't mine to sell. 'Tis Lord St. Alban's."

"He owns the Grange?"

Her head canted to the side. "How do you think you ended up here?"

"I thought you were doing him a family favor."

"Lord St. Alban and I are family in name only."

His eyes narrowed on her, shock receding, assessment growing. "Not friends either?"

"I'd never met Lord St. Alban until the day you fainted in his foyer. So, no, not friends either."

"And he's selling the Grange," Nylander said slowly. "So I'm assuming you'll never be friends."

Callie pinched her lips into a firm line to hold the bitterness inside. Somehow she'd opened herself up to this man. Wasn't it he who should be revealing himself?

She could be a fool, it was a fact.

"The Grange isn't entailed as part of the viscountcy?" he asked, the question smart and utterly surprising.

She gave a short, humorless laugh. The unexpected always had that effect on her. "Are you a student of English primogeniture and land laws?"

Nylander shifted his weight and crossed his arms over his chest. He could be very intimidating. If she chose to see him that way. But really all she saw was the muscle flexing and releasing beneath his plain linen shirt, drawing her eye toward the sinewy breadth of his chest. She remembered that chest quite well, the feel of it, the heat of it, the taste of it.

Her mouth went dry.

"I picked up a bit of knowledge here and there over the years," he muttered.

"Thinking of settling down and growing roots into the English countryside?" Oh, why would she ask such a thing?

"Aye."

She willed her body to go very, very still and not reveal the slightest inkling of her dismay.

"But it's near impossible for someone outside the peerage or landed gentry to own an estate like the Grange."

His words, their tone, chastised her with their naked desire. This was why Lord St. Alban wanted to sell the Grange to this man. His friend wanted it, craved it.

She snapped to. This man was her rival. Were his desires, wants, and cravings more valid than her own? Even if they were the same? And now, worst of all, her paranoia and insecurity had led her to reveal the sale of the Grange to him. *Blast.*

Well, she wouldn't take it any further. She wouldn't be

the one to inform the Viking that not only did St. Alban wish to sell the Grange, but he wanted to sell it to *him*. St. Alban could bloody well tell him himself.

Her desires, wants, and cravings were no less worthy than those of the man before her.

Is this fair play?

Life wasn't fair. And the Viking knew it as well as she. She wouldn't feel an ounce of guilt. Nothing had changed.

She was still the best captain of this ship.

His eyebrows drew together. "If the Grange is unentailed, then why didn't your late husband leave it to you?"

Another humorless laugh escaped her. It was the sort of laugh possessed of a razor edge sharp enough to cut a person on its way out. "Georgie believed the feeble female brain incapable of leading any endeavor, much less the running of an entire estate. He lacked the imagination even to conceive such a concept." She hesitated. "To answer your question, Georgie's will left the Grange to his heir, who he'd assumed would be his son."

"But, in the end, his heir was Lord St. Alban."

She nodded, wary of the canny light that had entered Nylander's eye. Puzzle pieces were beginning to snap into place for him. No good could come of that.

"Do you know of any interested buyers?"

She held his gaze, unwavering. "I know of one."

Understanding lit within his eyes, imbuing them with a silvery light. "You."

"The interested part, at least."

"And no other competitors?"

She shrugged one shoulder, hoping to convey disinterest, knowing she'd failed miserably. "There might be. I can't be sure who St. Alban has in the running."

It was just short of an outright lie, which would have to do.

16

A story lay behind the tight twist of Her Highness's mouth. But Nylander would never have that story if he pressed her head-on. There was a way of approaching a head wind when it stood between a ship and its destination. One had to angle the sails just so and use the wind to one's advantage, instead of fighting it.

"How did you come to be the viscountess?" he asked. If it was possible to see every muscle in another person's body tense, he was looking at it now.

"I've already told you—"

"*This* viscountess. The Viscountess St. Alban."

"Debt." The word emerged simply, succinct. "Georgie was in a mountain of debt to my father, who had a habit of acquiring the debt of lords and landed gentry when he could manage it. Usually at a discount from gaming hells happy to recover even a fraction of their losses."

"An ambitious man, your father." Nylander was careful to keep his tone neutral.

She laughed without mirth. He didn't like that laugh. "It would be one way of putting it. *Ruthless* would be another. Absolutely nothing stands between my father and his goals."

"No love or affinity existed between you and the late viscount?" Nylander asked, even though he knew the answer. After all, she'd been a virgin.

"Love and affinity weren't necessary to the acquisition of a title for my family."

"You're saying that your father—" He hesitated, suddenly wishing he could go back in time and restart this conversation, convince it to proceed in a different direction. No longer did he want to get at the truth of this matter. It was too ugly a truth. Yet that word—*acquisition*—nipped at him. It spoke of transaction of the fiscal variety. He couldn't let it be. "Your father sold you."

She cleared her throat. "It's a free country. I made my choices."

Cold, distant, and tough were her words, as if they, or the motivations behind them, no longer affected her. But her eyes, raw and skittish, belied her bluff.

"You were married three years?"

She nodded.

"Enough time to start a family," he stated, again pushing her.

Children come of marriage. Those had been her exact words as they'd stood outside the schoolyard, watching the children play. To be blunt, it only took about two minutes to conceive a child, if that was the main goal.

And they hadn't managed it in three years?

It didn't make sense.

Her gaze skittered toward him, and her jaw clenched. He'd struck his mark. "Perhaps," she began, "but no number of years is enough time if—" She bit off the rest of the sentence.

Her cheeks had grown flushed, and emotion rioted behind her tough exterior. Nylander leaned forward and placed his palms flat on the oak desk. "Not long enough if...?" he prompted. She would finish the sentence she'd started.

Her gaze fixed on some indeterminate point on her lap. She rolled her bottom lip between her teeth before releasing it on a rough harrumph of her throat. She had the most unladylike habits. He rather liked them. They were honest.

"If he is unable to perform," she stated without even a hint of emotion.

He leaned forward and cocked his ear toward her, uncertain he'd heard her correctly. "If he is unable to—"

"*Perform*." Bleak coal-black eyes stared out at him.

"Per—" He stopped.

Oh.

She shot to her feet, reached for the land survey at the center of the desk, and began rolling it up as if suddenly pressed for time. "Entirely my fault, it seems," she said, offhand, dismissive.

"I can't imagine that would've been the case," he said on a low grumble. Less than three feet of oak separated them, his words didn't need to carry far.

Her eyes flew up to meet his, still vulnerable, still raw, but he saw something new in their depths: fire. "Do not toy with me," she gritted out.

He moved not a muscle and didn't back down, as many must when this woman cast at them this particular glare. "I'm not the toying sort."

The moment elongated, and stillness filled the room, the only movement that of her eyes searching his, the air heavy with the unspoken… the unspeakable.

"I suppose you're not." She stacked papers into a neat pile and gave them an efficient *tap-tap* on the desktop for good measure. "Mayhap," she began, "you would like to take your drawing with you and make it more detailed."

He tamped down a groan of frustration. She was changing the subject. She didn't want to speak of her marriage, as was her right. He would follow her lead, as was the gentlemanly thing to do. "I'm no expert on such matters."

"Well, you're a natural at it," she continued. "Of course, I would pay you for your services."

"Pay me for my services?"

A thick tome slipped from her fingers and landed on the desk with a thud. "For your *drawing*."

She picked up her pile of books and strode toward the bookcase on the other side of the fireplace, which must have been recently stoked as it burned bright and hot. The stack, however, was too heavy for her to both hold and shelve. Without thought, he crossed the distance and silently held out his arms. Her profile to him, she closed her eyes and heaved a great sigh. Finally, she pivoted and faced him. Of necessity, they would have to close some distance to transfer the load.

She inched forward, hesitant, wary, calling to mind their awkward pas de deux in the cow house. It was her scent that reached him first. Fresh, citrus air. It reminded him of orange, lemon, and lime caught on the clean night breeze in a southern clime. It reminded him of the home he'd lost during his fifth year, his first home, his truest home. Unexpected that this perplexing English aristocratic woman reminded him of that time and place.

Only the rapid in and out of her breath sounded in the room. He slid his hands beneath the bottom book, skimming against smooth leather, alongside her bare forearm. She jumped, and her breath caught. Recognition spiked through him. He caught her eye just before it skittered away.

Separated by the width of a book, her gaze averted, light running along the fine hairs of her jawline, she muttered, "Do you have them?"

"Aye," he grunted.

She took the top book, slid it into place, and repeated the cycle, book after book, her gaze avoiding his as if her life depended on it.

How was it possible she'd been a man's wife for three years without consummating the marriage?

If he is unable to perform.

She was the most compelling woman he'd ever known. To be sure, she wasn't pretty in the conventional sense of the word, but convention had naught to do with attraction. And the woman was damned attractive.

Determination, steely and sure, surged forward, the determination to strip the truth from her would no longer be denied. The time had come to have it out in the open. No longer would he be a lady's private shame.

He would be acknowledged. She would confess.

He held out the last book, and just as she reached for it he caught her wrist. She tried to snatch her hand back, to no avail. "What on earth can you possibly mean by this? Kindly unhand me, sir."

He held her fast. "You."

"Me?" she asked, her wide eyes snapping fire.

"*You.*"

"You sound unhinged. Mayhap your fever has returned. Shall we send for the doctor?"

As impressive as her show of bravado was, she would have to do better to obtain her freedom. She would have to speak the truth. "That night at the inn," he began.

Face averted, attitude haughty, she asked, "Didn't we settle this earlier?"

"Bear with me."

He turned her wrist over, the warm, flickering light of the fire illuminating the blue veins that wound in delicate rivulets beneath her pale skin, disappearing beneath the tightly buttoned cuff of her sleeve. He worked one, then another, button free of its loop. When he reached the third and final button, she tried to twist away.

"Now back to that night"—the third button slipped free, and the sleeve fell open, revealing the hard blue beat of her pulse—"At first, I'd considered the possibility that it had been a dream. Can you imagine why?"

"Not at all." Her voice was composed of both solid ice and trembling heat.

"No?" He folded the linen fabric of her sleeve over on itself. "Something happened in that room that night, something that might be deemed too explicit for the delicate ears of a lady."

"You can keep the contents of your dreams to yourself. I don't care to hear the ravings of the fevered mind."

She was good. But not good enough.

He folded white linen on itself once again, baring the lower half of her forearm, which glowed translucent like the finest white marble. "There was one detail of the night that I recall with vivid certainty. The woman—"

"Mayhap you've conflated reality with dreams," she interrupted, a fighter to the end.

"The very real woman had a mark the shape and color of a tiny heart"—his fingers inched up her arm, skin against skin, pushing the fabric up to her elbow. Again, she attempted to wrench away from him—"on her inner arm"—the fabric became more difficult to negotiate the farther up it went, possibly from the density of the linen, likely from the thin sheen of sweat—"on the soft patch of skin"—one final push of linen—"here."

Both sets of eyes shot toward the only place he could be speaking of. Against pale skin, indeed, lay a tiny heart, the size of a beauty mark, the red of a ripe cherry.

With a great heave, she snatched her arm back and tugged her sleeve down in jerky increments. "How dare you?"

"How dare *I*?" Such nerve. "It seems you're the daring one."

Her strangled cry sounded equal parts mortification and distress as it echoed through the room. With her next breath, she seemed to recover something of herself. "I shan't explain myself to you."

Her words, her haughty demeanor, slapped across him with the force of a north wind in the dead of winter, shooting ice into his veins. "Right," he said, hard, acrid. "Why would you deign to explain yourself to a lowly sailor like me?"

She went still as stone, her wide eyes searching his.

"I know your type."

Her brow lifted, curious, befuddled. "My *type*?"

"Lady of the manor looking for a man who can *service* you right."

He knew the instant his meaning hit her, for a blush flared up the elegant column of her neck and formed twin patches of scarlet on her cheeks. "*Service* me?" she asked on a halting whisper, clearly shocked to her core by his bluntness. She rolled her bottom lip between her teeth and released it.

"*That* night," she began on a croak and cleared her

throat with her familiar, unladylike harrumph. "It was simply a night between a man—" She stopped. Abashment stole across her features. "I must say something about it. I thought, well, I thought you'd recovered."

"From my fever?"

She nodded. "I wouldn't have," she started and stopped. "*It* wouldn't have happened had I known you weren't actually recovered."

"So as not to take advantage of me?" he asked, incredulous. Well, this was a first.

Again, she nodded. "Because we both know it was nothing."

"Nothing?" He'd say it was a little more than nothing. If memory served, it had been quite *something*.

"Nothing more than an, uh, *occurrence* between a man like you"—she gestured up and down the length of him. He felt like a piece of meat on display at the market—"and a woman too unattractive to tempt her own husband."

"*Too unattractive?*"

Her fingers began worrying the fabric of her nightrail. The movement was small, but he caught it. Whatever she was about to say, she'd never said it aloud to anyone.

"It has been made abundantly clear to me all my life that I am *too* everything." She held up her hand, her fingers ticking items off a list. "*Too* tall. *Too* skinny. *Too* freckled. Hair *too* red, *too* frizzy. *Too* strong-willed." Her hands clenched into fists. "All the *too*-s add together to form the portrait of a *too* unattractive woman."

"People told you this all your life?"

"Some more plainly than others, but I've always understood the truth."

"The truth?"

"That they're right."

Her gaze held his, dared him to refute her words, and a sudden ache sprang to life inside him. He ached for her pain. He ached for her bravado. He ached to touch her, to make all her hurt and false bravery go away.

She laughed, the sound hollow and raw. "After all, you didn't remember me until just now."

A gut punch couldn't have floored him more effectively. "I've known."

"You've—" She stopped. "You've *known*? This entire time?"

"Aye." No use denying the truth.

She closed her eyes and inhaled a breath that shuddered and shook. "You *bastard*."

"Aye, that I am," he returned on a dry note. "But, Callie, here's what I don't understand."

"I haven't given you leave to call me—"

"*Callie?* I think we're past that."

"What is it you don't understand?" she asked on a whisper barely spoke.

"How is it you think any man could ever forget you?"

Her mouth opened and shut.

"It was mutual," he said.

"What was?" The words hardly carried on the slim air between them.

"The wanting."

Her pupils flared nearly to the outer edges of her irises, her lips parted, and a breathless, "Oh," escaped her.

At last, his words had the intended effect.

17

C allie's knees went to jelly, and it was all she could do not to lean against the fireplace mantle for support.

"Further," he began.

"Further?" she asked, the word a breathless gasp. What *further* could there be?

"I could tell you."

A beat passed. "Tell me what?"

"What else I remember from that night."

He pushed off his end of the mantle, and his hand, massive and strong, reached out and stroked the line of her jaw, a gentle, calloused caress. Her breath caught, and her eyes closed. It was all she could do not to sway into his touch, to feel it more fully. He found the back of her head and tugged the pins out of the loose chignon at the base of her neck. Her hair fell about her shoulders and cascaded to the small of her back. His fingers threaded through, drawing the silky red strands forward and allowing them to fall, individual threads catching gold in the flickering light.

"*This*, a red silken curtain." His words were a velvet rumble in his chest. His fingers tucked beneath her chin. "Look at me."

Her eyes blinked open and found his serious gaze fixed on her, pupils pushing irises into a thin blue ring. She was new to this, but could that be *desire*? Was it possible this man desired her?

"And I remember the lovely curve that lay beneath your nightrail."

"I don't have curves."

A smile curled about his mouth, and he shook his head slowly. "Whoever said that doesn't know you the way I know you."

"Oh."

She should run, but her knees quaked. They wouldn't carry her far. The fact of the matter was this: she was trapped.

Trapped by his physicality?

No.

By fear?

Not even close.

She stood, frozen in place, trapped by her own desire.

Thanks to the night he recounted more accurately with each tick of the clock, she understood where desire could carry her with this man, and she was powerless to resist its seductive call.

What he was offering, she wanted, badly. How she wished he would reach for her again, her hauteur aching to crumble to bits. What was pride when this glorious man called the curve of her waist *lovely*?

"I remember something else, too," he spoke into the space between them.

It was such a short distance, less than the length of a stride, close enough for him to reach out and touch her again. Yet she couldn't understand how to bridge those few feet. He might as well have been on the other side of the world.

"You wore a shift." He settled his shoulder against the stone mantle and watched her as if from a great distance.

Silence stretched between them, and it suddenly struck her. This massive, gorgeous man, who refused to release her gaze, was waiting... on her. That night at the inn, when she'd stood uncertain, poised on the edge of flight, he'd done the same and allowed her the option of staying or going.

Whatever came next would be initiated by her. She could go. Or she could stay. But if she stayed there was no doubt where this would lead.

Her fingers found the cinch of the sash at her waist and tugged. Her nightrail fell open, revealing the shift beneath. "*This* shift?"

His eyes roamed her, and he nodded once, as if words had deserted him. He shifted his stance, and she glanced down, the long ridge of his cockstand visible beneath buff superfine. Her gaze shot up to find an amused smile pulling at the side of his mouth.

Tonight, like the night at the inn, the wanting was mutual.

"I can't be sure if it's the same one."

He was pushing her, this situation, toward its edge. Where was that edge located?

She shrugged one shoulder, then the other, and her nightrail fell to the carpet in a linen puddle. "Can you be sure now?"

His smile fell, his pupils flared. She would take that as a yes. All she wore was the simple linen shift that stopped at the middle of her thighs. A fire roaring between them, both literal and figurative, they stared across the short distance at each other. How to bridge it?

Perhaps she shouldn't think about it too much.

Instinct would be her guide.

Outside herself, the person she knew herself to be, she lifted the strap of her shift off one shoulder and allowed it to fall down her arm. She repeated the motion on the other side and crossed her arms over her chest to prevent the garment from sliding to the floor.

Although his pose against the mantle suggested indolence, she suspected the opposite was true. Tension coiled in the lines of his magnificent body, suggesting tightly held control, a readiness for instant action. All she need do was speak the word.

She released her arms, and her shift dropped to join the nightrail on the carpet. She was entirely nude. Feminine power peaking inside her, she stepped out of the pile of clothing, her feet a slow prowl forward. Separated from him by no more than a foot, she stopped, heat and energy pulsing between them that had nothing to do with the fire roaring at their side. He didn't move a muscle, even as his eyes blazed.

Her hand, trembling and certain, reached up and flicked open the top button of his shirt, then another and another, until the fabric fell open to his waist, the golden dusting of hair on his chest narrowing to a thin trail below his navel. She touched light, brazen fingertips to the tattoo over his heart, the one she sensed was somehow more special than the rest, fine hairs tickling her palm.

"I remember this." She smoothed her hand across his chest to the defined muscles at his right shoulder, pushing his shirt off to reveal another tattoo. "And this."

"You like them?"

"Oh, yes," she said, her voice dark and husky and utterly unlike itself. "I would like to see more."

He shrugged off the garment and tossed it aside. He stood before her magnificent, the fire between them dimmed by the glory of him… Viking… Warrior angel.

Her fingers again felt him, drawn like a magnet to a lodestone. This time, they trailed lower, down his defined, ridged stomach until they reached the waistband of his trousers, the rigid length of his manhood a simple inch away.

She stopped. Something didn't feel right. It felt delicious and like everything she wanted, but not *right*. His words returned to her. *Lady of the manor looking for a man who can service you right.*

Was that who she was? Instantly, she knew. If she crossed this complicated inch, she would be. If she used whatever strange, ineffable sway she held over him, this way, in this moment, how wouldn't she be?

Her gaze met his, and she saw wariness there. "Is something wrong?"

She grew shy of him, of this power she held, of the path

she would pursue. With her decision not to touch him, the moment had grown more intimate. "It's just that I remembered something else I liked."

She moved forward, her chest separated from his by the slimmest molecule of air. Anticipation vibrating through her, she reached up and cupped the back of his head, silky, blonde hair weaving through her fingers, and rose to her toes. Her head arched back, and she closed her eyes, even as her mouth closed the distance to his, his breath a soft whisper across her mouth.

One more press of her toes against soft wool, one tug of his head lower, and she touched her lips to his. It was a kiss, sweet, tender, undemanding. It was the kiss of girlish fantasy. On a baritone groan, he pressed forward, leaned into her space, and the kiss transformed into something more, deeper. His tongue touched her lips, a light, seductive flicker, a suggestion of the pleasures awaiting her.

"*Callie*," he murmured against her mouth.

Her true name, spoken by this man, stole the breath from her. A petal protecting the closed bud of her core separated and peeled back.

He moved back an inch and eyes of the bluest sky held hers. "*Callie*," he repeated, and another petal lifted away. "I need to touch you."

Goose bumps scattered along her skin. What a thing to say... to *her*.

His hand brushed around her waist, tentative, a tremble in them. A tremble provoked... by *her*.

A shift, seismic and ineffable, occurred inside her.

His head slanted into the curve of her neck. Humid breath ran along her collarbone. Hot skin touched skin. Her hands clutched his shoulders, her legs jelly beneath her. His fingers tightened at her waist as he swiveled their bodies around like dancers until her back pressed against the wall next to the fireplace, the heat of it at her back, the heat of *him* at her front.

"I remember something else you like." His hand trailed along the curve of her hip, down her thigh, and anticipation gathered with every beat of her heart.

Instinctively, her leg lifted and wrapped around his hips, his fingers, calloused, strong, held her in place. She'd never been more open, more vulnerable, and, oh, how she ached with it.

She wanted his sweet, slow kiss. She wanted the carnal, hot *him*.

She wasn't the only one who ached. The ache of him stood erect and ready beneath the confining fabric of his trousers. She stroked its length, and his eyes drifted shut in pleasure. Emboldened, she worked the closure, flicking open, one... two... She was on the third button when his fingers wrapped around hers, stilling them.

"Not like this," he rumbled deep in his chest.

Every cell in her body rioted in protest. "Why not?"

"Trust me."

In a quick, efficient motion, he swept her off her feet and into his arms. When they reached the center of the Persian rug, he lowered her and sat back on his heels. She rose to her elbows and watched his gaze rove the length of her body. There shone appreciation, yes, but something more, something that invited another petal to peel away.

Lust.

This man, this glorious Viking angel warrior, this god among men, *lusted* after her.

His gaze met hers across the length of her body. "You are a glory."

He reached out and pushed open one knee. Alarm shot through her, and she closed it tight against her other knee.

"Do you trust me?"

It hit her: she did. With every fiber of her being. She nodded.

A smile, full of knowledge and promise, tipped up one side of his mouth. He tugged one knee, then the other, open and moved into the open space until he lay flat on his stomach between her legs. He dipped his head.

What was he—

Oh.

The hard, velvet tip of his tongue ran along her—

Oh.

Sensation, sweet and aching, flared from the point where his tongue touched her. No longer able to support herself, she fell onto her back, her knees now spread as wide as they would go as pleasure washed over her with every stroke, every butterfly flicker, of his slick, talented tongue. The sweetness and the ache began a slow coil, an interminable build toward something... *something*... just out of reach.

Out of her mind with need, she clutched his hair in a tight fist and pulled, spurring him on, her body winding tighter, all sensation pouring into her sex, into the place where his tongue licked, laved, stroked her, as she strove toward a destination her body demanded she reach, but she hadn't a map. How, oh, *how* was she to get there?

His eyes met hers across her body, and, frustrated, she cried out. He'd stopped.

"You don't have to control this." A smile that could seduce the delicates off a nun curled about his mouth. "Let it happen to you."

Muscle by muscle, she relaxed onto her back, and she let go. He bent his head and touched his tongue to her in a soft, direct brush, and a shudder raced through her, then another brush of his tongue, and another shudder, as she lay back and did nothing but *feel*.

Again, sensation pooled deep in her sex, coiling and expanding at once, until, at last, it broke through and washed over her. She cried out to the ceiling as her body shuddered in exquisite release, abandon sweeping through her and carrying her along its reckless tide as the hard tip of his tongue softened into a caress.

On a sigh, she fell back to earth, and her eyes fluttered open. His eyes fast upon her, he rose to his elbows, then to his palms and eased his divine, massive form forward. Poised above her, their breaths mingling, their gazes locked, he reached between them and positioned his hard cock at her slit.

Oh, how she ached for him, how it was all she could do not to lift her hips and take him in greed. Her fingers wove through his hair, and in one sure stroke he entered her, penetrating her to the core. He buried his face in her shoulder, his skin slick against hers.

"*Callie*," he breathed into her ear.

He was so *big*. How was it possible she could accommodate his girth, much less enjoy it. But, oh, how she did.

He gathered her into him, one hand at her back, one at her bottom, angling her hips so she could accommodate, oh, *more* of him as he stroked inside her, at first, gentle, restrained, until a relentlessness, a demand, began to build. His face slanted and his lips found hers, the taste of him sweet and male and *her*, too.

Oh, wicked thought, and, oh, how much more wicked that it increased her lust, her pleasure, tenfold. Her tongue tangled with his, him driving into her, her hips meeting his in reckless abandon, stroke for stroke.

He groaned into her mouth. "Oh, Callie, I can't hold on much longer."

Her mouth found his ear, licking it, eliciting another groan from his firm lips, a more punishing stroke from his hard cock.

"Then, don't," she whispered reveling in the wild abandon that was overcoming the glorious man above her.

His strokes became somehow more direct, more focused, and she felt it, whatever *it* was, springing to life inside her again. Her fingernails dug into his back, and her legs wrapped around his waist, one foot catching on the other ankle, squeezing him to her, insisting she never let go.

"*Callie*."

The spring released inside her, and she cried out her pleasure to the ceiling above, her quim clenched in sudden climax, the tight bud at her core blossoming like a flower, hot, wild, effulgent. The rhythmic exhalations of his effort sounded in her ear as he thrust and drove inside her, his manhood a rhythmic slide and drive.

"*Callie*, I must—"

He arched back and broke free of her legs, pulling out of her, taking his manhood in hand, his fist stroking his long length, his eyes roving across her body, the muscles of his neck and shoulders straining. His climax crashed in on him, and he groaned his release on a low, wild rumble.

He collapsed onto her, and she closed her eyes. For a swift moment of time, for all eternity, it was only he and she suspended beyond universal laws that no longer applied to them. Only they knew this place.

The cadence of their breath, heavy and humid, and the rhythm of their hearts, pressed against one another, joined in a pattern that slowed with every beat, were the sole reminders that they still existed on the physical, rather than astral, plane.

From the far reaches of the room rang a single chime of the grandfather clock, shattering the moment, announcing reality. One o'clock in the morning. The dead of night. It turned out the laws of the universe did apply here, escape an impossibility.

Covered by his solidity, his warmth, she gathered what little will to obey reality and wiggled out from beneath him. She rolled onto her side and pushed herself upright, each movement easier to negotiate than the last. It was as if her body didn't want to separate from his.

Well, her body didn't know what was good for it. *Or did it?*

"This mustn't happen again," she spoke into the room silent except for the odd pop and crackle of burning wood, now nearly reduced to embers so late the night had grown. "You're a sailor. A wench in every port, correct?"

His brow furrowed. "Something like that."

"Then you must find a different wench for this port." She was hardly able to believe the words falling out of her mouth.

"I could, but—" He hesitated.

"But?" She uttered the syllable on a breathless inhale, her heart a hammer in her chest.

"What if the wench I've found in this port suits me fine?"

Her breath hung in her lungs in a strange limbo between an inhale and an exhale. Had *this* man, this glorious, Viking angel warrior god, just spoken those words... to *her?* She swallowed in a futile attempt to moisten her parched throat. "Can't you see that you and I don't suit at all?"

Bitterness replaced vulnerability in the twist of his mouth. The eyes that stared out at her went hard and unknowable. "Of course, *my lady.* Have I your permission to leave the room?"

"Since when do you need my permission to do anything?" she asked around the lump that had formed in her throat.

Before her unblinking gaze, he jerked his clothes onto his body and strode from the room without another word, without even another glance her way. She gathered her shift and nightrail and came to her feet by slow, automatic increments. An odd mixture of confusion, despair, and relief swirled through her. Had what just happened really happened? The sweet ache between her thighs left no doubt. And she'd let him go?

It was no use dwelling on that. She hadn't a choice.

It was better to concentrate on the relief that she'd pushed him away. She'd had the opportunity to tell him the full truth tonight, that Lord St. Alban had a second buyer in mind, *him.* And she'd withheld the information.

More and more, she was resorting to underhand means in her endeavor to keep the Grange.

Less and less, it sat well with her.

She'd always gotten what she wanted through hard work and honesty. But of late? She'd made a deal with a pirate, and now she'd omitted the full truth about St. Alban's offer to Nylander, the man she'd done *that* with... *twice.*

Could the end possibly justify these means? Had she truly thought through the cost it would be to her?

It seemed her desire developed a will of its own when it came to Nylander, and it wouldn't allow her to reason it away. Wild, unruly, willful, it was reason's opposite, its enemy. She must squelch it for it couldn't happen again. She'd committed to a course, and she must stay it. Even if… this was difficult… she was cheating to get what she wanted.

She'd never been this kind of person, driven to the point of ruthlessness, like… oh, even more difficult… like Father.

She clenched her eyes shut, as if she could shut out the truth as easily as the room around her. Could it be the truth, though? It seemed so. The end—her possession of the Grange, the future stability and prosperity of its tenants—would justify the means—her deception of a man who really had no business here in the first place.

Her father's single-minded drive had always been for himself. He'd ever denied this, saying he was conquering his small corner of the world for the family, for its future prospects, when, in truth, it was for his own vainglory.

Her motivation was different. It was for the benefit of others, and she wouldn't falter or fail them now. She was pursuing the correct course, even if the means were underhand and wrong. Some things were right and wrong at the same time.

What if the wench I've found in this port suits me fine?

She swallowed back a sob of ache. She couldn't allow herself to consider those words. Or her response to them.

What else could she have said? It was fact: they didn't suit. Given the chance, he would steal the life she'd built from little more than nothing from her, which had to be the very definition of them not suiting.

She would be a fool to give him that chance.

18

NEXT DAY

B elow a moonlit sky, oars sliced through water still as the surrounding night, sending the small dinghy skimming along the coast.

Moisture beaded on Nylander's brow and trickled down his temple. If he kept going in this direction, eventually, he would happen upon the right cove. A loop of thoughts, unbidden and incessant, circled his mind with the rhythm of the strokes.

He'd succeeded in stripping the confession from her. Lady Calpurnia Radclyffe, the Dowager Viscountess St. Alban, could no longer deny the shame of him or their night together. Except, afterward, it didn't much feel like success for, in reality, it changed nothing. She was still lady of the manor and he still the dirt beneath her feet.

In the moment, though, he'd been fired up with a need that insisted on having her speak aloud that she'd deigned to couple with the likes of him. Then they'd done it, *again*.

A tenacious nag of guilt tugged at him. He'd taken her virginity, then he'd taken her in the study. But the wanting was mutual, that was certain, which made no sense. *She* made no sense.

The oars slapped against water with more force than necessary, propelling the small boat to jump forward in the water on a wobble.

He'd allowed her to avoid him today. Well, that wasn't

185

precisely true or fair. He'd avoided her, too. He needed the mental space to think clearly, and that bloody woman jumbled his senses when she was near.

Further, he'd needed a clear head when the youth from the *Free Reaver* returned. He'd just finished tracking a missing hen to a distant paddock when the youth appeared at his side, missive extended. "Tell him I'll be there at midnight," had been Nylander's curt instruction. He didn't need to crack open the missive's seal to know its contents.

The youth's gaze startled upward, and blue eyes, stippled with flecks of cloudy gray, met his. Recognition jolted through Nylander. He knew those eyes. In fact, he was meeting their sire tonight.

The lad nodded once and scampered off.

Tonight, he was headed straight to the source to find out what the bloody hell was going on. Ignoring Jack and shadowing Her Highness… *Callie*, wasn't getting him anywhere, not fast enough.

The oars missed the water and kicked up an arc of seaspray into his face. Well, his dealings with Callie had gotten him somewhere, but nowhere good.

The truth was he could no longer avoid Jack. He'd done a lucky job of it for over two decades, but it appeared his luck had run out. He just couldn't let the matter go.

He navigated the dinghy around the bend of yet another cove and peered into the moonlit distance. No sign of the *Free Reaver*.

None of this was his business. He should turn this boat around and let matters that had naught to do with him resolve themselves.

But he couldn't. He'd never been able to resist protecting a woman who needed protecting, even when it was all but assured it would land him in trouble. And two things were certain: Callie was in trouble, and she was trouble itself.

Last night, he'd caught more than a glimpse of the vulnerability she'd revealed by bits and increments. Last night, he'd seen it in its full, ugly glory. She'd allowed him behind the facade she presented the world, the one that hid the insecurity brought on by years of being told she wasn't enough.

He understood something about that. It was the very same voice he heard inside his head. Against his better judgment, which had no say in the matter, he felt a kinship with the woman that went deeper than the physical act they'd shared.

"Can't you see that you and I don't suit at all?"

Her words still stung, but their truth was undeniable. She'd only spoken aloud the line that divided them. She was a lady, and he the scum of the earth. Yet this lady was out of her depth, and he couldn't ignore the fact that she'd begun to drown. She simply didn't know it yet.

The dinghy glided around yet another jagged outcropping along the silent coastline, and, at last, he spotted the outline of the *Free Reaver* in the distance, anchored and waiting, not a single light visible across the distance that grew increasingly hazy with a descending fog.

His gut churned in anticipation of the meeting. There was no help for it. Aboard that ship awaited a reckoning of more than one kind.

The rate of his strokes increased, and the boat raced across the water. Sweat now dripping in a well-defined rivulet down his spine, his heart thumping a hard, fast rhythm, he slowed his strokes once his dinghy entered the shadow of the barque. The dinghy came parallel and sidled up to the starboard side of the ship. He tapped out a quick rhythm on damp boards.

On the last tap, it hit him what he'd done and what it meant. He still knew the *Free Reaver*'s code after all these years.

Above, a rope ladder unfurled and landed with a light slap against oak on its way to meet him. He tied off his boat and made a quick ascent, hopping over the rail and landing on the deck with a muted thud. He glanced up and found a dozen or so men gathered round, tensed, waiting for him. Hanging on the periphery of the group, Nylander noticed the messenger lad, eyes wide and observant. He likely missed nothing.

"Took ye long enough," sounded a voice both familiar and dreaded, a voice he hadn't heard in five and twenty years. "Yer late."

Nylander met the gaze he sought. "And I see you're still the world's most punctual pirate."

Jack's head cocked to the side, the long, thin scar running from hairline to jaw shining silver in the moonlight. "Yer voice is deeper than I reckoned." His eyes sped over Nylander, up and down, side to side, as if taking inventory. "Ye speak like a lord."

The words sparked an unexpected flare of anger inside Nylander, one he immediately suppressed. If he gave it oxygen, it would blaze into a full-scale conflagration, and he would get nowhere. "And, Jack, you're as weathered and grizzled as I thought you would be."

Jack glanced about his compatriots, who watched their captain carefully, unwilling to commit to an emotion until he showed them which way he would take the insult. A sudden, jolly rip of a laugh tore out him, and his crew followed his lead half a beat later.

"Ain't no denying the truth. The years ain't been kind to me face, that's fer certain," he barked. "Take a good look, me boy, it's the same face that'll be staring back at ye in a mirror soon enough. But, eh, ye got a bit of yer ma in ye, so who knows, Johnny boy."

Nylander flinched at his childhood nickname. "My name is Nylander."

"That ain't yer name, and ye know it."

"It's been my name for over two decades, and you'll address me as no other."

The humor fled Jack's face, and it hardened to flint in an instant. "Shall we take our conference to my quarters?" he asked in a faux lordly voice. "*Captain Nylander.*"

"Nylander will do."

Jack heaved a great sigh—the man always did have a flare for the dramatic—and conceded. "Nylander." He nodded once in the direction of the lad and gestured toward Nylander to follow him.

As Nylander took the stairs leading below the quarterdeck, the scents, sounds, and sights of his youth rushed up to greet him in a wash of unsettling familiarity. He hadn't prepared himself for this. For the possibility that it could be exactly the same as it was when he'd last laid eyes on it as an eight-year-old boy. The same length of rope coiled in a forgotten corner, surely rotted into dust and fiber by now. The same smell of gunpowder and toil, acrid, pungent. It was a smell he could almost taste.

After a quick series of cramped corridors and staircases, they'd, at last, reached the captain's quarters. Nylander stepped inside a room that, like everything else aboard the *Free Reaver*, remained unaltered by time. His eyes shot left toward a far corner and located the small bed, low to the floor, neatly made. It was still there. His old bed, the last place in this world that he'd ever felt completely safe and untouchable. It had only taken an instant for him to be thoroughly disabused of that notion.

The youth crossed the room and settled atop it, his direct gaze meeting Nylander's without an ounce of trepidation. Nylander's gut roiled, and sweat broke out across his skin. The room felt smaller than he remembered.

Right. He clenched his jaw. Time to get on with it.

Jack had taken a seat in his favorite brocade chair that had been constructed for and stolen from a king, its silk now faded and frayed.

"The lad's eyes have a particular shade of blue," Nylander stated. For some reason, he needed to test these waters.

"Aye," Jack grunted. "He gets it from his pa."

Nylander willed himself not to react. In his gut, he'd known the boy was Jack's son.

"And that ain't all he gets from his pa, either." The beam of fatherly pride was unmistakable. "He'll run the *Free Reaver* one day. The Seven Seas, too, mark me words. The lad has nerve like you've never seen. Once he gets some schoolin' in him, there'll be no stoppin' him."

"I told you I don't want no schoolin'," the lad called out from his bed.

Jack waved his arm in Nylander's direction. "Now,

Lash, how will ye become a man amongst men, like yer brother here, if ye don't?"

The lad's mouth closed in a sullen line.

"Lash?" Nylander asked, unable not to. "Wasn't that your father's name?"

"Aye, Louis was me pa's given name." He reached for a decanter and began pouring whiskey into two filmy tumblers. "But everyone called him Lash."

Bitterness, raw and acrid, spread its spiked tentacles through Nylander. For his own protection, he needed to steer the conversation away from this topic. "I didn't come here to play drinking games with you."

"No man boards me ship a free man without tippin' back a glass with me."

Nylander strode forward, took the proffered glass, and shot his whiskey back. He was in no mood for a toast.

"So it's to be like that?" Jack asked on a humorless laugh. He sank back into his chair, his elbows settled on the armrests, his fingers steepled before him. For all the world, the man looked like a king. All he lacked was a scepter. "Awright, I know ye ain't accepted me invitation to talk old times."

Nylander pitched directly into the heart of the matter. "What's your game?"

Jack flicked his wrist like any elegant lord. "Takin' in the sights of the world. Same as any free man with a boat and a crew."

"What's your game *here*, on the north coast of Devon?"

"Takin' care of storage needs."

"Storage needs?" Incredulity swelled inside Nylander.

"Ye know how weighed down the *Free Reaver* gets."

The man could be cagey as a squirrel. "What's your business with Lady St. Alban?"

Jack's eyes lit with a canny glow. "Ye be wantin' to know about the lady's business? It's like that, eh?" His eyebrows lifted to the ceiling in undisguised insinuation.

Heat, instant and undeniable, suffused Nylander's body. *It's like that.* Of a sudden, he felt lower than the floorboards beneath his feet. It was tawdry and wrong and too close to the truth. "The lady doesn't tell me her business."

"Well, then I reckon that business will stay between me and the lady."

Nylander suppressed the frustration that was steadily building toward genuine anger. Anger would do him no good here. He needed to try a different tack. "Are you taking care of your *storage needs* in the caves in the cliffs?"

"Could be."

"You know they connect to the silver mine." It was a statement of truth, rather than a question. There was no way Jack Le Grand didn't know that bit of information.

"Aye."

"And you know the vein isn't exhausted." Another statement of truth.

Jack shrugged an indifferent shoulder. "That's fairly common knowledge."

Nylander pressed his lips together and waited. Jack had never met a silence he could resist filling. Understanding dawned across his craggy face, and he gave another one of his great belly laughs. "What? Ye think me and me crew are turnin' into miners? That we would submit to a life inside a tunnel beneath the earth when there's a blue sky above and an open sea beyond? For a bit o' silver?"

"In case you haven't noticed, your heyday of jolly old pirating has come and gone," Nylander said with no small amount of satisfaction. "With every day that passes, your way of life is a memory. Honestly, I can't fathom how you've evaded capture this long."

"That'll be between me and the Crown, won't it?" He barked out another laugh. "But let me tell ye this, Johnny boy. For a man with a ship like the *Free Reaver* and the crew I've got mannin' her, there be easier ways of procurin' silver than by tunnelin' underground like a rat in a hole."

Nylander weighed the man's words. He wasn't wrong. "What do you know about the Grange's cider operation?"

"What use I got for cider? Ye can get that slop anywhere."

It wasn't a denial, which was all but a confession from Jack Le Grand. Something here was worth pursuing. "What about the brandy operation?"

"Now brandy, that's a whole different beast. There's a nuance in a good apple brandy. Wyldcombe Grange has thirteen different varieties of apples, ye know that? Whatever Lord of So-and-So who planted that orchard knew what he was about."

"I've heard."

"A real *connoisseur*," Jack continued. "And, Her Highness, well, she's got the grit to do somethin' with it."

"Is that your business with Lady St. Alban? Brandy?"

"I'll tell ye this once," began Jack, joviality replaced by unmistakable menace. This was the Jack Le Grand he'd expected to see tonight. "Don't involve yerself in what's between me an' the lady." Unspoken threat underlay the words. "Ye'll know soon enough anyhow."

Goose bumps pinpricked Nylander's skin, causing the individual hairs to stand on end. Jack had a plan beyond *storage needs. Bloody hell.*

Again, Nylander changed tack. "What do you know of the wheel mill accident?" He wouldn't bother asking about the cows in the orchard. That was a trivial prank by comparison. "A man could've been killed."

"Now, why would ye be suspectin' me of that?"

"You're not answering the question."

"Wood cracks and breaks all the time."

"How do you know the cause of the *accident*?"

"Like ye said, a man almost died. Word tends to get round about that sort o' thing. But if ye be wantin' elaboration, I'll say this. A man *almost* died." He leaned forward in his chair, his gaze dead serious. "If I wanted a man dead, 'e'd be meetin' 'is Maker in short fashion, ye ken?"

Jack had put on his lowest-of-the-low-class voice, and when that happened, the conversation was all but over. It was his strategy for dealing with nobs, and it usually worked, as it made them underestimate him.

And now Jack was speaking to *him* that way.

Right.

Jack propped his elbows on his knees, his gray-blue gaze bright and keen. The man was about to state his business. "No chance you'll join us on the *Free Reaver*?" The question emerged low and serious. This was a Jack Le Grand rarely seen by others.

Nylander didn't hesitate. "No chance."

The man sat back in his chair fit for royalty, drumming his fingertips on the armrests. "Ye run the *Fortuyn* right and tight, that's sure."

"I'm satisfied with the work," Nylander bit out.

Jack's eyes narrowed. "Are ye now? Captainin' another man's ship? Riskin' yer neck on the open sea for another man's payday?"

"I'm well compensated."

Jack snorted. "I can tell ye one thing certain, Johnny boy. Ain't no man measurin' me compensation but me."

Jack was trying to manipulate every last one of Nylander's emotions, but he mustn't rise to it. "I have plans."

Jack's head cocked to the side, and his mouth curved upward, sly. Instantly, Nylander regretted his words. Those three words were three too many.

"*Plans?*" The man scoffed. "Spoken like a man who's taken the bait, hook, line, and sinker. And what *plans* might those be, if ye don't mind me askin'?" His accent grew broader, more vulgar, with each word he spoke. "Could it be that ye *plan* on purchasin' yer own ship?"

Nylander's lips pressed together in a firm line. He wouldn't speak of his wants and desires with this man.

"Now why would ye go and do a thin' like that?"

A frustrated "What?" was out of Nylander's mouth before he could control it. "Not a minute ago, you were encouraging me to be my own man."

"Aye," Jack conceded, the syllable a patient, gravelly grumble in his throat. "But here's what I've known about ye since ye were a wee lad. At heart, yer a landlubber."

"I've been on the sea my whole life."

"Aye."

"You know nothing of what's in my heart."

"More than ye ken, Johnny boy."

Nylander's breath froze in his chest. Sudden memory of the boy he'd been, flashed before him. This man had been the center of his universe, his idol, capable of no wrong. Until the day his idol had shown his true colors...

Bitter anger swept memory aside. Memory he hadn't allowed himself to revisit in decades. Memory he wouldn't revisit now.

"This conversation is over." He pivoted on his heel and strode toward the door.

"Over before it began, methinks," Jack called out, an infuriating chuckle quick at the statement's heels.

Nylander's hand closed on the door latch.

"I reckon ye remember how to find yer way to the deck," he heard at his back. "But ye'll answer me one question before ye go."

Against his better judgment, Nylander waited.

"Do ye intend to buy her?"

Nylander's brow crinkled in confusion. "The *Fortuyn*?" Hadn't he just stated as much?

"Wyldcombe Grange."

Every muscle in Nylander's body bunched. Unclear on the meaning behind Jack's words, he said, "Lady St. Alban has an arrangement with—"

"It's been St. Alban's intention from the beginnin' to offer Wyldcombe Grange to *you*," Jack interrupted. "He'll sell it to ye, too, if her ladyship can't cough up the money."

Nylander drew in a deep breath and exhaled it on a soft curse. No longer could he keep his back to Jack. The man had just stated his true business. Nylander turned, no choice but to engage. "How do you know this?"

"I make it worth a servant's time to wag the tongue as the occasion sees fit."

Nylander knew as much. "Why are you telling me this?"

"Figured Her Highness wouldn't."

The words struck Nylander like a bare-knuckle blow to the sternum. *Her Highness*. She knew. Of course, she knew.

"You made a deal with her, shook hands on it. Yet

you're giving me this information. She might be more careful in her friendships."

"Aye." Even though his nod was agreeable, Jack's eyes held a steel edge. "And in who she makes her enemy, too."

Nylander pivoted and jerked the door open. He stepped through its cramped opening and began navigating the maze of close corridors and short staircases, making his way to the quarterdeck without a single wrong turn. No care for the crew's silent watch on him, he strode to the railing and tossed the rope ladder over the side. He'd descended its hemp length in a matter of seconds and jumped into the waiting dinghy with a solid thump. He began rowing, the strokes short and choppy, much like his thoughts.

Betrayal, hot and livid, charged through him.

Betrayal he had no right to.

"Can't you see that you and I don't suit at all?"

He was nothing to Her Highness.

Well, that wasn't precisely true. He was something. He was a source of pleasure to her.

Which, in his experience, was worse than nothing.

As the minutes ticked by, tense muscles began to unravel beneath the intensity of the exercise. His strokes lengthened, and the dinghy assumed an easy glide over glassy water hemmed in by a mist that had only become more dense with the deepening night.

Alongside the anger and betrayal came bitter disappointment. Strangely, he felt let down by her. He'd thought her an honorable woman in her way. Sure, she made deals with pirates, but, in this, he would've thought her someone who fought fair.

Would he never learn?

She'd wanted the Grange. And she'd withheld the information that Jake wanted to sell it to him. Was that why Jake had asked him to dinner? To offer him the opportunity?

New emotion entered the fray, something perilously close to hope. The Grange could be... *his.*

His? His.

The Grange represented everything he'd ever wanted, and everything he'd never have. But now... now it could be *his*? Land, a place to settle and grow roots, not subject to the vagaries of the shifting sea. A place to call his own. A place to grow a family.

She'd resorted to trickery to keep it from him. Atop all the other layers that years of betrayal had hardened around his heart, formed yet another one. This one seemed harder than all the others combined.

That Jack had been indirect and calculating had been expected. The man toyed with and upended the lives of others for a living. Nylander should've known he would leave with more questions. The answers lay at the Grange.

What he needed was to tuck away all the emotion tonight's revelations and half-revelations had stirred up and try to formulate a concrete plan. A brandy operation was happening in the cliff barn. That truth had been before his eyes this entire time. The heated conversation between Callie, Will, and Cam on the hillside. The locals talking it up in the taproom of the Devil's Books. The way Callie had rejected out of hand his suggestion to use the area for grazing.

She'd spent all of today there. Oh, yes, it was central to the operation. It had been all along. He just hadn't known what he was looking at. And it was the key to her bargain with Jack. Still, he needed the specifics.

He'd thought to keep the situation quiet until he understood its scope more fully, but he saw now that the time had come to contact Jake. To confirm the sale of the Grange. To inform him that Jack Le Grand was sniffing about his lands. The one detail he would omit was Callie's involvement. He wouldn't expose her until he knew what she was about. Instead, he would continue to involve himself in her business and rattle her.

There was but one potential problem with that last part: desire.

Hers.

His.

He wasn't at all sure whose was the greater of the two.

He snorted. He had a job to do. *That* was his function at the Grange. Not to be a lady's hunk of flesh possessed of no higher function than to provide her pleasure. He had to press on.

"And who she makes her enemy, too."

What on earth had Jack meant? And what had Callie done to make the man her enemy?

More than one factor was at play, and only Jack knew them all. Callie might not think she needed Nylander, the man who didn't suit her at all, but she did.

She needed him to stop her.

19

NEXT DAY

Callie's boots crunched a quick step along the cart path, the newly blue sky having driven away the gray clouds and mist that had enveloped the estate for the last two days. Autumn light, crisp and clear, surrounded her and cast a golden glow onto the greens and browns of the countryside as the sun began its descent in the west.

She reached the top of a rise. There, in the distance, stood the cliff barn. Aside from the main house, it was the estate's largest structure, its new thatched roof burnished a rich amber in the waning light. From this approach, it appeared to have a single ground level with a hayloft. In fact, the barn had multiple levels as it was built into the side of a hill, the edge of the cliff some hundred yards to its backside. One would never suspect those other levels if one didn't know about them already.

But it was the middle level that made this barn most useful. For there was housed the Charentais alembic pot still. Below that was yet another level, more of a cellar excavated into Devon stone that had been shored up for the storage of their ever-multiplying barrels of brandy.

Making this barn even more perfect was its location and isolation. Jack Le Grand and his crew could access the brandy from the goat scramble that connected to the cove below. They would barely venture onto estate lands, and they would never interact with her workers.

Quick in, quick out, and done, as if they'd never been here in the first place. The estate would be hers, secured.

She was so close. Only two days until the Baptism of the Duke of Muck. Then the following day, she would have the monies for St. Alban.

So, so close. So close she could taste victory. She'd all but done it, saved the Grange.

Saved it? From whom? Was the alternative to her—*him*—really so bad? Did *he* justify all she'd compromised? Her solemn word? Her very integrity?

He'd wanted to incorporate this barn into his brilliant pasture reconfiguration. Of course, she'd had to quash that idea.

Him… here? That wouldn't work. But how useful the man could be.

Useful… A slow crawl of heat crept down from the tops of her ears to the tips of her toes. When angled another way, the word sounded… dirty. She'd experienced precisely how useful the man could be. *Twice.*

She went yet hotter. She unbuttoned the cuffs of her blouse and rolled the sleeves up to her elbows. A gust of sea air breezed over bare forearms and lifted the fine hairs in cool relief.

"How is it you think any man could ever forget you?"

The question had quite stolen all the breath from her body. It still did.

He'd *known* all along. She didn't know what to make of it, so she'd immersed herself in work to take her mind off her shamelessness. But it persisted, endured, and expanded, taking up most of the space in her brain.

Oh, how she wished she could undo those two nights.

Oh, how she wished she could do them again.

Another wave of heat crested inside her. She unbuttoned the two uppermost buttons below her chin. It did little to alleviate her discomfort. This heat wasn't so easily assuaged. A dip in the ice-cold sea held promise, but likely not. It was possible she'd spend the rest of her life a walking blaze of shame.

Still, he'd become so involved in her life in recent

weeks that it had come as quite a shock yesterday and today that he'd made himself scarce. There could be any number of reasons for his absence. His fever might have returned. Cook could have him occupied collecting eggs, milking cows, and baking breads, and, since Callie hadn't stepped foot inside farmyard, dairy, or kitchens, she simply hadn't seen him.

But another reason for his absence burned at her, one she suspected much closer to the truth: *twice* was enough for him to have had his fill of her.

He'd found her lacking.

Just like every other man.

The cart path opened into a small loading area, and she was slipping through an unobtrusive side door in a matter of seconds. The wide double doors at the far end of the aisle were closed, the interior of the barn the gray of shadow. No matter. It was only her in here, and she understood today's task well. The stalls left of the center aisle held barrels leftover from last year, and the ones to the right held this year's newly casked cider, not to be consumed for a few weeks yet.

She dug a piece of charcoal from her trouser pocket and set to work before daylight ran out. With the Duke of Muck just around the corner, she was here to inspect and mark last year's barrels, ensuring they would be loaded onto wagons tomorrow and driven into town for the festival. Cider wasn't good beyond a year.

As she made her way down the center aisle, stall by stall, her ears picked up the soft drone of voices on the level below. Nothing unusual in that. Old Pete had conscripted Will and Cam into service. Time was of the essence during the autumn months. Winter was for rest.

But it was another voice in the mix that loosed a faint tremble through Callie and made the fine hairs on her arms prickle to their very tips. It was unfamiliar.

Actually, that wasn't true. It was quite familiar.

Could it be? It couldn't. But... could it?

Ahead, tucked in a corner, stood a narrow flight of stairs that had more in common with a ladder than a staircase. As she crept down, step by awful step, dread snaked through her. She stopped her descent halfway and ducked her head below to take stock, praying to the heavens above that she wouldn't be spotted.

The barn doors at the end stood open, wide enough to admit a fully loaded wagon, the cliff's edge in the distance and the watery horizon beyond. By contrast, the interior was dark, making it impossible to see the occupants at the far end beyond their industrious silhouettes.

She crept lower, her eyes adjusting by slow increments. Of the twenty-four, this was the loveliest hour of the day. Her foot touched solid earth, and she soaked in the transitory glory of a setting sun, its warm glow suffusing the woolen fibers of her shirt and trousers, the muslin of her camisole, until it stole into her skin.

Up ahead, the Charentais still shone bright copper, its three massive containers of pot, condenser, and collector lined up in a neat row, connected by crooked copper tubes, catching these last rays of the day and throwing them about the room, dust motes floating in their stream. It received its name from its town of invention, Charente, France. It was a strange thing of beauty beyond its function of processing cider wash from liquid to fine vapor, then cooling it into condensate that wended through coil and condenser into the collector, creating the *brouillis*, a low wine. This distillate went through the same cycle again, thereby creating an even finer brandy, the *bonne chauffe*. It was this brandy that Jack Le Grand set such a high premium on.

It was this brandy that would save the Grange.

Her eye moved on, across the packed dirt and straw expanse of the central corridor, eventually, nay inevitably, snagging on one of the busy figures, the one *not unfamiliar*. He, Will, and Cam were unloading barrels of cider from a parked wagon and rolling them toward the still, where the liquid would constitute the wash for a first distillation.

The heat from a thousand setting suns fired through Callie as, finally, it hit her:

Nylander was *here*, in the cliff barn, fraternizing with

her men and assisting in the production of a brandy that he should know nothing about. The man had the most dreadful habit of making himself *useful*.

She exhaled a rough, unladylike hiss. That word might just be ruined for her.

He drew his massive body fully upright, his back to her. He was an exceedingly large man, his breadth and height dwarfing the large opening of barn doors. The rays of the setting sun gleamed against the white linen of his shirt, outlining his form beneath.

Her mouth went dry. Perspiration beaded her skin from temple to toe. Her nipples definitely pinched into buds hard as cherry pits, and her body went light and floaty at the sun-drenched sight of him. The man was nothing short of glorious as he used the back of his hand to wipe the sweat of exertion from his brow. The tips of his golden hair brushing his broad shoulders, he set his arms at his waist, akimbo, a Viking god surveying the land before him, land he would plunder and pillage and take for his own.

But only if she gave up.

Well, she wouldn't. She was so, so, so close. Just a few more days.

Oh, why wouldn't the blasted man just leave Devon and get on with his life? Even as her mind formed the thought, another part of her reacted with a tug away from it. That part, which she refused to explore, didn't want him to leave.

His head cocked subtly to the right, as if someone had called his name and he was awaiting confirmation of it. The sun took its opportunity to backlight his profile, providing a silhouette in exquisite detail: brooding brow, deep-set eyes, straight angle of nose, firm set of lips, strong curve of jaw, dimpled chin that she regretted not having run the tip of her tongue across. What a classically masculine profile Nature had wrought upon this man.

Before she could blink, he half-turned, and his eye found hers with unerring precision. The breath froze in her chest. It was as if… oh, terrible thought… as if he'd known all along she was here, watching him.

He'd *known* all along, indeed. If she could, she would evaporate into a million dust motes and float away on a beam of light.

Oh, mortification of the soul.

Oh, that she would come out purified on the other side.

As a grown woman and mistress of this barn, she must say something. Yet the seconds ticked by, and the longer they went without speaking, the tighter her tongue twisted into a knot inside her mouth. His expression was both assessing and contemplative and somehow shrank the distance between them. Her heart would burst through her chest any second now.

Someone must have called him—she couldn't hear through the wool in her ears—and he broke their contact. Like that, the ground between them expanded into a more manageable distance, and she stood in it alone, exposed.

How easy it was for him to move on from her, the woman who couldn't stop throwing herself at him, who gazed upon him as if he was a one-man Michaelmas feast.

"*Bonsoir, madame,*" Old Pete called out, rushing to greet her, looking more healthy and vibrant than she would have thought his ninety-something years allowed. The brandy-making business seemed to agree with him. "I must speak with you, posthaste."

She cleared her throat. "Well, you have me. What is it?"

"We must halt the brandy production."

All Callie's other problems fell away. "Stop production? Why?"

"The spigot from condenser to collector keeps getting clogged and needs a proper cleaning. An alembic still is hearty, but delicate, *non?* It must flow and be nurtured better than I have time to give at the production level you require."

"Can't you manage it?"

"What am I? The skivvy? In France, I would be a master." He drew himself upright with every bit of dignity he could muster, which was considerable and oh-so-very

French. "Here, if you want me, I shall be master. Does the master clean?"

"Umm," Callie prevaricated, more than a little flummoxed. "No?" Only last week she'd mucked out a horse stall.

Quick movement caught at the periphery of her vision just before a voice piped up, "I'll do it." Kip stopped before them, charmingly defiant, if there could be such a thing.

Pirates... Vikings... now *children* were involving themselves in this brandy-making business?

"Kip," she began in as matronly a voice as she could muster. "How did you find this place?"

"Same as everywhere." He tucked his thumbs into his waistband and rocked back on his heels. "On my two feet."

"I can't imagine this is appropriate for a—"

"Tell you whut," he interrupted. "You let me 'elp out Old Pete, and I'll go to school two days a week."

A bewildered laugh sprang up from her throat. Was this scamp bargaining with her so he could work at her less-than-legal brandy still? Further, should she take him up on it? It was more schooling than he was submitting to now.

"Four days," she countered.

"Three," he shot back.

She stuck out her hand, and Kip shook it, a bargain settled.

Nylander stepped into their small circle, an amused glint in his eyes. She kept the blasted man at the edge of her vision as Old Pete, emboldened by his win, expostulated at length about the setbacks, the successes, and the needs of the still. The Viking was too gorgeous to look at directly, anyway.

How had she gotten so tangled up with such a man? It defied all her twenty-five years on this earth had taught her about herself, men, and their relation to one another. She wasn't the sort of woman who had interactions with this sort of man. And, yet, they had... *interacted*... twice.

Old Pete led Kip away to explain the workings of the

Charentais still, all but leaving her alone with Nylander. Awareness tickled along her skin.

"This is quite an operation you have going here," he observed.

She kept her gaze firmly fixed on Kip and Old Pete, who was demonstrating the path the vapor took through the swan's neck of the apparatus.

"Just a little something the estate is experimenting with." She'd tried for offhand and failed, she was sure.

He whistled through his teeth and made a big show of looking around. She had no choice but to glance his way. Well, that was her intent. Once her gaze landed on him, it had no choice but to stay.

"I'd say it's a great deal more vast than a little experiment."

She shrugged, hoping to give off an air of indifference, knowing she was wholly incapable of such a thing.

His head angled to meet her gaze. "Is this *little experiment* legal?"

"Not precisely." His penetrating blue eyes left her no choice but to admit, at least, some of the truth. "All the orchards do it."

Or so she'd been told.

"So St. Alban doesn't know about it?"

Callie knew she was looking at the man like he'd gone daft. But, really, what a daft question. "Why would Lord St. Alban know? He's never shown the slightest interest in the Grange."

"He might be interested in knowing if any illegal activities were taking place on his lands."

Her gut dropped to her feet, and she gulped, like a guilty person. She couldn't help it. She was.

"Further, I would think any potential buyers would want to know." A beat passed. "If I were buying the Grange, I would want to know."

Callie couldn't seem to draw enough breath. Sweat slicked her palms, and, again, she gulped like the guilty. She must answer him directly and authoritatively. Nothing less than the survival of her efforts and dreams hinged on it. She drew herself up to her fullest height, which, frustratingly, wasn't taller than him, no matter how much length she willed into her spine. "*I* am purchasing the Grange. *I* know about it. And *I* am perfectly amenable to it."

Two ticks of the clock beat by before the blasted man responded with a slow, skeptical nod. A tiny movement she would've missed if she'd blinked. "The Grange does appear to be quite prosperous, I suppose you would have the monies to buy her."

Portent spiraled through Callie, and she squeezed her eyes shut.

"Have you a speck of dirt in your eye, my lady?"

Her eyes flew open. "I'm quite speckless."

"*Quite*," he said, dry, ironic. "Have you considered setting up a round-the-clock guard?"

"I hardly think that's necessary. This is Devonshire."

"This barn is close to the cliffs bordering the estate's lands, and haven't you heard?" He paused, drama building into the moment. "There are pirates in the area."

Her hands clenched and unclenched at her sides. "I pay no mind to baseless rumormongering, to be sure. And, frankly, I'm surprised a sensible man like yourself does."

Oh, that last bit was bold. She could hardly countenance the boldness this man brought out in her.

He gave her a smirk, and Callie felt like she'd stepped too close to the sun.

That smile did things to her insides.

20

"Have I given offense, Lady St. Alban?" Nylander asked.

Her eyebrows drew together, and she blinked once. Hurt flickered in her eyes, and he knew why. It was his use of her proper name, spoken like a formality.

Bloody hell. He couldn't stomach the idea of hurting a woman. In the past, it was a consideration that might make him soften and pursue a different path, one that would take her hurt away, even if for a few blissful moments.

"Can't you see that you and I don't suit at all?"

She'd established the rules of this game, not he. He would stay the path he was on. This morning, he'd walked to town and posted his letter to Jake. Now all he could do was wait and keep digging at the truth.

"'Ello?" he heard behind him.

Callie peered over his shoulder. "Yes, Pete?"

"Pierre," the man corrected. "I shall be known by my true given name henceforth." His French accent grew thicker with each word he spoke. "Along with this alembic still, I was brought here from Charente as a lad of fifteen years to operate it by the Second Viscount St. Alban. When he died and it fell into disuse, I did, too. But now it and I are of use again, and we shall not squander the moment.

Now"—he clasped his hands together on a single, papery clap—"if you're done arsin' around, let us work."

Callie's mouth snapped shut. Nylander knew better than to allow the laugh building in his chest release. Likely, she'd never been spoken to in such a manner, but *Pierre* was the sort who could get away with it. It was difficult to become too upset with a fussy perfectionist well on the other side of ninety years when he was as passionate about his trade as this man clearly was.

She made to step around him, and Nylander braced himself for the brush of her shoulder against his arm. Yet she managed it without touching. Disappointment shot through him, even as he inhaled her. There it was. *Fresh citrus… apple blossom… her.*

She stopped in front of Pierre, and instead of upbraiding him, she said, "Tell me what to do."

"The last five barrels of cider must be rolled off the wagon and placed beside the pot to be ready for tomorrow's distillation. You"—he crooked a finger at Kip— "come with me to learn how to clean the water bath and remove the blockages."

Kip sprang forward on the eager, springy legs of youth, a direct contrast to Pierre's slow, deliberate shuffle. That left only Nylander and Callie and the deafening silence between them.

"Well?" she said, the first to break it. "You heard the man. Time to stop arsin' around."

Humor shone in her eyes, and Nylander felt himself respond to it, despite everything he'd learned of her lies and betrayals. Right now, it was only him and her, and those other matters felt less important.

They made their way to the wagon, the ramp already in place off the back, and stared up at the pyramid of oak casks already tipped onto their sides. "We take them top to bottom," he said, pointing to the stack. "The top two will need to be pushed out, placed flat on the wagon bed, then tipped back onto their sides and rolled down the ramp. I'll position myself below. You guide from the top." He caught her skittish eye. "Got it?"

She nodded and followed him up the ramp. She seemed content to let him take the lead. Surprising. But was it? She was the most pragmatic woman he'd ever met.

He squeezed between the wagon wall and one of the casks, placing his feet at the head of the cask and his back against sturdy oak. "Call out when I've pushed it halfway."

After a silent *one—two—three* count, he pressed his feet against oak with all his might, the muscles of his thighs and his back straining, the stubborn cask refusing to budge.

"Halt! I see the problem," she called around the cask. "There are wedges between the casks. Let me just..." she trailed. "I've got them. Now try."

Nylander settled in and readied his muscles. Another quick *one—two—three*, and he pushed. This time the cask inched forward, increment by slow increment, until, again, she called out, "Halt!"

His heart beating the hard thud of exertion, he went still and let his breath catch up with him. He poked his head around the cask. "It's there?"

She nodded.

He unwedged his body and met her at the foot of the cask. "Now, let's rock it forward, gently, and let gravity slide it down."

She took his orders in silent assent. In unison, they grabbed hold of the base of the cask and quickly developed a rocking rhythm. At first, nothing happened, but soon the cider inside the barrel developed a wave-like motion of its own, creating a momentum that had the barrel sliding onto the wagon bed in a matter of minutes, them guiding it until it lay flat.

Cheeks flushed, the light of accomplishment in her eyes, she exhaled a short, breathless laugh. "I thought we would be sloshing around in cider wash and explaining ourselves to Pierre."

Nylander smiled. He liked the way she looked right now. "Ready to tip it onto its side and roll it down?"

A smile on her lips, she nodded. This woman enjoyed hard work. Employing the same method of using the momentum of the cider to move it, they tipped the barrel onto its side and rolled it down the ramp, her guiding from the top, him steadying from below to the exact spot designated by Pierre. Then they tipped it upright and repeated the process with the remaining four barrels in silence.

Words were unnecessary when they worked together. They just had a natural rhythm. It had been that way from the very beginning. The choking cow in the orchard. Even the milking in the cow house. They worked well together. It was when they were at their best.

Well, that wasn't precisely true. There was something else they were even better at together.

Bloody hell.

"Pardon?" she broke into his thoughts, confusion writ across her face.

Had he cursed aloud? *Bloody hell.*

She gestured toward a barrel. "This is the last of the lot."

"Aye," he grunted, gruff.

She positioned her body behind it. "Ready?"

"As I'll ever be," he returned.

Down the barrel rolled and completed its journey with its fellows. They heaved it into an upright position, their task complete. Across the barrel, Callie removed her leather work gloves and swiped the perspiration from her brow with the back of her bare hand. But she'd missed a single bead: the one trickling down the space between her sweet breasts. Awareness charged into the moment, and he went rock hard.

Knowledge suffused the air; the knowledge of Adam and Eve.

The entire time they'd worked together just now, they hadn't touched. He'd made sure of it, guarded against it, and he was certain she had, too. To avoid just this sort of moment.

But, now, it mattered not, as the specter of their sexual history loomed large, the elephant in the tiny room of their short relationship. For here was the difference between now and the orchard and the cow house: now they openly shared the knowledge of what it was to touch one another. No amount of avoidance would change it. In fact, avoidance only intensified the feeling. Every nerve, every molecule, every cell notched into higher awareness, primed for a touch of skin on skin. Another bead of sweat trickled down the ivory column of her neck and disappeared into the V of her shirt.

How he would love to cool her off.

How he would love to make her hotter.

"Lady St. Alban!" a voice called out. It was a child's voice.

Her eyebrows drew together, and she stepped around the barrel. "Jim? How did you know to find me here?"

A boy of some ten years rushed up to join them. "Mrs. Bailey told me."

It was possible Callie's eyebrows might form a permanent crease above her nose. She actually believed her brandy operation was a secret. For a woman so sensible and canny, she could be incredibly naive. A swell of protectiveness crested inside him.

"Ma said your final fitting is to be tomorrow."

"Tell her"—Callie darted a quick glance his way—"I'll be there at my usual time."

Like that, the openness of minutes ago snapped shut with finality. She wasn't speaking the time aloud because she didn't want him following her. *Right.*

"Yes, milady." The boy turned on his heel, his feet already kicking up dust.

"Stop by the house," she called at his retreating back, "and take some of Mrs. Bailey's fresh shortbread to your ma."

That left just the two of them again. Nylander couldn't help asking, "Final fitting? I didn't think you overconcerned with fashion."

"This fitting has naught to do with fashion."

He raised an inquiring eyebrow and waited.

"The master, or in this case, the *mistress* of Wyldcombe

Grange has certain duties for the cider festival and must wear a costume."

"Which is?"

"I guess you'll see. That is"—her eye met his—"if you're still here."

The question she'd left unspoken rang out loud and clear. By way of answer, he gave an indifferent shrug of his shoulder, knowing full well it would irritate her.

"It occurs to me," she began, high pique evident in every uppity syllable, "that you are quite recovered and have a life you might wish to resume."

His head cocked to the side. "Are you asking me to leave?"

"I wouldn't dream of asking such a thing of the viscount's oldest and dearest friend." Her tone suggested the opposite. "But you are the captain of a great ship and might wish to return to your duties."

He shrugged. "I've been considering a change of profession."

Her brow lifted. "Oh?"

"Devon has had quite an effect. It's made me reconsider the trajectory of my life."

"Is that so?" she squeaked.

"I feel a distinct affinity for the land these days. With your gracious permission, I should like to stay on through the festival and perhaps gain inspiration for investing in my own estate."

If a person could look like she'd just swallowed a fish—scales, fins, and all—Callie did.

"That's why I just can't understand," he continued.

"Understand what?"

"Why St. Alban would sell this estate? If the Grange were mine, I'd hold onto it with both hands and never let go."

"The Viscount St. Alban owns several estates." The acid in her words could eat through steel. "He won't miss this one."

Nylander absorbed her words. There was something he wanted to know. Something she likely didn't want to consider, but he must ask. "If you don't succeed in outbidding your rival for the Grange—"

"I know of no such rival."

"What will you do?"

"I suppose I would do what any woman in my position would do."

"Which is?" It wasn't simply that he wanted to know. He *needed* to know what would happen to her.

"Return to my father's house." Her fists clenched and unclenched at her sides. "I, um," she started and stopped. "I, um," again she started and stopped. She began moving toward the barn door. "I've business to attend to. If you'll excuse me."

She strode, nay, *raced*, through the open doorway with nary a backward glance. He followed in her wake at a discreet distance. Confounding woman.

There were two Callies, and, increasingly, he was having difficulty reconciling them. One made deals with notorious pirates and lied to get what she wanted. The other, he'd glimpsed just now. The one who submitted to hard, manual labor with eagerness, even joy. Her passion for what she'd spent the past few years achieving was evident and more attractive than he could've ever imagined.

It was this Callie who he suspected was the true Callie. It shouldn't matter, but it did.

Return to my father's house.

The statement, the bitterness of it, worked its way beneath his skin. To return to her father's house would utterly defeat Callie, and he didn't want to *defeat* her. He respected her too much.

The realization struck him like musket shot.

Here was the crucial thing: she couldn't continue on the way she was. He must stay the course. It wasn't only the Grange's future that depended on it, but Callie's, too, even though she didn't know it.

And, later, when this mess was resolved, well, then they'd see where they stood.

21

NEXT DAY

Impatient to be on her way, Callie mounted Arrow and whirled him around to face Will, already seated on his mount. Frost snapped the pre-dawn air crisp and sharp. Clear nights were the coldest. She tugged her wool scarf tighter around her neck and didn't give the encroaching winter another thought. She had bigger concerns.

"How many days since anyone has seen Tom?" she asked.

Will screwed his eyes up to the brightening indigo sky. "I'd say five, but it's only been two since he was supposed to have been back."

"And why wasn't I alerted sooner?"

Will shrugged. "This isn't the first time Tom has been late getting back with the flock."

Arrow pranced restively, mirroring her exact frame of mind. She smoothed a steadying hand along his mane and glanced about the yard. "What is taking Cam so long?"

No sooner were the words out of her mouth than the man entered the stable yard on his mount, a spare horse tethered loosely to his saddle.

He nodded, respectful and distant, treating her exactly like every man who worked her estate did. "Milady," he began and stopped, clearly uncomfortable.

She breathed in the huff of exasperation that wanted out. "Yes? Speak freely."

Cam darted a quick glance at Will, who nodded once, before proceeding. "The rough of the Exmoor ain't no place for a lady."

Callie bristled, but remained silent as she could see the man hadn't yet had his full say. This was nothing new.

"Tom and those sheep could be anywhere on the moor. It's a vast place, and you're not a Devonshire lass. You don't know it."

"It's a flock of unruly sheep and one presumably drunken shepherd. They can't have gotten too far."

The men shifted in their saddles, silent.

"Besides, the two of you know the moor like the backs of your hands." She whistled for Chance, who came bounding out of the stable, tongue wagging, ready for the day. "You're the best men for the job."

The words could have sounded like praise, but out of her mouth they didn't. She just didn't have a knack for that sort of thing.

She was about to spur Arrow on when she caught movement beyond the arc of flickering lantern light. A hulking form emerged from the night, rays of the rising sun catching glimmers of golden hair.

Of course. *Nylander*. The man had a nose for trouble.

Will shouted, "Oi! Who's there?" but then broke into a smile when he recognized the man who had been working side by side with him these last few days. Nylander gave the man a quick nod, but his gaze, questioning and hard, fixed on Callie. She wouldn't squirm beneath it.

"What's this all about?" he asked, as if entitled to an answer.

She considered swinging Arrow around and galloping away, leaving the question in her dust. But the option was stolen from her when Cam volunteered, "Tom is lost on the moor, like as not on a bender, but we're off to find him."

Nylander didn't hesitate. "Kip," he called out for the boy who was never too far away, "saddle Buttercup and be quick about it."

Not five minutes later, Kip led a surprisingly docile Buttercup into the stable yard, and Nylander mounted the beast like he'd been born to the saddle. Had the blasted man been practicing?

"Captain Nylander, there really is no need to concern yourself in this matter. Will, Cam, and I are quite capable of handling—" she began at the same time as Will said, "We could use the extra hand, that's for sure. Tom can be a rough character when he's jug-bitten."

To Callie's festering displeasure, that was it. The men had settled the matter amongst themselves, and she wouldn't argue the point. She'd rather take the lead than engage in pointless bickering that would only shine on her in a negative light. She was a woman, and women picked and fussed over trivialities while the men rolled their eyes to the sky. Well, she wouldn't.

Instead, she guided Arrow around, pulled her scarf over her nose to protect against the strafe of bitter, northerly wind, and set out at a gallop toward the dawn breaking in the east.

In silence, they rode, her in the lead, the deep blue of the night sky giving way to stacked bands of yellow, orange, and red that seemed content to sit on the horizon until the sun decided to make its lazy appearance and usher in the new day. It wasn't until full day was upon them that they came to the edge of the Grange's lands and the beginning of the wild, rugged Exmoor.

Callie tugged on the reins, and Arrow slowed to a trot. Her gaze fixed on the landscape ahead, burnished gold by the risen sun. As much as she would like to leave the men behind, she couldn't. In fact, she needed Cam and Will to take the lead.

She'd just opened her mouth to issue the command when she picked up the conversation happening behind her. Her mouth snapped shut, and her ears perked up.

"Aye, the rumors be true, that's sure," came Cam's voice. "Me pa saw the *Free Reaver* up the coast not three days ago."

"Now, what I can't figure"—Will was speaking now—"is what a notorious freebooter like Jack Le Grand wants with our little stretch of coast. It sure ain't exotic and rich like some of the lands he's bound to know. Doesn't make a whole lot of sense to me, truth be told."

A contemplative silence followed, the only sounds the muffled *clomp-clomp* of four sets of hooves against solid earth, the odd jingle of bridle or provision pack, and the unsettled in and out of Callie's breath, loud and ragged in her ears.

Of course, it would be known that Jack Le Grand was lurking about the area. Once spotted, such information wouldn't stay quiet for the amount of time it took a wildfire to spread during a drought. As much as her focus was on Wyldcombe Grange and matters related to the land, this was a coastal area, and many of its inhabitants made their livelihoods off the sea's bounty. They would notice, and they would talk.

There was something else, too. How easily Will and Cam shared this information with Nylander, as if he was one of them.

A stab of envy cut through her. She'd been mistress of Wyldcombe Grange for five years, and they'd never treated her the way they were treating him. *Unnatural.* That was how they viewed her. And, upon Georgie's death and her decision to run the Grange herself, she'd accepted it, even if the deepest part of her hated it.

Yet here was Nylander, listening, absorbing, conversing, a complete *natural.* A complete contrast to her. Her darkest fear raised its foul head. Perhaps... perhaps St. Alban had been correct all along. Perhaps Wyldcombe Grange should belong to this man. Men respected him.

To be fair, they respected her, too. She'd earned it. But, more than respect, men *liked* him.

No... *no.* Wyldcombe Grange was hers, or, rather, it would be. Nylander hadn't earned it. He hadn't poured years of toil, blood, and sweat into it. *She* had.

She guided Arrow around to face the men and brought their party to a stop. "We've reached the edge of the moor."

She addressed Will and Cam. "I believe this is where you take the lead."

The men nodded and trotted ahead on their mounts, leaving her to navigate the rough terrain beside a quiet Nylander. She couldn't quite call the silence between them companionable. It was too much to ask, considering their history. Yes, silence was preferable to speaking, because, oh, what an awful lot of history that had accumulated between them over these few short weeks.

At the periphery of her vision he rode like he'd been born to it. Insufferable man. His body was massive, but he knew how to use it.

She exhaled a rough breath. It wouldn't do to think about all the ways this man knew how to use his body. Still, he was more than a strong, beautiful, useful body. He possessed a natural command, an easy manner, a sober pragmatism, and a keen intellect. It was possible he was a perfect man.

The perfect man to upend her life.

A far-away sound, short and sharp, pierced the crisp, morning air, breaking the uncompanionable silence. Chance dropped to his belly, his head lowered, his body a straight, alert line. Callie's head whipped around, and she met Nylander's gaze. "Was that bleat of sheep or shout of man?"

"Halt," Nylander spoke just loud enough for all to hear and obey.

The horses slowed to a stop, and they listened, a breeze blowing off the sea, whistling past their ears, all sets of eyes scanning various points on the horizon. Another cry sounded in the distance. Chance gave an imploring whine, ready to race into the moor at her word.

"There!" Will pointed at a spot some quarter mile in the distance. "Do you see that?"

Callie followed the direction and, at last, saw it: a gray piece of cloth attached to a makeshift pole, flapping in the relentless moor wind atop a craggy outcropping. Relief soared through her, for beyond the flag, she also spotted tufts of white. "The sheep," she exclaimed. "Chance, off!"

Permission granted at last, the collie took off like a shot as they urged their horses into motion. When they reached the rocky hillock, they saw nothing of Tom, just the sheep and Chance, impatiently awaiting his next command. Laboriously, their horses picked through the rough, stony ground surrounding the small hill before happening upon the mouth of what appeared to be a small cave.

"Tom!" Nylander shouted. Will and Cam followed his lead and began shouting, too.

Callie slid off her mount and hiked up the short, rocky rise to the mouth of the cave. She poked her head inside and squinted into the darkness.

"Lawk's be, no need to kick up such a ruckus," emerged a cranky voice.

"Tom?" Callie asked, both shocked and slightly perturbed by the man's choleric tone.

She stumbled back and nearly lost her footing when out of the gaping mouth of the cave hobbled the irascible Tom, dragging his right leg behind him, dried blood staining his trousers up and down their length. "'Tis no other," he ground out. He slumped against a large boulder and released a pained grunt.

"Hey ho, Tom," Will called out, a relieved smile cutting across his face until his eyes dropped to the older man's upper thigh. His smile fell.

Cam drew near. "What's that?" he asked, pointing. "You been attacked by a wolf?"

"Water," Tom croaked.

"Of course." Callie rushed to Arrow and dug a canteen out of her provision bag. Tom accepted it with grim relief, pulling the stopper out and gulping it down with an alacrity she wouldn't have thought him capable of thirty seconds ago.

Nylander ascended the small rise to join them. "Careful," he said with his usual quiet authority. "Not too much at once, or it'll return on you."

Tom took a few more greedy gulps and swiped his hand across dry, cracked lips. "Nay, it wadn't no wolf. There ain't a single bleedin' wolf in the Exmoor."

Eyes wide and incredulous, Cam said, "A bear, then?"

Cam clearly persisted in the belief, likely gained in childhood, that the moor was littered with apex predators waiting for the opportunity to rip apart a man, or little boy, who dared wander into its uncivilized wilds.

"No bears, neither. Get yer wits about ye, man." Tom inhaled with theatrical drama. Despite his pain, thirst, and hunger, he was drawing out the moment, relishing it, making it his. After all, he was the one who had suffered for it. "I was attacked by a band of brigands."

The words hung on the silent moment that followed, and Callie's stomach dropped to her feet. *It couldn't be.*

Tom's eye met and held hers. "Aye, it could and it was, milady."

She blinked, feeling four sets of eyes upon her and one set in particular. Had she spoken the words aloud?

"What sort of brigands?" Cam asked, drawing the attention away from her. Bless him.

"The thievin', brutish sort. 'Ere's 'ow it 'appened." Tom's accent grew thick and clipped. Callie felt for the boulder at her back and settled against it. "Several days ago, the sheep got out of the north pasture, and I didn't notice until the next mornin'. Since the gate wasn't busted up or nothin', like as usual when they get out, I figured it was the wind that blew it open. After a day's ride, I finally found the dumb beasts, but they wasn't alone." Slowly, one by one, he met each of their gazes, his meaning clear. "That band of brigands roughed me up all nice like—just look at me leg—and made off with a few sheep. Scared me 'orse off, too, and it never did come back."

"It arrived at the Grange last night," Will said. "That was when we knew something was amiss."

"Reckon the bloody animal was good for somethin'." Tom accepted a small loaf of bread from Cam on a grumbled thanks.

"Did you get a good look at them?" Nylander asked, his voice soft and authoritative.

Callie went utterly still.

"Nay." Tom spoke around the bread in his mouth.

"They got me from behind, damn cowards." His eyes narrowed, and he stopped chewing. "I'll say this, though. They 'ad two defining features that I'd know anywhere with my eyes closed." He held up his forefinger. "One, they were foul smellin' buggers. I mean to tell you they smelled of the ripest shite on a hot summer's day ye ever smelt, beggin' yer pardon, milady."

Callie nodded, wishing the man would get to his other observation about the brigands.

Tom's middle finger joined his forefinger. "And, two, they didn't talk like they were from around 'ere." He gave his head a baffled shake. "Or anywhere else in this world I ever 'eard of."

Nylander nodded, silent and cool, and confirmation settled in Callie's gut. It had been the pirates. It could be no other motley crew of personages.

She glanced from Tom to Cam to Will and remembered herself, who she was to these men, and what they expected of her. "It is imperative that we get Tom back to the Grange posthaste and have his wound tended by a surgeon." She met Will's eye. "Can you guide him on the spare horse?" Will nodded, and her gaze shifted to Cam. "Can you take Chance and lead the sheep back to the Grange on your own?"

"Sure thing, milady," he replied, perhaps sounding a bit insulted. "Ain't a man round these parts 'oo doesn't know 'ow to lead a flock of sheep 'ome."

The men set about their individual missions. Cam hied happily off across the moor, and Nylander helped Will settle and secure Tom onto his mount. Once done, Nylander skulked off to the other side of the hillock and out of sight.

From his seat atop his horse, Will asked, "You won't be coming?"

"I think"—she glanced about for Nylander—"I'll see if the brigands left anything that would identify them." Surely that was what Nylander was doing at this very moment. And she would see what he found.

Will set his horse into motion, the rope connecting his

mount to Tom's pulling taut and encouraging it to follow. Tom emitted a pained groan, but said nothing more as their forms receded into the distance.

Which left Callie quite alone on the rock outcropping.

Alone with Nylander.

22

Callie's stomach grumbled.

The sun shone directly overhead, and still Nylander hadn't returned. She couldn't wait a minute longer. She would lunch without him.

The first saddlebag she opened contained oats for Arrow. Once she'd settled him with his feed bag, she found the saddlebag that Mrs. Bailey had packed. From its depths emerged a near endless bounty of sweetmeats, pies, cheeses, fruit, and breads. At last, she reached the bottom. There, she found a red woolen blanket. Mrs. Bailey had outdone herself today.

Callie snapped the blanket open, the thin cloth flapping in the persistent moor wind, and negotiated it flat onto the craggy ground. It wouldn't be exactly comfortable, but it would do. Once the various food items were arranged, she settled herself atop, snugging her knees to her chest, hands clasped around her shins.

The feast spread before her looked scrumptious and decadent, yet she was finding it difficult to partake of it. Her stomach seemed to be tied up in knots, even as it hungered.

Brigands, who emitted foul odors, spoke in foreign tongues, stole sheep, and had no qualms about gravely injuring a local man, had taken to skulking about the moor. *Pirates.* That was the truth of the matter. She knew it. Will and Cam knew it. The entire estate and town would know it soon enough.

Nylander strode into her line of sight. He knew it, too. The man missed nothing. Tension radiated off him as he explored the area, eyes scanning the ground.

Oh, the way that man maneuvered across the jagged terrain, sure-footed and confident, the steady strength of him apparent in his supreme control of his person. Perhaps it was an ability gained during his years at sea. Perhaps, but she felt it was something more, a power and grace unique to him. He was unbearably beautiful and skilled.

Her eyes darted away. She could suffer the torture of him no more.

As for what he sought, she felt no need to join him. There was no mystery in the *who* of who had perpetrated this act. The mystery lay in the *why*.

She wove frustrated fingers through her tightly plaited hair and loosened it. She had a feeling it wouldn't stave off the headache coming on. Perhaps the pirates hadn't known whose land, shepherd, and sheep they'd been abusing. *Perhaps.* Except she couldn't see how such a detail would get past Jack Le Grand.

Her gut told her that the pirates had known exactly what they were doing and to whom. What on earth could their motive be?

Further, what had *she* done? She'd miscalculated and done a very, very wrong thing by striking a deal with a devil she didn't know. She'd endangered people, the estate itself, and the very future she'd claimed she sought to protect.

"Mind if I join you in a *light* repast?"

Her head jerked up. Nylander gestured toward the various delicacies strewn about the blanket. Against her will, the irony drew a smile from her. She nodded and inched toward the edge of the blanket to allow for his hulking mass. The heat of him reached out and enveloped her in a warmth not unpleasant on this blustery day.

She jutted her chin toward an object in his hand. "What is that?"

He spread a rough, worn cloth on the blanket between them and smoothed it flat. "Something I found."

She leaned in to get a better look. Its colors were washed out and the pattern faded. "Surely, all manner of items find themselves blown onto the moor by tempestuous winds."

"Without doubt, but not this." He tapped his forefinger dead center on the ragged cloth. "This belonged to a pirate."

All at once, her body drew into a bundle of tense muscle. "How can you know that?"

"Red, yellow, black"—his finger traced the cloth as he spoke—"these are the colors of the *Free Reaver*. And, if you look closely, you can just make out the outline of a skull and crossbones." His head angled to the side, and his piercing blue gaze met hers. "It appears the pirate rumors are true."

Callie gasped. She couldn't help herself. A testing note wove through his deep baritone, a keenness in his eye. She recovered her good sense enough to say, "I can't imagine what pirates would be doing on the moor."

"Can't you?"

She wouldn't answer. Instead, she continued in a rush. "Look around you. This place is so desolate and rough. There can't possibly be any buried treasure here."

"No?" His intense, blue gaze surely stripped her layers down to her soul.

She swallowed and shook her head.

"Well, you'll find out soon enough, I suspect." He spoke the words on a low, hard note and released her gaze.

Breath that had been frozen in her chest also released. How long had she been holding it? She'd gone light-headed. But then this man's very presence made her go giddy with alarming frequency.

Apparently content to let the matter drop, he stretched forward and grabbed the nearest food item, which happened to be a mutton pasty. He tucked into the pie with a verve that would've made Mrs. Bailey proud. He was a big man. Of course he had big appetites.

A lightning hot blush flashed through her. She knew exactly how big his appetites were. Other parts of him, too.

She needed to occupy her mind on other subjects. Otherwise, she might burst into flame right here on the moor. She stared out at the vast wilderness spread before her and spoke the first words that found her tongue. "I can't imagine how Tom felt out here all those days, alone."

Nylander, very carefully to Callie's eye, set down the remainder of his mutton pasty, swiped a linen napkin across his mouth, and leaned back onto his elbows, a leisurely pose to the unobservant eye. But the air between them had changed.

His attention fixed on the distant moor, he said, "He thought he'd been abandoned by his God and his fellow man."

His words made her feel worse about Tom's ordeal, for she doubted them not. But it was the way Nylander spoke, so matter-of-fact and flat, that struck a wrong chord inside her. It revealed something fundamental about him. What wasn't he saying?

She leaned onto her elbows, mirroring his pose as they stared in parallel across the dramatic landscape of the moor. She'd never really given the moor much thought, focused as she was on the daily running of the Grange. But here it lay before her wild, free, and spectacularly untamed. She would like to know more of it.

Much like the man beside her.

"You make it sound like you've experienced such a thing." She needed to test this idea, to draw him out.

"That I have."

Three simple syllables. *That... I... have.* The meaning within them, anything but simple.

Instinctively, she recoiled from the complexity, the implicit darkness. This was Nylander, her most capable rival. "I'm sure you rescued yourself."

They were awful words, callous, unfeeling, but necessary. Separated from him by no more than twelve inches, she needed to achieve another sort of distance. And the uncomfortable silence that stretched between them told her that she was achieving her objective.

Oh, wretched victory.

"I was in the middle of the sea," he said, faraway, his attention fixed on a distant past.

"Swam to shore, then," she said. Why was she being so horrid? *Distance.* She must keep it.

"I was a lad of eight years."

Shock streaked through her. Was this a test to find out how horrible she could be? Well, she wasn't equal to it. *"Eight?"*

Nylander nodded, refusing to meet her eye.

"Where were your family? They couldn't have been too far away."

A laugh, dark and humorless, escaped him. "My pa wasn't too far off, but then the ship he was trying and failing to capture hadn't been either."

"Your father was a—"

Nylander nodded. "He was."

A *pirate.* She would've thought herself beyond the reach of shock, but there it was in the catch of her breath. "How did you come to be in the sea?" she found the wherewithal to ask. She needed the full telling of this story, and she wouldn't rest until she had it. "Wouldn't a child have been kept below deck somewhere?" She didn't know the first thing about ships, but that sounded approximately correct.

The wind blew an apple across the blanket, its green skin a bright contrast as it rolled along red wool. Nylander grabbed it and began absently circling it beneath his palm. "Not that day. My pa wanted me to see the family business up close."

Her eyebrows drew together. "Your mother had nothing to say about that?"

"My ma died of the pox around the time I reached my fifth year."

A knot of grief formed inside Callie's chest at the subtle note of love in his voice. She knew what it meant to lose a mother as a child. Nothing in the world could reconcile one to the grief, even if one's mother was a whore, for surely that was yet another truth that lay unspoken between the cracks of Nylander's words.

His father had been a marauder, his mother a whore. Both had deserted him, one by choice, one not. But he'd known safety and love with his mother, no matter her profession. Then it had been stripped from him. Callie knew that feeling, too.

"A gangway had been dropped between the two ships, and my pa's men were readying themselves to board and begin the fight for the trade ship. I was completely absorbed in the action. That's why I didn't see it coming."

"What?"

"The well-placed shove at the base of my spine."

Callie's hand flew to her mouth.

"Overboard I went, instantly plunged into the drink."

"Could you swim?"

"Aye, my pa had made sure of it."

"But how… why?" she sputtered, unable to find rhyme or reason to the words proceeding from Nylander's mouth.

"I spotted a raft ten feet away and swam to it," he continued. "Once I'd draped myself across it, I began shouting. No one paid attention. Then—" He stopped. Bitterness flattened his lips and twisted at his mouth. "Above my head, the gangway was pulled back, and the barque began moving away."

Dread twisted her gut into knots. "*Away?* Without you?"

"I shouted like a banshee until I lost my voice." Nylander's eyes closed for a fraction of a second, but long enough to see the past clearly, she suspected. "Finally, I found him."

Relief soared through her. "Your rescuer?"

"My pa standing at the railing, watching me, growing smaller and smaller until he eventually disappeared into the horizon."

She might be sick. "How did you survive?"

"I'd just given up on that possibility when a hand grabbed the scruff of my shirt from behind and yanked me up into a dinghy."

"The trading ship."

"Aye. It belonged to the powerful Van Rijn family."

"They took you in."

"As their own." For the first time since he'd begun his tale, his head angled her way, and he met her gaze. "I was raised alongside the man you know as Lord St. Alban. He was a few years older than me and the best at everything he did. I had no choice but to worship him. I know him as Jake."

"*Jake?*" Callie's mouth twisted in reflexive distaste. Her feelings about *Jake* couldn't be more opposite of Nylander's. "He doesn't seem like a *Jake* to me."

"I doubt you really know."

"Fair point," she conceded, feeling the closeness between them begin to evaporate beneath the loathing she bore the Right Honorable Viscount St. Alban, *Jake*. "I met him only once, and that meeting did nothing to endear the man to me. I must ask, though, how did you come to be raised alongside him?"

"His uncle, from his mother's Dutch family, took me in. Raised me as his son, in fact, and taught me about the value of family."

"How lovely," she said before she could think better of it. It wouldn't do to allow emotion to get carried away around this man. But... it was lovely. The adoption of an unrelated child was such an unusual step. Most men wouldn't consider it. Take Georgie, for example.

Memory surged forward, deep and long-suppressed, of a night. She'd pleaded, *begged*, him to allow her to take in a child. Not even a boy, but a girl who wouldn't inherit, whose presence he would never experience if he chose not to. Outraged, he'd refused to consider the possibility. Oh, how she'd mourned that little girl, one who had never existed and never would.

"Jake and I grew up like brothers," Nylander continued.

Callie snapped to. His tone had grown harder, somehow more grounded in the present.

"Which is why I can't fathom something."

"What is that?" she asked, wary.

Nylander shifted forward and threw his arms wide as if inviting the entire western horizon into his embrace. "Why would Jake release this wild and glorious land from his grasp?"

Dismay at the sudden curve in the conversation struggled to the surface in the form of a grimace. "I believe we've already covered this. Lord St. Alban"—she wouldn't be calling him *Jake* any time soon—"doesn't care for the land."

"I don't think I've explained myself clearly." Nylander shifted and angled his body toward her, subtly encroaching into her space. Her heart banged out a hard thud. "Why would Jake allow Wyldcombe Grange to leave his family?"

No longer was Nylander looking backward into his vulnerable past, a past still raw and unresolved. He'd returned to the present and was asking her a very straightforward question, a hard glint in his eye.

She shrugged a shoulder in false indifference and reached for a sticky bun she had no intention of eating. She tore off a small piece and rolled it between forefinger and thumb. "I know nothing of the man's mind, to be sure."

"But you see, I do, and I can't fathom it. He was taught, the same as me, that land is what binds a family together, gives it stability."

"You'll have to ask him."

"I intend to, the first chance I get."

Callie tore off another piece of roll, and her heart thundered in her chest. No matter how she wanted to, she couldn't look away from Nylander now. His head canted slightly to the side, he was watching her too closely. Not in an intimate way, not in the way her body craved, rather from a distance. He was looking at her like a Viking, and she'd be damned if a flicker of desire didn't flutter through her.

But that was of no consequence right now.

Right now, she needed to pursue the unnerving direction of this conversation and ask him a question, one whose answer she wouldn't like. She was certain of it. "Are you upset St. Alban didn't offer you the estate since you're" —she gulped in the face of his vibrant blue stare, the inches between them at once a great distance and terribly, terribly close—"you're family?"

She'd had to ask. She couldn't go on not knowing.

Nylander leaned in, further invading her space, no more than a few inches separating them now, his eyes twin blue seekers of truth. "What if I said *yes*?" The question rumbled velvet in his chest. It might've made her heart skip a beat or two.

"I, um," she began, each syllable a granular rasp in her throat.

Although her mind knew he was referencing her question, her body possessed a different sort of knowledge and heard, or ached to hear, an altogether different *yes*.

If only he would move a little closer...

IN BOXING TERMS, Nylander would say he had Callie "on the ropes." He could continue working her over with this line of questioning, but...

In the full light of a yellow sun, he could see how the flare of her pupil pushed her iris, only a few shades lighter, into a thin, sable ring. It was the flare of want, and it swept all rational thought from his mind, leaving only irrational desire in its stead.

He could seduce her, here and now. It could be a cold and calculated thing. Except his body's response to her was neither cold nor calculated. It wanted her, deeply, with a longing he'd never felt for another woman.

She tugged at the collar of her high-necked blouse, revealing a stain of red creeping up the ivory column of her throat. His mouth went dry. "Why do you hide yourself so?"

"How do you mean?"

He reached out and covered her fingers with his. A tremor shuddered through her, and she snatched her hand away, leaving only his fingers on her throat, the beat of her pulse a fluttery throb beneath his fingertips. He took a button between forefinger and thumb. "Why do you choose blouses that button up to your chin?"

She swallowed, the subtle undulation of her throat moving against his fingertips. "I'm not covering up any-thing anyone wants to see."

That he didn't see the vulnerability that lay within her eyes. That he could ignore it.

With a quick flick of his fingers, he slipped the button through its loop. "Who wouldn't want to see this place right"—he splayed the fabric wide—"*here.*"

Before he could think better of it, he angled forward, allowing not only the momentum of gravity to carry him, but the impulse of the moment, and pressed his lips to the hollow cup at the base of her throat. Her skin, warm and cream dappled with red rose, moved beneath his mouth as shallow exhalations of breath whispered into his ear. Gooseflesh raced across his skin.

He shifted back, not two inches, slanted his face up and took in the elegant curve of her jaw, her determined chin, her parted lips, the upturned tip of her nose. The scarlet had stolen higher, pinking her cheeks in a hot blush, her eyes bright as if with fever, assent in their depths.

He freed the next button, and the next, the only sound in his universe the sharp intakes of breath into her lungs.

"Or this place?"

His lips touched the space between her breasts, their delicate curves just visible.

He should stop right here.

She should stop him.

But she didn't, so he wouldn't.

He flicked open another button and pushed the coarse linen of her blouse wide, exposing a thin camisole and her small, well-formed breasts beneath, the pink of her nipples peeking up at him.

"May I?"

She took her plump lower lip between her teeth and gave a slow nod. Through gossamer linen he sucked one sweet bud into his mouth, and she gasped. He rolled it gently between his teeth and flicked his tongue across its hard tip, and she groaned, a low, animal sound that shot straight to his cock.

"*Callie*," he spoke against her small, perfect breast.

"Oh," she gasped, "say my name again."

"*Callie*," he murmured and shifted to take her other breast in his mouth.

Her fingers threaded through his hair, freeing it from its leather queue, and clenched into tight fists, pulling him closer. Her head arched back in abandon when his tongue swirled around the hard bud. One hand released its grip from his hair and reached between them. It found his swollen cock, a feather touch through fabric.

Another animal groan sounded, this one from him. Then she squeezed.

"*Callie*," scraped against the back of his throat.

A smile, sure, triumphant, tipped up the side of her mouth. In an instant, release was upon him. He'd thought to drive her wild, but it was he who teetered on the edge.

He wanted her.

He *needed* her.

What pulsed between them was based on mutual desire. And while there was so much that felt right about it, down to his very soul, he knew it was wrong, wrong, utterly and completely wrong. He wouldn't be able to easily walk away from this woman if he had her again. And based on her own words—"*Can't you see that you and I don't suit at all?*"—he knew he would have to.

She was a lady. He was a nothing. The past had taught him that lesson. Why would the future be any different?

He gathered whatever last shred of willpower he possessed and broke away.

"Why?" she cried out, cheeks flushed, eyes flashing, thwarted desire radiating off her in waves.

He repositioned himself so he once again sat parallel to her. Gaze fixed on the horizon, he watched from the corner of his eye as her shaky hands buttoned blouse and tidied hair. A feeling of exposure permeated the air. Sexual exposure—desire, ache, want, need, lust—but more: emotional exposure. The sort of exposure he'd thought to avoid. What the *bloody hell* had he gotten himself into?

"About the Grange," she began, her composure regained. The only remnant of the last five minutes was the red fading into pink at her throat. Her eye, hard and flinty, met his. "Were you saying *yes*? Would you like Lord St. Alban to offer it to you?"

"Yes."

It was only the truth.

Without another word, she shot to a stand and began gathering up the remains of their picnic, stacking breads, cheeses, and pies haphazardly in her arms and stuffing them into her saddlebag. His eye never truly off her, he stood and folded the blanket, but not before snatching up the pirate cloth and shoving it into his pocket.

She was definitely upset, possibly appalled at herself, which was partly her doing and partly his.

She wanted the Grange.

He wanted the Grange.

She wanted him.

He wanted her.

Somehow these wants had swirled together and, for him, become increasingly inextricable. *Bloody hell.*

Without another glance, she swung up onto her horse and began picking her way carefully across the moor. Alarmed, Nylander gave a short, sharp whistle, the same he'd heard Callie use, and to his utter surprise, Buttercup ambled into view. Unable to wait for the unruly horse to make it to him, he rushed over and mounted the beast in fewer than five tries, which gave him no small amount of satisfaction. He urged the beast on and kept Callie in his sights the entire ride back to the Grange.

Matters had escalated, on all sides. Between him and her, which was obvious, but also with Jack Le Grand. The assault of Tom hadn't really been about sheep thieving. It had been a message. To whom? And why?

Callie thought she'd made an honest bargain with Jack Le Grand. Nylander held no such illusion. Not just because of these "accidents" and assaults, but based on the man's own words.

And who she makes her enemy, too.

Jack could be a formidable enemy when he put his mind to it, and Callie would need an ally very soon.

She would remain in his sights until they reached the Grange.

Until he understood what was between her and Jack.

Until she was safe.

23

NIGHT

Callie smoothed decadent silk down her rib cage and tried not to squirm. "Are you sure about this costume, Jane?"

Jane removed the straight pin from her mouth. "Is the fit uncomfortable?"

"The fit is impeccable, and you know it. But it's so," Callie trailed, certain Jane would understand precisely what she'd left unsaid.

A smile that could be called naughty curled about Jane's mouth and twinkled in her eyes. "It is *so*, isn't it?"

"It's a complete break with tradition, and you know how people around here feel about change."

"I think they'll come around to it." Jane's head canted to the side. "I just need to adjust that hem a bit."

Callie stood still as a post while Jane unpinned and re-pinned the fabric. Once done, she released the garment and stepped back, her sharp gaze scanning the hem for anything amiss. At last, she grunted her approval and met Callie's gaze. "I'll send Jim over with it first thing in the morning."

Callie rolled her shoulders, allowed the garment to slide to the floor, and stepped out of its billowy cloud of silk. She handed it over to Jane. Really, it was quite a departure from any costume she'd ever seen for the Baptism of the Duke of Muck. But she trusted Jane's judgment.

She'd just pulled up her trousers and was reaching for her blouse when Jane said, "I have something else for you to try."

"Oh?"

Jane held up a flimsy scrap of cloth sewn together in a strange puzzle of fabric pieces that crossed and connected and buttoned in odd ways to form a garment utterly unlike any Callie had ever seen. "What am I looking at?"

"A solution to your problem."

"Which problem is that? Lately, they've managed to accumulate at a rather alarming rate." More than Jane could possibly know, in fact.

"The problem of your, well, your tender..." Jane gestured in the general area of her own rather sizeable bosom. "Of the chafing you've been experiencing when you run."

Callie accepted the odd garment and held it up to the dim, flickering light of a nearby lamp. Following its tangle of lines, she began to make out the rhyme and reason of the piece. These strips of muslin would wrap around her shoulder blades to go beneath her armpits and over her shoulders. These two small swathes of fabric formed the front where her breasts would fit. These three small buttons would fasten at her breastbone and hold the garment together and all her jiggly bits, what little of them there was, in place.

Callie couldn't help feeling awed and slightly overwhelmed. This might be the nicest thing anyone had ever done for her. She met Jane's eye over the garment. "You're a genius."

Jane beamed with pleasure and pride. "I think this will solve the problem of the soreness and chafing on your breasts that you experience on your longer runs."

Callie avoided Jane's gaze. "This should solve that problem perfectly."

It wouldn't do to dwell on the reason her breasts were sore tonight, so deliciously sore. They wouldn't soon let her forget this afternoon and Nylander's talented mouth.

"Are you going for a run when you leave here?" Jane asked.

Callie nodded.

"Then why don't you try it?"

"Certainly." Callie presented her back to Jane and tugged her camisole to her waist. She slipped one arm, then the other, into the straps and began adjusting to the unusual feel of the garment. Not since she'd given up corsetry had she experienced something so confining on her body.

She'd just taken the first button between forefinger and thumb when she heard behind her, "There have been a great deal of rumors bandied about the Grange of late."

Callie's fingers froze. "Oh?"

"Word has it the Charentais still is running again."

Callie forced out a laugh. "It's fairly well known that Old Pete never stopped using it."

"Old Pete? I heard he goes by *Pierre* now."

Callie's fingers unfroze and began buttoning with lightning speed. She needed to get out of here. "He does."

"And the operation has grown in scale."

"Well, we do have more apples and cider than we know what to do with."

"Hmm." Jane didn't sound at all convinced. "And other rumors are flying about, too."

"Oh?" The garment was completely fastened, but still Callie couldn't turn around.

"About bloodthirsty pirates." Jane paused. "About your Viking guest."

"People must find entertainment somewhere."

"That they're linked."

Callie forced her body around. "Linked? That's preposterous."

"They arrived around the same time. That's the connection people have made in their minds. And I'll admit it's a curious coincidence."

"Captain Nylander is friend to Lord St. Alban. They grew up together. And aside from that fact, I've never met a more honest and honorable man in my life. They aren't linked. I'd stake my last farthing on it."

Jane's eyebrows lifted clear to the ceiling. "Your last farthing? Is that so?"

Callie felt a blush coming on. Perhaps she'd been a trifle vociferous in her defense of the Viking. She reached for her blouse and had it buttoned to her chin in a thrice of seconds. "Jane, I must go now. Thank you for this wonderful garment."

"You'll tell me how it works at the festival tomorrow?"

"Of course," Callie called over her shoulder, feet already itching to race out the door and be free of this conversation that had gone horribly awry.

Her run would sort it out.

It never failed her.

BREATH, regular and even. Feet, steady and sure. Waning moon, bright enough to illuminate the path and the river that flowed alongside it. Worries, set aside and left behind.

This was the beauty of the run. It was much like the distillation of fine brandy. It had a head, a heart, and a tail.

The *head* of the brandy process was the first quarter of the distillation. Those gallons were sour, even poisonous, but necessary, and must always be cut and discarded. The same was true of a run. The first minutes of the run could be rough going, her body protesting that it was cold in her lungs, it was hard on her feet, it was too much tonight. But she just had to keep going, let the run flow through her, one foot in front of the other in dogged repeat.

Moisture would break on her brow. A rhythm would develop. Her body would, at last, accept its fate, and her cares would fall away. Here, she entered the *heart* of the run, its essential spirit, its finest and sweetest section. Her mind could open into blankness, and she could find the expanse and freedom to sort through her thoughts.

Tonight, her run was less about the joy of it than about the raw need to clear herself, mind and body, of Nylander.

He wanted Wyldcombe Grange. He wanted a family. He wanted something rooted so deeply that it could never be stripped away from him. It was a soul-deep need.

It was the same soul-deep need inside her.

Beyond the physical, which was considerable, how connected she'd felt to him on that desolate moor, only him and her and his confessions. His mother, the life she'd led implicit in her cause of death. The abandonment by his father. His desire for the land, a home.

And, oh, how she didn't want to feel this connection to him, for he wanted the same life as she, a fact she couldn't begrudge him. But he could only gain it at her expense.

For him to have the life he wanted, she couldn't have the life she wanted.

This was the problem between them at its core, implacable, insurmountable. As strong a connection as she might feel to him, he was still her rival. In effect, her enemy.

Behind her sounded the crunch of bracken, and a sliver of anxiety slid in. She dismissed it. She'd chosen to run along the river tonight on a trail known only by locals. She was safe on this path. Likely, the sound had only been a skylark or a nightjar scurrying beneath protective fronds, perhaps late for its winter migration south to the northern shores of Africa.

She ran past the anxiety and left it behind. On nights like this, it was only her and the path and the moon. Although, tonight the moon was becoming obscured by a roll of clouds moving in from the west. She picked up her already blistering pace and thought to turn back. She had no intention of being caught out in a midnight storm.

Again, her ears picked up the crunch of scrub and bracken, this one not so easily dismissed. It was closer. But that wasn't what threatened to turn a sliver of anxiety into a full-panic. The sound was... *rhythmic.*

And gaining on her.

She increased her pace and resisted the urge to look back, her arms pumping fast in rhythm to her feet, her breath coming in short, hard bursts. Even the quickest glance over her shoulder would slow her down, and she would have to take her eyes off the ground. With the ever-thickening clouds obscuring the moon, she couldn't risk looking up and tripping on a root.

The sound, its rapid clip at her back, drew closer. Adrenaline pumped through her veins, and no longer could she deny it: she was being pursued, tracked like an animal. And not by animal, but by man. Someone was coming for her.

And after today on the moor, she had to allow the possibility that it could be a pirate.

No longer could she avoid it. She must look back. She had to know how close her pursuer was, if there was more than one, and, most importantly, she must come up with a plan to elude him or them. Her feet fast and sure, she twisted around and made out a human form, shadowed and solitary, not twenty feet behind her. He was faster than her, his heavy, determined tread gaining ground with every step, his strides longer and quicker.

Ahead, her salvation appeared in the form of a massive boulder that marked the Y where this river converged with another, aptly called Riversmeet. On the other side of the boulder was a narrow path that dropped off at a steep pitch before wending its way to the river below. If her pursuer wasn't from the area, he wouldn't know it.

Her pace increased into a flat-out run. Her only chance was to make it to the boulder well before her pursuer. The rough in-and-out of her breath loud in her ears, puffing white with every exhalation, she rounded the boulder and instantly ducked down, her body gone still as the stone that sheltered her, her hand clamped across her mouth to muffle the roar of her ragged breath, her ears attuned to the heavy tread of her pursuer. Not three feet removed from her head, his boots thundered past and followed the bend in the path.

Relief soared through her, and her breath whooshed out of her lungs in ragged relief. Enervated by exertion and terror, she sagged against cooling stone. She'd done it.

Above her head, the clouds broke, and the dirt beneath her bottom instantly transformed into mud. *Blast.*

She unraveled her body to a wary crouch and poked her head up just enough so she could scan the heath. Through the rain gaining momentum with every drop, she saw nothing and no one. Another wave of relief pulsed through her. One hand braced on the boulder, the other wrapped around a clump of crumbly shrub, she hoisted herself forward and up in a bid to regain the path and make her way back to the Grange. Except the slick mud beneath her feet had a different idea about how she should proceed.

Her footing slipped out from under her, and her right hip came down hard, landing on slick ground with a sickening splash. A loud, "Oof," escaped her, and adding insult to injury, gravity began to carry her, on her back and headfirst, down the path toward the roaring river below. Her hands grappled for purchase, but found none, her body gaining momentum with every inch descended.

At the head of the path, receding fast, a figure rushed into view. It was her pursuer, and she knew him. *Nylander.*

She wasn't sure whether to feel more relieved or affrighted.

Both seemed reasonable responses.

24

Nylander blinked, unable to believe his eyes.

There Callie went, sliding down, down, down the path growing muddier by the second. Instinctively, he started forward. Instantly, he, too, lost his footing on slick mud, landing square on his arse.

"*Bloody hell!*"

All the while she continued her descent to the bottom of this trail and whatever lay at its end. Ten, fifteen, twenty feet away, away, away. He had to get to her.

He planted a bracing palm on unstable ground, rivulets of fresh rain flowing around his wrist, drops the size of apples soaking him to the core. Next month, those drops would be sleet, and the next, snow. For now, it was simply water that would have been refreshing after his run and under different circumstances.

He shifted his weight into his hand, and it slipped out from under him. Face first, he splashed into mud, bracken, and rock. "*Bloody fecking hell!*" he shouted, louder, just in case the gods hadn't heard him the first time.

Again, he tried. A hand, a knee, a foot. Nothing found purchase. And further she slipped from him. Another, "*Bloody fecking hell!*" escaped him.

Again, he struggled to seize control. Again, he couldn't.

If he could just—

He stopped struggling.

Really, there was one way to catch her.

He succumbed to the inevitable, the combined forces of slick mud and gravity, and started sliding feet first. With his greater weight, he was already gaining on her and would reach her in a matter of seconds.

Careening down the steep slope, he tried digging his heels into sloshy earth to slow his descent. To no avail. He just kept going and gaining on her. *"Callie!"* he shouted to give her fair warning.

Through the wind and rain, now coming down in sheets, her eyes found his and went wide. Since he couldn't make himself stop, he shifted his feet sideways to avoid ploughing into her, which only seemed to invite gravity to speed him up.

Next thing he knew, he was nearly upon her. So he wouldn't barrel over her, he caught her about the waist with one hand and attempted to plant his palm into the earth with the other in a futile stab at slowing them. It only succeeded in making matters worse as momentum and gravity drove the full length of his body on top of hers.

"What the blast are you doing, Viking?" she shouted into his face, her eyes incredulous and fierce.

He wrapped his arms and legs around her, squeezed tight, and flipped around, so it was she who now stretched full-length atop him.

"Have you lost your blasted mind?" she screeched.

"Be still, woman," he shouted back.

She went stiff, her body resembling more plank of wood than woman.

At last, they met the bottom on a hard *thud*, and he held her tight as they rolled, finally stopping on a rocky embankment in a heap of cursed invectives and tangled limbs, her sprawled atop him, their chests heaving in unison, the river rushing beside them not five feet away. By the healthy sound of the swollen waters, they'd stopped just in time.

She planted both hands to either side of his head and pushed herself up. Not ten inches away, murderous, coal-black eyes stared down at him. Her hair had unraveled from its long plait and streamed about both their faces in sodden strings.

"What the *blasted hell* was that all about, Viking?"

Nylander didn't have a ready answer. Instead of trailing behind Callie like a shadow, as he'd done so many times, he'd thought to catch her and pretend he'd been out for a moonlight stroll, so they could walk and talk side by side. Something had shifted between them this afternoon, and he wanted to explore it. Then she'd caught sight of him and started running in earnest, from *him*, and everything went downhill, literally, from there.

Now their eyes remained locked, and awareness flared through him. This awareness had naught to do with the outside elements. Not the pointed shard of rock at his back. Or the cold rain pelting his face and soaking him to the skin. It was *her*, the way she was pressed against him. Her chest lifted, her hips had no choice but to press more fully into his.

His cock took notice. Her next question died in her mouth, and her eyebrows drew together. In the light of day, he would have detected a blush.

She felt it, his manhood, rigid and ready.

For a delicious instant, it felt like the moment could tip in either direction. Then her eyes narrowed, her lips pinched together, and she pushed off him and shot to a stand. "Oh!" she yelped, hopping on one foot.

Alarmed, Nylander sprang to his feet, ready. "What is it?"

"It seems that during our little conflagration on the hill there"—Mrs. Bailey couldn't devise a pastry tarter than Callie's mouth—"I managed to tweak my ankle." She set the foot on the ground and gingerly tested her weight on it. A silent wince crossed her features. "What were you doing? Chasing me like that?"

Thunder crashed, lightning streaked the sky. The eye of the storm was upon them. "We need shelter now," he shouted through the rain that had begun pelting them like it held a grudge. "Do you know of a place?"

Callie pointed beyond his shoulder. "There is a cave the local youths enjoy. But—"

Nylander exhaled a rough breath. "What is it?"

"It's a bit of a climb. With my ankle, progress might be slow."

"Oh, bloody hell, woman." A grim set to his mouth, he strode over and took her in his arms.

"What do you think you're doing? I can walk," she protested. Still, her hands clutched at his neck to secure her body in place. Soaking wet, the woman didn't weigh anything.

"Tell me where to go."

Fast and steady, his feet followed her directions and found them ascending the rise to the cave in a matter of seconds. At its dark, gaping mouth, he asked, "Can I set you down?"

He felt her nod against his neck, and he shivered, and not from the cold or wet.

He found a flat stretch of wall and settled her against it. "Do you know if there's a lantern?"

"With the youths using it, there must be."

He began his search, feeling his way deeper into the cave, step by cautious step, the darkness swallowing him inside. He felt along the wall, damp with moss and humidity, his fingertips trailing along the base. It must be here somewhere. At last, his fingers touched cool metal and glass. "Found the lantern."

"Flint and striker can't be far."

He dropped to his knees, the better to feel along the ground… *There.* "Got it."

He struck flint and striker together, and in a matter of seconds the dark flickered into orange light, shadows dancing about ceiling, walls, and floor. Outside, the storm raged on.

"Come closer," he commanded, like he was speaking to one of his crew. She stood outside the small circle of light, and it bothered him.

"Why were you following me?" emerged softly from the darkness.

Nylander froze in his crouched position. "You know there are pirates about."

It didn't answer her question, but it was a statement of truth and enough to snap her mouth shut.

His eyes cast about until he found it: a blanket. Actually, two. He reached for one and held it out. "Take this. You must be freezing."

Anything to get her into the light and closer. He didn't like her standing out there like a wet cat. Outside, the storm might rage, but inside, stillness pulsing with tension, prevailed. At last, she limped into the light and eased onto a flat rock opposite him with a wince. He tossed her the blanket.

She snatched it up and held it out in front of her. "It won't do any good, unless—" She bit off the rest of the sentence.

She didn't need to finish it. He knew how it ended. *Unless we strip off these wet clothes.* "We could be here all night," he said instead.

Her dark eyes, fathomless as the sea on a moonless night, would obliterate his presence, if they could. But he saw agreement there. She nodded absently. "If we don't, we might catch an ague."

"I'll turn my back while you"—he wouldn't say *strip*—"disrobe."

Disrobe, a discreet, unsalacious word. A word he'd never spoken in his life.

"Is it only your ankle that's paining you?" he asked to get off the subject of disrobing.

She shifted. "My right hip is a little bruised."

He tamped down the impulse to ask if she needed assistance as she leaned down and untied the laces of her boots. She removed the left one with no problem, but the moment she tested the right boot, her mouth went tight at the corners.

"You'll need to get that boot off your foot."

"It can stay."

"I don't know of any way to remove one's trousers other than to remove one's boot first."

Her mouth gave a twist, sour and stubborn.

"Oh, blast it, woman." He crossed the distance between them and had her foot in hand in a matter of seconds, fingers already unlacing her boot. "You need to get this boot off."

She tried to wrench her foot away and again winced. "It'll be fine by tomorrow."

Nylander jabbed a finger toward the mouth of the cave, torrents of rain coming down in sheets. "We'll be lucky if *that* abates *tonight*."

Her mouth closed in a grudging line. He would take that as acceptance.

One hand closed on her boot heel, and the other removed the laces entirely from their holes. It would hurt her less this way. "I'm going to slide it off on the count of three. Ready?"

She nodded. Her knuckles showed white as her hands clenched the stone at her sides.

"*One... two... three.*" As gently as he could, he angled the boot and coerced it off her foot in as slow and steady a motion as was possible given the damp cling of her woolen sock to leather. The boot off at last, she released the breath she'd been holding on a relieved grunt.

"Does it need a—" He stopped. He wouldn't ask if she needed a massage. Instead, he returned to the opposite side of the cave. It was safer over here. "I'll turn my back while you—" He hesitated. Would he never finish a sentence again?

"*Disrobe?*"

"Aye."

Back to her, he evaluated his person. Boots, socks, shirt, trousers, smalls. They all had to go. With every article of clothing he removed, he heard a corresponding slap of wet cloth against stone from her side of the cave. Sock, sock, *slap, slap...* shirt, *slap...* trousers, *slap...* smalls, *slap.*

He stood naked as Adam, and behind him, safely on her side of the cave, stood Eve. The thought had him reaching for his blanket. There was quite a bit more of him to cover now than there had been before that thought sprang to mind.

"You can turn around now."

He snugged the blanket around what little of him it covered and faced her with an air of nonchalance, as if he wasn't currently tamping down a massive cockstand. She sat on her flat stone perch, curled into herself beneath her blanket, except for the length of one slender, creamy leg revealed from knee to toe. That inviting stretch of skin wasn't helping the problem he was battling beneath his blanket.

"Might as well make ourselves comfortable."

"Hmm," he grunted. *Not bloody likely.* Frustrated and grumpy, he asked, "Why do you run in the dead of night?"

They wouldn't be in this current predicament if she didn't.

"You've been hearing tales of the Wyld Hare, I take it."

He nodded.

She shrugged. "I enjoy it."

"Is it a common activity around these parts?"

"I've never encountered anyone else doing it."

"Then why do *you* do it?" He sensed more beyond the words she spoke. Unspoken ones hung out of reach.

"My mama."

"She ran?"

Callie snorted. "Couldn't imagine." Her eyes flashed with humor. "She would've liked you."

Nylander lifted his brow in silent question.

"You're rather like Thor." Her humor fell away. Eye on the flickering flame of the lantern, she huddled deeper into herself. "When I was in my tenth year, my hale and hearty mama began to grow thin. Of a similar height with me, she was broader and carried a deal more weight. It suited her nature. *A jolly belly for a jolly laugh,* she always said. By my eleventh year, the pounds kept steadily falling away and her energy faded. Although they wouldn't speak in front of me, I took to listening at doors and learned there was a deformity, a lump in her bosom that was the problem." She swallowed. "And there was no help for it."

He wanted to reach out to her. But he didn't.

"I flew out of the house as fast as my legs would carry me, in no direction in particular. Ours was a sprawling estate. I could just run and run. My lungs burned, and it hurt like hell, but I ran for a full hour that day. I came home with blisters on my feet and utterly, completely exhausted. Too exhausted to think about what I'd heard. After the blisters healed, I did it again. I ran on the day she died, and again on the day of her funeral. I never stopped."

Without her having to speak them, he heard them now, those unspoken words. "It's freedom."

Her gaze fixed on the lantern at her feet. "I can sort myself out on a run."

He waited for her eyes to lift. "What were you running from tonight?"

"You, of course."

It was literally true, but there was more to that *you*. He saw it in her eyes. He dare not move a muscle.

"There is something I must tell you. Something I've been keeping from you."

At last, she would be out with it, and they could move forward. *They?* There was no *they*.

Not yet, anyway.

"'Tis to you that St. Alban wants to sell the Grange." The confession emerged in a tremulous rush. "I've known it since London and have deliberately withheld the information from you."

He nodded and held his tongue.

"St. Alban has given me until the festival to secure the monies."

Surprise jolted through him. "That's tomorrow. Do you have them?"

Her coal-black eyes transformed into cold, hard diamonds. It was the wrong question. "That'll be my business."

There. Confirmation. Jack Le Grand would be providing the funds. Or, at least, that was at the heart of her bargain with the pirate, except it wasn't going to plan. Recent "accidents" and assaults didn't add up. Her monies were anything but secured, and she knew it.

"Is there anything else you would like to tell me?"

She gave her head a curt shake. "It's nothing I can't handle myself."

She thought to handle Jack herself? He couldn't dream up a more frustrating woman.

"If I can't secure the funds, are you going to buy the Grange?"

She'd just made her deepest fear a tangible thing by speaking it aloud, and he couldn't help but admire her for it. She was brave to her core. The only way he could honor her courage was to be honest. "Yes."

She flinched, as if he'd struck her.

"Would that be such a terrible thing?"

A small, humorless laugh startled out of her. "If you'd asked me the same question even a few days ago, I would've said yes. I would have listed all the ways it would've been the worst catastrophe in the world." She held up her fingers and began ticking items off a list. "For the Grange. For its tenants. For Upper Wyldcombe Lacey." She hesitated. "For *me*."

"And now?"

"I'm not so sure. Perhaps I made the wrong choice to stay after Georgie's death. Perhaps it's prevented me from having the life I really want."

"And the Grange isn't it?"

She shook her head.

"What is it you really want?"

He waited. She might not answer. She didn't owe him that. He had no right to her deepest desires, not the ones that went deeper than her skin.

"A child." The words, stark and simple, echoed about the cave. "No one liked Georgie, not even my father. But that hardly mattered, because everyone would get what they wanted from the marriage." Again, she held up fingers to tick items off a list. "Father would get a title into the family. Georgie would get a much needed infusion of fresh funds into his bank accounts. And I would get a child." Bitterness twisted her face, her short laugh. "The marriage happened, but the promised child didn't. And nothing—not fortune, not status, not connections—mattered in the face of that particular misery."

"You could have remarried." He hesitated. "You still can. You're a young woman of great ability and talent." *Any man would be lucky to have you,* he left unspoken.

"Most men don't regard a woman who strides around in men's trousers and barks orders at them all day as the ideal wife and mother."

"Most men are fools." The words were out of his mouth before he had a chance to stop them.

They were unwise and careless words.

They were the most honest words he'd ever spoken.

The moment shifted on its axis.

Secrets may abound between them, snugged deep inside hard, twisted shells, but as they stared into each other's eyes across flickering flame, deeper truth showed itself. Raw, vulnerable, the real Callie stared out at him, and he couldn't help but give her the real Nylander in return.

On this day, they'd entrusted the most vulnerable pieces of themselves into each other's keeping. Only these selves populated this cave. He'd never experienced a day, not a single instant, like this with another person, and he suspected she hadn't either.

Headlong, they'd slipped into an important moment. Nothing in his life had ever mattered more. It fed a side of him that he hadn't known existed.

And it was ravenous for yet more.

For everything.

Of her.

She shifted on her stone seat. Again, that wince.

"Is it your ankle?"

"It's really nothing."

For the second time tonight, he crossed to her side of the cave when he knew full well he should stay away. No good could come of it. Still, he couldn't see her in pain and do nothing. Her foot was in his hand before he could fully process that he was touching her, again. He couldn't seem not to.

Below, from his supplicant's position, he found her staring down at him, not like a goddess, but, eyes narrowed, considering, like a very curious woman. "Why do you have to be so, so…" She was searching for a word. "So *nice.*"

This pulled a laugh from him. "Many epithets have been cast at me over the years, but never that one."

"I have a feeling that's because they haven't glimpsed the real you."

He focused on her foot and allowed her words to slide off him like water off a duck's back. It wouldn't do to take those words inside. They might fill him with boundless joy. "How does it feel when I press along here?"

"Fine." She sounded annoyed. Better.

"And here?"

That pulled a squawk from her. "*Not* nice."

He began rubbing the area and remained silent.

Her eyebrows crinkled together, like a woman of science studying an especially curious specimen. "You're really nothing like a Viking."

He released her foot and sat back on his heels. "I never claimed to be."

A laugh conscious of itself sounded from her. Her hand emerged from her blanket and reached out to touch his cheek. He went very, very still as she caressed the line of his stubbled jaw. "In this imperfect world, you're just so *perfect.*"

Bitterness, uncontrollable and familiar, roiled his stomach. It always came back to this with her ilk. "I've been told. A perfect specimen of man. A perfect *fuck,*" he flung at her.

She blinked at the vulgarity, but she didn't pull away. Instead, understanding dawned in her eyes. "I can't deny that, but where you are most perfect"—her hand trailed beneath the blanket down to his chest and stopped directly above his heart—"is *here.*"

It answered with a hard thud, and his breath froze between an inhale and exhale. Time wound to a stop.

"Has no one ever told you?"

No one had. Well, mayhap his ma, so many years and lifetimes ago. But he couldn't speak the words, not beneath the spell Callie was weaving around him. She pushed the blanket aside, revealing the tattoo above his heart. Feather-light fingertips traced every straight and curve of black ink. "Is this script?"

"Aye."

"What does it say?"

"It's the meaning of my name."

"Which is?"

"Dweller on new land." His blood fizzed hot and fast through his veins as if he'd exposed a raw nerve to oxygen. "'Tis the fate of all sailors to seek new lands."

"And this is the name you gave yourself?"

"Aye."

"But it isn't *seeker* of new lands. It's *dweller*."

She would catch the distinction.

"Writ above your heart. It isn't simply the meaning of your name. It's your heart's desire."

This woman… She *knew* him.

He'd experienced a good variety of intimacies with a good number of women, but never an intimacy like this. She didn't simply care about what lay between his legs, she cared about what lay inside his heart. Something new and wondrous was happening inside this cave.

"You're shivering."

Was that concern in her eyes?

"It's nothing," he dismissed.

He wasn't trembling from cold.

"It's not nothing," she pressed. "You have needs, too."

"I've been colder."

Why was he pushing her concern away?

"That's not relevant," she said in her tart, schoolmarm voice. When had he grown to like it so much? "Your needs matter. Take my blanket." She shifted to remove it.

As much as he'd like to see her in her full, naked glory,

he couldn't lower himself to that level. It was cheap. "I'm not taking your blanket. You need it more. You're small."

Her eyebrows met and held before she barked out a laugh. Free and unguarded, it was a laugh of utter abandon, and the loveliest sound he'd heard in all his life. "You're the only man in the world who sees me as *small*."

Again, that uninhibited laugh sounded, and unfettered joy surged inside him.

"You're a blasted difficult man to care for, you know that?"

"I've been told."

Solemnity replaced impulsivity in her eyes. "Won't you allow anyone to care for you?"

Her question stole the answer from his mouth. She shifted forward and winced.

"Your hip."

"Don't worry about my hip."

"You're a sight difficult to care for yourself, you know that?"

"Aren't we quite a pair?"

"Aren't we?"

She pressed herself up just high enough to slide off her stone perch and onto the ground. There she sat opposite him, legs crossed, his mirror image. The timeless feeling that had entered the cave continued to cocoon them.

He reached out and tucked a damp string of flame-red hair behind her ear. "I love the color of your hair."

The words—*that* word—were out of his mouth before he could control them. And, inside this protected bubble the two of them had created, he didn't want to.

"You *love* it?" she whispered.

"Aye." Emboldened, he continued, "And I love the smattering of freckles across your nose."

"You *love* them?"

She sounded breathless, and a wave of joy crested at the sound of her breathlessness.

"Aye."

"Your eyes," she began, a hitch in each syllable. "There's a forever blue sky contained inside them, even on the cloudiest day. It's the most truthful blue in the world. I lo —" She swallowed. "I love it."

"You *love* it?" His heart might stop. Could too much joy be lethal?

She nodded. "And I love—" She tripped over that word again. Like him, she didn't have much practice speaking it. "I love the crooked curl of your mouth when you smile, like now."

His smile crooked further. "You *love* it?"

Solemnity, vulnerability, shone out from her eyes as she nodded and angled her body forward, over her crossed legs, over his crossed legs, until her lips stopped a hairs-breadth away from his. "Right," she murmured, her breath whispering across his mouth, "here." She pressed her lips to the curled up corner of his mouth in a kiss gentle, pure, sacred.

She shifted back. He could howl for the loss of her.

"And I love"—he leaned forward, pitching into her space—"this blush right"—he slanted his face into the bare patch of skin between the top of the blanket and her jaw— "here."

He pressed his mouth to the pulse point of her neck, her heartbeat thrumming beneath his lips. She exhaled a soft sigh into his ear, and his manhood stirred. The sweet purity of their intimacy slid into the carnal.

She edged backward, ever so slightly, and knowing eyes met his. Her grasp eased on the blanket enough so it slipped off her shoulders, barely held at breast level, re-vealing the hollow at the base of her throat, the creamy slope of her shoulders in the flickering light of the lantern.

She released the blanket entirely, and rough wool dropped in a gray puddle at her hips. Here she was, re-vealed in all the ways she feared: vulnerable, exposed, naked, not only in the flesh, but in her dark, solemn eyes.

For him.

This glorious woman was baring her entire being, for *him*.

He allowed his blanket to fall. He wouldn't have her alone in her vulnerability.

She would see his, too.

For her.

She reached out and touched his face. He reached out and touched hers.

Again, she angled forward. "I love the tremble of your fingers when you touch me," she murmured against his lips.

The lightning streaking the sky outside didn't come close to packing the electrical punch delivered to him by the soft press of her lips. It shimmered through his veins with light and energy, longing and joy.

His fingers reached around and tangled in her hair, pulling her forward, deepening the kiss. She rose to her knees. Her face slanted down, and his head tilted back, refusing to break from her as she straddled his legs. His arms encircled her back and drew her closer so her chest pressed against his, and her slick, soft cunny against his cock, rigid, ready.

"*Callie*," he groaned. He might never let her go.

She trailed feather-light kisses until she reached the cup of his ear. "I want you."

He pulled back and met her eyes. He needed to see if what he thought he'd heard within her words was really there. And, with a sense of wonder, he saw it was.

The wanting wasn't merely, or purely, physical. A possibility lay within those words, within her solemn eyes, that she wanted more of him than his body and the pleasure it could provide her. It was possible that she wanted *him*... *all* of him. How they'd arrived at this place after weeks of a cat-and-mouse game, he wasn't certain, but they were here, *now*. It was what mattered.

It was all that would ever matter.

Her lips trailed to the crook of his neck, and his breath caught in his throat when she sucked the sensitive flesh into her mouth. Goose bumps prickled across his skin, and he took her hips in hand.

"Oh, yes," she breathed against his neck, her sweet breath filling the space with a sultry warmth. "*I need you now.*"

From here, his body knew what to do.

His cock pressed against the slick, sweetness of her quim, and her hips gave a subtle rotation. On the roll forward, she took him inside on a long, slow grind. A moan, deep and animal, crawled from her very depths. Her long legs wrapped around his back.

"*More*," she groaned.

His fingers closed hard on her hips, steadying her, as he impaled her on every last inch of his thick length until he was fully seated. Raw lust licking at him, he pulled back, then drove into her, eliciting that raw, animal groan of hers that incited a hunger in him that grew more ravenous with each stroke.

Her eyes drifted shut, and her mouth parted, shallow breaths rasping from her lungs with every thrust, abandon seizing her and... taking her away from him.

"Open your eyes," he demanded.

Eyes lust-glazed and wanton slid open and met his. But he saw something else, too, beyond mad desire: connection... soul-deep intimacy.

This feeling wasn't his alone.

Her hands cupped his face, and her mouth closed in on his. Her tongue glided along the seam of his lips, pressed into his mouth, and tangled with him. His hands wrapped around her sweet arse and squeezed, driving her harder on his cock. Her mouth tore away from his, and her head tipped back on her neck as she released the longest, most sultry moan ever to cross a pair of lips.

He licked up the elegant length of her sweat-sheened neck and pressed his mouth to her ear. "You like it hard?"

He thrust, she gasped, and a wicked smile curved her lips. "I *love* it."

His heart kicked a fierce beat inside his chest, and he folded her deeper into his embrace. He would feel all of her at once. He would take her into himself, if he could. "Far be it from me to deny a lady what she *loves*."

Another time, with another woman, the statement would have been an irony laced with bitterness. Not tonight, not with *this* woman.

He took one cherry-hard bud into his mouth and sucked. Like an apple blossom, she bloomed before him, her sweet surface scent complicated with one deeper, more complex, more animal. A scent that spurred on the animal inside him.

In and out, he drove into her, one relentless thrust after another. Her fingers wove through his hair and formed tight fists, threatening to pull it out by the roots as she steadied herself against the pleasure that had begun washing over her in waves that were arriving by increasingly tighter sets, deep groans now punctuated by sharp gasps.

She was close.

As was he.

"You're there," he murmured against her breast.

His fingers found her mons pubis, golden red in the flickering light. If it was possible he grew harder as he pressed through soft curls and sweet slit toward the hood of her sex, slick and swollen with lust. He rubbed it between forefinger and thumb, and squeezed, gently. Her hips gave a hard buck, and her wild, unfettered, "Oh!" sang in echo through the cave.

One more thrust of his cock, and he squeezed her again. "*Come for me, Callie.*"

Her breath hitched in her chest, her back arched, and, for an untamed moment, time stood still. Then she broke, her quim clenching and pulsing around his cock.

His face buried in the hollow of her neck, he followed her over the edge of release. Her fingernails bit into his shoulders, and his seed spent inside her, transporting him to a plane known only to him and her.

An airy sigh whissed in his ear, pulling him back into his physical form, his cells bursting to life on a rolling wave, attuned to the press of her hot, sticky skin against his, her delicious weight sunk into him. He blew cooling breath along her neck, her clavicle, between the delicate curves of her breasts to her navel, her pebbled nipples. Her eyes shut, a sated smile curled about her mouth.

This act had never brought him an ounce of satisfaction or fulfillment beyond release, his and his partner's. Now he was full to the brim, overflowing with satiety. With this woman, it was a different act altogether.

His thumb hitched beneath her chin and tipped her face up. Eyes shining with wonder and uncertainty met his. They only reflected the emotions that surely shone out from his. This day and this night had shifted the earth beneath their feet, and he was no longer sure of his footing. But it was within this newly loose soil that hope could bud and grow.

"How is your ankle?"

She shrugged.

"Your hip?"

"Never felt better." She laughed. "In fact, no part of me has ever felt better in my entire life."

Her laughter infected him, shimmering through his veins, shooting light from his fingertips for all he knew.

Her head canted to the side, and her eyes screwed up to the ceiling. "Can you hear it?"

"What is that?" He was thoroughly distracted by the perfect cup of her ear and began bussing kisses along its delicate curve.

"The storm. It's exhausted itself."

Mid-kiss, he stopped.

"I think it's safe to leave."

Safe?

It was safe here, her body snugged into his, the outside world be damned.

"Perhaps we should," she trailed.

Return to the Grange was left unsaid.

His return to earth, to reality, was swift and hard. "Aye, perhaps we should."

He reached for her blanket and draped it across her shoulders. She took his chin in hand, made him meet her eye. "But that doesn't mean we have to return to… *before.*"

She spoke the words shyly, as if she'd just learned them and was still unsure of their meaning. They were the bravest words he'd ever heard. Words his own insecurities had held bound inside his mouth. His heart soared.

Through their tangled mess of secrets and lies had emerged this one true thing.

And after the tangle was unraveled and sorted, it would remain.

He would see to it.

———

CALLIE LAY a quiet figure in bed, in her pitch black bedroom, and listened to the sounds of night beyond her window. Day would be breaking soon.

She touched fingers to lips, to the exact spot where he'd kissed her one last time before retiring to his chamber, solitary, a gentleman.

They'd picked their way home on muddy trails, across wet heath, their progress slowed by her stiff ankle. By the time they'd reached the house, it had worked out whatever small injury it had sustained earlier. It would be ready for tomorrow.

There had been something she'd been less sure about, though. On their return, they'd walked side by side, but not touching. For a dreadful instant, uncertainty had quaked her. *What if—?* Then his hand found hers in the dark. Reassurance in their dry warmth.

It was perfect. *He* was perfect. How was it possible that such a perfect man wanted to take her cold, clammy hand in his? It didn't seem like it could be. But the proof was there, in his firm, reassuring touch.

And now she lay alone, delicious ache pulsing through her. Something had happened between him and her on this day, on the moor, in the cave, beyond the physical. It was wondrous and new and a feeling she'd never experienced in her five and twenty years.

They'd shied away from speaking it aloud, from giving it solid form. It was too new. Something that would evaporate into nothingness if not properly tended. If cared for, perhaps, perhaps, it could grow into the tangible, the solid. Into something she could grasp with both hands and never let go.

Perhaps... but how?

Of one fact she was certain: it didn't stand a chance of developing into something she could hold in her hand, in her heart, if she didn't change course.

While she'd revealed to Nylander that he was St. Alban's first-choice buyer for the Grange, she'd withheld her bargain with Jack Le Grand.

Her reasoning why was obvious: shame, ugly and rotten to its vile core. The way she'd gone about securing her monies, the bargain itself, was underhanded and wrong. The person who had struck that deal with a ruthless pirate, who was endangering the Grange and its occupants, wasn't the person she'd thought she was. But it was the person she'd somehow become.

For here was the thing: the bargain had been for her own benefit. For her pride and not for the good of the Grange. It was the sort of deal her father would strike. It had been a selfish act, one that needed rectifying.

Outside her window, the first bloom of dawn appeared as did a solution to her problem. Tomorrow—*today*—was the Duke of Muck. She would break off the deal directly after.

Tonight.

Twin pangs of loss and relief skirred through her. She would lose the Grange, but she would rid it of Jack Le Grand. Only then, would she begin regaining her integrity.

The Grange would be in good hands with Nylander. She knew it down to her gut. It was strange to think, but he, too, had striven his whole life to achieve it, not underhanded, not like her, but nobly. He was everything a man should be and deserved the Grange. He would run it with integrity, and it would continue to prosper beneath his sure hand.

She touched awed fingertips to the plait of hair resting on her shoulder. He, that admirable, noble, gorgeous man, loved its color. Fingertips feathered up to the bridge of her nose. He loved her freckles. The way his eyes had held hers... It was possible he loved...

The thought skittered away. She couldn't find the

courage to hold it in place and examine it. But even a crumb of the thought was enough to send that delicious ache racing through her as the rising sun burnished the room with its golden light.

She wouldn't get any sleep this night. How could sleep possibly compete with this glorious feeling charging through her veins?

26

DAY

Festoons of crepe paper crisscrossed High Street from opposing building roofs, fluttery above Nylander's head, striking stark white against the placid, blue sky that indicated no memory of the storm that had raged the night before. Spontaneous strains of lively fiddle and competing scents of freshly baked treats swirled around him, while children ran and wove through the adults, whose strides were only slightly more measured.

This was festival day, and no one could remain unmoved by its unmoored and easy gaiety for long. Upper Wyldcombe Lacey was a town transformed.

Again, Nylander scanned the sea of heads stretching up and down the length of the street, looking for *her*.

He hadn't spoken to her since last night, since they ambled back to the Grange together and he'd left her in her bedroom, alone. The hardest thing he'd ever done in his three and thirty years. He'd wanted nothing more than to lie with her, wake up next to her.

This morning, she'd been completely absorbed in preparations for the festival, and he'd left her to it while he made himself useful delivering last year's cider to the public houses and stalls lining High Street. On this day, there was to be free cider for all, courtesy of Wyldcombe Grange.

That wasn't to say he hadn't caught a few glimpses of her. He had. And once he'd even discovered her watching him, silently, even shyly. A woman, a *lady*, had never looked at him the way she had. It warmed him through his skin clean to the marrow in his bones.

Today was the autumn festival.

Tomorrow, possibly a future.

He dug his hands into his pockets and felt the slender missive. His sense of optimism faltered. It had arrived by special courier from London at daybreak. In it, Jake confirmed the sale of the Grange. Then he'd gone on to say he'd taken steps toward resolving the "other matter." Excise men weren't far behind the missive, if not ahead of it. The law was coming.

Bloody hell. He should've known better than to mention Jack Le Grand's name. At least, he'd kept Callie out of it. She'd waded too far out of the shallows. Now a riptide was muscling in. He wouldn't let it pull her under.

Jack Le Grand, on the other hand, deserved everything coming to him.

"Why if it isn't the Viking sea lord come to pillage and plunder," grated an overfamiliar voice behind him.

He pivoted and confirmed that it was Liza Bickle, radiating mischief. "Mrs. Bickle," he said, his indifference impossible to mask, "I take it you're enjoying the festivities."

She cast a malevolent eye about and shrugged a shoulder. "Never did care for apples." She snaked an arm through his and snugged close into his side, the smell of her strong enough to peel the paint off the prow of a ship. She stretched up to speak directly into his ear, her breath somehow worse than her body's odor, as if a small rodent had died in her mouth. "If ye come along with me, I'll show ye what I do care for. It involves a bit o' pillage and a whole lot o' plunder. I think ye'll like it." She winked. "Or yer money back."

Nylander opened his mouth to express his deepest regret that he wouldn't be able to take her up on her offer when Mrs. Jane Smith strode into view, a storm cloud on her face. "There you are, Captain Nylander. I've been searching the street high and low for you." She claimed his other arm and tugged in the opposite direction.

Liza Bickle wasn't about to concede the ground she'd staked. "Oi! Ye can't march in 'ere like the Queen of Sheba and claim another woman's man."

Nylander's brow lifted, but again Mrs. Smith spared him from speaking. "Liza Bickle, I've heard about you." With the air of a general on the march, she puffed out her considerable chest. "This man is spoken for."

"By 'oo?" Liza Bickle sputtered. "*You?* Yer a married woman."

"The *who* is none of your concern."

"Speakin' o' pillage and plunder," Liza Bickle trailed. Her head canted to the side, and speculation entered her eyes. "Ye've been makin' yer recovery at the Grange. I reckon there's been a bit o' plunder 'appenin' on the regular."

Mrs. Smith gasped and shooed the other woman away. "Back to London with you, Liza Bickle. You've overstayed your welcome in Devonshire."

Liza Bickle cast one last knowing smirk over her shoulder and slinked into the crowd, a saunter in her step, leaving behind a scandalized Mrs. Smith and a bemused Nylander. It wouldn't do to admit to the upright Mrs. Smith that Liza Bickle hadn't been entirely, or even mostly, wrong.

"My savior." He gave a slight bow. "I'm in your eternal debt."

"Of course," Mrs. Smith said, the fading remnants of a bristle in her matter-of-fact tone.

He glanced down and found her cheeks vermillion with a blush. He cleared his throat politely. "A nice day for a festival."

The weather was the safest course of conversation with a blushing woman.

"Oh," Mrs. Smith exclaimed, "do you have the time?"

He craned his neck to get a good look at the sun's position in the sky. "I'd say we're approaching noon."

Blushes gave way to an all-business tone. "We must

hurry!" Her feet were already scurrying into motion, pulling him up the hill. He only now noticed the entire town was proceeding this direction, and they were simply entering its tide. "I want to see how Calpurnia's costume looks in the full sun."

"Ah." He had difficulty envisioning Callie wearing anything so frivolous as a costume. He rather liked that about her. Her utter lack of frivolity.

"Oh, yes," Mrs. Smith continued, "as head of Wyldcombe Grange, 'tis Lady St. Alban who is Master of Ceremonies." She gave her head a little shake. "*Mistress* of Ceremonies. This is her first year in the role since the past few years she's allowed the mayor to fill it. I still can't believe she's doing it herself this year. You've got to admire the woman for that."

"For what precisely?" What was all this talk about *costumes* and *roles*?

Mrs. Smith's eyebrows lifted. "That's right. You've never witnessed the Baptism of the Duke of Muck. Well, no matter, you'll see later. You're in for a treat." A bemused smile poked a dimple into life at the center of one round cheek. "Her Ladyship just can't help defying tradition at every turn. Such is the lot of a woman who wants a say over the running of her life."

"It was my impression that the wilds of Devon must breed a new sort of woman."

His comment provoked a laugh. "Captain Nylander, surely you jest. If rumor is to be trusted, you're a well-traveled man. Is there a single society in the world who lets a woman have a say over her life?"

"Well, there were the Amazons of Greece."

"An ancient society that is no longer in existence, may I remind you," she pointed out, smug in having proven her point.

"Captain John Nylander?" he heard behind him.

Before he faced the man, or men, more like, Nylander scanned what he already knew. London accent. A bit of education. Steel-edged. Pugnacious.

Excise men.

Mrs. Smith had already turned and exhaled a soft, "Oh."

When he pivoted and squared up to the men, his suspicions were confirmed. Officious thugs in suits. Excise men.

"Aye," he confirmed, equally hard.

Another soft, "Oh," escaped Mrs. Smith, whose eyes had gone round as saucers.

"A matter has come to our attention," began one. "About Jack Le Grand," finished the other.

Bloody hell. "You won't make much headway today." Nylander indicated the tide of bodies jostling around them with a jut of his chin. "It's festival day."

The excise men looked about, as if they'd only just noticed that they stood in the midst of a jubilee.

"I suggest," Nylander continued, "getting yourself a glass of cider and an apple tart. This can wait until the morrow."

The men glanced at each other, then back at Nylander. "All right," said the one. "Tomorrow," said the other.

As their backs disappeared into the crowd, Nylander released a breath that was two parts relief and one part foreboding. Those men had a job to do, and they wouldn't leave until they'd done it. *Tomorrow.*

"What on earth?" Mrs. Smith asked, the question rhetorical.

If she only knew. *Tomorrow.*

"Now, we must hurry." Determination in her step, she pulled him onward and upward.

They reentered the flow of the increasingly dense crowd and reached the summit of the hill, where they stopped dead center in the squirming mass of humanity, a raised dais not fifty yards beyond. Distant figures bustled back and forth across its hollow boards, clearly preparing for a speech.

"Calpurnia's costume is a bit of a departure from tradition, but I couldn't seem to help myself," Mrs. Smith said, brimming with delight, hands clasped before her.

Nylander squinted into the distance. Where was Callie anyway? The only people he could make out on the stage were three rather elderly men and a woman in an emerald-green dress.

"Couldn't help yourself?" he only just thought to ask.

A sly smile formed about Mrs. Smith's mouth. She nodded toward the figure clad in the emerald dress, who was now stepping up to the podium and clearing her throat to address the crowd.

His mouth went dry. *Callie*. But the fact it was *her* wasn't what startled a thin sheen of sweat along his spine or made him stumble over an exposed root.

She stood before the entire town clad in her *costume*. Comprised entirely of emerald silk, the gown gathered in all the right places to accentuate the elegant length of her arms and legs, the undulate curve of her waist, the gentle rounding of creamy breasts above deep, square neckline. Hair twisted in a loose braid over her shoulder, wisps of flame red hair quivering in the light breeze, completed this perfect vision of poised femininity.

Statuesque, striking, she was a queen.

Except, she was so very much a woman.

And she was *his*. Or was she? How could it be true?

Mayhap he'd interpreted last night all wrong. For how was it possible that the *lady* standing above him, about to address this multitude like the queen she was, had gazed upon him the way he thought she had this morning?

It couldn't be.

She opened her mouth to address the assembled mass. Then her eye snagged on his, and she went mute. Even as the crowd grew restive, Nylander refused to surrender her gaze and what he found there. Could it be?

It couldn't.

A shy smile curled about her lips, and a pretty blush pinked her cheeks. Darkness gave way to light.

It could.

An officious elderly man shuffled forward and spoke a discreet word into Callie's ear. Still, her eyes remained locked onto his. Hushed whispers began swirling through the crowd as people took note of the recipient of her gaze. A jocular elbow cut a light jib into his ribs. Her blush deepened into embarrassed scarlet, and her gaze darted away. It was as if the summer sun had slipped behind a black cloud.

She cleared her throat. "Righteous seekers of the Duke of Muck," she called out, eliciting a few wry chuckles from the crowd. "Today we celebrate not only the bounty of this year's exceptional harvest, but all the work that made it possible. From the picking of the apples to the churning of the butter and to the baling of the hay. Every person gathered here makes today possible, year after year." She spread her arms wide. "This is your festival. This is your day. Make merry and celebrate, 'tis well-deserved. Let the festivities begin, and may the fleetest of foot win the day!"

"Is that a challenge, milady?" a man called out, the question playful.

An enigmatic smile played about Callie's lips. The crowd went dead silent. "Aye," she said, "that it is."

The assembled erupted into raucous laughter. The official who had whispered into Callie's ear rushed to the podium as fast as his elderly legs would carry him. "Mind you, pace yourselves!" he called out to the already dispersing crowd. "That's right, I'm looking at you, Harry Broadbent!"

His words of warning fell on deaf ears as the townspeople scattered and parted for the children's parade already on the march, drummer boys at the lead, followed by girls clad in white linen dresses pirouetting in twirls and loops, tossing fall leaves into the air, showers of orange, yellow, and red swirling about their heads in fluttery wisps.

"I believe you know how to proceed from here," Mrs. Smith tossed cryptically over her shoulder. She strolled away to the beat of the parade.

Alone, Nylander set his trajectory toward the stage and the woman still upon it, her back turned to him as she spoke with the men who remained. "A nice day for a festival," he called up to her.

Her head startled around, presenting her strong profile, and her body followed a beat behind. Eyes bright and shining, she smiled down at him. "A perfect day." A pause. "I *love* it."

Like that, last night was between them. The confessions. The connection. And it was good. Better than good. "You *love* the weather?"

She broke into a broad smile, and his heart lifted. "Mm-hmm."

He extended a hand. "Are you finished up there?"

She placed one hand in his—a jolt of lightning might have fired through him—and gathered her skirts in the other before jumping from the stage on a short hop. She gave a small wince on the landing.

"Is it your ankle?" he asked.

She nodded. "A little stiff is all. Nothing a little movement won't work out. It'll be right as rain by dusk."

"Will you walk with me?"

"I have a little time for a stroll."

"Do you have another pressing engagement?"

"You could say that." Her smile turned cryptic.

There was something about this festival that everyone but him understood. He held out his arm for her. "I'll take what time you'll grant me."

A sudden and charming shyness came over her as she threaded her hand through his crooked arm. Again, last night charged between them, the air vibrating with their bodies' memory. The breath held in his lungs, the feeling of having too much and not enough at once. The feeling of green youth lost, regained. Optimism for the day, for the future, flowed through him on a happy wave. Humbled, *proud*, that was how he felt to have this woman on his arm.

Wordlessly, they entered the flow of the crowd, their gazes fixed on its scene of merry, boisterous revelry. "Your dress," he began, "is most becoming."

Becoming?

"Thank you," was her demure reply.

"Why don't you wear dresses more often?"

"They're highly impractical for the work I do. Besides
—" She hesitated.

"*Besides?*" he prodded.

"I don't know of any men who would like to see me
dressed so."

"I can think of one."

2 7

A rush of heat flooded Callie, and the tame blush she'd been experiencing since the moment she'd locked eyes with Nylander across the crowd went wild with sudden abandon, crawling across her décolletage, up her neck, all the way to the tips of her ears.

Of all the reactions he could have had to her blush, he chuckled. "With all those high-necked shirts you wear, I've never had the privilege of witnessing the full glory of a Callie blush in the daylight."

The blush heated up another degree. He liked her red splotches? She might love that about him. A change of subject was in order. "Shall we follow the children's parade to Stickling's Green for the games?"

"The games?"

"Have you never experienced an English village festival?"

"Never."

"Well, you're in for a treat."

And she was the one to provide it to him. She rather loved that, too.

On they strolled in a silence that wasn't strained, but not without a specific sort of tension either. A heightened sense of being. A charge, floaty, electric, vibrating. They passed booths selling fairing cakes, gingerbread, and cream tea. Free cider for all at every other stall. Her nose caught the scent of cinnamon and apple. Enticed, she pulled him toward it.

"Mmm, apple turnovers." Her stomach growled.

Nylander produced coin and, before she could blink, she had one of the warm, crisp treats in hand. It was only after she'd consumed the entire pastry in four bites that it occurred to her she'd been rude. Sheepish, she glanced up. "I didn't offer you any."

His lopsided smile appeared. "I might love that you didn't."

Her heart flipped inside her chest every time he used that word, *love*, in connection with her. She loved it.

She held up her hands. "And now my fingers are all sticky."

His smile fell. He took her hand and lifted it, turning it, caramelized sugar glistening in the sunlight. His eyes narrowed, and he brought it to his face, to his lips... *Was he about to—?*

In popped her middle finger into his mouth.

He sucked. She gasped.

His tongue circled once, twice. Her knees threatened to buckle.

"The town," she rasped. "Everyone will—"

"Know?" he finished for her.

She nodded, and his smile turned devilish. Intently, he moved from finger to finger, and she stood there, permitting him. A female passerby might have emitted a breathless, "Oh, my," but Callie couldn't be sure through the cloud of cotton in her ears.

Oh, the feel of his tongue on her skin. Pure decadence in the middle of town. She was powerless against its pull. He gave her pinky one last lick, and she thought she might collapse into a puddle of jelly.

"I think that takes care of your little problem."

Her mouth gaped open and instantly snapped shut. *Little* problem? There wasn't anything *little* about the problem this man excited inside her.

"Shall we proceed?"

She swallowed and rubbed her fingers together. They

tingled and nerve endings thrilled along her skin, but not a sticky bit remained. "Umm, yes." *Eloquent.*

He held out his arm in formal invite, and she slid her thoroughly cleaned hand through. On a delicious cloud, they made their way to Stickling's Green, its air of excitement and festivity infectious as the town's buildings fell behind and the field opened before them.

"See anything you would like to try your hand at?" She gestured to their left. "Perhaps the grinning contest?"

Two men sat perched on opposite stools, not two feet separated from one another, each pulling one face more grotesque than the last, trying to get his opponent to break and smile.

"It's a most serious business, as you can see."

Nylander shook his head. "Not a chance."

Callie gestured to their right. "Or how about the whistling match?"

"I'll content myself with watching."

More than a dozen contestants stood gathered round in a large circle, silent lips puckered in anticipation, an officious man at the center. His arm lifted high above his head, and the participants' mouths pursed tighter, ready. The official's arm slashed down, and the whistling commenced.

Nylander smiled. "'Drunken Sailor.' Slower than I've ever whistled it, though."

"I take it you've never seen a whistling match?"

"Nay."

"Well, the song starts off slow. Then the tempo increases with each new verse."

"That doesn't seem too difficult."

"Another layer of difficulty is added when Merry Andrew enters the fray."

"Merry Andrew?"

"He's the—" She stopped and clapped her hands when a bright figure danced into view. "There he is!"

A masked jester, dressed in pink, yellow, and green, slinked, step by exaggerated step, into the center of the circle, arms extended wide, and began whirling like a dervish. Callie knew that jester. He was—

"Kip," Nylander finished her thought aloud.

She couldn't contain a squeal of delight. She'd never squealed in delight in her life. She rather loved it, too. "It seems the boy has found his place."

"And what, pray tell, is that?"

"Chief mischief maker, of course. He's our very own Norse god, our Loki."

"Can't think of a lad better suited to the role."

Kip came to a stop and swept off his mask, his cape dramatically swishing about him. He sniffed the air and lowered his head, singling out a most intent whistler.

Callie's hands clasped before her. "The real fun is about to begin."

Kip rushed forward and began pulling faces at the whistler, who for his part bravely stayed the course and soldiered on in his song.

"It's the Merry Andrew's job to get the whistlers to break and laugh. The last whistler whistling will be crowned winner of the contest."

Disgruntled by his inability to "break" the whistler, Kip moved on and began weaving in and out of the circle, poking a finger into the odd rib here and there, blowing air into whistlers' ears, and making a general monkey of himself. As the song's tempo sped up, so did Kip, his antics reaching a more frantic and fevered pitch, his unpredictability rising with every note, his faces and tickles doing their job and eliminating contestants until only two remained, both focused and seemingly immune to Kip's capers.

He swung to a sudden stop and heaved a huge, theatrical sigh as he looked from one contestant to the other, finally lifting both hands into the air and dropping them in exaggerated defeat. The next moment, his face dramatically brightened, and he pointed a finger to the sky. Of a sudden, he bent over and lifted his robes over his back, the twin white mounds of his buttocks shining bright as the moon on a clear night.

Shocked silence broke into guffaws, hoots, and skirls, as one, then the other, whistler lost his composure. Like that, a winner was crowned. Kip swept his cape around his slight form and scampered off.

"He's a boy of many talents." Nylander's words emerged dry as dust. "That lad needs someone to keep an eye on him."

"Indeed." Callie couldn't contain the laughter that bubbled up.

"Shall we see what further frivolities await us?"

Callie hiccupped on a laugh—*hiccupped!*—and nodded. She wasn't sure what had happened to her usual self today, but that Callie was nowhere to be found. In her place was a woman who felt free and light as the air she breathed. *The man beside you might have something to do with it.* Nay, not merely something.

Everything.

They approached a rather nasty mud puddle, and Nylander deftly steered her around it, but not before filmy dreck caught and clung to the hem of her skirts, seeping up emerald silk, forming a brown ring around the circumference. "Your dress," he began, worry in his tone. "It's ruined."

Callie flicked a dismissive wrist. "It's not the worst treatment this dress will receive today."

His eyebrows crinkled together. "Why does everyone keep speaking that way?"

"What way?"

"Like a possibly catastrophic event will be occurring later."

She gave him a saucy smirk. "You'll see." Was it possible she was becoming a *flirt?* She flung one arm wide. "Now that you've seen our humble festival's offerings, what competition will it be for you, my captain?"

His arm reactively squeezed, and a frisson of excitement raced through her. She hadn't intended to say it, but he'd heard it. *My* captain. And she wasn't about to take it back. Reckless, but she couldn't seem to help herself.

Recklessness felt safe with him.

She gestured to her left. "A game of quoits?" Her hand flicked to the right. "Or how about skittles?"

His eye snagged on a game farther afield, and he pointed at the thirty-foot-high pole in the center of the green. "What is *that*?"

"See the large lump at the top of the pole?"

He squinted. "Aye."

"That's a joint of mutton. The first man to scale the pole and grab the meat, gets to keep it."

"Is that all?" he scoffed. "I've climbed masts higher than that."

"There's just one small obstacle." She couldn't quite contain the smile building. Smiles were tending to accumulate at a high rate around this man. "The pole is greased."

As if to illustrate the difficulty of successfully snatching a joint of mutton off the top of a greased pole, a man stripped off his shirt, cracked his knuckles, and attacked the pole, clawing his way up, barely making it six feet before sliding to land on his generous rump with a solid thud. Small snickers and outright jeers rippled through the crowd.

Nylander shrugged off his overcoat and handed it to Callie. "That's the one for me."

She accepted the garment and folded it over her forearm. "You must enjoy a challenge."

His eye, keen and serious, met hers. "Never could resist one."

His words stole all the breath from her body. All she could do was stand there, hold his coat, and watch him stride determinedly away toward a greased-up pole and a mutton trophy with his name surely writ upon it. He pushed into the fray and made quick conversation with the man who looked to be in charge. Before she could blink, Nylander had pulled his shirt over his head.

It was as if a lightning bolt had struck earth. The crowd went electric at the sight of him, the corded muscles of arms, chest, and back rippling beneath exposed flesh. But that wasn't all that had the town struck dumb. It was his tattoos, littered across his skin, harkening to places unknown, to a life lived beyond the confines of the north Devon coast.

Slowly, Callie approached, her gaze never once leaving him. In the full, midday sun, the man was nothing less than magnificent. That was the truth, and everyone understood it.

He surveyed the pole and ran a finger down its length.

"Pig lard," one man piped up, "in case yer wonderin'."

"That would explain the smell," Nylander responded, eliciting a few chuckles.

He reached around the pole, hugging white pine tight to his chest, pig lard making a squishing sound that elicited a few sickened groans. Then he did the same with his legs. Instantly, he slid to the ground, landing flat on his bottom with a solid thunk. While the crowd roared with laughter—mayhap buoyed by a relief that he wasn't quite the god he appeared—he pushed to his feet and dusted himself off. With a wry smile, he snatched his discarded shirt off the ground.

"What?" a rough man's voice shouted. "Givin' up already?"

Again, the crowd howled. Even so, Nylander began to reassess the pole, and silence descended. He flapped his shirt open and began rubbing it up and down the pole as high as he could reach, sloughing off layers of pig lard with each pass.

Unwittingly, he was also offering quite a view of his torso. The play of muscle beneath tan skin was very much appreciated by the female contingent of the crowd, if their collective held breath was any indicator.

Clutching the shirt in one hand, he wrapped his arms and legs around the pole, locking one foot around the other ankle. This time he found purchase and didn't slide. He began shimmying up, increment by increment, wiping at the pole along the way. Every few feet he lost a bit of ground and slid an inch or two. Then his powerful thighs squeezed together and stopped any momentum that wanted to land him flat on his bum again.

Hands clenched into fists at her sides, Callie willed him up that pole with every last cell in her body. Buoyed by the crowd's increasing good will and his own determination, there was no way that joint of mutton wouldn't be his. Was it strange that she might envy a slab of meat?

The higher he climbed, the more wound up the crowd became until, at last, he reached the top and grabbed the joint of mutton. Triumphant, he waved it over his head, inciting the crowd into a frenzy. Meat firm in hand, he released his thighs and began sliding. His feet struck earth with a heavy thump to a hail of hearty congratulations and jocular slaps on the back.

He set the meat onto the ground long enough to shake the pig lard out of his shirt and slip it over his head. His gaze cast about until it found her. He stalked forward, and her heart gave a little skip. The champion of the fall festival was moving toward *her*.

The crowd intuited his intent as they parted, opening a clear path. A fiery blush blazed across her skin, but she cared not. How could she? Not when the glorious Captain John Nylander held her in his sights with that hot glint in his eye.

He drew within a few feet of her and stopped. Silently, he held out his trophy. "For you, my lady."

He could've been holding an armful of diamonds, and his gift couldn't have meant more to her.

It meant everything.

Transfixed silence surrounded them, but Nylander hadn't a care, not while Callie's wide, serious eyes held his.

One side of her mouth, then the other, curled up, and there it was: her smile. She brought her hand to her lips to cover it. He wished she wouldn't. He liked her this way.

Someone approached, haltingly, and cleared his throat. Her smile slipped. "Yes, Will?"

"I'll be taking the mutton."

"Is the pit ready?"

"Aye."

The man reached for the joint of meat. Nylander frowned, but gave it up. Will lugged the mutton away, a crowd forming at the man's back. "That was for *you*." He couldn't seem to keep a note of petulance out of his voice.

Callie's smile returned. "I'll have some after it's been roasted. But it's more symbolic than anything. The town will have meat today, courtesy of you."

Nylander allowed his disgruntlement to fall away.

Callie sniffed the air. "You smell like a farmer."

"Pig lard."

He thought she would crinkle her nose and distance herself from him. Instead, she said, "I don't mind," and laced her arm through his. The woman really was unlike any other.

The breeze picked up the harmonious scents of baked goods and apple cider and swirled them through the air. Children, with no care for the adult world, brushed past them, intent on their game of chase and their unsupervised good time. Nylander had never experienced such a joyous day, or had the opportunity to allow such joy to flow through him.

So, too, did Callie feel it. It was in the way she greeted the townsfolk, unreserved smile on her lips and in her eyes. They had never seen her like this, which was apparent in their reactions to her. Bewilderment. Confusion. Then, one by one, they decided they liked this version of Lady St. Alban and returned her smile.

It was as if he and she combined through some mysterious alchemy to bring out the best qualities in each other.

A pair of familiar forms snagged at the periphery of his vision. *Excise men.* Foreboding cut into his joy like a sobering tonic.

Tomorrow.

Today, he had this woman and this joy running through his veins. He wouldn't let tomorrow, and whatever it may hold, dilute it.

"Oh," Callie exclaimed, her hand tightening on his forearm as she pulled him through a loose crowd of onlookers, "the apple bobbing contest!"

Before them was a circle of girls and young women gathered around a large tank of water with apples floating on its surface.

"I've never ducked for apples."

He heard something in her voice. Something last night and this perfect day gave him permission to pursue. "Why not?"

Callie raised a single, imperious eyebrow. "Under no circumstances does a *Calpurnia* duck for apples."

"What about a *Callie?*"

A conspiratorial smile formed about her mouth. It felt like a gift, the best he'd ever received. "I rather suspect she does. But—"

The smile slipped, and an anxious knot formed in his stomach. *"But?"*

"Only unmarried young women play."

"Isn't that you?"

Her smile slid back into place, and all felt right with the world again. She slipped her arm from his and stepped up to the tank to the raised eyebrows of her soon-to-be competitors. She rolled her sleeves above her elbows and wrapped her fingers around the metal edge, body braced and tense, determination clear in her eye. His Callie was a competitive one.

His Callie.

Aye, that she was.

The master of ceremonies harrumphed. "Are the ladies all on their marks?"

Anxious nods of assent and a few yeses scattered around the tank.

"One... two... three... to the apples!"

No one needed to be told twice, a dozen heads ducked into the water, face first, mouths open, teeth intent on being the first to crunch into sweet, crisp flesh and come up the winner. Out of time with each other, heads popped up sporadically, heads soaked, eyes squinched shut, mouths sputtering for air, and then it was into the drink again. There was no room for vanity in an apple bobbing contest.

A few participants stepped back in forfeit, while others steamed on. Callie fell into the latter category. She came up blinking and sputtering more times than he could count, but never once did her focus waver. An apple floated into reach on a splashy wave, and teeth bared, resolve in her eye, she went for it, face buried in the turbulent water. Of a sudden, she sprang up, the apple, bright and red, between her teeth.

"We have a winner!" the master of ceremonies cried out.

The shoulders of the other participants slumped in defeat, their hands clapping in half-hearted applause.

"The next to marry will be our very own Lady St. Alban," the man continued.

The applause fell off, punctuated by a few fractious murmurs. Callie glanced about the gathering sheepishly, and the flush of vigor transformed into a full-on blush. The man's words rather went along with Nylander's way of thinking, truth be told. But that truth could wait until later. Until after tomorrow.

The master of ceremonies winked. "And don't forget to tuck it under your pillow tonight, milady."

Apple in hand, Callie returned to Nylander. Wet strands of hair clinging to her cheeks, she stopped not two feet from him. The woman was likely soaked to the skin. She was the most adorable thing he'd ever seen.

Adorable? A word he'd never once used, or even thought, in his life. He'd been reduced to a man who thought words like *adorable*, and he minded not one whit. "Your dress is definitely ruined now."

She shrugged. The hand holding the apple lifted and held, and it struck him: she was offering it to him.

It felt Biblical. She was Eve, and he Adam. Fate offered no choice but he take it. His gaze never once releasing hers, he brought the fruit to his mouth. He took a bite, and her mouth formed an "O" of surprise.

He stepped forward, into her orbit, and lowered his face, unable to resist her apple-sweet, forbidden mouth a moment longer. Her head tipped back and an acquiescent sigh escaped her parted lips as her lashes fluttered shut. Luscious anticipation glittered through his veins. This kiss would be the start of something new and wondrous. It would seal the beginning.

A horn blared, piercing and tinny, and a hue-and-cry raised in the distance.

Callie's eyes flew open, wide and frantic. Her mouth not an inch from his, sweet sugary breath whispering across his lips, she spoke, "It's time."

"*It's time?*"

Her eyes darting from side to side, she sprang away from him, and he felt her absence like an ache in his body.

But there wasn't time for such mawkishness. The woman was poised on the edge of flight, like a criminal.

Or prey.

She hiked her skirts to her knees and met his eye long enough to say, "Wish me luck?"

Alarm clanged through Nylander and sent his pulse racing. She might be poised for flight, but he felt the fight rearing up in him. "*Luck?* For what?" The questions met her back as she raced off, her feet fleeter than a deer's.

"There she is!" cried out a group of lads with no more than thirty years between the three of them. "Get 'er!"

The hairs on Nylander's nape prickled to a stand. He followed the chase, others joining the fray every few steps. On the periphery of the mob, he spotted the old man from the Devil's Books. With his weather-beaten face and un-concerned gait, this man was bound to know what was going on.

When Nylander asked just that, the old man issued a phlegmy chuckle. "The Baptism of the Duke of Muck." Another wet laugh sounded, this one productive. "Well, *duchess* in this case."

They were back on High Street, and Nylander caught a flash of green silk streak past the opening between two buildings, the increasingly large mob not three seconds behind. They were gaining on her, likely because her stiff ankle was slowing her down.

"Aye," the old man continued, "she'll lead them on a merry chase, the Wyld Hare will."

"Will someone please state plainly what the bloody hell is going on?" Nylander wasn't keen on fighting this entire town for her, but if it turned out he needed to, well, he would.

"Cool yer blood, me boy," the old man said, dismissive. "The Duke of Muck washed up on these shores nigh two 'undred years ago. Shipwrecked, 'e was one stormy night. Wadn't long before 'e started infecting the town with 'is drinkin', whorin', and gen'ral licentiousness. A proud sinner was the Duke of Muck, and 'e wore out 'is welcome right quick with 'is wretched, immoral ways." He held up a finger while he hawked up a wad of phlegm and spit it onto the ground. "So one night the town rousted 'im up from 'is favorite 'ore's bed and chased 'im naked to the sea. When they got 'im there, they did like good Christian folk and baptized 'im."

Nylander hardly heard the end of the tale, for he'd become stuck on a single word. *Naked.* His hands curled into hard fists. "They don't think they're going to strip Call—her ladyship *naked*, do they?"

Over his lifeless corpse.

"Yer a feisty lad, aren't ye?" An inquisitive blue eye peered up at him from beneath its wrinkled lid. "None of them lords and squires 'oo've owned Wyldcombe Grange over the years would've agreed to it, if that was the case." Mischief twinkled out at Nylander. "Not with their bodies soft and buttery as clotted cream."

Another flash of green striped across Nylander's vision. Callie was, indeed, leading a merry chase. As he neared the beach where High Street ended into the sea, the density of the crowd intensified, and he became separated from the old man. He kept pushing through, taking notice of the expressions on everyone's faces. Warm smiles, easy with sun and cider, abounded. This was no angry mob.

Callie wasn't in danger. He relaxed a bit. A man he'd never seen in his life shoved a glass of cider into his hand. "Well done with the pole. Never been able to manage it meself."

Another man slapped him on the back. He'd been at sea with sailors, had experienced their rough camaraderie, but it was a community of shifting sands. Not solid like the land. Not like this place. These jocular slaps on the back and proffered ciders told him that he'd been accepted. This could be his community. Not just *his*, but *theirs*, his and Callie's.

Their community.

Their future.

A loud, rhythmic clanging of cymbals crashed through the air, marching closer, firing up the crowd, who parted to make way for a group of three, two men and their prisoner, the Duchess of Muck.

Callie. Filthy and bedraggled, she played her part without restraint, leering and snarling at the townsfolk as they began chanting, "Repent! Repent!"

They reached the end of the road, the shore's edge, and stopped, a throng filling in behind them. The crowd quieted before descending into a tetchy silence.

"Duchess of Muck," one of Callie's jailors shouted for all to hear, "do ye repent of yer sins?"

A pin could've dropped with a loud clatter, so quiet had the crowd gone.

Callie dropped to her knees and lifted her hands to the sky. "I repent!"

Her other jailor scooped a large quantity of water into a large bucket, and, before Nylander could glean the man's purpose, sloshed the bucket's full contents into Callie's face, surely dousing her clear through to the skin.

Sodden and sputtering, she reached out blindly. A tankard of cider was shoved into her hand. She brought it to her mouth and began downing its contents, gulp after gulp. Wet, red strings of hair clinging to her face, her eyes blinked open, and she turned the glass upside-down, proving she'd drained the glass to the last drop in one go.

"The Duchess of Muck has repented, and the harvest is good!" the master of ceremonies cried, and the crowd roared its loudest cheer of the day.

"Didn't know she 'ad it in 'er," a male voice said somewhere behind him.

"Mama," came a girl's awed whisper, "'Er Ladyship is so *brave.*"

Pride like no other swelled up inside Nylander. He pushed his way through the excitable horde until, at last, he reached her. He stopped just shy of her, wanting to take her in. She radiated a joy like he'd never seen.

She'd been accepted. Like him, she was part of this community. They would build a life together here. The certainty planted roots deep into his heart, deep into his soul.

As one, they stepped forward, the puckered tips of her breasts a hairsbreadth away from his chest. 'Twas only him and her in this space.

It was all that mattered.

It was all that would ever matter.

Her face tipped up, and his slanted down. "You know what I love most?"

"What?"

"Not a *what*, but a *who*."

"Oh," she sighed.

The sun dipped below the horizon, inky night chasing day into darkness. His lips touched hers, and her arms curled about his neck, her lithe body straining up the length of his. The tip of her tongue skated along his bottom lip, and his hands found the indent of her waist, holding her steady, pulling her into him.

His tongue met hers in a tangle, and through the cocoon surrounding them floated scandalized tuts, rowdy woots, and one definite, "*Finally.*"

Then ripped another sound: a great explosive *barrroooom!*

Callie's eyes flew open and held his. This wasn't a poetic, metaphorical *barrroooom!* borne of their blossoming desire. Rather, it was an explosion borne of the physical world that shook the earth beneath their feet and streaked the sky above a not-too-far distant hill. For a trio of rapid heartbeats, shocked silence descended upon the town as the acrid scent of smoke carried in on the wind.

"That came from the Grange's lands," Callie whispered, eyes wide, frantic.

Gut-deep fear pulsed through Nylander. "Who was guarding the cliff barn?"

"No one, except—" She shook her head, anguish in her eyes.

"Except?" he prodded.

"Pierre."

Another explosion sounded, this one larger than the last, and the town broke apart on a roar and burst into hysteria.

Before Callie could tear herself away, Nylander tightened his grasp, protective. He searched her eyes. He didn't much care for what he found there.

Fear... panic. Those were the expected emotions. He saw others, too. *Knowledge. Remorse.*

Callie twisted out of his arms and ran toward the orange light streaking the distant sky. His feet kicking into stride to catch her, or at least keep up with her, uncertainty sank long claws into him. Had he lost her before he'd ever really had the chance to have her?

Tomorrow had arrived a day early.

29

F rantic breath puffing white in the crisp autumn night air, Callie ran. Faster than they'd ever run in their five and twenty years, her feet ate up the distance between her and the orange-stained horizon, clouded by tufts of dense gray smoke.

It wasn't the main house. The fire was too close to the water. It was the cliff barn.

The brandy... it was surely adding fuel to this fire. That was the last two years of her life gone up in flame. And she knew in her gut she'd had a hand in its destruction.

This perfect day had been a mirage... an exercise in self-delusion. Before her was reality, her dreams incinerating into memory. Even though she heard Nylander's heavy tread close at her heels, he was behind her, too. In more ways than one.

She swiped at the moisture on her cheeks and ran past the thought. She couldn't let her heart ache now. There would be plenty of time for that later... the rest of her life.

Across damp gorse and scratchy heather, she raced, her dress clutched at her thighs, her lungs burning with exertion and smoke from the barn. Heat intensified the nearer she drew.

Still, a measure of hope gathered in her chest. Although there had been the two explosions, the fire hadn't really caught hold. *Yet.*

But the barn wasn't her first concern.

"Pierre!" she shouted into the darkness, her voice a jagged scrape across her throat. *"Pierre!"*

A figure shambled out of an amorphous clump of shrubbery. "Pipe down, the Maker isn't ready for me yet." There stood Pierre, as laconic and French as she'd ever seen him. She could hug the man. "Good thing I needed to piss when I did."

Nylander rushed up, his breath puffing loud and hard. "Where's the well?"

Before Callie could direct him, Will and Cam joined their group. "Will, you and Cam get the Newsham pump," she commanded. To those who were just arriving, she cried out, "Everyone grab a bucket, a glass, anything that will hold water and get that pump filled!"

"A Newsham pump?" Nylander asked to her back as she was already on the move to help Will and Cam set up the device.

"For extinguishing fires," she called over her shoulder. "I bought one last year when we increased our production."

They found Will and Cam tugging, pushing, and pulling the heavy and awkward machine out of a storage shed. They weren't getting very far, very slowly.

"Here," Nylander called out, brushing around Callie, "I'll take the back, each of you take a side."

As they made slow progress across a grassed-over path, Callie grabbed the hose attachment and went to check the progress of the bucket brigade that snaked in a wavy line from well to barn. "Pierre! Kip!" she called.

Kip bounced into view, eyes bright with alarm and excitement, and Pierre shouted, "What is it now?"

"Kip, run to the Grange and gather every bucket you can find." The boy nodded and scampered off. She turned to Pierre. "Make sure this line extends to the Newsham pump." She pointed toward the spot where the men had pushed the machine. "If the fire reaches the rafters, what remains of the still can't possibly be salvaged."

"Are you implying the still is the cause of this conflagration? That it exploded?"

"Pierre, we haven't time for that right now," she shouted.

But, of course, it was the still. What else would cause such an explosion?

Yet her gut told her it wasn't negligence on Pierre's part that had started it. Rather, purpose on someone else's part. *Jack Le Grand.* Explosions didn't happen randomly when a pirate skulked about the vicinity.

Pierre snapped to and shuffled to his duty, shouting orders to anyone who would listen. Callie raced back to Will, Cam, and Nylander, who had just pushed the pump into position. With trembling, panicked hands, she attached the hose as buckets began sloshing water into the pump's lead tank. It was too early for hope, but there was a chance they could salvage something from this disaster.

Nylander appeared at her side, his face black as a thundercloud. Ache panged in her gut for the man who had been hers last night and today, a Nylander she would never have again. Not once he knew how this disaster had started.

And her part in it.

"Do you know who did this?"

She nodded. Nothing useful would come out of denying the fact. "Do you?"

"Aye."

He *knew.* A knife twisted in her gut. He was never going to be hers, not if he *knew.* She inhaled the sob that wanted release.

"The explosion came from beneath the still," he continued.

Confusion coupled with alarm spiked through her. "It wasn't from the still?"

He shook his head and pointed. "See that?"

She did now. Between the barn and the cliff's edge, the ground was cratered in.

"The explosion originated below."

"The brandy," she whispered.

"Surely blown into smithereens and adding fuel to the fire."

The breath left her body in one great whoosh, and she wrapped her arms around her gut from the pain of it. To hear it spoken aloud—the utter and complete destruction of her hopes and dreams—it was too much.

"Is there another entrance to that cellar?" he asked, the question cutting through the wool in her ears.

Callie snapped to. "The old mine shaft." She began running. "This way."

Lungs full of acrid smoke, she found the familiar sheep path that led around the barn and down the cliffside, her feet picking across rocks and tufts of grass with the expertise borne of experience. Nylander was just behind her, his feet imprinting on her every step. After one switchback, then another, she slowed, her hand feeling along the cliff wall for the cave's opening as they stepped off the defined portion of the trail and onto the goat scramble, bits of stone crumbling beneath their feet as they scooched along the cliff's face.

"Is this safe?" came his voice behind her.

"Safe enough for wild goats."

"Reassuring."

His dry humor warmed her, even as it made her long to howl with despair. Her palms scraped and bleeding, she, at last, found the opening. "We're here," she whispered. "Three more steps for you."

Callie scuttled into the cave blacker than night and acrid with gunpowder. Nylander slipped inside behind her. They were forever finding themselves in deep, dark caves.

"'Bout time," sounded a voice full of gravel and whiskey.

Flint scratched striker and the cave flickered into light. Callie's eyes adjusted to the brightness and saw Jack Le Grand standing beside a lanky lad with skin the color of creamy tea.

"Took ye long enough to get down here, Johnny boy."

"Johnny boy?" Callie asked. "Who is—"

The question died in her mouth.

Jack Le Grand was a powerfully built man. But also a shadow of the man he would've been thirty years ago.

That man stood beside her.

The truth clicked into place. It had been there all along, in their build, their hair, their eyes, their bone structure. In the same lopsided smile.

But that was as far as the resemblance went. For all that Nylander was the spitting image of Le Grand, he was nothing like him.

"This man"—she pointed at the pirate—"is your father?"

"A loosely defined version of one, yes."

Forgetful of her place and the circumstances of this meeting, scorn and rage bubbled up and all other concerns fell away. This was Nylander's *father*. The man who…

"*You,*" she growled.

"'Tis I, Jack Le Grand." He tipped his hat, and his gold hoop earring caught a glimmer of lamplight. "The one and only."

She advanced a step forward. "You… you *monster.*"

A well-worn chuckle sounded from the pirate. "Ye ain't the first to call me that. And won't be the last neither."

"You threw your son into the sea. You left him to drown and be eaten by sharks. What sort of man abandons his son like that?

"Abandoned him?" Bewilderment knitted the pirate's weathered brow. "I gave him the best life a father could."

Nylander scoffed beside her, but her attention remained fixed on Jack Le Grand. "Can it be that you actually believe your words?" she asked.

"Why wouldn't I?" His eye shifted toward Nylander. "The *Free Reaver* was no good place for ye back then."

Nylander pointed at the lad, whose light hazel gaze watched the proceedings in silence. Those intelligent eyes missed nothing, Callie was sure. "How is it any different for him?"

"Haven't ye heard?" Jack Le Grand asked. "The *Free Reaver* has her letters of marque, bought 'n' paid for and signed by King George himself." He gave a formal bow. "She's gone right respectable. Although I must say, livin' on the straight arrow is provin' to be a sight more dangerous than bein' the danger itself. Pirates are a right nasty lot."

"How does that justify you leaving your son for dead?" Callie asked.

"That's where yer wrong, luv." Jack Le Grand settled one hip against a boulder and sucked his teeth. "Years, I'd been goin' round and round with the Van Rijns. For all our fallin's out, I knew them for good, Christian people. They were on the side o' right more times than yers truly, that's sure. I knew they'd take Johnny boy. I'da staked me life on it."

"Except you didn't," Callie cut in. "You staked his."

A sheepish look crossed the pirate's face. "I'll concede that point. It were a gamble." His gaze never once left Nylander. "But look how it paid off for ye."

Nylander's eyes narrowed. "The past is done. Why did you blow up the barn?"

"Ye truly don't know why."

Understanding hit Callie a beat later, and her gut sank into the stone beneath her feet. "You did it for your son," she whispered, the hiss and truth of her words echoing off the cave's walls. It had been the truth from the beginning. And she thought she'd been in control? She'd been nothing more than a pawn in a game she hadn't realized she was playing.

"This is why you agreed to the twenty thousand pounds up front. You never intended to pay it."

The pirate snorted. "Figured that out all by yer lonesome, did ye?"

Her gaze found Nylander's, frightened to her bones of what she would find there and the answer to the question she must ask.

"Have you been in league all this time?"

30

Nylander's world upended on itself and went topsy-turvy. "In league?"

"Of course," Callie said, a shell hardening over the hurt in her eyes. "It makes perfect sense. This whole time, you knew."

"Knew what?" he asked, slowly, to buy time. Her insinuation was clear.

"That Lord St. Alban wanted to sell the Grange to you," she replied, her tone growing hard as well. "And you worked together with this"—she pointed an accusatory finger toward Jack—"with your *father* to sabotage my chances of purchasing the Grange."

Nylander's gut dropped. "You have it all wrong."

"It explains everything," Callie continued, unheedful, and began ticking items off her fingers. "The cow in the orchard. The damage to the wheel mill. The lost flock of sheep. You had access to it all."

"No."

"The *seduction*."

Jack gave a randy whistle.

"It was all part of your plan," Callie continued. "And today? I thought it was real." Her voice hitched on that last word. *Real.*

"It was absolutely real. Every moment."

How had it gone so wrong, so fast? It didn't seem possible.

"That a man like *you* could find a woman like *me*—" She stopped. *Attractive. Desirable.* Those were the words left unspoken. "Now everything you ever wanted is yours for the taking." She lifted empty hands and let them drop to her sides. "You won. I would say fair and square, but this fight was never fair."

She turned to flee, but Nylander caught her arm as she brushed past. She smelled of dirt and grass and ocean spray and sweet apple cider. She smelled of everything he loved in this world, including herself.

"*Callie,*" he said, low, for her ears alone.

Her eyes startled up to meet his. For an instant, confusion and indecision shone up at him, enough to give him a glimmer of hope. The next, they went flat and unreadable.

The sound of heavy footsteps rushing into the cave sounded behind Nylander, and he had just enough time to register the stricken expression on Jack's face before a shout sounded. "Halt in the name of the King's justice!"

Callie gasped, and Nylander pivoted to find the excise men, faces like granite, serious fists clenched and ready for a fight, if it came to that.

Nylander didn't hesitate. "There's the man you seek." His finger pointed dead-square at Jack.

Incredulity spread across his face. "Grassed out by me own blood?"

Nylander hadn't time for Jack's bruised feelings as the excise men's gazes had shifted.

"And she is?"

He stepped in front of Callie, blocking their view of her. "The Dowager Viscountess St. Alban," he stated, imbuing the title with its full, aristocratic consequence to dazzle and distract. The ploy appeared to work as they shifted on their feet in the presence of their *better.* "Jack Le Grand is the man you seek."

The excise men nodded and stepped forward. Nylander made eye contact with Callie and jerked his chin toward the cave's entrance. This could turn ugly, and he wanted her out of here.

Protest in her eyes, her mouth began to form the words that were surely following. He shook his head and mouthed, "Now."

Still, she stood rooted in place, as if she wanted to tell him something. He must convince her to leave this second. *"The fire,"* he whispered.

In an instant, panic replaced stubbornness, and her feet were moving. At the mouth of the cave, just before she disappeared into the dark, she gave him one last look. He couldn't read it, that look. Then she was gone.

A void, black and heavy, opened inside him. She thought him in league with Jack to steal the Grange out from under her. His hands fisted, and he returned his attention to the group. The excise men had Jack cornered, closing in by small steps.

"Now, you can keep your pretty face intact," began one of the excise men. "If you come with us all docile, like a lamb," finished the other.

Jack barked out a laugh. "Me face ain't been pretty in more years than ye've been on this earth. So if ye be lyin' about that, I gotta wonder what else ye be lyin' about?"

Nylander's fists clenched tighter, and he stepped forward. "Would you mind if I have a word with me dear old pa?"

As one, the excise men nodded and stepped back.

Nylander prowled forward. The loss of Callie settled deeper into his soul with each step, with every beat of his heart. He'd lost her. Because of the man before him, who looked upon the world as one big joke. "You're like gangrene," he growled. "All you touch turns to rot."

Jack cocked his head. "Is this about Her Highness?" He sucked his teeth. "Let her go, Johnny boy. Any woman that would truck with the likes o' me ain't worth havin', that I kin tell ye fer free."

Nylander's world went dull and flat and meaningless. The blackness he'd been holding at bay was given free rein, and he swung around and landed a solid right hook to Jack's jaw. The pirate stumbled back and just caught himself on a boulder before he hit the ground. Seized by blind fury, Nylander advanced. He grabbed the man's collar and jerked him upright, positioning him for another blow. He reared his arm back and hesitated. If he struck Jack again, he wouldn't be able to stop until the man was nothing more than a pulpy mass of bones and skin.

He hadn't yet lowered his fist when a strong, trembling hand wrapped around his upper arm. His gaze cut to meet Lash's steady and wide upon him. Ever silent and observant, the lad could be easy to forget. Which would be a mistake, Nylander knew down to his bones. Only a fool would underestimate the lad and the man he was destined to become.

Nylander knew something else, too: he would have to work his way through Lash if he was to continue going after Jack. The fight drained out of him. He wouldn't be exchanging blows with this lad, his half-brother, not in an eternity of lifetimes.

Ahead, Jack made a big show of working his jaw and swiping a trickle of blood from the corner of his mouth with the back of his hand. "See what I mean?" He looked to the excise men. "I knew me pretty face wasn't gonna make it out without a few bruises."

They shrugged and settled in against the cave wall, apparently content to let this family drama play out without interference.

What a bloody fecking day. The numbing effect of adrenaline fading fast, Nylander winced and shook out his hand. He'd likely broken a few knuckles on that bloody bastard's face.

"Judgin' by yer right hook, the sailor's life has been treatin' ye well." Jack slouched forward and braced his elbows on his knees. "Could use me beloved boy on the *Free Reaver*. The straight life on the high seas is a sight more dangerous than an out-and-out pirate's."

Bitterness, acrid and metallic, hit Nylander. "You have your beloved boy sailing with you."

Jack's head cocked to the side. "And ye think yer not me beloved boy? Ye think I truly gave you up?"

"I have no reason to believe otherwise."

Jack's chest puffed up with indignation. "Whose colors do ye think ye've been sailin' under all these years?"

Nylander held his tongue. This conversation wasn't worth his breath.

Jack jabbed his thumb into his chest. "Mine, that's whose."

"You're going soft in the head," Nylander scoffed.

"What? Ye've never once been attacked. Ye think yer the luckiest sailor who ever navigated the high seas?" Jack sifted his weight to rest his elbows on the stone at his back. "No one's that lucky."

Dread snaked through Nylander.

"Ye've sailed beneath my protection, Johnny boy. Ye think anyone would dare touch ye, the son of Jack Le Grand? I kept one finger on ye, made it me business to know all that affected ye. And who needed to know it, knew it."

"I can hold my own."

"Of course, ye can. Like that one"—he nodded toward Lash—"yer me *beloved* boy."

"Get this in your head, Jack. I'm your *nothing*. After that day, we can never be anything to each other. And not after what you've done to Callie."

Jack waggled a leering eyebrow. "*Callie?*"

Nylander ground his teeth together and kept his mouth shut.

"Why can't ye see?" Jack asked. Was that a ribbon of hurt threading through the question?

"See what?"

"I've given ye everythin' ye ever wanted."

The words hit Nylander with the force of a blow. Jack truly believed them.

Jack held up one finger. "A family with the Van Rijns." Another finger joined the first. "Land with Wyldcombe Grange. Why can't ye see?"

Nylander did see. In Jack's twisted version, he'd acted

out of fatherly love. "You haven't given me everything I've wanted. You've only pushed her out of my reach."

Jack waved his words away. "Women come and go, Johnny boy. Ye've had one, ye've had 'em all."

"I know all about your view of women."

"Well, yer ma had her charms, that's sure. And Lash's ma, she's somethin' special."

"All done with your family chat?" asked one of the excise men as he pushed off the wall. The other dug a pair of cuffs out of his voluminous overcoat. "You gonna come easy?"

"Aye," Jack assented.

A gun cocked, and, in an instant, the cave went on alert. Four sets of eyes swung toward the source. There stood Lash, eyes wide, hands trembling, gun pointed dead center at one of the excise men's chest. "You'll not be layin' a finger on me pa."

Nylander started forward, but Jack met his eye and gave a slight shake of his head. Nylander froze. The situation was spiraling out of control, as situations tended to do around Jack. Yet he was the only man in this cave, right now, who could stop the spiral.

Jack held up a steadying hand. "No, son, I can't let ye ruin yer life o'er the like o' me. I'll be goin' with these men. The King's justice needs to be served and all."

"But, Pa—"

Jack shook his head. "Ye stay with yer brother and learn from him." His canny eye shifted to Nylander. "And, ye see the lad gets some schoolin' in him."

Lash lowered the gun, and Nylander secured the weapon from the lad's slack hands. The excise men grabbed Jack.

"Ain't no need fer these cuffs, boys. If I wanted to escape, ye couldn't hold me."

His captors might've rolled their eyes skyward, but they made no further move to bind Jack. As they strode past, Jack turned to his sons one last time. "Ye ain't seen the last of me, me boys."

The trio disappeared into the night, leaving Nylander

alone with Lash, a lad he hardly knew, a lad whose welfare was now his responsibility. A lad whose eyes reflected back at him a pain that had been inflicted on him twenty-five years ago. For he, too, had once loved Jack that deeply.

"He's not worth it," Nylander said, knowing full well the lad wasn't ready to hear those words. "He'll only break your heart."

Lash swiped at his eyes with the back of his hand. "What do you know?"

Of broken hearts? Quite a bit. "Follow me," was all he said.

He strode out of the cave, the lad's soft tread at his back, and into the fallen night. Of necessity, they shortened their step when they reached the inches-wide goat scramble and the cliff's edge, their progress slow and painstaking on this return trip without Callie as a guide.

At last, they reached the top, and the fire appeared in the distance, its fiery orange a few shades dimmer than it had been a half hour ago. The fire was getting under control.

Outside the edge of light, figures silhouetted by varying shades of darkness and light scurried to do the bidding of the woman at the helm. *Callie.* The township hustled to fulfill her commands, every last one, confident their mistress knew what she was about.

"Come," Nylander tossed to the lad at his side, feet already on the move. "We need to see this through."

Careful to keep his distance from Callie, Nylander and Lash found a section of thatch along the barn's back roofline that needed more dousing. All the while, he kept half an eye out for her. Believing what she did of him, she wouldn't want him here.

The dull, flat feeling that rendered the world blank and meaningless again hollowed out his insides. She believed him in league with Jack Le Grand. Why shouldn't she? If he'd just told her at the very beginning what he knew, there might've been a chance for them.

Likely not.

His luck didn't work that way.

The last twenty-four hours had been nothing more than an exercise in delusion of the most massive proportions. Had he really thought he'd be lucky enough to spend the rest of his life with her?

He was the scum beneath her feet.

The air saturated with smoldering ember and thatch, Lash met his eye. "Where to next?"

"The fire is under control." He sounded as dull and flat as his soul felt. "It's time to leave, now."

"Where are we going, then?"

"To London."

Nylander's feet kicked into motion, away from the cliff barn, away from *her*, determination gathering steam with each stride. He had a few matters to sort out in London.

Jake wouldn't like the way he wished to resolve the matter of Wyldcombe Grange, but he would do as Nylander requested.

Then it was on with his life.

Without her.

———

DIRT AND GRAVEL crunched beneath Callie's swift feet, the only sound in the interminable night, as she made swift progress toward the main house. Only the race of her heart was faster.

Where was he?

He'd returned to help with the fire alongside Jack Le Grand's lad, but in the chaos of it all, she'd lost track of them. Once the fire was nothing more than damp, smoldering ashes, she'd discovered they were gone.

Her feet, blistered and sore, notched up their pace. There was something she must tell him.

No, not *tell*.

Ask.

She would sink to her knees and ask, nay, *beg* for his forgiveness for thinking, even for a moment, that he'd been in league with a villain like Jack Le Grand. Shameful, unthinkable, utterly, disgustingly wrong, were the words she'd spoken to him.

In that moment, she'd let every bad word she'd been called to her face and behind her back—*unnatural, mannish*—whisper in her ear. How could a Viking warrior angel like Captain John Nylander possibly feel the way she wanted him to feel? There must be trickery involved, the malicious whispers went. They'd overridden not only her good sense, but, most importantly, what she knew of him in her heart.

And when the excise men had rushed in and he'd protected her, the knowledge of how deeply she'd wronged him sank sharp claws into her as she'd rushed to tend her duty as temporary mistress of Wyldcombe Grange.

The roof had been saved. The Charentais still was salvageable. It would live on to distill apple brandy another day.

The brandy, every last cask, was lost to the explosion. She wouldn't be purchasing the Grange. That, too, was lost to her. In truth, it had never really been within her reach.

But that wasn't at all what she must tell him. Not even close.

The house drew closer, and just ahead, in the stable yard, movement caught her eye. She slowed her feet to a stop as two riders, Jack Le Grand's lad and *him*, mounted their horses in the distance. She backed off the path and faded into shrubbery gray with shadowy night.

He was leaving. Before… a hollow void, as deep and infinite as the universe extending above her head, opened inside her… before she could ask, *beg*, for his forgiveness.

There would be no absolution for her sins. Which was exactly what she deserved.

A quick twist of the reins and a soft click of the tongue, and the horses whirled onto the path. The riders raced past her without the faintest notion of her presence. She clambered out from behind the protective shrub, her eyes squinting into the distance, determined to keep on him until the night swallowed him whole.

As if her heart had been putting off the inevitable, it

now took leave to fully break in two, then four, and on and on, until the pieces of it were nothing more than powdered dust. Wyldcombe Grange... Nylander... they were lost to her, decidedly and irrevocably.

And now, oh, irony of ironies, those which were lost would belong to each other. The Grange would be Nylander's. He'd won it.

He would make a bloody good squire. He had the respect and admiration of the tenants and town, which was something she'd never been able to accomplish in her years here. This outcome had been destined from the very beginning.

Except, hadn't there been a moment tonight? On the shore wild with laughter and revelry, when she'd downed the glass of cider and the townsfolk had roared their approval, hadn't she been like him and one of them in that moment?

She took one step forward, then another, away from memories that would drive her toward madness if she allowed them purchase. Through the kitchens, up the grand staircase, she continued until she found her bed, where she laid her exhausted body, still clad in the emerald silk dress, now ragged and sodden. Her soot-flecked head found the pristine white pillow, a pillow no longer hers.

It would belong to the man she'd lost.

31

CHRISTMAS EVE

"How about this?" Jane slipped the wire hook into the eye and stepped away, her head tilted in assessment.

Callie rolled her shoulders, testing the fabric encircling her chest, and released a sigh of relief. "Much better."

"And the waistband on the trousers?"

Callie buttoned them with ease.

"Not too snug anymore?"

"They're perfect."

Jane's eye fell on Callie's midsection. She resisted the urge to squirm.

"How curious that your body decided to gain weight in your breasts and around your waist. I can't say I've seen a case quite like it. This usually happens to a girl of twelve, not five and twenty."

"Mayhap I'm like a late blooming flower." Callie swallowed, the deceit stuck in her throat.

Jane tapped a pensive forefinger to her lips. "Unless, of course..."

A tiny charge sparked in the air. It was obvious what was left unsaid, and Callie was content to leave it there. She wasn't ready to say it out loud. She'd only just admitted it to herself.

"I suspect," she began on a false high note, "Mrs. Bailey's Christmas holiday fare may be the culprit. Mayhap her cooking has caught up with me after all these years." To add outright lie to fib, she squeezed out a hollow laugh. "I'll tell her to start minding the butter."

Jane's expression turned skeptical. "That's quite a few *mayhaps*." Mouth in a firm line, she began sticking straight pins into their cushion, respooling the leftover thread from today's alterations, and carefully replacing the tools of her trade in their individual stations. Callie watched, wary. Jane wasn't finished, she could feel it.

At last, Jane stood straight, crossed the room, and took Callie's hands in hers. "I expect you're busy with matters on the Grange. But Calpurnia, pet, when you're ready to speak of other matters, any matters at all, you know where to find me."

Unexpected emotion surged forward, and Callie nodded. She gathered up her altered trousers and released Jane's hands. "I must be going now."

In a moment, she found herself on Jane's front stoop, swiping a stray tear. She was a right, soupy mess these days.

She popped her collar up against a biting northerly breeze and stepped onto High Street. Throngs of villagers were flowing toward the bay, the opposite direction of where she was headed. "What's all the fuss about?" she asked in the general direction of anyone who would answer.

"Tall ship just arrived," came a hurried response.

Callie dug her heels into cobblestone and stopped herself from following the momentum of the crowd. Nothing new in the town getting excited about a recently arrived tall ship, bringing all manner of goods, some expected and ordinary, others exotic and unique.

She had no intention of joining the fray. In fact, she'd already taken too much time out of her schedule to see Jane today. But there had been no help for it. She hadn't been able to button her trousers.

And it was obvious as day that Jane suspected why. Nay, not suspected, *knew*. Mrs. Bailey's buttery Christmas cooking had naught to do with Callie's expanding waistline or tender breasts. What, really, had been the point of withholding the truth? Soon, she would be gone from the Grange, and no one would be the wiser.

Nylander would return, deed in hand, to claim his rightful place and boot her from the premises.

How soon? It was only a matter of time.

In all honesty, it would be no small relief. She would no longer have this ax suspended over her head. These last few months, she'd been busier than she'd ever been in her life. When she'd awakened after the night of the fire, she'd lifted her head off her soot- and tear-stained pillow and resolved to make the Grange whole before Nylander returned to claim it.

Her life, it would never be whole again. But the Grange could and would be.

She'd started by confessing to her men and offering to turn herself in to the law. To a man, they heard her confession and rejected her offer.

"If you don't mind me saying, milady," Will said, "we thought something like that was afoot. You might work on your lying skills. Besides, you been making it right."

"Weren't no real harm done," Jess dismissed, working his shoulder to demonstrate its wholeness. "If they wanted me done for, they'd a done it."

"We don't need the London law breathin' down our necks," Tom said and spit.

"But I—" Callie began to protest.

"Will ye do it agin?"

"Never."

"Then leave it be. We take care of our own in the west."

She'd had to fight back the tears—when wasn't she fighting back tears?—at the grace she'd been granted.

Lastly, she'd spoken to Pierre. The man was singularly attached to the Charentais still. Fortunately, he had Kip, who was only too happy to be his arms and legs in the repairs. The boy was thriving. That she wouldn't be here to see what sort of man he'd become, tugged more tears from her.

"I only wish you'd told me you were in a pickle," Pierre

opined. "I could've introduced you to some freebooters a sight more honest than that old bugger, Jack Le Grand."

It still shocked her how sanguine the men had been about her shameful bargain, the way they'd shrugged it off. Just when she had to leave, they'd accepted her as one of them. Again, tears welled up, and this time spilled over.

Now, all she could do was wait for the ax to drop, should be any day now. She'd had the large travel trunk that she'd brought with her five years ago lugged down from the attics. In her bedroom, it waited, mouth yawning open, for her to toss what few belongings she possessed into its great depths. She would be gone within an hour of the new master's arrival.

She found that her hand had settled on her stomach, ever so gently rounded and noticed only by her. Thus far. When she returned to her father's house, for that was a foregone conclusion, she would have to confess all.

Well, mayhap not *all*, but enough to explain this rounding belly.

Her father possessed a far-flung estate in Yorkshire that he'd come to own when he'd purchased a minor lordling's debts. For all his faults, he would let her live there due to a combination of fatherly affection and the need to put distance between him and her shame.

Perhaps, she thought, her daydreaming eye upon the hilly horizon, colors dimmed by the deep frost of winter, the estate would need improvements. She could start over. No one in Yorkshire need know that her widowhood had begun over two years ago, well before any child could have been conceived.

There was but one problem with this daydream: her heart was here.

She neared the top of a hill, and the Grange rose into view, a roll of puffy gray clouds behind it. Snow was in those clouds. They would wake up to a world transformed on the morrow.

An estate worker—Billy, if she recalled correctly— reached the top of his side of the hill just as she reached hers. He stepped aside to let her pass. "Yer headin' the wrong direction, yer ladyship," he said. "The merchant ship is the other way."

This young man had always been cautious around her before the festival. But here he was speaking to her like one of his own, a tease in his words.

"Well, Billy," she began, "you'll just have to pick out something pretty for your best girl."

"That I will." He jammed his thumbs into his waistband. "She's been wantin' an ivory comb from China somethin' fierce, like the one 'er sister got off a ship last year."

"How lucky it's arrived on the eve of Christmas. You'd better hurry so you get the very best one."

He gave Callie a serious nod and raced down the hill like a shot.

As she approached the Grange, a vision of *him* replaced the view. Of working side by side with him. Of being held in his arms and made to feel precious, like the only woman in the world.

She missed him, as a lover, as a companion. A man who always knew the correct course of action and pursued it. She missed his familiar, windswept scent. He smelled of the ocean after a cleansing thunderstorm.

She approached the Grange from the side, rather than from the main road's head-on approach, whose purpose was to give visitors the opportunity to appreciate it in its full grandeur. Long, curved road with plane trees to either side. Rolling, green hills dotted with fluffy white sheep. The house itself, Palladian, grand, its golden stone, brought in from the Cotswolds, glinting mellow in the sun. She preferred the back way. Here, behind the grand facade, pumped its living heart, steady, stalwart, and true.

A gust of northern wind blasted in from the sea, and she tucked her chin into her upturned collar. But not before she caught competing whiffs of Christmas goose and shortbread flavored with a hint of orange wafting toward her from Mrs. Bailey's kitchen. She wasn't sure which she preferred, the savory or the sweet. *Both,* her stomach growled, wolf-like.

She'd told Jane a bald-faced lie when she'd said she

would ask Mrs. Bailey to mind the butter. Her step quickened on the anticipation of culinary delight.

"Your ladyship," came the proper tones of the footman behind her, arresting her step just as her feet reached the kitchen's threshold.

She pasted a neutral expression onto her face and squared her shoulders, when all she really wanted to do was fling herself to the ground like a toddler in the throes of a proper tantrum. *Shortbread,* she wanted to cry. But she was a *Lady,* therefore she must act like an adult woman worthy of the respect afforded her.

"What is it, Ollie?"

He held out a packet wrapped in brown paper and secured with twine. "This arrived for you."

Her stomach dropped to her feet as she took the packet between fingers that had begun to tremble. Neither thick nor thin, it contained the heft of importance. The ax that had hung suspended over her head for the last few months? It had just fallen.

On Christmas Eve.

Packet clutched tight to her chest, she dismissed Ollie and fled through the kitchen, unheedful of the scent of shortbread that had so tantalized her moments ago. Winged feet navigating the maze of hallways, she reached her study in a matter of seconds. She kicked the door shut behind her and slumped against solid oak, her breath coming in quick, shallow pants.

She turned the packet over and found *Callie* scrawled across the outside in an unfamiliar script. Only Nylander called her by that name. Her fingertip traced her name surely writ by his hand. She brought it to her face, pressing it flat against her nose, and inhaled. It smelled faintly of the sea, of *him.*

She stalked across the room and seated herself behind her grand desk on the half hope that its stalwart heft would shore her up for what she must do. For it was clear that she must read the contents of this packet. She grabbed a pen knife and sliced through twine with the same grim determination one used when stripping a bandage off a not-quite-healed wound. Corner by corner, she peeled back the brown paper until the white contents of the packet stared up at her. She took a deep breath and focused on fine, black print.

Page one was the bill of sale of the unentailed estate, Wyldcombe Grange, and its six thousand acres from the Right Honorable Jakob Radclyffe, Fifth Viscount St. Alban, to one Mr. John Nylander for the sum of £100,000. Paid in Full.

Her breath stole away, and she sat back in her chair, eyes clenched shut.

Paid in full.

Her eyes flew open, and she bent her face close to the document to confirm the sum. That *Paid in Full* caught between her teeth. Nylander had the available funds to pay such a price *in full?* It boggled the mind. She'd been prepared to approach Lord St. Alban with a plan to pay yearly, but this...

She flipped to the next page. Here was the deed. Ownership of the Grange transferred from the Right Honorable Jakob Radclyffe, Fifth Viscount St. Alban to Mr. John Nylander. Even though she'd known this document was an inevitability, moisture blurred her vision. She blinked it away.

It was official in black and white. She'd lost the Grange.

She turned the page and gave it a quick skim. Her heart froze in her chest. She tried reading it again, this time slowly, but the words refused to make sense. Her mouth went dry. She pressed her forefinger to paper and read as slowly as it moved, willing herself to comprehend words like *transfer* and *ownership* and *to* and *Lady Calpurnia Radclyffe, Dowager Viscountess St. Alban.*

Time slowed until the clock stopped ticking altogether.

She read and reread, slower each time, words broken into syllables, syllables into individual letters, and then reformed into words, which remained immutable. Mr. John Nylander had transferred ownership of Wyldcombe Grange and its attendant lands to one Lady Calpurnia Radclyffe, Dowager Viscountess St. Alban for the sum of—

She lifted the deed to confirm no more documents lay below.

—£0.

A long, blank line where her signature was required stared up at her. If she scrawled her name across it, she would be the owner of Wyldcombe Grange.

Everything she ever wanted was in her hands.

She blinked, and time resumed its steady tick-tock.

Not everything.

She caressed her stomach and glanced around. So much of what she'd spent her adult life craving could be hers. All she had to do was sign.

And it lacked all substance without *him*, the man who was sacrificing everything he ever wanted to give her her heart's desire. What would possession of the Grange mean without him?

She held the papers to her nose again, taking in his fading scent. A thought blasted through her with the force of an exploding star. She shot to her feet and gathered up the papers into an unkempt mass before rushing across the study. She swung the door wide. "Ollie! Ollie!"

The footman appeared at the end of the hallway and approached her with his usual dignified gait. She tapped an impatient toe. Why wouldn't the man hurry up already? Couldn't he see she had a matter of pressing importance?

At last, he stopped before her, all dignified patience. "How may I be of assistance, my lady?"

She held up the mass of papers. "When did these arrive?"

Ollie's eyes screwed up to the ceiling. "I'd say an hour past."

"And how did they arrive? By post?"

"The post doesn't arrive for another two hours."

"Then who brought them to you?"

"The stable lad brought it to Mrs. Bailey, who gave it to me. This brings me to another matter of importance. That lad needs a firmer hand guiding him if he is going to—"

"Kip?" Callie interrupted.

Ollie drew himself up. "Yes, my lady."

"Thank you, Ollie," Callie called over her shoulder, already on the run. The instant her feet hit the stable yard, she began shouting, "Kip! Kip!"

In what felt like an eternity of seconds, but couldn't have been more than thirty, Kip sauntered out of the stable, a piece of straw between his teeth. "What's all the fuss about, milady?"

The boy really was an impudent rascal. But that was neither here nor there at the moment. "Who gave you the packet of papers to deliver?"

Kip shrugged. "Some old salt."

Callie's eyebrows met in the middle. "An old salt?"

"You know, a sailor."

An old salt... a sailor... the tall ship in the harbor... Nylander was... *here.*

She nearly hugged Kip in gratitude, but she resisted. The lad likely wouldn't appreciate it. Instead, she settled for a quick, "Thank you," before rushing off.

It might not be too late. But...

What if he was only delivering the packet before sailing away? If the tide was going out, he might already be weighing anchor.

She would never see him again. She would never have a chance to make this right. To make *them* right.

And she must.

She darted toward the quickest path to the village and stopped. She glanced down at herself, clad in trousers and shirt buttoned up to her neck. First, she would change clothes, and she knew exactly what to wear, even though the stains had never really come out and the hem was tattered to bits and a few buttons would surely resist fastening.

He'd given her everything, and she would do the same for him. She would offer him everything the magical night and day they'd shared had promised, and more.

If he would have her.

Nylander planted his feet wide to brace himself against the subtle roll and sway of the sea below, arms akimbo, his usual stance at his usual place on the quarterdeck at the base of the main mast.

It was familiar. It was home. After spending all his days serving the sea's whims, and dreaming of different ones, he'd at last resigned himself to his fate.

"So this is the place, eh?" came the First Mate's voice.

"What place is that, Mr. Smythe?"

"Where you recovered from your fever."

"Aye," Nylander grunted, his gaze fixed on the hive of activity aboard the *Fortuyn*, and most definitely not on the distant shore.

"We thought we'd lost you to the land." Mr. Smythe huffed a small laugh. "Some of the men laid odds on it."

"Not a chance." The reply was clipped and curt and efficiently closed the door on this conversation. Mr. Smythe discreetly stepped away to see to his duties.

It wasn't simply that Nylander had spent his entire fortune in the space of an afternoon inside a fuggy London solicitor's office and had no choice but to keep captaining the *Fortuyn*. On the sea, a fortune could be made, lost, and remade in the span of a few years.

No, it wasn't that he was starting from zero that kept him tethered to the sea. He'd forgotten the place life had handed him and reached too far, too high. And his crash back to earth, to reality, had been jarring and exquisitely painful. He'd not be forgetting his place again.

Which was here, the captain of a tall ship provisioned for another trip to the Mediterranean. Apparently, the Ottoman sultan was so delighted with his pair of Thoroughbreds that he wanted to reciprocate by gifting a pair of Arabian stallions to the lord who had provided them. For the voyage out, the *Fortuyn* was outfitted with ironware, woolens, linens, and textiles.

He wouldn't think about the other life—the one on the shore that his gaze kept avoiding—that he'd come close to having. So close the taste of it still tickled his tongue in the small hours of the night. It tasted of apple and earth and the salt of honest, sweat-soiled toil.

Buzzing around him, lugging ropes and canvas, whistling the odd sea song, securing cargo, was his real life as they prepared to set sail. They wouldn't touch land again until Gibraltar.

He allowed the feeling of satisfaction to settle over him when the ship operated like a well-executed piece of machinery. He didn't need to bark orders at these men: they knew what they were about. Even if it wasn't precisely a joy—all traces of that emotion had been stripped from him two months ago—he felt less numb for this moment. It didn't repair the gaping black void in his soul, but it did offer him a moment's relief.

"There's a boat drawing nigh," the coxswain called in his direction, spyglass pressed to his eye.

"Must be Gibbons and the men returning." Nylander didn't bother looking. Along with a small delivery to the Grange, he'd instructed the men to secure a few casks of the Grange's cider from the Devil's Books. Their price had been bloody extortionate, but it hardly mattered. It was something of his time here to bring with him. He'd ever had trouble releasing lost dreams to the wind.

"Nay," the coxswain continued after a bit. "This vessel is a sight smaller than the jolly boat Gibbons took out. This is a dinghy." He twisted the spyglass to focus it. "Besides all that, couldn't be Gibbons, not unless 'is hair turned to flame while 'e was on shore. And 'e grew six inches to boot. *And*"—he paused long enough to build a little drama around his next words—"'e's taken to wearing ladies' silk dresses beneath 'is overcoats."

Nylander's gut flipped. It might not be her. "Is the dress green?"

"Aye, 'tis."

It was *her*. His hand shot out, snatched the spyglass from the coxswain, and pressed the brass oculus to his eye.

It was most definitely her, silk dress flashing green beneath a worn winter overcoat, huffing, puffing, and having a devil of a time maneuvering that dinghy across waves choppy with a newly arrived breeze. A breeze that was the *Fortuyn*'s signal to weigh anchor and set sail before the snow began falling.

He wouldn't look away. As long as he kept his eye on her, she couldn't vanish. It was clear that she hadn't much experience with the mechanics of rowing. Her oars struck the water out of sync with one another and at ineffectual angles, splashing sea foam onto her lap and doubling the work she had cut out for her. Adding to her burden, she didn't seem to understand how to use her legs in the effort, and her arms had a heaviness to them like they felt like falling off.

This struggle of a titled lady grappling with the sea in her silk dress might've been comical if it didn't feel so deadly serious. Like his life depended on its outcome.

"Lower the dinghy," he barked to anyone who would snap to and take the order.

Once readied, he wasted no time boarding the small vessel and setting its oars into motion across waves growing choppier with the breeze that was strengthening into a wind. A quick, practiced rhythm developed between arms and legs, and he was covering the distance with one stroke that took Callie ten.

He glanced up and saw that she'd stopped altogether, her eyes a squint across the distance that separated them. With every pull of his oars, he drew closer, and the question he should've asked himself the moment he saw her through the spyglass hit him: Why was she here?

When his boat bumped against hers, he didn't ask quite so delicately. "What the bloody hell are you trying to accomplish? Your death?"

Her mouth opened. "I—" Her mouth snapped shut, and she stared out at him. Her cheeks were stained scarlet and her eyes bright with exertion. Perspiration blotched the green silk of her bodice, and flame-red hair clung to her cheeks in damp strings. If the gust of wind that blew past him was telling the truth, she smelled.

A large wave rolled beneath his boat, then hers, rocking them violently from side to side. He reached for a length of rope and worked at tethering her dinghy to his. "We need to get to shore."

Eyes wide, her arms braced to either side of the narrow vessel, she nodded. He set his oars into motion and made for the nearest cove, a few hundred yards in the distance. His load doubled, progress was slower, but soon enough the bottom of his boat was scraping against sand and rock. He jumped out, grabbed the rope linking his boat to hers, and pulled her in until she was beached as well.

He reached out a hand. She took it, and his pulse jumped in his veins. With that simple touch, he felt more alive than he had in months.

"I could carry you to shore." His instinct was to gather her in his arms and protect her from the weather about to break over their heads. He resisted the urge, and added, "To save your dress." That last part emerged with the awkwardness of a green youth who'd found himself alone with the fairer sex for the first time.

A little smile ticked up at the side of her mouth. "There's no saving this dress, I'm afraid." Her smile fell. "I think it's better if I go under my own steam."

"Right," he said. *Of course*, he didn't say.

He handed her down and stepped aside, gesturing for her to lead the way. As he waded to shore through frigid, ankle-deep water, again the question came to him: Why was she here?

She stopped on the edge of the waterline and faced him, waiting for him to join her, choppy waves skating across brown sand until they were nothing more than tiny licks at her boots. She looked an utter, bedraggled mess. Brown overcoat heavy atop the silk dress that sagged in a limp, sodden mass beneath, damp hair hanging about her face and shoulders.

But there was something more to the way she looked. A nervous energy vibrated about her. Eyes unnaturally bright, her hands clenched and unclenched anxiously at her sides. She had something to say.

To him.

He refused to give that last bit air to breathe. It might encourage hope.

He stopped at the water's edge. It wouldn't do to get too close.

"What took you so long?" she blurted.

The question took him by surprise. "To do what?"

"To come back."

"I didn't know I was—" He stopped. *Welcome*, he didn't say. Too much complication resided within that finish. He kept it simple. "There were matters that had to be sorted in London. Family matters mostly," he added and instantly regretted it. She didn't want the details of his damaged family.

She nodded, thoughtful. "The lad who was with Jack Le Grand in the cave, is he your—"

"Brother? Aye. Had to see him sorted and in school. I'm his guardian now, which was a whole other laborious legal process." Why was he explaining all this to her? Best to get to what she was really here for. "You received the deed?"

"I did."

"Did you sign it?"

"I did not."

His brow furrowed. "Do you have a question about it?"

"One."

She rolled her bottom lip between her teeth. He tried not to watch, and failed.

"Why?"

"I don't know the first thing about managing a five foot square of land, much less an estate like the Grange." He tried to believe the next words out of his mouth. "I would've run it into the ground."

"You would've been the best thing to ever happen to the Grange."

Nylander shifted on his feet and tried to let her words wash over him without soaking in. Without letting a belief in them take hold.

Fire snapped in her eyes. "Stop that."

"Stop what?"

"Avoiding praise."

Taut silence stretched between them. She was awaiting his response. Well, she'd be waiting for a good long while. He took the conversation another direction. "Underneath your coat."

"Yes?"

"Your dress."

"What about it?"

"It seems mightily impractical."

"You liked it, so I wore it. I thought it might—" She threw frustrated hands into the air. "I didn't plan for ocean spray and choppy waves and wind and"—she exhaled a defeated sigh—"*sweat.*"

"It seems to be falling off you."

Self-consciousness quenched the fire in her eyes. She squirmed inside damp silk and tugged at various places to situate the garment better on her body. Nothing helped. In fact, she might have made it worse. A pink shadow, that may or may not have been a nipple, peeked above the low neckline. Nylander used every bit of will-power he possessed to keep his eye fixed on hers and not explore the possibility further.

"I couldn't button it."

He stepped forward without thinking. "Let me assist you."

Callie splashed a hasty step backward. "We'll get to the dress later. You've already done enough as far as it goes."

What in the blast was the woman going on about?

With a decisive sweep of her hand, she cleared her face of the red frizzy strings of hair that clung to it with sea spray and, yes, sweat. Somehow, she managed to maintain a regal bearing. "I owe you an apology."

"You don't owe me anything."

"I was utterly, shamefully wrong to have believed for even an instant that you were in league with Jack Le Grand."

He shook off her apology. He had to. "You weren't in the wrong for believing it. I would have."

Her eyebrows drew together. "Why is that?"

A short laugh escaped him, its bitterness leaving a metallic taste in his mouth. "The offspring of the unholy union of an infamous pirate and a dockside whore? It wouldn't be natural to believe otherwise."

Her visage went as dark as the clouds overhead. "I care not one whit about your parentage."

"You do, you just don't realize it," he began, unable to plug the truths that wanted release, that had plagued him all his life. "When you know a thing like that about a person, you can't unknow it. It's a knowledge that loosens a poison that infects and kills the entire relationship. This isn't the first time it's happened, and it won't be the last."

It will be the last, Callie ached to shout at the blasted, cross-grained man. Except he wouldn't believe her.

"But..." She struggled for words, the right ones. The ones that would take his pain away. "You're *you*. That's all that matters to me. It's all that will ever matter."

He crossed his arms over his chest, a skeptical look in his eye, silent. She had her work cut out for her, and she wouldn't be leaving here until she'd done it. "I'm the daughter of a *respectable* union and look at what I did. I struck a deal with a notorious pirate."

His broad shoulders shrugged, laconic. "You were pushed to it."

"Don't make excuses for me."

"Your back was driven to the wall."

"Stop that," she demanded. "I need to know. Can you forgive me?"

"There's nothing to forgive. Again, who wouldn't have done the same?"

"*You.*"

His lips pressed together, and the muscles of his jaw worked as if he was grinding his teeth.

"*You* would've found an honorable way to accomplish your goal, because that's what *you*, the son of a pirate and a whore, are. *You* are honorable." When he opened his mouth to protest, she held up a staying hand. "Why did you sign the Grange over to me? You placed your heart's desire in my hands."

"You wanted it."

"But you wanted it, too. In fact, it's everything you ever wanted."

"Not everything. Not even the main thing."

Words abandoned her.

"I love that about you," he said.

"What?"

"The way you roll your bottom lip between your teeth when you're thinking."

She released her lip. Their little game had returned. Here, at last, was her opening, and she must seize it with both hands. She couldn't lose him. Not again. "Your hair. I —" She hesitated, still unaccustomed to speaking the next word. "I love it. The way it riffles in the breeze like summer barley."

His brow lifted.

"I love your forearms when you milk a cow. The way your muscles roll beneath your skin like you're the most alive man in the world."

The beginnings of a smile crinkled at the corners of his eyes. How she wished he would follow through with it.

"But most of all, I love"—she swallowed around the lump in her throat. She suspected it was her heart—"*you.*"

The smile that had begun, fell away. "That can't work."

"Why?" she cried out.

"Look where I come from. Where you come from. Where I belong, and where you belong. The gap between us is too wide."

"Where *I* belong? Where *you* belong? Can't you see? We belong together. Nothing else matters."

"Those differences are all that matter in this world."

"Then let's blow up the world."

"Callie—"

"All that matters is *you... me... here... now.*"

"You've never lived out in the world."

Something about his resistance worried at Callie. It was as if he—*Oh.* Frustration with the blasted man gave way to understanding. "You don't know, do you?"

His eyes narrowed. "What is that?"

"That you could be loved." She allowed a beat to pass. "That you are worthy of love."

He flinched.

"Love has done nothing but hurt you. It failed you. But" —she reached inside her bodice and dug out papers that were mostly dry—"you and I can fashion a new world. A better world."

"Callie—"

She shook the deed at him. "Right here, we have all we need to make our world what we want it to be. You are worthy of being loved. And I can't think of a love more worthy than yours. To be loved by a man like you... to be loved by *you...* there is nothing in the world I crave more."

"Not even the document you hold?"

"It's nothing without you."

The balance of her future hung on those words, immutable, true.

He moved forward, his boots a soft splash in the water, halving the distance between them before she could blink, his gaze holding hers in its blue thrall.

At last, she did blink and snapped out of her trance. "Wait."

He halted, and his brow knitted in confusion.

"I, um," she stammered. "I can't think when you're close."

"Maybe we don't need to think right now."

Again, he halved the distance between them, and halved it again. He was so close his warmth reached out and invited her to nestle inside. He tucked her hair behind one ear, then the other, and she wanted nothing more than to turn her face and melt into his strong, calloused hand. Instead, she placed her own smaller hand on his chest, on the tattoo above his heart.

"*Dweller on new land*," she uttered. "Come, dwell *here*, with me, in this land. It'll be our new land, together."

Unnamed emotion clouded the blue of his eye. He took her waist in hand and drew her close. His mouth found her ear. "I've loved you since the moment your eyes threw murderous daggers at me across Jake's study and all the other moments since, even when you're driving me mad." The velvet gravel of his voice threatened to turn her knees to jelly. "Maybe especially when you're driving me mad. I love you, Callie, and I'll protect you to the end."

So many emotions surged, she couldn't differentiate one from the other. They just swirled together and made her feel whole and loved and utterly ferocious. "And I'll love you to my very last breath."

He shifted to meet her eye. "We'll build our world of two, just you and I."

"Just you and I," she repeated. "Oh." She broke from his embrace and stepped back. Her heart thundered in her chest. Now was the time. "There is something I must tell you."

His brow furrowed in bewilderment.

"About my dress."

"There is something you must tell me about your dress?"

"It won't button up anymore."

"Here"—he reached for her—"let me see what I can do."

She evaded him. "You can't do anything." She shook her head. "Well, that's not precisely true. You've already done quite a bit."

"You're not making any—" He stopped cold. His brow

released a hard beat of Callie's heart later, and his gaze dropped to her stomach. "Are you saying—"

"Aye. It's a world of three we're building."

His face softened and warmed her to her bones. "May I?"

Words choked in her throat, and she nodded. Trembling fingers traced over her belly, from hipbone to hipbone.

"You're willing to give this little mite my name?"

"I can't think of a more noble one."

He went solemn and serious. "You're mine forever."

As if Nature would punctuate his point, the sky released a single glittering snowflake that landed on the tip of his nose and instantly melted. Then another caught in his hair, and another in his eyelashes. He blinked, and Callie laughed. All around them the world was transforming into a wonderland, magical and perfect.

She moved fully into his embrace and lifted her heels until she reached the tips of her toes. Her mouth found the cup of his ear. "Just try to get away."

His face angled, and his mouth found hers on a low growl. She swayed into him, the length of her body pressed full into his.

He broke away on a groan. "The crew."

"The crew?" she asked between shallow breaths.

"You can bet we're giving them an eyeful."

She supposed he was right, even if every last fiber of her being protested otherwise. "Shall we adjourn to our home, Captain Nylander?"

"John."

"*John*," she repeated softly. Direct and strong, his name suited him.

In the world of their own creation, they would ever be straightforward, plainspoken John and sweet, feisty Callie.

It was the only world that would ever matter.

EPILOGUE

SUMMER

"Are you sure?"

Unable to take her eyes off the babe suckling at her breast, Callie spoke a simple, certain, "Yes."

"Don't feel like you have to use it."

John sounded uncertain, even nervous, and utterly unlike the husband she'd come to know these last six months. At last, she pulled her eyes off the babe—really, she was the most beautiful babe in the world with her strawberry blond hair, her father's blue eyes, and cheeks, oh, those cheeks plump as apples—and craned her head around to give him her full attention. Well, *almost*. The babe never left the corner of her eye.

"Do *you* want to use it?"

"I just thought you might reconsider when the time came."

"It's a lovely name."

"But it was—"

"Your mother's," she finished for him when he hesitated.

"I would understand if you don't want to saddle her with the name of a—"

"Woman you loved very much," she again finished for him.

He smiled, self-conscious. "She always said Rose was too prim a name for the likes of her. She was Rosie."

Callie's smitten gaze returned to the squirming bundle in her arms. Really, how could he expect to hold her attention for any length of time? "I know something about prim names. It doesn't get much primmer than Calpurnia."

"And since Rose will be her second name, we can call her by her first name, Lenora."

"While I'm sure my mother would like that, I think she'd take one look at this girl and agree with me."

"About?"

"She is a Rose, through and through."

He drew them deeper into his embrace. "Lenora Rose Nylander," he murmured, as if testing the weight of it in his mouth. "A Lenora Rose knows what's what in this world."

"That she will." Callie smiled. "Her honorary uncle Kip will see to it."

That drew a laugh from her husband.

"Where is the lad, anyway?"

"Showing Lash the cider house."

Lash's carriage had arrived last night when Callie had been deep in the throes of a labor whose ferocity was already fading in her memory. If anyone had asked her then, if she'd ever repeat the torture of childbirth, she would've cursed their name. But now, as she gazed upon this bundle of sweetness, the intensity of those feelings faded. What was a little—or a great deal—of pain when *this* was the outcome?

"How is Lash adjusting to country life?"

"I think he's ready for school break to end so he can return to London and Westminster. The lad is accustomed to a faster pace of life than can be found here. It seems he and Jake's nephew by marriage have become fast friends."

"And Jack?" Callie asked, trying for offhand and failing. "Any word of him?"

"He's paid restitution, so it's a matter of him serving out his sentence in a few years."

"Then he'll be sailing the Seven Seas with his letters of marque, no doubt." Acrimony mixed into the sweet moment. She would never forgive the man for his multitude of sins. *Never.*

"Aye."

"You'll have to keep an eye on Lash." She liked the grave, quiet lad. He was rather like his brother. Loyal like his brother, too. Future trouble might lie within that loyalty.

John nodded. "The family Jake married into has government connections. The lad will be protected."

Callie let the subject slide away. She touched her nose to the top of Rose's head and inhaled. Oh, there wasn't a thing she didn't love about the girl. "John?"

"Aye?"

"I think my heart might burst from happiness."

He squeezed her and Rose into his broad chest, his arms strong and steady and safe. "Aye."

He was a man of few words, her John.

But within that single *"Aye"* existed the world.

A world that suited Callie in every way.

The End

ALSO BY SOFIE DARLING

All's Fair in Love and Racing
Odds on the Rake
The Duchess Gamble
Wager With a Siren

Shadows and Silk
Three Lessons in Seduction
Tempted by the Viscount
Her Midnight Sin
To Win a Wicked Lord
At the Pleasure of the Marquess
One Night His Lady
Nell and the Runaway Duke

It was Only a Kiss

ABOUT THE AUTHOR

Bestselling and award-winning author Sofie Darling's passion for historical romance began in middle school the moment she cracked open *Wuthering Heights* by Emily Bronte. An instant and enduring love affair was born.

Sofie spent much of her twenties raising two boys and reading every romance she could get her hands on. Once she realized she simply must write the books she loved, she finished her English degree and set pencil to paper. (Ticonderoga #2 is her quill of choice.)

When she's not writing heroes who make her swoon, Sofie enjoys a nice weekend hike, a visit to a crumbling medieval castle whenever she gets the chance, and a slightly codependent relationship with her beagle, Bosco. Visit her website.